a novel

REARVIEW MIRROR

Stephanie Black

Covenant Communications, Inc.

Published by Covenant Communications, Inc.
American Fork, Utah

Printed in the United States of America
First Printing: October 2011

17 16 15 14 13 12 11   10 9 8 7 6 5 4 3 2 1

ISBN-13: 978-1-60861-463-9

Acknowledgments

Thank you to the people who took time out of their schedules to read and offer feedback on the manuscript: Sue McConkie, Bonnie Overly, Jonathan Spell, Dianna Hall, and Shauna Black. Test readers are solid gold; getting their feedback is a vital step in plugging holes and strengthening story and character. Another big thank you goes to those who answered my questions and shared their expertise: Gregg Luke, Amy Black, and Marshall McConkie. And thank you to Stan McConkie Jr., who came up with the title.

Particular thanks goes to Dr. Samuel Maio. When I asked Sam about the life of an English professor, I had no idea of the extent he'd go to in answering my questions. He not only provided answers, but also dug far more deeply into the questions and offered tons of suggestions for creating a background and professional life for my main character.

As always, thank you to all the staff at Covenant, including my editor, Kirk Shaw, and cover designer, Jennie Williams. And thank you to my husband, Brian, for all his encouragement and support over the years.

Chapter 1

SLEET WHIPPED LINDA TAYLOR ACROSS the face. She bent her head and trudged along the muddy path that led deeper into the wooded acres of her property. Bare branches dotted with spring buds wouldn't provide much shelter, but this was exactly what everyone wanted for her, wasn't it? Linda, cold and wet and alone. Shoved aside.

On the top of the bank that sloped down to the creek, she stopped and listened to the water rushing onward to oblivion, unheeded. Just like Linda. She *tried,* but did anyone care?

The wind tore at her hood, pulling it off her head. Sleet and rain soaked her hair, but she didn't bother to fix her hood. It would only blow off again. She'd freeze out here, but better frostbite than going home to be insulted and ignored.

She glanced over her shoulder, but saw only the empty path, bumpy with roots, and the gray-brown branches of trees trembling in the wind. No one cared enough to follow her. When she was dead of hypothermia, they'd realize what they'd done to her. Linda wiped her face with numb fingers. She'd forgotten her gloves. Why hadn't someone at least brought her some gloves? How could she possibly remember her gloves when she was so upset?

How could it be so dark this early in the afternoon? The sky was almost black. The creek gushed high up the banks, frothy and agitated. Linda leaned against a sodden tree and watched the water splash and foam around the chunks of granite that barely showed above the surface of the swollen creek. She was like those rocks—solid and reliable and always there—and *this* was her reward? Standing alone and drenched and rejected?

The roar of the creek and the pounding of the rain would make it impossible to hear footsteps on the trail, and soon Linda's neck ached from her repeated glances over her shoulder. No one was coming. Sleet slid under her collar in freezing rivulets. The legs of her slacks were now so wet she could have wrung the fabric out over her houseplants to give them a good drink.

Her body was convulsing with shivers by the time she glimpsed the figure moving toward her, face obscured by an umbrella jerking in the wind. Swiftly, Linda turned so she was gazing at the creek. Not until her peripheral vision revealed that her rescuer had stopped a couple of feet to the side of her did Linda turn to offer a brave smile. "You shouldn't have come after me. It's better for everyone if I—"

The shove came like a sledgehammer smashing into her chest. With a screech, Linda flew backward, her shoes skidding on decomposing leaves, her arms flailing. She grabbed for a branch and missed; a boulder caught her in the back of the legs and she landed hard on her backside, the air forced from her lungs. Mud crumbled beneath her, and she felt herself sliding toward the creek. She clawed at the roots exposed at the edge of the water, but her stiff fingers couldn't find a handhold. Thrashing, screaming, she slid into the creek.

The current seized her, dragging her along. Her arm slammed into a rock. She tried to scream, but her throat filled with water. Choking, she struggled to find her footing—she could feel the bottom—

The water spun her around, throwing her toward another rock.

* * *

"This just became a *much* better day." Fiona Claridge stopped in front of her office door and picked up a package wrapped in blue cellophane and tied with a silver ribbon. After a walk across campus that had left her umbrella broken, her shoes waterlogged, and her hair damp and straggling free of the pins that held it in a French twist, a surprise gift was a warm flicker of cheer.

"Lucky you." James Hampton pulled his glasses away from his eyes and peered through the lenses as though studying a clue through a magnifying glass. "That package has chocolate vibes."

"Please, yes. I'm starving." Fiona lifted a silver gift tag so she could read the message.

"Who's your admirer?" James asked.

"It just has my name on it." Fiona flipped the tag over. The other side was blank. "The message must be inside the package."

"Or it's from a secret admirer."

"It's probably an attempted bribe."

James grinned. His cropped brown hair was sticking up, thanks to the hat he'd yanked off, and bits of slush clung to the shoulders of his coat. "I'd sell an A for two dozen homemade chocolate-chip cookies."

Fiona laughed and unlocked her office door. She set the package on her desk, opened her briefcase, and took out a plastic grocery sack. "Here it is. Finished at last. It took me nearly a year, and it would have taken me ten years if Shannon hadn't badgered me about it."

"Under pressure from the knitting police, were you?"

"She made it her personal crusade to ensure that I finished *something*. Otherwise, all her work teaching me was in vain."

"You wouldn't be in this pickle if you hadn't caved and told her you were interested in learning. You put her off for years."

"It was vacation syndrome. Sitting there at the reunion, relaxing with my sisters . . . forgetting that the instant the next semester started, I wouldn't have time to breathe, let alone pick up a ball of yarn." She handed the sack to James. "Next to that fancy package, I'm embarrassed that I went with a grocery bag."

"What's the point of expensive wrapping paper?" He reached into the bag. "It gets ripped up and thrown away. I use old newspapers myself. Ah, Fiona—" He drew the scarf out. "It's amazing. Incredible!"

"It's a scarf, James. Not a Rembrandt."

"Yeah, but it's so . . . it's great." He wound the dark blue scarf around his neck. "I'm deeply honored to be the recipient of your first knitting project."

"I believe the scientific term for you is 'guinea pig.'"

He laughed and fingered the fringe on one end of the scarf. "Seriously, this is fantastic. No wonder your sister pushed you to learn. She could sense your innate talent."

Fiona smiled. "Either that or she's a knitting zealot hunting for converts." She picked up the package on her desk and untied the silver ribbon. Underneath the cellophane was a box wrapped in silver paper.

"Here goes the waste of some expensive paper." Fiona tore the end of the package open.

James sat in a chair facing her desk. "Recycle it. Then you can feel virtuous."

Fiona ripped the paper off and opened the box. Balls of wadded paper surrounded a smaller white box that looked as though it might hold jewelry.

"'A riddle, wrapped in a mystery, inside an enigma,'" James quoted.

"Thank you, Winston Churchill. Well, it's not chocolate." She lifted the lid of the smaller box. Inside the cotton-lined box lay a folded piece of paper and a set of car keys.

Puzzled, Fiona held up the keys and raised an eyebrow at James.

"Good grief," he said. "Your admirer gave you a *car*?"

"It must be a joke." Fiona unfolded the paper. In black type, the note read, *Want to kill again?*

Her heart jerked, and a rush of blood burned her cheeks. She folded the paper and returned it to the box.

James sprang to his feet. "What's wrong? What does it say?"

Fiona swallowed. "It's—not from an admirer."

"Let me see it." He reached for the note.

She held the box away from him. "It's—a prank . . . it's nothing—"

"Fiona. What does the note say?"

She drew a deep breath and pushed back a damp tendril of hair. She'd have to tell him. At least it was James, not someone who didn't know.

She handed him the note. He unfolded it and read the message.

"That's cruel," he said quietly, folding the note. "And ridiculous." He put it back into the box and closed the lid. "You need to call the police."

Fiona sank into the chair James had vacated. "And tell them what?"

James pulled his gloves out of his pockets and put them on before gathering up the boxes, the cellophane, and the wrapping paper and placing the materials inside the grocery sack Fiona had used to hold the scarf. "A package like this is . . . I don't know the legal term, but it must be a crime. They need to find out who's responsible."

"I don't think it's technically illegal. The note writer didn't threaten me." Avoiding James's gaze, Fiona focused on the rows of books filling the shelves in her office. "Someone was angry and decided to lash out at me. They had their fun. It's over."

"You need to report this."

Fiona realized she was absentmindedly rubbing her forearm, her fingers following the sunken scar beneath her sleeve. She folded her hands in her lap.

"Do you have any idea who might be responsible?" James asked.

She tried to think about his question but felt as though someone had grabbed her and shaken her thoughts into a jumble. "I . . . don't know."

"A student?"

"How would a student know—" She stopped, realizing it was a silly question. If someone googled her name, they'd find newspaper articles about the accident. "I did make one of my students extremely angry a few weeks ago," she admitted.

"The one you caught plagiarizing a paper. I remember. Sounds like you've got a suspect, then."

"James, we're only an hour from Canfield. It could be someone who grew up with Mia, someone who learned I was at Hawkins and decided to . . ." She let her voice die. She'd convinced herself that the hour between Canfield, Massachusetts, and Bennett, New Hampshire, was enough of a cushion, and she didn't need to worry that any of Mia's old friends would have reason to venture into small college-town Bennett. But what if someone had heard Fiona was here and had sought her out? She shouldn't have taken the job at Hawkins College. Never mind the fruitless months of job hunting—never mind the dozens of positions for which she'd applied before she'd been fortunate enough to land a tenure-track job at Hawkins. Better to wash dishes for a living than to teach at a college an hour from the people who had loved Mia Hardy.

James rested his hand on her shoulder. "No matter what, you need to report this. Go to your department chair. Make it clear you will *not* stand for this garbage. They need to talk to your student."

The heat had drained from her cheeks, and now she felt colder than she had outside in the driving rain and sleet. "I don't want to make this bigger than it has to be."

"Then cut it off now before the culprit decides to *do* something bigger."

"I don't know that it *is* a student who's responsible."

"This isn't from someone angry over Mia's death. If her family or friends blamed you, they wouldn't have waited eight years to strike. This is the work of a kid who needs to learn that cruel, immature acts have consequences."

He's probably right, Fiona thought. And maybe the culprit could learn that lesson a little less painfully than Fiona had.

* * *

"You're kidding, right?" Nicholas Cortez took a wild swing with his racket and missed. The ball rocketed into a corner and bounced crazily.

Kimberly Bailey raised her racket in both hands and stomped her feet in a victory dance. "Bad luck, Nicky! Dinner's on you."

Panting, Nick bent and rested his hands on his thighs. Kim buzzed around like a hummingbird when they played racquetball. How did she move so fast? "No fair. You distracted me."

She tugged the elastic band off her ponytail and shook out her hair. "If you're so dumb you can't whack a ball and listen to me at the same time, apparently my branch of the family got the brains, and yours got the . . . nah, we got the looks too."

"Sure you got the looks, if you like short and skinny and pale instead of tall, dark, and handsome," Nick said. Kim had inherited her petite blonde prettiness from her mother; she didn't look anything like Nick. *No way!* was the usual reaction when he introduced Kim as his cousin. "You didn't *really* do it, did you?"

Kim retrieved the ball and bounced it on her racket. "I told you I was going to."

"I thought you were just venting."

"She had it coming."

He mopped sweat off his face with his arm. "You're cold, Kim. So your parents repossessed your car for the rest of the semester. Get over it."

Kim tossed the ball into the air and gave it a whack so powerful that Nick half expected it to smash through the wall. "She cost me Paris."

"Whoa—*what?* They canceled your trip?"

Lips pinched tight, Kim didn't reply. She whacked the ball again, the noise echoing around the court.

"You didn't tell me that," Nick said.

"Do I have to tell you every dumb detail of my life?"

Nick swore under his breath. *Paris.* Kim had been looking forward to that trip for ages, rambling about visiting the Louvre and sketching the Arc de Triomphe and other topics that made Nick want to jam his earphones in his ears and turn up the volume.

"Give them a little more time to cool off," he said. "They'll change their minds."

"As *if.*" Another smash of the racket.

Nick swung his own racket, knocking the flying ball away before it could take his head off. "Sheesh. Settle down."

Kim lowered her racket. "They were iffy about the trip, anyway, because they didn't think my stupid grades were as high as they should have been last semester. And now—Claridge killed it for good."

The desolation in her face made Nick squirmy. "Yeah, well, if you don't like what your parents do when you get in trouble, maybe you shouldn't go out of your way to stir *up* trouble."

To his relief, anger burned away the pain in her eyes. "Like you're so pure."

"Maybe I'm smart enough not to get caught."

"She targeted me. She hates me—it's so obvious. The only reason she noticed my essay is because she was *looking* to take me down."

"Seems like a stretch to call it *your* essay," Nick said.

Kim swung her racket at him. He leaped backward.

"Everybody's done it," she said. "But *my* paper is the one she goes after. She could have just given me a zero on the essay—whatever! But an E for the whole *class*? For one little mistake?"

"Uh . . . you know Claridge didn't make up that penalty just for you, right? That's what school policy says. You plagiarize, you fail."

"Since when do *you* read all the fine print about policies?"

"I always read that stuff. If you want to gamble, you'd better know the stakes."

"I read it too," she snapped. "And I know she could have recommended a lighter penalty if she'd wanted to."

"I guess she didn't think you deserved a lighter penalty, and neither did her boss or whoever else talked to you. Tough luck for you to get nailed by a school that doesn't like bratty plagiarists. And double tough luck to have parents who check your grades like you're a snot-nosed junior high kid. That's gotta be embarrassing."

"Your parents do it, too!"

"Not like yours do. They just ask me for my final grades."

"Oh, and that's *so* much better."

It *was* a lot better than the way Kim's parents hovered, forever poking their noses into the online postings, but Nick figured he'd better not say so or Kim would put a dent in his skull.

"Maybe I ought to turn you in for cheating on your chemistry midterm," she said.

"Who says I cheated?"

"You passed, didn't you? You must have cheated."

"If I did," he said, "I'm obviously better at it than you are. And you've gone from dumb to dumber, giving Dr. Claridge that package. You think she won't know who it's from? Do you *want* to get kicked out of school?"

"Knowing who's mad at her and being able to prove who gave her a gift are two different things." Kim's gray eyes reminded Nick of the patch of ice-coated concrete that had yanked his legs out from under him a month ago when he was sprinting across campus late to class. "When she's having nightmares, I hope she *does* know I did it. It'll kill her to not be able to prove it."

"What if she can prove it? What if the cops get involved? They could check your Internet history and find out you researched her."

"First of all, the cops have better things to do. Second—I didn't use my own computer. I used one at the library when I was home a couple of weeks ago getting yelled at."

Nick stared at her. "Wow. You're sneakier than I thought."

She flopped to the floor and lay on her back staring at the lights overhead. "Okay, I didn't *plan* it that way. I was super bored, waiting for my brother to finish his study session so I could take him home—driving that cheesy SUV, by the way, because they won't even let me *touch* my Mustang—and while I waited, I went online and did some research."

"Looking for pictures of Claridge in her underwear, guzzling beer at a frat party. So you could post them around campus."

"It was worth a try."

"Yo, genius. If there were embarrassing shots out there, the Hawkins people would have found them before you did. You think this place would hire a party girl?"

"Okay, I didn't really think I'd *find* anything, but then—jackpot! She gets all up in arms about a little copying and she *killed* her own roommate? That woman is *twisted*."

"It was an accident," Nick pointed out.

"Caused by 'driving too fast for conditions.' If you make an accident happen, is it really an accident? Sounds like homicide to me."

"Like *you* don't drive like a demon mainlining Red Bull."

"So I'm a better driver than she is."

"You're a luckier one. Did she get hurt bad?"

Kim shrugged. "Yeah, she got messed up. The article didn't give details, but I know she's got a big scar on her arm. Not that she ever shows it in class—she always wears long sleeves, but I saw her running at the indoor track this morning. I'll bet her legs have scars, too. She was wearing long exercise pants even though it was way warm in there. And she's got a scar on her face. A big one."

"In the middle of her forehead? Shaped like a lightning bolt? Maybe she's a wizard."

"A *witch,* not a wizard, and she *is* a witch, but not that kind. The scar's right here." Kim touched her hairline near her left temple and traced her finger down to her cheekbone. "It's usually hidden by the way she wears her hair."

"I thought she wears her hair up in that twisty way." Nick had never had a class with Dr. Claridge, but Kim had pointed her out on campus. Nick hadn't noticed any scars. All he'd noticed was that Fiona Claridge was young and pretty with light hair—blonde? Light brown? She looked kind of elegant, like a character from those Jane Austen chick flicks his sister loved. She just needed the long dress and a big stone manor house. And a butler.

"She wears those bangs that get longer on the sides," Kim said. "But when I saw her at the track, she was all sweaty and had pushed her hair back."

"If you saw her close enough to notice the scar, I'm betting you were stalking her."

Kim giggled. "Maybe I wanted to see how she was doing."

"You're dumber than a clod of dirt. First you send that package, then you parade yourself in front of her?"

"Didn't you hear what I told you? I *want* her to know I did this. I want her to know I found out what a monster freak she is. She knows, but she can't touch me. That's why it's awesome."

"What if someone saw you leave the package?"

"No one did. The hall was empty. Plus, I had a big hat on and an old coat I never wear. And I stole my roommate's boots which have, like, four-inch heels, so I was a lot taller than normal."

Sticky with sweat, limbs rubbery from the racquetball workout Kim had put him through, Nick wanted to bail out of this conversation and go shower. "Good for you. You showed her. I'm going to get dressed."

"You don't think I'm done, do you? One wimpy package?"

"You're kidding. More?"

"That was just the overture, baby."

Nick didn't know whether to laugh or hit Kim over the head with his racket. Kim could get so weird sometimes, grabbing on to something and letting it take over her life. Most of the time it was funny, like when she got fired from that store at the mall for being rude to a customer, and she'd come back half a dozen times, in difference disguises, to release big bags of crickets.

"If you're this obsessed, I'm not going to feel sorry for you when you get caught," Nick said.

"She targeted me, Nick. This is personal. I'm not going to just forget about it."

"You cheated and you got caught. End of story. Get over it."

"Want to help me?"

Nick sighed and slumped down with his back against the wall. "Yeah, I want to help you. I want to help save you from a life of crime. I'm calling your mom to tell her what you're up to."

"Oh, you want to spill each other's secrets? I think I'll call *your* mom." Kim made her voice prim. "'Aunt Olivia, I thought you should know that when Nick was a senior in high school, this football player called him a bunch of nasty names, so he broke into the guy's house while he was on vacation and—"

Nick grimaced. "Fine. The pact of silence holds."

"Good boy." Kim poked his shoe with her racket. "I want you to break into Dr. Claridge's office for me."

"Why?"

"You'll find that out later. It's more exciting if it's mysterious."

"Forget it. Maybe you want to get kicked out of school, but I don't."

"You know my roommate, Madison?"

Long black hair, skin so smooth it reminded Nick of the ivory satin his sister had worn on her wedding day, and a body that would make a supermodel look like an underfed rat. "Yeah. Ooh. Yeah."

"How would you like a date with Madison?"

"I thought she had a boyfriend."

"They broke up." Kim pretended to wipe tears from her eyes. "Poor Maddy. So right now she's free and lonely."

Nick tried not to drool. "What makes you think she'd go out with me?"

"She owes me a favor."

"Ouch. So I'm a favor."

"Take what you can get. You know you'd kill to spend a few hours with Madison."

"I might."

"Get me into Dr. Claridge's office. Come on, Nicky. How long has it been since we've done any Mission Impossible stuff? Is life over at twenty? Seems that way, for all the fun we've had lately. Aren't you bored? Don't you want some adventure?"

Nick pictured the curve of Madison's lips. Kim did have a point. "Yeah, life's been kinda dull lately," he said.

Kim grinned.

Chapter 2

FIONA PAINTED A THICK LAYER of paint stripper over the top of the doorframe, set the timer, and walked to the window, where she could breathe clear, damp air instead of chemical fumes. The spring weather had been surprisingly mild today, but with the sun setting, the air had chilled. Soon she'd need to shut the windows.

She should have been grading essays for her first-year writing classes—she'd be up until two in the morning trying to catch up after taking this break—but she'd been so twitchy after spending hours hunched over her desk that it was either take a break or lose her mind.

She turned and surveyed the bare wood of the mantel she'd finished stripping two weeks ago—beautiful wood once obscured by layer after layer of paint. This eighty-year-old fixer-upper had enough projects to keep her time and her salary occupied for years, especially considering the slower-than-snail's pace at which she worked.

Good.

She leaned against the window and stared at the black outlines of trees silhouetted against a twilight sky streaked with lavender and coral pink. A beautiful sunset. One of the many sunsets Mia had never seen.

She drew a deep, slow breath, breathing in the scent of crumbling leaves exposed by melted snow and the freshness of trees beginning to bud. She'd tried not to let the package and note bother her, knowing that the more distress she felt, the greater the victory for the culprit. But she hadn't been able to get Mia out of her mind.

Thank heavens for James. He'd sought her out multiple times this week—a couple of times to chat with her at her office, once to urge her to accompany him and a few other colleagues to a new seafood restaurant that had recently opened in downtown Bennett, and once to show her a new 3D cell puzzle his sister had sent him. They'd ended up wasting an hour playing with it, piecing cell organelles together while Fiona teased James about his biology-professor nerdiness in getting such a kick out of the gift, and James countered with gibes about how many copies of *Jane Eyre* Fiona owned.

James never directly mentioned the package, but she knew he was checking to see how she was doing and offering his support. It was like him to be that thoughtful, even though the cruel reminder of Mia must have stung him. Her thoughts slid backward to the night she'd been heading out for a late-night grocery store run and had opened the apartment door at exactly the wrong moment, making herself an unintentional witness to James and Mia's first kiss. James and Mia had jumped apart so awkwardly that Fiona had had to bite her lip to keep herself from laughing.

She'd nearly convinced herself the package had come from someone in Canfield—someone still mourning Mia—until she'd seen Kimberly Bailey at the track two days ago. Kimberly had passed close to Fiona several times and had looked over at her, a sweet smile on her face. The message was clear: *Gotcha.*

She shouldn't be surprised that Kimberly had decided to seek revenge. It had startled and unnerved Fiona at how personally Kimberly had taken the fact that Fiona had caught her plagiarizing an essay—and how much she shrugged off her own responsibility. *"You were totally hunting for something to pin on me. You've always trashed my stuff, even when it's twice as good as the slop everyone else turns in. Why should I keep trying when you've been cheating* me *out of decent grades since day one?"* Kimberly had finally stalked out of the meeting, leaving Fiona in the humiliating position of defending herself to department chair Sarah McKinley—no, she had *not* graded Kimberly unfairly; no, she had *not* targeted her in any way; she'd noticed the essay because it didn't seem to be in Kimberly's usual style—in fact, was less clever, less insightful, and relatively colorless compared to Kimberly's usual work. After reviewing several of Kimberly's graded essays alongside other student essays, Sarah had agreed that Kimberly's accusations were false, but Fiona could only pray any negative vibes lingering from the whole mess would fade long before Fiona's tenure decision.

The timer dinged. Fiona picked up her putty knife and went to attack the liquefied, bubbling paint on the doorframe.

She'd told Sarah about the package; Sarah had consulted with Dean Everly, and to Fiona's acute discomfort, she'd found herself in a meeting where Hawkins College President Trenton Kregg had—kindly and bluntly—asked that she let the matter die; there was no proof of any student involvement, and any investigation would only stir up pointless trouble. Mortified to have the college administration discussing something as personal and painful as the note writer's reference to Mia's death, Fiona had quickly agreed that silence was the best course. She'd tossed the car keys into the lost-and-found—chances were Kimberly had swiped them from some other student—and hoped this ugly episode was over.

Would Kimberly try anything else? No. She'd found a creative way to vent her anger, and now she could move on, while Fiona settled back into the normal craziness of struggling to dig herself out before the next session of class and the next avalanche of student essays came rumbling down the mountain. Had she really once pictured the life of an assistant professor of English as an idyllic existence of contemplating great books and discussing them in cozy seminars with students who shared her passion for literature?

And since when does anything turn out exactly the way we imagine it at age twenty-one? She wiped a mass of gelatinous old paint onto a newspaper and scraped another section of the doorframe. She *did* enjoy her job. Life was good. If she could keep things as they were, that would be enough. More than enough. More than she deserved.

The phone rang. She set down her putty knife, tugged off one glove, and went to answer it.

The name on the caller ID surprised her. *Willis, Bradley.* It must be Carissa. Mia's sister. She hadn't talked to Carissa in a couple of months.

Exhaling in an attempt to relieve the anxiety constricting her lungs, Fiona reached for the phone. *Calm down. Since when do you get nervous talking to Carissa? Don't let that ridiculous package shake you like this.*

"Hello?"

"Fiona? This is Carissa Willis."

"Carissa, how are you? It's so good to hear from you."

"It's been too long, I know. You're all of an hour away, and I don't see you any more than I did when you were at Princeton. Life is nuts."

"How are Brad and the boys?"

"Everyone's fine. The kids are getting so big. David's such a reader now. He's going to be a total bookworm."

"I approve."

Carissa laughed. "And how are you? Is Hawkins treating you well?"

"Yes, things are good."

"Is James settling in? I can't believe you two are both teaching there. Talk about a cosmic coincidence."

"It definitely is, and he's happy to be here. It's almost a miracle to land a job in academia at all, let alone land your dream job."

"Hawkins is his dream job?"

"So he claims—mainly, I think, because finding a job as quickly as he did is something that usually only happens in dreams. It's been good having him here."

"Tell him I said hi."

"I will."

"Fiona . . ." Carissa's tone went somber. "I'm afraid I have bad news. Alan Taylor's mother passed away earlier this week."

"Oh no. Oh my goodness. What happened?"

"They . . . found her in the creek that runs through the woods behind their house."

"Oh no." Thoughts of walking with Alan through the acres of tree-covered land behind the Taylors' home flashed into Fiona's mind. She forced the memory away.

"She must have fallen down the bank," Carissa said. "And the water in the creek was so high . . . it was the day of that nor'easter—was the storm bad up where you are?"

"Yes." Fiona tugged off her other glove and sat at the kitchen table. "She was out in the storm? Why?"

"Gavin said that's how she dealt with stress—wait, did you ever meet Gavin? Alan's younger brother?"

"No. He was on a mission when Alan and I . . ." Fiona didn't finish the statement, and Carissa quickly filled the silence.

"Anyway, Gavin said she vented stress by walking around their property, no matter how rotten the weather. Maybe she was upset about something. Gavin's here in Canfield now—he got laid off, and he came home to save money while he's looking for a new job."

"I thought he was in medical school," Fiona said, remembering what Linda had said in her Christmas letter.

"He *was* in med school, but he dropped out a while back. He got a job with a pharmaceutical company but got laid off, so he's looking for something new."

It didn't surprise Fiona that Linda hadn't mentioned Gavin's change in plans. Likely she was determined that he *would* become a doctor, and even if Gavin had changed his mind, Linda hadn't changed hers. For as long as she could get away with it, she'd act as though medical school were still a go.

"Alan's here," Carissa said. "I saw him last night—I took dinner over to him and Gavin. He's—did you know he moved back from Virginia a year or so ago? He and his wife are living in Waltham."

"Yes, I know. Linda still sends—sent—me Christmas letters." Linda's gleeful report that Alan had come home to Massachusetts had rattled Fiona, even as she'd told herself her fears were years out of date. Alan was married, no doubt happy. He'd moved on without her.

At least not *all* the damage she'd done in her life was permanent.

"The funeral will be on Saturday at eleven, at the church," Carissa said. "I wanted to let you know just in case, but I understand it might be awkward with the Taylors . . ."

"Of course I want to come." The words formed automatically, but the instant Fiona spoke, she felt sick. *Could* she face Alan Taylor again? Could she face not only his family and friends, but Mia's family and friends?

Do it. Don't be such a coward. Can't you give the Taylors that much?

"It would be wonderful to see you," Carissa said. "Do you need directions to the church?"

Fiona swallowed. "No. I can find it."

"Come over for lunch after the funeral. It's been too long since we've had a chance to hang out."

"Thank you." She tried not to sound hesitant. She didn't mind the idea of lunch with Carissa—bubbly, gracious Carissa could make things comfortable and keep the conversation flowing—but she had the feeling Carissa's husband wouldn't be thrilled at Fiona's presence. She'd always had the sense that Brad didn't like her.

No, not always. Since the accident.

"Bring James, too, if he wants to come," Carissa said. "I'm on my own—Brad can't get off work—so I could sure use the company. Much as I love my kids, sometimes I'm dying to talk to adults."

Relieved, Fiona said, "I don't know if he'll be able to come to the funeral, but I'll let him know."

"Tell him he should come to my house just for the scientific pleasure of seeing what three little boys can do to a formerly spotless environment in less than a year. He could write a paper about it. 'Hands of Pure Destruction: A Study in Chaos and Doom.'"

Fiona laughed. "How are you enjoying your parents' house—or I should say *your* house?"

"*Love* the space. Hate caring for the yard. No wonder my mom decided she'd had enough and wants to buy a condo when they get back from their mission." Carissa chuckled. "I'm kidding. I love the yard, and the boys are great at pulling weeds. Just don't tell Mom what we've done to her dining room carpet."

After a few minutes of chitchat, they said their farewells. Her knees a little weak, Fiona returned to the doorframe to scrape off the rest of the paint.

Linda Taylor, dead. Alan must be having a terrible time right now. He'd lost his father when he was ten, and he'd been close to his mother—too close. Linda's overbearing personality and her tendency to interfere in her children's business was one of the things Fiona had decided she couldn't deal with long-term. She thought of the most awkward conversation she'd had in her life—Linda warning her what a fool she'd been to break off her relationship with Alan and that if she let Alan slip away from her, she'd regret it for eternity.

Water under the bridge, Fiona thought. Though the occasion of Linda's funeral was a tragic one, there would be some peace in seeing the Taylors again—supporting them at this time of loss and knowing all the upheaval and hurt feelings between Fiona and Alan were past.

Peace. That's all she wanted.

* * *

Carissa Willis tried to hang up the phone, but her hand trembled so much that she miscalculated and banged the phone into the edge of the base, knocking it off the table.

Blinking at the tears welling in her eyes, she bent and picked up the base. Why was she still shaking? She'd done the right thing, called Fiona Claridge, sounded like the concerned friend solemnly reporting on a mutual friend's tragic death. The words had been right, the tone had been right, everything had been right.

She hadn't wanted to call Fiona, but Fiona would want to know of Linda's death, and calling her was the natural thing to do. She couldn't let anyone—especially Brad—start thinking her behavior in relation to Linda's death was strange.

You did the right thing. Get a grip before the kids see you. If six-year-old David walked in and saw her flushed and teary, he'd know something was wrong. And she could imagine him reporting it to Brad in his chatterbox way—*"Dad, Mom was crying."* She could pretend it was grief for Linda, but she doubted Brad would fall for that.

Maybe she'd done more than she needed to, inviting Fiona to lunch, but it would have seemed odd to let her come to Canfield without making a courteous effort to visit with her for a couple of hours.

Calm down. At least now, with Linda dead, maybe everything would be all right. Carissa knew it was wrong to feel relief, but she couldn't help it.

Death was the only thing that could have shut Linda Taylor's mouth.

* * *

"This thing itches." Nick readjusted his shaggy wig.

Kim pushed his hand down. "Quit messing with that."

"I look like an idiot."

"You always look like an idiot."

Nick rolled his shoulders inside the heavy sheepskin jacket Kim had found for him to wear. The weather was mild tonight, and he was sweating as they walked across campus. Sweating and itching. He jammed a finger under the back of his wig and scratched. "How come you get the Barbie-doll look and I get the caveman getup?"

"Typecasting." Kim flipped her fingers through her long, platinum-blonde wig. "Quit whining. Shaggy hair is *in*."

"I like my hair short."

"Join the Marines. And *stop messing with your wig*. Can't you act natural?"

"You didn't tell me there would be costumes involved." Nick lowered his voice to a whisper as they passed two girls holding Dunkin' Donuts cups and chattering loudly.

"Duh, Nicky," Kim said when the girls were out of earshot. "Do you want someone to be able to report that they saw Nick Cortez near Dr. C's office?"

"So instead they'll report that they saw a caveman—with fleas." Nick scratched again. Kim slapped his hand.

As they walked up the sidewalk to the Gilmore Building, Nick's adrenaline began to pump. He grinned, fingering the miniature tool kit in his pocket. Kim was right—it had been *way* too long since they'd had some fun. He still didn't know what she wanted to do once she was in Dr. Claridge's office, but whatever it was, it would be creative. Kim wouldn't settle for something dull like dumping desk drawers and spray-painting profanity on the wall.

The building was silent, and their footsteps echoed as they walked up the stairs to the second floor. "What if she came back after you saw her leave?" Nick whispered. "She might be lurking in her office right now, waiting to ruin your life."

"Knock first to see if anyone's there," Kim whispered back. "What kind of a pea-brained burglar are you?"

"And if she answers the door, we . . . what? Sell her some Girl Scout cookies?"

"We run."

The second-floor corridor that housed Dr. Claridge's office was deserted. With a mischievous look at Kim, Nick flattened himself against the wall and crept toward the office, his gaze darting in every direction and his thumb and index finger forming an imaginary gun. Kim clamped her hand over her mouth to stifle her laughter.

"Watch my back," Nick whispered when they reached the correct door. He offered his index finger to her. "Here, you take the gun."

She smacked him on the side of the head. "Hurry!"

Nick knocked on the door. No answer. He pulled out his tool kit and set to work. Apparently, no one worried much about theft around here—the lock opened so easily that he was disappointed. He'd hoped for a little more challenge.

They slipped into the dark office. Kim closed the door behind them and switched on the light.

"Nice job," Kim said. "You may look dumb, but you're good at crime."

Nick sprawled in Dr. Claridge's desk chair and looked around. The office was small—really small, with no window. Fiona Claridge was young enough that she couldn't have been teaching at Hawkins for long, and obviously, she didn't rank. No stray papers or coffee cups littered the desk. Apparently she liked things tidy—Nick's mom would approve. On top of the filing cabinet sat a framed snapshot of a group of women and a houseplant with lots of trailing tendrils. Gold-framed diplomas hung on the wall, along with a watercolor of a New England country road, complete with fall foliage, a stone fence, and a red barn. A bookshelf was crammed with the type of books Nick preferred to read in CliffsNotes form, along with textbooks.

"What kind of a nut job signs up for a life of forcing people to read *The Scarlet Letter* and correcting their grammar?" he asked.

"Don't look at me. I'm not an English major." Kim pivoted slowly, studying each corner of the office. "And keep your gloves on. You don't want to leave any fingerprints, just in case."

"They're on, they're on." Nick picked up a photo from the group of family pictures on the desk. A bunch of smiling people in matching T-shirts. Must be a family reunion. He held the picture out to Kim. "So which one is she?"

"You've seen her before."

"Yeah, but there are too many blonde women in this picture. She must have a lot of sisters."

"She's the one with poison dripping from her fangs."

Nick chuckled and set the picture on the desk. He picked up a photo of an older couple who must be her parents. No pictures of anyone who looked like a boyfriend or husband. "So what's the punch line this time? Dead fish in her files?"

"Yuck." Kim stopped, her gaze focused on the plant on top of the filing cabinet. "That'll be perfect."

"Perfect for what?"

From her pocket, Kim removed a small black object and handed it to Nick.

"A camera." He examined it. "With audio. You're kidding."

"Here's the receiver." She held up a flat, palm-sized object with a small screen. "I'm going to hide it under the couch in that lounge area down the hall. It'll record everything and I can check it whenever I want."

"You're sticking a camera in her office? What are you hoping to record? You think she's up to something nasty that will get her fired?"

Kim shrugged and took the camera back. "I just think it'll be fun."

"Uh-huh," Nick said. "You're getting freaky weird on me. Can't we just do the dead fish thing?"

"Too crude." Kim parted the leaves of the plant.

"So what happens when she waters that plant?"

"It's silk, you dunce."

"Have you heard rumors? Is she sleeping with a student or something?"

"We'll find out, won't we?"

"You must suspect something, or you wouldn't be trying this."

"Anyone that heartless *must* be up to something. Just think how much fun we could have if we snare a few choice videos."

"What rumors have you heard about her? You must have heard rumors."

Kim shrugged, but her reddening cheeks belied the casual gesture. She positioned the camera and moved the framed photo a little to the left. "Who says I've heard rumors?"

Nick frowned. Her voice was sharp—not angry-sharp, but hurting-sharp.

"Kim," he said. "Did Dr. Claridge do something else to you besides flunk you? Steal your boyfriend or something?"

"Shut up and think about Madison Brower," she said.

Chapter 3

JAMES SWITCHED OFF THE ENGINE and looked at Fiona. "Are you all right?"

"Yes." Fiona wished she'd done a better job of hiding her apprehension. She'd tried to keep up a normal amount of talk on the drive to Canfield, but she'd found it difficult to think of conversational topics. James had seemed to struggle as well; he'd been unusually quiet.

Through the windshield, she looked at the church steeple. She associated this building with Alan, but James would associate it with Mia's funeral.

No wonder he was quiet.

At least Fiona didn't have to live with memories of the funeral. She'd been two thousand miles away, in a hospital in Utah while doctors reconstructed her crushed arm and leg with titanium rods and plates. She hadn't had to see Mia's coffin or witness the tears of friends and family or see the pain of an entire ward mourning the loss of a young life—all while knowing *she* was the one who'd brought this pain.

She'd have to face some of those people now, but eight years had passed. Few to none of them would even know who Fiona was. And of Mia's family, only Carissa would be here. Her parents were in Texas on a mission, and all of Carissa's siblings had moved elsewhere.

She wondered what James was thinking right now. He must be remembering—must be hurting.

"Are you worried about seeing Alan again?" When James was concerned about someone, he could speak in the most warm, gentle voice Fiona had ever heard—a voice that dissolved defensive barriers and made the hearer certain there was nothing James cared about more than helping with the problem at hand.

"He is so sweet! *He's just so . . . so . . . attentive? Is that the word I want? I don't mean in a smothery way. I mean, he cares, he really cares."* Mia's words replayed in Fiona's head. She pictured Mia grinning, eyes bright as she lay on the carpet in their apartment with her feet on the couch and her arms flung behind her head. *"I think I'm in love."*

"Fiona?" James reached for her shoulder but dropped his hand before he touched her.

"I'm sorry." Fiona tried to close Mia out of her thoughts. It was like trying to close the door on an overfilled closet; no matter how she pushed, the door couldn't click into place with everything piled against it. "No, I'm not worried about seeing Alan—not in that sense. But this must be such a difficult time for him." She reached for the door handle. If she kept sitting in the car, James would keep asking questions, and she'd end up admitting that she *was* worried about seeing Alan—selfishly worried. At a time when she should have been solely focused on comforting the Taylor family, she was hoping for some comfort of her own—to see Alan look at her with forgiveness, or kindness in his eyes—or even lack of interest, if that was the best she could hope for. If she could blank out her roiling, painful memories of Alan with new memories—replace the hurtful things she'd said to him with gentle words—

"Don't come here again, Alan. Don't call me, don't text me, don't contact me in any way. I don't want to hear from you—ever. How can I make this any more clear?"

"How long has it been since you saw him?" James asked.

"Six years." Fiona stepped out of the car. James's matter-of-fact question helped jolt things into perspective. Why was she so edgy? It was unlikely that Alan would do anything more than greet her and thank her for coming, ask her politely about her life and work, and move on to the next guest.

Lining the hallway outside the Relief Society room were easels displaying pictures of Linda Taylor and her family. Fiona stopped in front of each easel and looked at the pictures without seeing any of them. Her heart pounded and blood burned her cheeks. She shouldn't have come. Why would Alan's family want her here now?

"Talk to you for a minute?" James whispered.

Caught off guard, she nodded and let James lead her away from the easels toward a deserted corridor of classrooms.

He steered her into a classroom and turned to face her. "If this is too difficult," he said quietly, "we can go somewhere else until time for the funeral to begin. You don't have to attend the viewing. Or we can skip the services altogether."

If anyone else had said those words, Fiona would have been embarrassed at how clearly her face had exposed emotions she wanted to hide. But this was James; she didn't have to put on a good front for him.

"I'm sorry," she said. "I didn't think I'd get so nervous."

"Don't apologize. I know things got tough with Alan and it was a bad time for you all around. If you don't want to talk to him, you're not obligated to do so."

A bad time. A tactful, oblique way to refer to Mia. Why was she so selfish that the only pain she could focus on was her own?

"I want to do this. Linda would . . . appreciate it."

"With all due respect, Linda is dead and won't care one way or the other. You don't have an obligation to put yourself in an uncomfortable situation."

"It won't be like that. Alan's married now. Everything is fine. I want to support the family. It's the least I can do."

James studied her, and Fiona could read the thoughts behind those glasses that she teasingly accused him of wearing in an effort to look scholarly: *If everything is fine, why are you red in the face and trembling?*

"I thought I was more level-headed than this," she said, trying to smile. "It must come with the academic mindset—treating history as though it's current reality."

"That excuse would be credible coming from a history professor. Not an English professor."

"Treating fiction as though it's current reality," Fiona amended.

"Anytime it gets too hard for you, say the word and we'll leave."

Fiona nodded. She already felt better. The spasm of panic was easing.

She stepped into the hallway. James kept a light hand on her elbow as they moved toward the Relief Society room; she appreciated the friendship conveyed in his touch.

A man strode around the corner. Renewed trepidation hit Fiona as she saw his face. The handsome features were thinner than Alan's, and he looked taller—or perhaps it was simply his leanness making him appear taller than he was—but the family resemblance was strong. Alan's younger brother, Gavin. She'd never met him in person, but Linda had shown her enough photos of him to fill a gallery.

As they came within speaking distance, Fiona had no idea what to do. Should she greet him? Introduce herself? Gavin looked as though he was on an errand. This wouldn't be a good time to stop him and try to have a conversation. But to nod and smile and let him pass seemed so—

Gavin stopped in his tracks and stared at her. He looked so startled that a new surge of blood scorched Fiona's cheeks. She hadn't expected Alan's brother to recognize her, let alone gape at her in shock. What had Alan and Linda told him about her?

You mean besides that you shattered Alan's heart and killed Mia Hardy?

"You're Fiona Claridge," he said.

"Yes." Fiona offered her hand. "You must be Gavin."

He shook her hand, his movement abrupt and almost robotic. He was still staring at her as though he didn't know what to make of her. The unsettled feeling inside Fiona turned into nausea. If Gavin was gawking at her like this, what would Alan's reaction be?

"I'm so sorry about your mother." Fiona tried to sound graceful, but it was difficult with Gavin staring at her.

James extended his hand. "James Hampton. I knew your brother at BYU."

Gavin shook James's hand without looking at him. His eyes—blue-green, with dark brows like Alan's—stayed focused on Fiona. The dazed look cleared from his face, and fury flared in his eyes.

"What are you doing here?" He spoke quietly but with an intensity that made the soft words pierce her ears more sharply than yelling.

"I—came to support—"

"*Get out. Go,* before—" He stopped, looking over Fiona's shoulder. She turned and saw a heavyset woman in a purple dress hustling along the corridor.

"Gavin, dear, how are you?" The woman brushed past Fiona and threw her arms around Gavin. Gavin returned the hug in the same tense, mechanical way he'd shaken Fiona's hand.

"My back is killing me; that flight was terrible!" The woman released him, straightened Gavin's tie, and brushed a piece of lint off his shoulder. "Linda would have throttled me if she knew I cut things so close, but what could I do? Ava had her baby yesterday, and gracious, I couldn't leave before the little one arrived! How are you holding up, dear?"

"I'm okay," Gavin said. He glanced at Fiona with a look so hard that it seemed to shove her backward. The message was still there in his eyes: *Get out. Now.*

Oblivious, the woman turned and grasped Fiona's hand. "My goodness, honey, but you look familiar. I'm ashamed I've forgotten your name."

Fiona wanted to flee the building. Considering Gavin's reaction to her presence, she didn't dare talk to Alan or anyone else. "I—don't think we've met. I was just—"

"Oh, my goodness! Oh, I knew it was somewhere in this old brain. I've seen your picture. You're Fiona Claridge."

Mouth dry, Fiona nodded.

"My dear, it's so good of you to come! Linda told me all about you. I'm her sister, Marilyn Patterson."

"It's—very nice to meet you."

"And who is this handsome young man?" Marilyn shook James's hand.

"James Hampton." James's voice was calm and pleasant, as though Marilyn hadn't just interrupted Gavin in the process of throwing them out. "I knew Alan at BYU."

"Oh, a friend of Alan's! How nice. My goodness, Linda would be so happy to have you both here. How *is* Alan doing? I need to go find him, the poor boy. He's probably thinking I've abandoned the family."

"We . . . haven't talked to him yet." James shot a glance at Fiona. "He didn't know we were coming. I'm not sure—"

"Come with me, you two," Marilyn said happily. "He'll be thrilled!"

"I—maybe we'd better—" Fiona fumbled to think of a way to excuse herself and James, but Marilyn grabbed Fiona's elbow with one hand and James's elbow with the other and marched them toward the Relief Society room. From the consternation on James's face, she could tell he didn't have any better idea than she of how to worm out of this.

Gavin fell in step behind them. Fiona wondered if he'd tell Marilyn he didn't want them at the funeral, but he said nothing.

"I heard Linda talk about you *so* many times, Fiona," Marilyn said. "She adored you."

Fiona was certain not all of Linda's remarks had sprung from adoration, but it was tactful of Marilyn to pretend so. "Thank you. I'm so sorry for your loss."

"Gracious, it *was* a shock. Not how I expected Linda to go. You'd expect her to wrassle a creek into submission—not drown in it!"

"I'm so sorry."

"I'm sure she went out fighting," Marilyn said. "Heaven help that creek—Linda will probably haunt it."

Since Marilyn was smiling, Fiona smiled back, wishing desperately that she could slip away. But what good would it do now? If she left, Marilyn would tell Alan she'd been here. Better to face him than to leave him wondering at her odd, cowardly behavior in showing up to the funeral but running away before she talked to him.

A jumble of people and conversations filled the Relief Society room, and Fiona felt a flicker of hope. There were so many people here—she would only be one face among the multitude of friends and family who had come to pay their respects to Linda Taylor. She would have her brief contact with Alan, shake his hand, express her sympathy, and slip back into the crowd. And Alan *wouldn't* react the way Gavin had. She knew him better than that. Even if he didn't want her there, he'd be polite.

White roses decorated the lid of the closed coffin. Fiona was glad to see it closed; the thought of seeing Linda's face brought wrenching anxiety, as though Linda might open her eyes, glare at Fiona and say, *"I told you you'd be sorry, didn't I?"*

Alan was standing to the right of the casket, talking to an elderly couple. A spurt of adrenaline made Fiona's skin prickle as she looked at him.

Her memories of him were so tangled up with guilt and pain that she'd forgotten how when Mia had introduced her to Alan Taylor, it had taken all her self-control not to stare at him. The perfect angles of his face . . . the green eyes . . . the way a cowlick made his thick brown hair stand up a little on the right; he could never get it to lie flat at that spot and kept his hair short so the cowlick blended in.

He looked older now, and it only made him more attractive—stronger, more mature. But the shadows under his eyes and the tautness in his expression made him look both vulnerable and remote, a familiar expression that started Fiona's apprehension on another climb. *Take it easy. Alan's changed; you've both changed. He lost his mother a few days ago—how do you expect him to look?*

Marilyn released Fiona and James and charged toward Alan. "Alan, dear!"

Alan gave a quick nod of farewell to the elderly couple and stepped forward to meet Marilyn's hug.

"I got here as soon as I could," Marilyn said as she pulled back. "Ava's baby came yesterday afternoon."

"Congratulations!" Alan smiled at his aunt. His smile sent another shot of adrenaline through Fiona's bloodstream. She'd forgotten how appealing he looked when he smiled.

"I found some friends of yours out in the hallway." Marilyn swung around and waved toward Fiona and James.

Alan's gaze met Fiona's.

"Hello—hello, Alan." Fiona's tongue got stuck partway through the greeting, and she had to swallow to moisten it.

Alan didn't speak. His expression had frozen, and his skin went ghost-white.

Fiona's heart hammered insanely. "I'm so sorry about your mother."

He blinked. A small, choky laugh rasped from his throat, but his eyes were still strangely blank, as though her presence had stunned all emotion into numbness.

"How are you doing?" she asked. When Alan didn't respond, her words remained stranded in the air—awkward, ridiculous.

"Carissa Willis told us what happened." James moved half a step past Fiona, drawing Alan's attention. "I'm sorry."

Slowly, Alan extended his hand. "James. It's been a long time." The words emerged stiff but courteous, and the rigid look on his face eased a little as he shook James's hand.

"It's good to see you again," James said. "I'm sorry it's under these circumstances."

Alan nodded, his gaze moving back to Fiona. "Fiona." He spoke her name at last, his voice soft. "You came."

He stepped toward her, one hand lifting, then both, then one, like he couldn't decide if it would be appropriate to hug her or shake her hand. Seized with the same confusion, Fiona reached hesitantly for his hand, but when their fingers met, this businesslike contact seemed too cold. She stepped forward and embraced him.

Alan's arms went around her. The smell of him—the same soap he'd used since college—brought a surge of memories. "I'm so sorry," Fiona whispered.

They broke apart. "It's good of you to come." Alan had obviously regained control of himself—his voice was smooth, almost elegant. Alan had a beautiful voice. No one could recite Byron and Frost like Alan. "I heard you were teaching at Hawkins College."

"Yes," Fiona said, the burning cramps in her stomach gradually easing. Gavin might hate her, but Alan clearly didn't. "James is there, too."

"Wouldn't your mother be thrilled to pieces to have Fiona here today?" Marilyn straightened the ropes of purple and blue beads she wore around her neck. "What a wonderful surprise!"

"Yes, she'd be very pleased," Alan said.

"Linda was an amazing woman." Marilyn leaned toward Fiona and lowered her voice. "Amazing and stubborn. I *told* her—how many times did I tell her?—that marching off into those woods wasn't a good idea. Didn't I tell her?" She squeezed Alan's elbow. He jerked slightly, as though her grip hurt. Marilyn quickly drew her hand away.

"I'm sorry, hon. Did I poke you?"

"No, not at all." Alan gave a thin smile. "I slipped and cut my elbow when I was out . . . looking for Mom."

"You poor boy." Marilyn patted his shoulder. "It's a wonder you didn't end up in the creek with her. Those paths are overgrown, and Linda was no spring chicken—and no athlete either." Marilyn patted her wide hips. "Neither am I, you can see. Fiona, you'll come to the graveside and to the luncheon afterward, won't you? You and James, of course."

Caught off guard, Fiona glanced at James. Gavin was still standing behind them, and she didn't dare check to see what expression had appeared on his face at Marilyn's invitation. "Thank you, but we wouldn't want to intrude on the family." Before Marilyn felt obligated to insist, Fiona added, "And we have a lunch engagement with a friend here in Canfield."

"Who's that, dear? I used to live here, so I might know them."

"Carissa Willis."

"Oh goodness, Carissa will surely be at the graveside—she's Ginny Hardy's daughter, and Ginny was so close to Linda. I know Carissa will want to be there in her place. Do join us at the cemetery, even if you can't come to lunch. It would mean a lot to Linda to have you there."

"Please come," Alan said.

Fiona smiled noncommittally, stalling so Gavin would have a chance to object if he wanted to.

Gavin said nothing.

Whether or not Gavin openly objected, Fiona didn't want to go to the graveside. Now that Alan had greeted her warmly with none of the rancor or misery that had filled their last meeting, she wanted to take that new memory and slip away before anything could mar it. The selfishness of that desire embarrassed her; she was supposed to be here supporting the Taylors, not seeking her own peace of mind.

"Thank you," she said. "We'd be honored to come."

A young couple approached Alan, obviously wanting to talk to him. "I'll see you later." Alan smiled at Fiona and turned toward the couple. As he lifted his hand to place it on the man's shoulder, his gold wedding band caught Fiona's eye.

Now that she'd seen Alan, she could finally believe what she'd been telling herself for years—that Alan was fine. He'd moved on.

Relief made Fiona feel both oddly weak and oddly light on her feet as she and James walked away.

* * *

Dark clouds filled the sky, and a damp spring wind blew her skirt around her legs as Fiona lingered at the edge of the group gathered at the graveside. After offering kinds words and handshakes to assorted family members, she'd drifted tactfully to the periphery of the gathering. Despite Marilyn's and Alan's invitation, she felt like a stranger here, and she preferred to remain a stranger—she tensed every time she introduced herself, wondering if the person shaking her hand recognized her name and was thinking, *"Oh, Fiona Claridge. The woman who—"* followed by disturbing thoughts of Mia or Alan. But to her relief, she had sensed no animosity. Even Gavin hadn't said anything else rude, though he'd kept his distance. Apparently Alan was willing to forgive what she'd done to him, but Gavin wasn't.

Fiona's thoughts drifted to that Christmas Eve she'd spent with Alan's family. She never should have come to Canfield for Christmas, but Mia had been so excited to have her visit. By the time vacation approached, Fiona had already begun having doubts about her relationship with Alan, but she'd told herself she was visiting Mia, not Alan, and she wasn't sure about Alan yet anyway—maybe she *wasn't* ready to break it off. Maybe she needed to give the relationship more time. Besides, she'd already purchased the plane ticket, and she couldn't go home to Arizona for Christmas that year. Her parents were in Nevada, assisting Shannon after the birth of her first baby, and Fiona didn't want to crowd herself into Shannon's one-bedroom apartment.

Justification. Rationalization. In her heart, she'd already known that for all she'd been head-over-heels for Alan at first—and part of her still *was* head over heels—he was wrong for her. What an awful, selfish mistake it had been to come to Canfield. She thought of the way Alan had invited her to go for a drive after dinner on Christmas Eve—her conflicting emotions as she got into the car—the growing certainty that she wanted to end the relationship fighting against reluctance to hurt Alan. She couldn't break up with him on Christmas Eve. After the holidays—back at school—that was the time to tell him.

She didn't realize how far she'd led him on until he'd parked in the church parking lot and remarked that he would have preferred a view of the temple spire, but with snow forecast, he didn't want to drive all the way to Belmont.

She'd never thought the sight of a diamond ring could catch her so off guard or make her feel so sick.

Fiona pushed the memories back. Alan would think she was ridiculous if he knew she was standing here stirring up guilt over pain he'd long since forgotten. Alan was happily married. Fiona was part of his past, nothing more.

James was standing a few yards away, talking to one of Alan's uncles—a zoologist who had cornered James upon learning he taught biology at Hawkins. As soon as James finished his conversation, they could leave. They were due at Carissa's soon. Carissa had already left to finish preparing lunch.

"So—you and James are together now?" Alan's voice startled her. She hadn't realized he'd come up behind her.

Putting a smile on her face, Fiona turned toward him. "No. We're just friends."

"Wild coincidence, him ending up at Hawkins with you."

"It's a remarkably small world at times. How are you holding up, Alan?"

He shrugged. "I'm hanging on. Fiona . . . I know it's clumsy timing, after all these years, but I want to tell you I'm sorry for everything."

The apology surprised her. "So am I," she said. "And it's past, Alan. Ancient history. So update me on your life. You're back in Massachusetts now."

"Yes, it's good to be on the home turf, or nearly. We live about twenty minutes outside Boston. I'm working for a start-up company. Graphic design, web development, that kind of thing."

"They're lucky to have you." Fiona thought of the strikingly beautiful e-cards that used to show up regularly in her inbox, filled with intricate graphics, changing images, strains of classical music, and Alan's own lyrical poetry. Alan was a genius on the computer.

"I'd love to meet your wife." Fiona gestured toward the woman she'd seen next to Alan during the funeral and graveside service. Petite and curvy and pretty, with glossy mahogany-brown hair. She hadn't dared go up to introduce herself, since she had no idea what—if anything—Alan's wife knew about her. "Summer, right?" Fiona added, remembering the name on the wedding announcement.

"Yes," Alan said. Fiona expected him to escort her over and introduce her to Summer, but he didn't move.

"Carissa told me you're restoring an old house," he said.

"'Restoring' is too strong of a word. I've been doing some painting, and so on. A tiny old fixer-upper was the only thing I could afford, so Home Depot and I are well acquainted."

"Given that you're only a couple of years out of school, I'm impressed you can afford anything in this market."

"Well—the only reason I could is because of a very generous gift from my grandfather. He's ninety-five and has decided he'll get more pleasure out of watching his family enjoy his gifts now than letting his lawyer read the will after he's gone."

"It's admirable that you're fixing up the home yourself."

"I'm learning as I go. *Very* slowly."

"You're outdistancing me. When I try DIY projects, the only thing I learn is how to swear."

Fiona laughed. It was good to hear Alan joke. He'd been so bleak, so miserable, the last few times they were together. "I actually love it. It's a sanity project. When I feel I can't read or write one more word, I pick up a paintbrush. But I have almost zero time for it—it took me three months to paint one room. I don't think I'll ever finish, but it makes it more *mine*, fixing it up with my own hands."

"Building your own ivory tower."

She smiled. "The ivory tower is a tad crazier than I imagined it would be."

"What classes are you teaching?" Alan asked, but his tone was absent, and he was looking at Summer, who had started walking toward them.

"Two first-year writing courses and two upper division American literature courses. It's the writing courses that are killing me. Department policy requires that I assign weekly essays—"

"Forgive me for interrupting you," Alan said. "I'd better go find Gavin. The rain is going to start at any moment, and we'd better head back to the church."

"It's—been good to see you," Fiona said. Alan nodded and walked away.

Off balance at his abrupt departure, Fiona expected Summer to turn and go with him, but she continued to Fiona's side.

Fiona smiled at her. A Mother Nature name suited Summer Taylor. She had a fresh, natural beauty and wore little makeup—she didn't need it with those clear blue eyes, long and dark lashes, and olive skin dotted with a few freckles across her nose. "I'm Fiona Claridge, an old friend of Alan's," Fiona greeted her. "I was so sorry to hear of Linda's death."

Summer gave her a long look. "So you thought his mother's funeral would be a good time to slobber all over Alan and make your dirty secret public?"

Summer's coldness hit like a blast of ice water in the face. "My—dirty secret?"

"Don't act stupid. I know what's going on."

"I have no idea what—"

"That's a big scar." Summer's eyes traced the scar from Fiona's hairline to her cheekbone. "If I were you, I'd consider plastic surgery."

Fiona's hand went involuntarily to her face where her windblown hair had exposed the scar. "I came to the funeral to support the Taylors," she said icily. "Not to 'slobber all over' anyone. Alan's aunt invited me to the graveside."

"Funny how it wasn't Alan's *aunt* you were flirting with."

Fiona couldn't fathom how her brief conversation with Alan could have looked like flirting, even from a distance. "I spoke with Alan about work and my fixer-upper house. That's all."

"I'm sure you'll think of some better ways to comfort him later over his mommy's death."

"You are completely irrational. I would never—"

"I know what's going on. I have proof, sister."

"Proof of what?"

"You'll get what you deserve." Summer swung around and started walking away. "I hope your guy friend is driving you home," she called back over her shoulder. "I hear you have some problems behind the wheel."

Chapter 4

As soon as they finished dessert, Carissa's four-year-old son dragged James off to the family room to see his new Wii game. The two-year-old tagged along, shrieking something incomprehensible about Mario and Luigi, leaving Carissa and Fiona alone in the dining room.

"I'm sure Brad's sorry he missed seeing you and James," Carissa said.

Fiona doubted Brad was sorry at all, but she smiled politely. "Tell him I said hello."

"Would you like a little more pie? Please say yes, because I want some, and as long as you're eating too, I won't feel like a pig. Take one for the team, will you?"

Fiona laughed and passed her plate. "Just a sliver." Carissa's French silk pie was the creamiest, richest chocolate concoction she'd ever tasted, and she welcomed an excuse to eat more of it.

With their plates restocked, they ate silently for a moment. Fork in hand, Carissa leaned across the table and said softly, "I didn't get a chance to ask you after the funeral. Did it go okay with Alan, or was it really awkward?"

"Alan was fine," Fiona said. "But I shouldn't have come. Gavin was *not* pleased—he wanted to grab me by the collar and throw me out the door. And I offended Alan's wife."

Carissa drew back, her gaze dropping to the tablecloth, and fidgeted with her fork. It was a gesture that reminded Fiona of Mia. Carissa and Mia didn't look a lot alike, beyond similar coloring—auburn hair, pale skin that could sunburn in a rainstorm, and brown eyes—but the lowered gaze and the fidgeting with whatever was in her hand was very Mia—Mia when something made her edgy.

"What happened?" Carissa asked without looking up.

"She walked up to me," Fiona said. "I introduced myself as an old friend of Alan's and she promptly accused me of coming to the funeral to hit on him. She seemed to think we were—that we're . . . involved. Or at the very least, that I'm pursuing him."

"Oh, Fiona! I'm sorry."

Not for anything would Fiona repeat the other things Summer had said—the cruel references to the accident. "I'm sorry for coming. I had no idea it would make her think I was chasing Alan. I can't fathom what's going on in her head. Obviously she knows I'm an ex-girlfriend, but it's been six years since I've even heard from Alan! What in the world could make her think I was involved with him? She said something about having 'proof.' Proof of what?"

Carissa poked at her pie, misery in her face. "I don't know anything about any proof, but I think—" She stopped and shoved a bite of pie into her mouth.

Fiona thought of pretending not to notice that Carissa had stopped herself from revealing something, but she felt so jarred and bewildered by Summer's words that she couldn't pass up the chance to learn what had set her off.

"You think what?" Fiona asked.

Carissa's cheeks went pink. "It seems . . . tacky . . . to talk about Linda's quirks now," she said, an uneven edge to her voice that made her sound almost as angry as embarrassed. "But I think Linda liked to throw your name in Summer's face."

"*What?*"

Carissa drew a deep breath, and Fiona had the impression she was struggling to calm herself. Discussing Linda must be difficult for her—she'd known the Taylor family all her life and Linda's death must have been a terrible shock. "I'm sure it's not news to you that Linda really liked you and wanted you to marry Alan," Carissa said.

"But that was so long ago—"

"I don't think Linda had ever . . . given up. From that first time she met you when she came out to BYU while you and Alan were dating, she picked you as his bride. I know all this through my mother. Linda and my mom were good friends."

"But . . . I was out of Alan's life before Summer ever entered it."

"Well . . ." Carissa took another bite of pie, and Fiona figured she was wrestling with her conscience over wanting to say something and fearing it was inappropriate. Carissa didn't like speaking negatively of anyone.

"Linda was a talker, I know," Fiona supplied. "I suppose she liked telling Summer all about anything to do with their family."

"Probably." Carissa averted her eyes. "But . . . please don't repeat this to anyone. I feel bad saying it, but I think it's only fair that you know. Linda didn't like Summer. She thought you'd come to your senses and you and Alan would marry. When Alan got engaged to Summer—from what my mother told me—Linda tried to talk him out of it, telling him he was making a mistake and you and Alan were meant for each other."

"Did Summer know this?"

"Linda . . . um . . . she said all this in front of Summer."

Horror stabbed Fiona. "Alan and Summer have been married for three years. Didn't things ever improve between Linda and Summer?"

"Not much, from what my mom said. They tolerated each other, but I don't think Linda ever got to the point of being happy about the marriage or really embracing Summer as a daughter-in-law."

"Linda didn't still talk about me, did she?"

"I don't know. She'd still mention you to my mother sometimes. I don't know if she talked to Summer about you."

If Linda was insensitive enough to refer to Fiona when objecting to Alan's engagement, she probably hadn't been shy about referring to Fiona at other times. No wonder Summer had been rude to Fiona. Seeing her must have felt like a punch in the stomach. Still—what kind of proof could she think she had against Fiona? Even if Linda had flat-out lied about Fiona's interest in Alan, Summer must have known what Linda was like. She'd know not to believe her—wouldn't she?

Unless Summer's marriage was already so troubled that she was ready to believe the worst?

Feeling sick, Fiona put her fork down. As desperately as she wanted to believe Alan's marriage was happy, she'd suspected something was wrong when Alan had ignored her request to be introduced to Summer and had walked away as soon as Summer approached them. "I never would have come to the funeral if I'd known."

"I know. I'm so sorry. I would have warned you, but *I* didn't know until this morning. My mother called to ask me to give her sympathies to the Taylors today and let them know they were in her prayers. When I mentioned you were coming to the funeral . . ." Carissa's voice faded. "By then you were probably on your way, so I just hoped for the best. I'm so sorry. It's my fault for telling you about the funeral."

"It's not your fault. I should have known better than to come."

"You were just being kind."

Fiona didn't want to admit how much of her desire to come had stemmed from selfish motives. In an effort to find her own peace, she'd angered Gavin, hurt Summer, and stirred up more conflict between Summer and Alan. Summer had been rude and aggressive, but it was hard not to sympathize with her insecurity.

At least you know Alan's forgiven you. And maybe now that Linda wasn't here to drop hints that Summer had not been her choice as a daughter-in-law, things would improve between Summer and Alan.

Carissa tactfully changed the subject. "So . . . it's good to see James again. I always thought he'd end up in some high-tech research lab, not teaching at a small New England liberal arts college."

"He loves teaching," Fiona said. "Interacting with the students is his favorite—"

The phone rang. Carissa jumped to her feet. "Excuse me. If I don't get that, Peter will, and he'll babble the caller's ear off."

Carissa returned a moment later, brow furrowed in an expression that was either confusion or anxiety. "It's for you," she whispered. "It's Alan."

Fiona's nerves tingled. "Thank you." She took the phone. Carissa made a quick exit, leaving Fiona alone.

"Alan, hello."

"I'm glad I caught you," Alan said. "I'm deeply sorry about Summer. I heard what happened. Her behavior was completely inappropriate."

Had someone overheard their conversation and reported to Alan, or had Summer told him? "I never would have come if I'd had any idea it would be hard on her. Please let her know I'm sorry for upsetting her."

"She's the one spitting venom and *you're* apologizing?"

"I hope I haven't—caused trouble between the two of you."

Alan chuckled, a dry sound empty of amusement. "Fiona . . . it wouldn't be possible to make things worse between Summer and me. We're getting divorced."

"Oh no! Alan, I'm so sorry."

"I'd hoped she'd have the class to keep up a good front at the funeral. My family doesn't know yet—except Gavin—and Mom's funeral wasn't the right time to tell people. Summer had no right to take her anger out on you."

"I'm . . . afraid I upset Gavin as well."

"What did he say?"

"He just didn't want me there. I understand. He was probably worried about Summer's feelings."

"Don't let Gavin bother you. He shoots fire, but he cools down fast. Thank you for coming today. It means a lot to me."

"I'm sorry it caused problems." Fiona restrained both the urge to ask Alan if he and Summer had tried counseling and the even more tactless urge to point out that with Alan's interfering mother gone, things could get better for him and Summer if he'd give it a chance. She had no right to give him advice, nor did she have any idea what issues—besides Linda—had wrecked the marriage. Besides, she knew Alan would resist the idea of counseling. "I'm sorry for everything you're going through."

"Thanks, Fiona. Thanks for caring. Mom always—" His voice cracked. "Mom always said you were a jewel."

Fiona bit her lip, finding it impossible to respond graciously to Linda's compliment when if Linda had complimented Summer instead, maybe Alan's marriage would have gotten off to a better start. "Hang in there."

"I will." His voice sharpened. "I'd better go."

Fiona pictured Summer walking into the room and catching Alan on the phone with her. Hastily, she said good-bye and hung up.

She pushed back from Carissa's dining room table and went to return the phone to Carissa, her remaining hopes for Alan's happy life with Summer steadily crumbling inside her.

* * *

Clouds darkened the Monday morning sky and raindrops speckled the kitchen window as Fiona put her plate and cup in the sink. The prospect of another storm made her think of Linda Taylor sliding down a muddy creek bank and drowning in a rush of water.

She closed her eyes and inhaled, trying to force extra oxygen and extra energy all the way to her toes and fingers. Eyes still closed, she exhaled. She would not dwell on Linda today or on Alan and Summer or on Saturday's funeral debacle. She'd never contact any of the Taylors again, and the only connection she'd keep with them would be fervent prayers that Alan and Summer would be able to work out their problems.

Today would be routine, uneventful—and crammed with her efforts to finish marking the latest batch of essays before her students started complaining. She put on her raincoat, grabbed her umbrella and briefcase, and opened the front door.

A rectangular object wrapped in a rain-speckled grocery sack sat on the mat. Without picking it up, Fiona gingerly opened the grocery sack and saw a white candy box tied with an orange-and-pink plaid ribbon.

Sure it's candy. Just like last time. Dread at what might be inside the package made it hard for Fiona to breathe. Was Kimberly Bailey stupid enough to swagger up to her house and drop a cruel package on her doorstep? Fiona's first impulse was to kick the package down the porch stairs and leave it there in a mud puddle, but instead she picked it up. She couldn't ignore this. If Kimberly was vicious enough and unbalanced enough to continue lashing out at Fiona—and to take things up a notch by targeting her at home—Fiona needed to report it.

She pulled the box out of the sack. Tucked partway under the ribbon was a note that looked like an afterthought—an unevenly folded piece of notebook paper. Fiona tried to tell herself not to read it, but shouldn't she at least see what she'd be slapping on Sarah McKinley's desk as soon as she arrived on campus?

Stepping inside the house, she unfolded the note.

Fiona—sorry about the delivery method. I was going to ring the bell, but your lights were off, and I didn't want to risk waking you up. I just wanted to wish you a good morning. And it's okay if you eat fudge for breakfast.

James

She blinked at the note, feeling as though she'd opened a door expecting chill darkness and had gotten sunlight in her eyes.

Candy from James? What a sweetheart he was to try to cheer her up after the stress of the weekend. She'd told him everything about Alan and Summer on the drive home from Canfield.

Residual adrenaline from the jolt of finding the package made her fingers shaky as she slid the ribbon off the box. Fudge sounded like a perfect breakfast food. She lifted the lid.

Inside, a knife with a long steel blade lay on a bed of cotton. Taped to the cotton was a note:

Try stabbing your victim next time. It's cheaper than crushing her head with your car. Or maybe you ought to cut your own throat before you hurt someone else.

Chapter 5

"YOU'RE OKAY? YOU'RE REALLY OKAY?" Sitting on the edge of Fiona's desk, James studied her, his brow creased.

"I'm okay." Fiona rubbed a smudge off the closed lid of her laptop, thinking bleakly of all the work she hadn't gotten done today. "I'm just disappointed that I didn't get any fudge."

James tried to smile, but his eyes were so troubled that the expression failed. "*Do* you think Kimberly Bailey is responsible?" he asked. Given that James's name was on the note, he'd been included in this morning's session in President Kregg's office. The verdict this time: Fiona needed to go to the police. Even though the note writer hadn't directly threatened her, the inclusion of a weapon was enough to tip the balance. Kregg's fear that an unstable student might do damage outweighed his fear of stirring up scandal.

"James, I told the police precisely what you heard me tell President Kregg and Provost Clarke—Kimberly took it very personally when I caught her plagiarizing an essay and felt I had maliciously targeted her. She was furious and said some harsh things. Then the day after I received the first package, she seemed to make a point of seeking me out on campus, and she appeared very smug. But none of that is even close to being proof of anything. The culprit could easily be someone from Canfield. After we went to the funeral together, someone there might have thought of using your name to get me to open the second package."

"Someone who knows what my handwriting looks like."

Fiona pictured the neat, squarish, mostly caps handwriting on the note. It had been close enough to James's handwriting that she hadn't questioned it. "You wrote in that memory book Linda's sisters were making. Anyone at the funeral could have taken note of your hand-writing."

"And obviously a student of mine could have taken note of it as well," James said grimly. He'd been openly dismayed when he'd learned the name of Fiona's angry student, and Fiona had been surprised to learn that James knew Kimberly well and liked her—she was an ex-tremely bright student who did stellar work in his introductory cellular biology class and was thinking of switching her major to biology.

"James, I could easily be wrong in suspecting Kimberly." Fiona didn't want to admit that one segment of Kimberly's tirade against her was true—Fiona *hadn't* liked her. In class Kimberly had often looked bored—staring into space, checking the clock, or even resting her head on her desk. When she did offer comments, she had a knack for offering insightful analysis painted with condescension or sarcasm— an attitude that literary analysis was mostly nonsense that professors made up, but look, I can play the game, too. Fiona had wondered why on earth she'd signed up for a course in nineteenth-century American literature if she found it such a waste of time—until she heard Kimberly complaining to a friend that she was stuck in there because her parents had this *thing* about educated people knowing classic literature.

But Fiona was positive she had *never* graded Kimberly unfairly, nor had she been seeking to catch her cheating.

"I could be completely wrong," Fiona repeated.

"Does Sarah think you're wrong? Has she talked to Kimberly yet?"

"She's talked to her. Kimberly denied everything. Sarah tactfully suggested that if Kimberly was feeling frustrated, she might want to talk to someone in the counseling department, but Kimberly gave her a blank look and said she was fine; what was the big deal about a grade? I'm sure she'll do the same if the police approach her. She's smart enough not to give herself away, and there's no proof."

"'Smart enough not to give herself away,'" James quoted. "So you *are* convinced she's guilty."

Fiona folded her arms on the desk and rested her cheek on her arms. She was due in class in twenty minutes. How was she supposed to teach when she was so tired that she'd be lucky to keep her eyes focused, let alone make sense of her lecture notes? Last night's insomnia had left her fatigued, and stress had killed any remaining flicker of energy. "James, it was the way she looked at me. The . . . glee in her face. The challenge. As though she *wanted* me to know she'd found a way to hurt me, but I'd never be able to prove it. And yes, I know my interpretation is completely subjective. Maybe she was smiling sweetly to say she forgave me."

James touched her arm. "You're in bad shape, aren't you? You should go home. Stick a note on the door telling your students class is canceled."

"Are you joking?" She sat up straight. "Cancel class when there's a good chance Kimberly tried again to smear my reputation when she was talking to my department chair a couple of hours ago?"

"Sarah would have told you if she had any concerns about you."

"Maybe. But this is still not a good time to look like a slacker."

"You've had a bad few days. Those vicious packages, the stress of seeing Alan again, the cruel things Summer said—"

"So I'm a nervous wreck. But I can't cancel class. I just wish I hadn't been idiot enough to go to that funeral."

"Beating yourself up about a well-meant decision that you can't change accomplishes nothing. Summer and Alan's problems are Summer and Alan's problems—not yours. Let it go."

She sighed. "I should have known it would hurt Summer to have me there."

"There's no way you could have known that Linda tried to use you as a wedge between Summer and Alan."

"I should have suspected she didn't have a good relationship with Summer. She never mentioned Summer in her Christmas letters. She'd talk about Alan and Gavin, but never Summer."

"Fiona, whatever problems Linda had with Summer are *not your fault*. Let it go. This is not your problem."

"I . . . sent Summer a note."

James raised his eyebrows. "An apology?"

"Yes. I wanted her to know I was sorry my being there had hurt her, that Alan and I were finished long ago, and I never would have come to the funeral if I'd thought it would offend her. She'll probably burn it, but at least I tried."

James slid off the desk and settled into a chair. He sat slouched there, his chin in his chest, the overcoat he hadn't bothered to remove bunched around him. "That was nice of you."

She could read his expression—James was afraid her contacting Summer would stir up more trouble, and half of her agreed with him. But the other half had nagged her relentlessly until, at four o'clock in the morning, she'd finally climbed out of bed and penned a note of apology.

"After finding out the type of things Linda said to her, I couldn't let it lie," Fiona said, hoping to clear the frown off James's face. "I had to at least try to make amends."

"Explain to me why you're blaming yourself for things Linda Taylor said."

"I'm not. I'm blaming myself for not having enough sense to stay away from the funeral. And why would Summer claim she had 'proof' of something—apparently proof I was pursuing Alan or that we were having an affair? How can she have proof of something that doesn't exist?"

"Summer is not behaving rationally. Her marriage is a mess, and she's looking for someone to blame. She probably made up the line about proof in hopes you'd slip and give her some proof. You'll let it go now, right? You've apologized. You'll let it go."

"I'll let it go."

"Did you—mention Summer's name to the police?"

"I didn't want to, but I didn't see how I could hold it back. They wanted the names of anyone who might be angry with me, and obviously she is. Whether or not they'll talk to her, I have no idea, but I hope I haven't . . . caused more trouble between Alan and her."

James pulled his chin out of his collar and straightened in his chair. "Summer and Alan's problems are *not your fault*."

"I know. But I can't help feeling bad for both of them."

"I understand. Just make sure you don't start blaming yourself." James checked his watch and rose to his feet. "I know you need to go teach, so I'll stop pestering you."

"Feel free to pester me anytime. And I'm sorry you got pulled into the situation with these packages."

"Don't worry about it." James adjusted the scarf around his neck. The weather was too mild for a scarf today, and Fiona suspected

James was wearing it more to show his appreciation for her work than for warmth. "Fiona . . . I want to talk to Kimberly."

"Do you think that's a good idea?"

"Yes, I do. I have a good relationship with her, and I've seen a different side of her than you have. I'm not going to accuse her of anything. I'll just test her a bit and see how she reacts. And if I think you're right about her, I'll kindly get across the message that in the end, she's only hurting herself. Maybe she'll listen to me."

She might, Fiona thought. James was far more gifted at connecting with people than Fiona was. If anyone could talk a headstrong troublemaker out of making more trouble, it was James. "I hope she does listen," Fiona said softly. "Thank you, James."

"I'll do my best," he said.

* * *

Eyes chilly with hatred, Kimberly Bailey raised the knife and took another step toward Fiona. Fiona tried to retreat, but her limbs were numb. The best she could do was drag her feet backward one slow, excruciating inch at a time. Kimberly lunged and pressed the flat of the knife against Fiona's throat, pushing hard.

"I'll kill you," Kimberly whispered. "Like you killed Mia. You should have died in that accident. It was *your* fault. Murderer."

Fiona choked, gasping for air against the cold pressure of the blade. Her arms flopped and her hands batted clumsily at Kimberly's hands—batted at nothing . . . at darkness. The room was dark and quiet, the only sound the hiss of the wind against rattly old windows.

She sat up in bed, breathing deeply. She could *feel* where the blade had pressed against her throat. It had been a long time since a dream had been so vivid. Rubbing her throat with her fingertips, she sank back against her pillow. *Don't let Kimberly's "gift" shake you like this. That's what she wants. She'd be thrilled if she knew you were having nightmares.*

Fiona tried to relax her muscles and return to sleep, but soon the effort made her twitch. She'd be better off abandoning sleep and reading for a while. Fumbling in the dark, she turned the switch on her nightstand lamp.

Nothing happened. The power—the clock on her nightstand was dark, too. Power outage.

After that frightening dream, the darkness evoked horror-movie prickles. Annoyed that she was so susceptible to her imagination, Fiona pushed back the covers and stepped onto the cold, hardwood floor. Holding her hands in front of her to keep from knocking into something, she shuffled to the closet and grabbed her bathrobe off the hook. If her heart would stop pounding like she was about to be murdered, maybe she could handle this with some degree of logic.

Was the power out for the neighborhood, or had something tripped her circuit breaker? She trudged over to her window and parted the curtains. Across the street and a few houses down, a porch light glowed. The problem must be with Fiona's house.

Trailing her fingers along the wall, she headed for the stairs. In the kitchen, the light on the stove glowed, but the microwave was dark, and when she tried the light switch, it didn't work. She opened the cupboard near the back door and groped inside until she located a flashlight. The beam of light cutting through the darkness made her feel a little better.

The stairs chilled her bare feet as she descended into the basement. Even on a bright summer afternoon, this basement was creepy, and Fiona shuddered as the flashlight beam passed over bits of mortar crumbling from the old stone foundation and a large spider clinging to a web strung across one corner of the room. She should have moved into a cheerful, modern apartment.

Take a deep breath. It may look like a setting Poe would have loved, but it's just a dusty old basement, not a torture chamber. There's nothing scary here, unless you have a phobia of cobwebs.

But she should have put on shoes. No telling what might crawl across the floor at night.

Carefully lighting her path, she moved toward the circuit breaker. At least the previous owner had upgraded the electrical system before Fiona moved in. She knew very little about electrical wiring. That was one facet of home repair she preferred to leave to experts.

She opened the panel and shone the light on the switches. Most of the switches were in the off position. What could have tripped so many of them? Thank heavens for the circuit breaker, or she might be dealing with a house fire instead of a blackout. She'd call an electrician first thing tomorrow.

As she reached to flip a switch to on, a creak overhead made her jump. Another creak . . . and another—it sounded like someone walking. *Stop it. This house always creaks.*

More creaks—almost rhythmic. Were those the same type of noises Fiona had made when walking down the stairs from her bedroom to the kitchen?

Heart hammering so violently that she felt dizzy, Fiona swung around and aimed the flashlight at the basement stairs. Was someone in the house? Kimberly? Maybe leaving vicious packages wasn't a big enough thrill anymore?

"Get a grip," she whispered. Kimberly was a coward. Anonymous packages were her style, not breaking and entering. No one was in the house. The creaking noises were the house settling or the wind. Only that bad dream, the blackness, and this eerie basement had shaken her enough to make her perceive footsteps from random creaks.

Motionless, Fiona strained to hear any sound from upstairs. A few faint creaks. A long stretch of nothing. A faint rattling noise. The old singled-paned windows were prone to rattle—or might someone be trying to open a window . . . or a door—

Stop this. Fiona swung around and rapidly flipped the switches on the breaker. She stood for a moment, waiting to see if whatever problem had tripped them would trip them again. If that happened, she'd go to a hotel before she'd spend the rest of the night in a pitch-black house dreaming about knives and footsteps and Kimberly Bailey.

The switches stayed on. Fiona walked to the center of the room and yanked the chain that hung from the lightbulb on the ceiling. In the light, the basement looked grimy but harmless. No one was in her house. Kimberly wouldn't have the guts, and no thief would be desperate enough to think this tiny, grubby fixer-upper had anything worth stealing.

Leaving the light on behind her—she'd turn it off in the morning, since the thought of walking upstairs in the dark made her shudder—Fiona headed up the stairs. *Paranoid. Good luck on getting back to sleep now that you've scared yourself to death.*

In the kitchen and living room, she switched on all the lights. Everything was quiet. Nothing was out of place.

Embarrassed at herself, but unable to completely shake the skin-crawling sense that her home had been invaded, Fiona checked the front and back doors—both locked. She really needed to get a dead bolt on the back door—needed to replace that entire rickety old door, in fact. But Bennett was such a low-crime area that she'd put off replacing the door. Tonight that seemed like a stupid decision.

She checked the windows in every room, along with the closets, behind the furniture, and under her bed. No one was there, nothing had been disturbed, and the window locks—such as they were—were all engaged. She should make replacing the windows a higher priority on her home-repair list. *And why don't you put bars on the windows and motion sensors on the lawn while you're at it? You need to calm down.*

Fiona groaned softly. Kimberly would laugh until she cried if she knew how spooked Fiona had been tonight.

Until her adrenaline ebbed, there was no point in trying to go back to bed. Wrapping herself in an afghan Shannon had knitted for Christmas, Fiona settled in her recliner and opened a worn copy of *Gone with the Wind*. A book with a weather-themed title seemed appropriate tonight, given the way the windows—and her nerves—kept rattling.

Chapter 6

FEELING THOROUGHLY STUPID AND THOROUGHLY terrified, Carissa Willis hid behind the massive trunk of an oak tree and watched the Taylors' house. Gavin *had* to be leaving soon. When she'd dropped by at nine that morning with plate of warm cinnamon rolls—the neighborly Relief Society sister checking in on him—she'd casually inquired about his plans for the day. He'd told her he had a job interview that morning in Springfield. She hadn't dared ask him the time of the appointment—Gavin would have wondered why she was so curious—so she'd complimented him on jumping back into life and had added something trite about how pleased Linda would have been. But now, after spending an hour cowering behind a tree, she wished she'd risked asking the time of the interview. It was past ten and Gavin hadn't left the house.

It was a chilly, overcast spring day. She'd dressed warmly and it wasn't raining, but she felt stiff and cold. She jogged in place for a few seconds, fingering the keys in her pocket—the spare keys to Linda Taylor's house that had hung on Carissa's mother's key rack since Carissa was a child. When Carissa and Brad had purchased her parents' house and her parents had left on their mission, the keys had remained.

The rumbling sound of the garage door opening made Carissa sigh with relief. She leaned against the scratchy bark, waiting for the sound of a car driving away. She didn't need to worry about anyone spotting her. Her brown coat and tan jeans made her blend in with the multitude of trees that covered the Taylors' property. Even when she tried to make herself noticeable, she was blah and uninteresting; certainly no one would notice her now.

Carissa pulled her hood tighter around her hair. She'd thought maybe a brighter shade of auburn would add some appeal to hair that got duller and less red the older she got, but the dye job had ended up looking fake. Not that Brad had noticed.

Keith thinks you're beautiful.

She shoved the words out of her mind. She never should have listened to Keith's flattery.

Where was he now? Back in Indiana? Carissa wished desperately that he'd change his mind about opening his practice in Canfield, but she knew he wouldn't. He loved Canfield and had been so excited at the thought of coming home. When she'd called him in a panic, telling him of Linda's threats, he'd said he'd already heard from Linda, and he wanted to meet with her and smooth things over, and Carissa didn't need to worry. Had he had a chance to talk to Linda before . . . before—

Carissa shivered at the thought of Linda in that icy creek. *Don't think about Linda.*

Carissa had forced herself to call Keith a couple of times to see if he'd talked to Linda and what she'd said—had Linda told anyone?—but he hadn't answered his phone and hadn't called Carissa back. The last time she'd talked to him, the day before Linda died, she must have scared him off completely. She couldn't blame him if he wanted to hide from her after the way she'd blubbered, wailing about what an idiot she'd been and how she'd wrecked her life and could he please, please go somewhere else and never come near Canfield again.

Even if Keith *had* met with Linda, Carissa doubted he'd been able to smooth anything out. No one could smooth Linda Taylor out of a righteous huff, especially not a righteous huff centering around the juicy indiscretions of Carissa Hardy Willis. *"I'm sure you think this is none of my business, dear, but if I stood by and let Ginny Hardy's daughter lose her immortal soul, I wouldn't be much of a friend, would I? Of course, you'll want to do the right thing. Talk to Brad and the bishop, dear. You have two weeks, or I'll need to help you along a bit."*

Talk to Brad. The idea made her sick to her stomach. She'd make everything right someday, but right now she *had* to find those pictures and get rid of them.

She peeked out to see Linda's car reversing along the driveway. Gavin must have decided to take Linda's Ford Flex to his interview instead of his own rust-stained Honda. When the sound of the engine had faded, Carissa picked up the bucket of cleaning supplies that sat at her feet and darted around to the back of the house. From experience with bringing in the newspapers and mail when the Taylors were on vacation, she knew one of the keys she held fit the lock on the back door. The other key on the ring opened the studio at the edge of the Taylors' yard. She hesitated, looking over her shoulder at the small white-shingled building that Linda had ordered built when she'd decided she wanted her sons to take music lessons but didn't want to hear them practice. Linda's cell phone couldn't possibly be in there—did anyone even use the studio now?—but she'd better check it anyway.

In the studio, the piano was covered in dust, and boxes were stacked against the walls. Linda must have used the studio for storage. No way would she have left her phone here.

Carissa relocked the studio and hurried to the house. On the back porch, she slipped out of her boots so as not to risk leaving dirty footprints inside. Bucket of cleaning supplies in hand, she padded into the kitchen in her socks. This would have been so much easier if Gavin had accepted her offer to clean the house for him, but he'd refused, insisting he could handle it and Carissa was busy with her own family. But still, she'd brought the bucket of supplies just in case. If Gavin returned unexpectedly early and caught her here, she'd brandish a bottle of Windex and claim she'd decided to come clean up anyway as a surprise.

Not that the place needed cleaning. Linda had trained Gavin well; the kitchen was spotless except for one plate and one cup in the sink.

The easiest way to start searching was to dial Linda's number and hope that, miraculously, the battery on her phone hadn't died yet and Linda didn't have the ringer silenced. Carissa hadn't dared call from her own phone, but she'd be safe calling from the Taylors' phone. She lifted the phone from the kitchen wall mount. Halfway through punching in the number she'd memorized, she froze. What if Linda had left her phone in her car—the car Gavin was currently driving?

It probably wasn't in the car, but Carissa couldn't take the chance. She slapped the phone back on the hook and stood for a moment, drawing slow, lung-filling breaths and letting them out. It had been a dumb idea anyway—surely the battery was dead by now.

She had to stop shaking. If she started searching when she was trembling like this, she'd knock things over and drop things. She flexed her fingers and flapped her hands, trying to work out the tension. *You can do this. Find that cell phone.*

She'd be methodical about it, searching each room in the house. If she was lucky, the phone would be somewhere obvious. She knew Gavin and Alan hadn't begun sorting through Linda's belongings. She'd elicited that information when, wide-eyed and compassionate, she'd said to Gavin how difficult it must be for him, sorting through his mother's things and deciding what to do with them. Gavin had said they hadn't even started thinking about that. Everything was as Linda had left it.

Lucky for Carissa. The question was—had Linda spilled her secret to Gavin or Alan? She'd promised she'd keep her mouth shut until the deadline she'd set for Carissa had expired. But would Linda really have been able to resist telling her sons?

Gavin doesn't know, Carissa told herself. *If he did, he'd have acted embarrassed and awkward around me. Find that phone and he'll never know.*

Linda wouldn't have taken her cell phone on that last walk. Linda had told Carissa's mother that she never took her cell on her "stress walks" because she "needed to be completely alone." Carissa doubted a need for solitude had impelled Linda to leave the phone behind. After her drama-queen exits, she probably didn't want her family to have any way to contact her except to go racing after her.

Carissa set the bucket next to the wall shelves displaying Linda's collection of elephants—stone elephants, crystal elephants, porcelain elephants in multiple colors. It wasn't *really* wrong coming in here, was it? She *did* have a key, so she wasn't breaking in. And she wasn't going to take anything. She just needed to delete those pictures.

She scanned the kitchen counters and checked the drawer near the landline phone where Linda kept office supplies meticulously organized in plastic dividers. Pens, pencils, paper clips—the sight of a coiled black cord made Carissa gasp with relief. A cell phone charger. Maybe Linda had kept her phone with—

No phone. Just the charger. It was a good find anyway—chances were she'd need the charger to power up the phone enough to delete the pictures.

The phone was probably in Linda's purse. Carissa checked the coat closet, but the purse wasn't there. She checked the pockets of all the jackets in the closet. No phone.

Her footsteps sounded heavy and clumsy as she hurried up the stairs toward Linda's bedroom. Entering the bedroom felt more intrusive than entering the kitchen and living room, and Carissa's heart rate increased along with her shame. If her parents could see her, they'd be horrified—but not half as horrified as they would have been if Linda had followed through on her threat to send them those pictures.

She'd hoped the phone or the purse would be sitting on the dresser, but the only thing on the dresser top was family photos: Linda's late husband, a bunch of kids and young adults whom Carissa didn't recognize—must be nieces and nephews—Alan and Gavin, a wallet-sized picture of Alan and Summer—and a five-by-seven of Alan and Fiona. Carissa grimaced. If Linda had wanted to wreck her son's marriage, she'd probably died happy at the thought that she'd succeeded.

Carissa picked up the picture of Linda and Randall Taylor. She remembered when Randall had died—Carissa had been, what, twelve at the time? She remembered her mother crying at the news and asking her not to tell Mia any details—ten-year-old Mia already had nightmares about burglars and house fires, and if she learned Randall Taylor had died in a fire at the Taylors' cabin, she'd be traumatized for months. Carissa shuddered and set the picture down. How awful for Gavin and Alan to have both their parents die sudden, tragic deaths. Which would be worse? Asphyxiating on hot, toxic smoke like Randall had, or getting bashed against rocks by an icy, roaring stream—

Don't think about it. Are you trying *to freak yourself out?*

Carissa wiped her sweaty fingers on her jeans and opened the top dresser drawer. No cell phone—just a jewelry organizer filled with a multitude of chunky, colorful necklaces, and earrings and brooches in the shapes of flowers and animals. Carissa remembered how, as a child, she'd watched eagerly each Sunday to see what fancy jewelry Linda would wear. The purple and blue peacock pin had been Carissa's favorite—oh, and that glittery green frog pin; she remembered staring at it all through a Primary lesson, wishing she could touch it. And the silver whale necklace with the turquoise eye, and the bracelet of large purple-and-yellow-enameled pansies—

Carissa closed the drawer, feeling queasy. Linda would never wear any of this jewelry again. She wondered what Alan and Gavin would decide to do with it. Somehow she couldn't imagine Summer would want any of her mother-in-law's costume jewelry. Maybe one of Linda's sisters would want it?

Stay focused. The closet. Carissa hurried to open the closet door. With a tremendous surge of relief, she saw a big, red faux–alligator skin handbag hanging from a hook. She grabbed the bag and unsnapped the pockets on the outside. No phone. She plunged her hand inside the purse. Frustrated at the awkward way her sweat-sticky fingers fumbled through the contents of the purse, she finally emptied it onto Linda's bed so she could search more easily. Wallet, coupon case, tissues, lipstick . . . even a flashlight, a first-aid kit, and a book of inspirational quotes—good grief, was there anything Linda *didn't* keep in her huge purse? Just her cell phone, apparently. *I should have worn gloves,* Carissa realized. She was leaving fingerprints all over the place.

The thought made her giggle nervously. She'd been a police officer's wife for too long if she was worrying about fingerprints. Linda's death had been ruled accidental. The police would have no reason to care who had handled her purse.

Carissa replaced all the items in the purse and hung it in the closet. Where in heaven's name had Linda left her phone? Carissa continued through the bedroom, opening every drawer and even looking behind the bed, in case it had fallen there. No phone.

Tension cramped her stomach as she exited the bedroom and headed for the room Linda had used as an office.

Half an hour later, sweat was rolling down her sides, and only constant blinking kept tears from spilling down her cheeks. The phone wasn't here. Linda must have left it in her car, or maybe she *had* had it with her when she'd gone on that final walk. Carissa hoped so. If the phone had been in her pocket, then the water would have destroyed it. But what if it *was* in her car or somewhere else where Gavin or Alan would find it? Before getting rid of the phone, they'd be sure to look at the pictures she'd saved. Her sons would want to savor every last taste of her life, including any photos she'd taken in her final weeks.

Carissa fought an urge to start searching the house again. The phone wasn't here, and she had to get out before Gavin returned.

So frustrated that she wanted to scream, she stalked back into the kitchen to collect her bucket of cleaning supplies.

The doorbell rang. Carissa jerked toward the sound and her arm banged into a wall shelf, knocking over a porcelain elephant. She grabbed for the elephant, but it hit the floor and shattered.

Paralyzed, Carissa stared at the shards of porcelain. Had the visitor heard the crash? Did they know someone was here? Holding her breath, she waited.

After a long moment of silence, Carissa let the air out of her lungs along with a moan at how pathetic she was. What had she expected— that the visitor would keep ringing the doorbell, shouting, "I know you're in there!" and then tell Gavin his home had been invaded?

Biting her lip, she counted to fifty. When all remained silent, she crept to the front door and snuck a look out the peephole. No one. She glanced out one of the narrow windows that flanked the door. Leaning against the porch wall was a box with a shipping label. Wonderful. She'd freaked out over UPS.

Tears spilling over, she returned to the kitchen and started collecting bits of porcelain. What could she do about the broken elephant? She ought to replace it, but how? She had no idea where Linda had purchased it, and it was an unusual piece—a pink elephant painted with red and blue swirls. She'd have to hope Gavin didn't notice it was gone. He probably didn't pay close attention to Linda's collection, and there were at least two dozen other elephants on the shelves. But the pink elephant had been one of the biggest. How could he not notice its absence? And breaking it and not owning up made her as good as a thief. Maybe she should tell Gavin she'd come here to clean and had broken the elephant. She could apologize and offer to pay for it.

If that's your story, you'd better get cleaning. The thought of sticking around the Taylors' home and mopping the already-clean floors shredded her nerves. She had to get out of there.

She dropped the pieces of the elephant into her cleaning bucket, retrieved the broom from the pantry, and swept up the smaller pieces. Even if Gavin did notice the elephant missing, he wouldn't have reason to suspect Carissa of doing anything wrong.

At least until he looked at those pictures.

* * *

The flush on her cheeks and the shine in her eyes made Kim laugh as she studied herself in the mirror. "Could you try not to look *quite* so excited?" she whispered.

She tugged the hem of her silk blouse so it fell more evenly and picked a stray hair off her shoulder. Skinny jeans, dangly silver earrings, and high-heeled boots completed an outfit that looked classy enough to be eye-catching but subtle enough so it wasn't obvious she'd dressed up. Okay, maybe it was a *little* obvious—a woman would notice, but a man wouldn't. He'd just think wow, she is *hot*.

Kim took her brush out of her backpack and played with her hair for a moment. Sleek blonde hair curved around her face and brushed her shoulders with graceful wisps. Perfect—somehow both sexy and innocent. She pivoted, checking to see how she looked in profile. This restroom on the third floor of the Murphy Sciences Building was deserted, and she could take all the time she wanted making sure she looked her best. She touched up her lip gloss and spritzed her neck with a small amount of body spray. Not too much—heavy perfume would be a tacky turnoff—but enough to give her an appealing, feminine scent.

Perfect. Her makeup made her eyes larger and bluer and her lips fuller, but it all looked natural, not pancaked on. And the natural blush in her cheeks accented her cheekbones and made her eyes sparkle.

She draped her chocolate-brown leather jacket over her arm and picked up her backpack, careful not to mess up the line of her shirt. Moving with casual grace, she exited the restroom and strolled along the hallway. A couple of guys sitting in the lounge area looked up as she passed, and they *kept* looking—she could tell they were watching her all the way to the stairs. *Sorry, boys. I'm taken—or will be soon.*

She stopped in front of James Hampton's office door. She was a couple of minutes early, but that was all right. She had the feeling he was someone who admired punctuality. When he'd pulled her aside after class that morning and asked her to meet with him, triumph and excitement had erupted inside her like fireworks. She'd been holding her breath, waiting for this moment since she'd watched the recording from Dr. Claridge's office where Dr. Hampton had said he wanted to talk to her. This was the perfect chance to help him see what an ice-hearted devil Fiona Claridge really was.

She knocked.

"Come in," he called. Kim opened the door and stepped inside. She loved his office. His shelves were filled with cool, crazy models—glass flowers, a plastic model of the parts of a cell, a twisty DNA strand made up of colored balls.

"Hello, Kimberly," he said. "Thanks for coming. Please, sit down."

"Thank you." She made herself sound a little hesitant, as though she wasn't sure what to expect. When he'd approached her, he'd simply asked if he could meet with her in his office this afternoon. He hadn't told her why. It would be natural for her to look both interested and bewildered.

She sat in the chair across from his desk and set her backpack on the floor. He smiled at her—ooh, that *smile*, as though seeing Kim had made his day. Maybe it had!

"How are your classes going?" he asked. "Obviously, bio is fine."

She smiled back. Her scores in his class were nearly perfect. "I guess I've got a knack for it. Or a really great teacher."

He laughed. She loved the warmth of his laugh—he sounded so amused, so admiring, as though Kimberly was one of the wittiest people he'd ever met. "You've got a knack for it," he said. "I think, Kimberly, that you're smart enough to do well at anything you try."

"I hope that turns out to be true if I ever try skydiving," she said, and he grinned.

"If you decide to try it, let me know how it goes. The only way I'll ever skydive is vicariously."

"I'll text you from ten thousand feet." She mimed pushing keys. "Cold and windy. Small problem with parachute. Take care of cat for me."

He laughed. "I can see you having the guts to calmly text your last words as you hurtle toward the ground."

"It's not guts so much as a lot of practice with texting. Autopilot."

"You're a bright girl," he said. "And a gutsy one. But in freefall, the sensation of falling is lacking. It's good to think about what you're doing and open that parachute before it's too late."

Interesting approach into a touchy subject, Kim thought, making her expression attentive and slightly confused.

"Anger fades," Dr. Hampton said. "But the consequences of actions taken in anger can be much longer lasting."

She furrowed her brow. "True," she said, making it clear by her puzzled tone that she had no idea what he was leading up to.

"You had some difficulty in your American literature class." His eyes were so *warm.* He wasn't condemning her over a silly essay. She'd known he wouldn't. No reasonable person would.

"Yes." Kim lowered her gaze, hoping she looked penitent. "I . . . I made a mistake. It was so dumb. I was swamped, completely out of time, and I panicked and—and—took the easy way out. I felt horrible about it. I've never plagiarized anything before." She played with the cuff of her blouse, as though too embarrassed to look up at him.

"I understand making a bad decision under stress." His voice was kind and soft, like a gentle hand touching her cheek. "But you need to take responsibility for the consequences of that decision—not attempt to place blame on someone else. Anger is an excuse, Kimberly. An attempt to shift blame. You cheated. You violated the honor code. You knew the terms before you made that decision. You have no one to blame but yourself. Lashing out only hurts you. You might get a few moments of satisfaction, but in the process, you could take a mistake and blow it up into something that could rip your life apart. Do you understand that?"

She blushed. It *was* uncomfortable talking about this, knowing Dr. Hampton was wondering if she'd left those packages. "Did—did Dr. Claridge tell you I was rude to her? I guess I was. I . . . I was just so flustered and she—she—" Ooh, this was thin ice. If she stepped right, Dr. Hampton would end this interview convinced that Fiona Claridge was a stonehearted monster. If she stepped wrong—*crack.*

She looked up. Dr. Hampton was watching her steadily, his expression attentive. Kim wondered if he ever wore contacts—not that the glasses weren't cute, but she was curious what he looked like without them.

"I feel awful," she said. "I know I shouldn't have lost my temper and said nasty things to her and Dr. McKinley." *Step carefully.* She couldn't fudge on what had happened in front of Dr. McKinley. It was too risky; what if Dr. Hampton wanted to compare notes with Dr. McKinley? "I did go to Dr. Claridge's office the next day and tried to tell her I was sorry. I kept *trying*, and she kept cutting me off and . . . and she was so cold, like she was made of stone, like she couldn't even hear what I was saying, and I got mad again. But I know I shouldn't have yelled at her. I guess . . . I owe her another apology, right?"

His brows drew together, and she knew he was scrutinizing her, hunting for signs of duplicity. "That would be a start."

"I'll do it, if you say so. I'm . . . pretty nervous, though. Like I said, when I tried to talk to her, she . . . well . . . she . . . said some things that really hurt. Personal things, I mean, not things about the essay."

"Like what?"

Kim shifted in her chair and twisted the silver bracelet around her wrist. "It's . . . well . . . um . . ."

"What did she say?" His tone was gentle. Reassuring. She felt so *safe* with him. No way would Dr. Hampton criticize her or analyze every decision she made and shred it, like her parents did all the time.

"She—she called me a . . . spoiled brat, said I was wasting my parents' money, and it was obvious I didn't have the brains for college anyway, and why didn't I drop out and do something I'd be good at— like—like—" Kim straightened her shoulders as though mustering her courage. "Like working street corners in Vegas."

The shock on Dr. Hampton's face was a sweet sight to Kimberly, but she quickly averted her eyes as though embarrassed to repeat Dr. Claridge's ranting. "I know I shouldn't let it get to me. But I've always been insecure in school, worried I *wasn't* smart enough—my parents are super hard on me—and when she said those things, it stirred everything up again, made me wonder if I *did* belong in college, or if I'm just a worthless—"

"You are one of the brightest students I've ever met," he said. "Don't destroy yourself. I think it would be best for everyone if you stayed away from Dr. Claridge."

Kim nodded meekly. "Okay. And I'm really sorry about the plagiarism. I'll never do anything like that again."

"Glad to hear it." He sounded uncertain. She'd thrown him off balance. Good. She memorized the expression on his face. She wanted to sketch it later—that look that spelled the beginning of the end of whatever relationship he had with Fiona Claridge.

"I guess I shouldn't take it so personally—what she said to me," Kim added. "It's not like I'm the only one."

"What do you mean?"

"Well, she's . . . harsh with a lot of people."

"In what way?"

Kim squirmed in her chair and averted her eyes. "She ripped one of my friends apart over an essay, saying she'd read better stuff from a third-grader. And there was that guy—really shy guy, you know, the kind who hunches in his seat like he wants to be invisible—and she just lost it with him in class, in front of everyone, and went off on how she couldn't believe anyone so stupid could . . . well, anyway, let's just say I don't know anyone who would go to her for help." She formed her lips into a shaky smile. "Thanks for talking to me. You are . . . the most amazing teacher I've ever had. You care so much about your students."

"I try," he said, but he wasn't smiling.

"You've made a huge difference in my life. I hope . . . if I can ever help you with anything . . ."

"Thank you." He stood up.

She rose, knowing he was dismissing her. She was tempted to say something a little more overtly flirtatious, but that would be pushing things too far. He needed time to mull over Dr. Claridge's cruelty and realize how beautiful and interesting Kimberly Bailey was.

He moved to open the door for her.

"Thank you," she said. "I feel a lot better after talking with you."

He nodded.

She stepped through the open doorway, fervently hoping he'd say something to keep her there a little longer.

"Kimberly," he said, his voice quiet.

Kim's heart pinwheeled in her chest as she turned to look at him standing in the doorway. Today's baby blue shirt and royal blue tie made the dark blue of his eyes even more vivid. The intensity in his gaze made her heartbeat accelerate. She took a step toward him—a small movement, but enough to take her a little closer to him than people usually stood when talking. He'd get the subtle message: if he wanted to close the distance between them, it was okay with her. She felt a little lightheaded, imagining him bending down and touching his lips to hers—

"I've known Dr. Claridge for years," he said, his voice still quiet. "Lying to me about her doesn't help you at all. *Leave her alone.* The only person you're destroying through this childish revenge scheme is yourself. You have great potential. I don't want to see you tossed out of Hawkins with a criminal record."

Before she could answer, he stepped back and closed the door in her face.

Chapter 7

THE RINGING OF THE PHONE made Fiona jump. Annoyed with herself, she slid her computer aside and reached for the phone. She'd been edgy all evening, and it infuriated her to acknowledge that she was still unnerved over the thought of Kimberly Bailey—or someone else—creeping onto her porch and leaving that knife. She would have loved to be able to shrug the incident off as a pathetic prank, but the only pathetic thing about the situation was the way she kept jumping every time the house creaked—jumping and clutching at the flashlight in her pocket, afraid the power might go off again. The electrician hadn't been able to find anything wrong with the house's electrical system and couldn't explain so many breakers tripping, which made her worry that an undiagnosed problem would cause another blackout.

At the name on the caller ID, her nerves went from jumpy to frayed and snapping. *Taylor, Linda.* Who was calling her from the Taylors' house? For a moment she was tempted to let the call go to voice mail, but she forced herself to pick up the receiver. If she'd had the guts—or the idiocy—to send a note of apology to Summer, she ought to have the courage to talk to whichever of the Taylor clan wanted to contact her now.

"Hello?"

"Fiona?"

"Yes." The familiar male voice triggered an uneasy sense of déjà vu. Alan.

"This is Gavin Taylor."

Gavin. Not Alan. Now that Gavin had spoken more than a single word, it was easy to tell the difference. Gavin's voice was more brisk, less resonant. She drew a breath, ready to offer Gavin the same apology she'd given Summer—she was sorry for causing distress and never would have come to the funeral if she'd known it would hurt anyone—but Gavin spoke first.

"I apologize for how I acted at the funeral," he said. "You startled me when you showed up out of nowhere."

Fiona's death grip on the phone loosened a little. "Don't worry about it. I shouldn't have come. I had no idea there were issues that might make my presence unwelcome." How stiff could she possibly sound? "I'm sorry," she said. "The last thing I wanted to do was hurt your family."

Gavin said nothing, and Fiona wondered if his apology for his own behavior didn't include forgiveness for hers. "I'm sorry," she repeated. "How are you doing?"

"Okay, I guess. It's just very empty here."

She knew what he meant. After Mia's death, Fiona had never returned to the apartment she'd shared with Mia and Carissa. After she was released from the hospital, she'd stayed at her aunt's house in Lindon until she was strong enough to return home to Arizona. Her mother and Rebecca had taken care of packing up her things.

She'd feared that emptiness too acutely to even set foot over the threshold.

"I'm so sorry," Fiona said. "This must be such a painful time for you."

"Yeah. It's unreal. Every morning, I still expect to see her come through the door after her walk. Fiona, I've got a job interview in Nashua tomorrow, which puts me in your neck of the woods. If you're free tomorrow night, there are some things I need to discuss with you."

"With . . . me?"

"It has to do with Mom's will."

Oh no. Fiona's shoulders drooped and her eyes closed. Surely Linda hadn't been tactless enough to leave something to her. *She told Summer to her face that she would have preferred you as a daughter-in-law,* Fiona reminded herself. *If she was insensitive enough to do that . . .* Fiona had an uncomfortable vision of herself being presented with Linda's diamonds while Summer inherited her old Tupperware. "She didn't . . . mention me in her will, did she?"

"She did," Gavin said. "Very generously."

Oh no. Please no. "Gavin, you're all very kind, but I don't deserve anything from your mother, and I wouldn't be comfortable accepting it. I can send a letter to her lawyer—"

"We're talking about Mom's final wishes." Gavin's voice hardened, and Fiona knew she'd offended him. Guilt stabbed her in one of the few places not already smarting from the fear that Linda might have posthumously snubbed Summer in favor of Fiona. Fiona wanted to insist that she could *not* accept anything from Linda, but how could she tell that to Linda's grieving son?

"It's very kind of her to think of me," Fiona said, wondering if she'd ever said anything less sincere in her life.

"Are you free for a little while tomorrow night?" Gavin asked. "I can stop by whenever it's convenient."

"I'm free." Better to get this awkward meeting over with. At least it was Gavin coming over, not Alan. Had Gavin volunteered to talk to Fiona about the will so as to avoid inflaming Summer's suspicions by having Alan visit her?

"What time?" Gavin asked.

"Anytime. I'll be home grading papers." She glanced bleakly at the computer screen displaying the essay she'd *almost* finished marking before the phone rang. "Or if my brain starts frying from too much reading, I'll be painting walls."

"I'll stop by between eight and nine. What's your address?"

She gave it to him, along with directions.

"I'll see you tomorrow night." Gavin's cool tone lingered in the neutral zone between friendly and curt.

"Thanks, Gavin." Fiona felt less than thankful as she hung up. It embarrassed her that she'd come across as ungrateful in trying to refuse Linda's bequest—whatever it was—but there was no possible way this wouldn't cause more friction between Summer and Alan.

But maybe it wouldn't be too bad. Maybe Linda had only left Fiona a token.

Her remembering you "very generously" doesn't mean a token. And if it were something insignificant, Gavin wouldn't be in such a hurry to meet with you to discuss it.

If Linda had left Fiona money or something else valuable, Summer would be that much more convinced that Fiona and Alan were having an affair—with Linda's blessing. Fiona tried mentally to shake off the sensation of sticky spider silk tangling around her limbs. Even from the grave, Linda seemed determined to draw her into the Taylor web.

Chapter 8

"This smells delicious." Fiona dipped her spoon into the takeout container of lobster bisque.

James sat next to her on the bench and opened his own container of soup. The day was cloudy and in the low sixties, and James had texted her this morning to invite her to a "pseudo-picnic" near the fountain in front of the Murphy Building.

"The soup is a peace offering." James handed her a packet of oyster crackers.

"Why would you need a peace offering?"

"Because I've come to confess. I've done something rotten."

"I *thought* I heard a heart beating beneath the floorboards this morning. Was that your guilty conscience?"

He grinned. "Lemonade or Sprite, Edgar?"

"Lemonade."

He handed her a bottle. "I didn't kill anyone, but I wanted to." He ripped open a packet of pepper and sprinkled it on his soup. "I talked to Kimberly Bailey yesterday."

Interest and apprehension crackled along Fiona's nerves. "I still don't know why that would require a peace offering to me. Unless the offering is from Kimberly and you're just the messenger."

"I wouldn't hold my breath for *that* message—unless you like turning purple and passing out. First of all, I think your instincts are right. I think she did give you those packages. I'm sorry to say that, because I hate to see her fouling up her life like this. But I think you're right."

"She didn't admit something, did she?"

"You kidding? Of course not. She put on a good show. Bambi-eyed innocence, lots of compliments about how I was the best teacher in the world, a big show of remorse over what was allegedly the first time she'd cheated, and a sob story about how she'd been so snowed under that she got desperate."

"Was she convincing?"

"It was too perfect. Overdone. I could almost see her reading from cue cards. But when she started with the personal digs on you, that's when I blew it."

"What did she say?"

"Apparently you're a cold-hearted fiend who told her she was too stupid for college and she ought to go sell her body for cash."

"*What?*"

"Then, while looking wounded and reluctant to repeat such vicious remarks, she told me she'd heard you say those kinds of things to other students. Bottom line: you're cruel and heartless, no student likes you, and she's an innocent victim of your spite."

"What did you do?" Fiona hoped he couldn't hear the edginess in her voice—the fear that maybe, even momentarily, he'd believed Kimberly.

"I held it together really well until I was escorting her out. Then I said I'd known you for years, that lying to me about you didn't help her at all, and she'd better leave you alone. Then I shut the door in her face. I was afraid if I talked to her any longer, I was going to strangle her."

Fiona's tight shoulders relaxed. "If you stood up for me, why do you need to bring lunch as a peace offering?"

"Because my goal was to get her to stop bothering you, and instead I'm afraid I made things worse. She's going to be embarrassed and angry, and the last thing she'll want to do is let me think I won. I'm afraid she's going to keep after you—and escalate things."

Fiona ate a few more spoonfuls of soup, contemplating James's words. "That might be true. But it also might be true that your talk was enough to scare her into stopping. If she knows she can't fool you, maybe she'll be nervous enough to quit. I don't think she *really* wants to risk getting thrown out of school. At some point her cockiness is going to give out, and she'll realize she might get caught."

"Maybe. I hope so."

From the way James's brow was furrowed and his mouth open, she knew he was debating saying something. She dropped a few more crackers into her soup and waited, but he didn't speak. After a moment, he resumed eating.

"I'm sorry I didn't handle her better," he said between spoonfuls of soup. "I wanted to coax her into seeing that she was only hurting herself. Instead . . . yeah. So much for that."

"Thanks for not believing her about me."

He laughed. "Let me get this straight. We're dealing with Fiona Claridge, the woman who feels so guilty about rude things someone *else* said that she writes a note to a paranoid, unbalanced woman, apologizing for tweaking her paranoia. And you think you need to thank me for not believing Kimberly's lies about you?"

Fiona sighed, watching the water gush from the fountain into the concrete basin surrounding it. "I don't think Summer is unbalanced. Just bitter and desperate, and it's hard to blame her. The bad news is, things are about to get worse." She told him about Gavin's phone call. "I don't want anything of Linda's, but when I tried to tell Gavin I didn't deserve it—whatever it is—I could tell I hurt him by trying to reject his mother's gift."

"Maybe he thinks you *do* deserve it. She might have left you her toilet scrubber."

Fiona forced a laugh, but it would have been easier if James had looked amused at his own joke. Instead, he looked worried.

"I'll gladly take her toilet scrubber," Fiona said. "At least no one would be upset with me."

"One of these days you need to figure out the difference between feeling guilty over something *you* did and something someone *else* did."

"I don't feel guilty. I feel extremely awkward."

"You also feel guilty. And you're stuck between Scylla and Charybdis."

"You get five points for that allusion. And yes, no matter which way I veer, I'm in trouble. If I accept whatever Linda left me, that will drive an even bigger wedge between Summer and Alan. But if I refuse to take it, that will hurt and offend Gavin and Alan, who are intent on carrying out Linda's wishes."

"It will offend *Gavin*. You don't know how Alan feels. Maybe he's on your side."

"True." Fiona felt somewhat better. If Alan could intercede with his brother, maybe they could defuse the situation. Surely Alan would agree that it was ridiculous to think of something that had belonged to his mother going to the ex-girlfriend who'd rejected him eight years earlier.

"I'm betting she made the will years ago." Fiona leaned back on the bench, admiring the way the blue of James's scarf matched his eyes. She'd picked that color of yarn perfectly. He wasn't wearing his overcoat today, but he was still wearing the scarf with his jacket. "She probably made the will while Alan and I were dating and never got around to changing it. If it *is* something of significant value, Summer could contest it in court."

"And clearly you wouldn't fight her. Maybe you two could arrange a secret transaction. You take your inheritance, thank Linda's lawyer, then meet Summer in a back alley and hand over the Monet."

Fiona laughed. Talking to James was like sunlight shining through a rainstorm—the raindrops were still there, but the gloom wasn't. "I'm hoping all this worry is for nothing—that Gavin will hand me a box containing a couple of crystal elephants from Linda's collection, we'll shake hands, and that will be that."

"You do realize that you're worried about driving a wedge between a couple that has already decided to divorce. The wedge can't get much bigger."

"I know. But from what Carissa told me, it sounds like Linda was a big part of the problem. Maybe with Linda gone, Summer and Alan will finally be free to reconcile."

"Just remember that the offense came from Linda, not you. No matter what you do or don't do about her will, it's not going to change how Summer feels. There's no point in your worrying about it. You didn't do anything wrong."

Fiona smiled wearily and dropped the last cracker into her soup. "I want Alan to be happy."

"I know you do. But there's a difference between wanting him to be happy and feeling responsible if he's not."

"I don't feel responsible. I'm just sad that . . . things have been hard for him."

"I understand." James passed her another packet of crackers. "Mind if I follow you home tonight? I'm worried that Kimberly has had enough time to come up with some revenge for our little talk, and I don't want you alone if there's another 'gift' on your doorstep."

"If she wants revenge for your talk, maybe I'd better follow *you* home."

"She won't go after me. She'll take it out on you. She seemed very intent on—" James hesitated, looking up at a budding tree overhanging the bench. "—intent on making a good impression on me."

James looked so embarrassed that Fiona asked the obvious question. "Does she have a crush on you?"

He shrugged. "Who knows?"

James did, from the way he was turning crimson. "Maybe that's a good thing," Fiona suggested. It didn't surprise her that Kimberly might have a crush on James. He was young, handsome, funny, and kind. "If she wants to impress you and knows you don't like what she's been doing to me, that might be enough to put an end to it."

"Or it might make her work harder not to get caught while she tries to push you over the edge."

"She can try," Fiona said. Remembering how frightened she'd been after that nightmare about Kimberly followed by the power outage, Fiona didn't sound quite as firm as she wanted to as she added, "She won't succeed."

* * *

Gavin Taylor scratched his head, studying Carissa clutching her bucket, car soap, and portable vacuum. "Carissa, you are way too nice. There's no reason you need to clean our cars for us. I've already had the Relief Society president call half a dozen times trying to bring in meals or send someone to mop the floor or whatever the sisters do when they go all compassionate on you. I'm *okay.* I can handle things."

"I know." Carissa smiled. "But I want to do *something* for your family, and I know you'd never ask for anything. So here I am, cleaning tools in hand. Just surrender the keys and let me get to work. I'll feel much better if I can help you out a little."

"It's been raining so much—what's the point of washing the cars?"

"The forecast for the rest of the week is either sunny or partly cloudy."

Gavin grinned. "You checked?"

"Of course." He had a very charming smile, Carissa thought. He looked a lot like Alan, but his features were thinner with sharper angles, and his eyes were bluish where Alan's were green. Gavin was three years younger than she was, and she hadn't known him very well growing up, but she remembered him as a fiery contrast to Alan's quiet self-control and courteous—almost old-fashioned-chivalrous— manner. Every girl in the ward had had a crush on Alan, Gavin, or both at some point. Carissa was surprised Gavin wasn't married by now—she'd have expected some lucky girl to snatch him up.

And what are you staring at, Mrs. Frumpy? Are you hoping Gavin finds bad dye jobs attractive?

At least there was nothing shocked or uncomfortable in the way Gavin was looking at her. Plainly, he hadn't seen the pictures, which meant he probably hadn't found Linda's phone.

"Hand over the keys and let me get to work," Carissa said. "Otherwise, I'm pushing my way inside and scrubbing your floors."

"Fine, I surrender."

"Here's something for when you get hungry this afternoon." Carissa handed him a bag of chocolate-chip cookies.

"You people sure take good care of me."

"We don't trust bachelors on their own," Carissa said, and he walked off laughing.

She kept the teasing smile on her face until she was vacuuming out Gavin's car and Gavin was inside, out of sight. She'd decided to start with his car. She didn't want him to think she had any reason to be particularly interested in Linda's car.

After another nearly sleepless night of worry, she'd known she couldn't rest until she'd checked Linda's car. Her own mother had always placed her phone in the cup holder while she drove, wanting to be able to swiftly check the number if anyone called so she'd know whether she could ignore it or if she should pull over and take the call. She never talked on her cell phone while driving. After Mia's death, she was a fanatically careful driver.

Carissa knew it was a long shot. If Linda had left the phone in the car, Gavin would have seen it yesterday and probably would have taken it inside—but maybe not. Yes, he'd been able to cope with driving her car, but driving a new car Linda had only owned for a few weeks wasn't likely to evoke the same pain as handling something as personal as the phone she'd pressed to her ear countless times, a phone that probably held traces of her makeup or perfume. The personal items were the hardest to deal with. Carissa remembered crying as she and her parents had gathered Mia's belongings from the apartment she'd shared with Carissa and Fiona—crying as she handled Mia's favorite sweater; blinking through a waterfall of tears as she tried to decide what to do with a pile of Mia's shoes; bawling over the familiar citrus scent from a bottle of Mia's body wash.

Carissa swallowed. The last thing she needed this morning was the distraction of missing Mia. Thank heavens Mia wasn't here to see how low Carissa had sunk.

Gavin's car wasn't as clean as the house had been, and tension made her muscles ache as she worked feverishly, wanting to finish so she could move on to Linda's car. *This is ridiculous,* she thought, squirting window cleaner on the inside of his windshield. She should check Linda's car right now—Gavin wouldn't notice or care—

The ringing of a phone startled her. She'd been so focused on Linda's phone that for a moment, she had the crazy impression that it was Linda's phone ringing, that it was here in Gavin's car, maybe under the seat. The thought passed; the ringing was coming from her pocket.

Carissa pulled out her phone. The name on the screen made her heart swoop toward her shoes. When was the last time Brad had called her in the middle of a shift? Maybe he'd found out—maybe someone had told him—

"Hi, sweetie." Did her voice have to come out all high and super-fakey-cheerful like that?"

"Do you have a minute?" he asked.

"Sure." Carissa hoped the breakneck speed of her pulse rate wouldn't translate into trembling in her voice. "What's up?"

"Our department has been contacted regarding a missing person—not officially a missing person yet, but his girlfriend is making a stink. He lives in Indiana, but was last seen here in Canfield. I think he was one of that group of old friends that you went to dinner with the other week. Dr. Keith Murray."

Carissa felt as though someone had stuffed a handful of rocks down her throat. "Yes, he was there. He's—missing?" *His girlfriend? He has a girlfriend?*

"Apparently, he was supposed to have arrived home last night and didn't show," Brad said.

"Maybe he . . . missed his flight?"

"The girlfriend says she can't get in touch with him—hasn't been able to get in touch with him all week—and now that he didn't come home, she's sure he's in trouble." From the dryness in Brad's voice, Carissa could tell he thought the girlfriend was overreacting. Heat filled her cheeks. A girlfriend. What had happened to *"You're even more beautiful than you were in high school." "I couldn't stop looking at you at dinner the other night." "I'd love to get to know you again." "You're gorgeous, you know that?"* He'd used her, flattered her, flirted with her—and she'd drunk it in like it was sweet, clear truth.

"Maybe he's avoiding her," Carissa said. "If he hasn't answered her calls all week, maybe she should take a hint."

"Yeah, that's what we're thinking at this point—we checked with the doc he used to work with in Indianapolis, and he laughed and said Murray wanted to ditch the girlfriend but didn't have the guts to tell her to her face. Said the woman wants to move to Canfield with him, but no way is he going to let that happen. But it would be nice if we could come up with something to settle her down. At that dinner, did Murray say anything about a change in his schedule?"

"As far as I know, he was planning to go back yesterday. He is—he's going to move here permanently in mid-May. He was here taking care of some things related to opening his practice. Doing a little traveling, too, I think. He loves New England and is—is very excited to be moving back."

"What was the night of that dinner?"

"March. March 30."

"Did you or any of your friends see him or talk to him after that night?"

Carissa's tongue was so dry that she had to swallow to get enough moisture to make a sound. She opened her mouth to say no, she hadn't talked to him, but stopped herself. *Phone records.* If the police were looking for Keith, they'd eventually check his cell phone records.

They'd find Carissa's number there. "He—uh—we spoke on the phone a few times. He wanted advice—he was looking for office staff. Receptionists, and so on. And he had some decorating questions—wanted recommendations for painters and so on. He probably called a lot of local people for advice." Shame seared her heart. She was lying to Brad. And not just to Brad. He was asking this question as a police officer. She was lying to the police.

Brad's voice was gruff—almost cranky, as though he'd already wasted too many words on Carissa today. "When was the last time you talked to him?"

"Um . . . let me think." She knew exactly when it was—Sunday, April eighth, when she'd called him in a panic about the pictures. "Um . . . was it the seventh? Was that a Sunday? No, the eighth. I'd talked to some of the women at church, getting info about window treatments, and wanted to pass that on to Keith."

"Does he still have family here?"

"No. His mother died a few years ago, and his dad remarried and lives in South Carolina."

"Who else was at that dinner? I know you mentioned Anne Marie Anderson."

Sweat rolled down Carissa's back. If the police questioned her other friends, what would they say about Keith and Carissa? Had anyone noticed how much time Keith had spent talking to her? Or the way she and Keith had lingered in the parking lot, chatting, after the dinner broke up? *Please don't ask me for their names. Please don't talk to them.*

"Carissa?"

Tears stung her eyes. She gave the other four names, feeling as though the words would swell and cut off her air. *Stop panicking. No one would have noticed anything wrong that night—you were just talking. What's wrong with talking to an old friend?*

"Thanks," Brad said crisply. "Gotta go."

"So—the police don't really think he's in trouble?" Carissa asked cautiously.

"Looks more like he's dumping a girlfriend and she's in denial. See ya."

"Bye." With trembling fingers, Carissa slid her phone shut. What an *idiot* she was, on every level. Keith was a smooth-talking slimeball.

He was probably ignoring her calls the same way he was ignoring his Indiana girlfriend's calls. But—what about Linda? He'd planned to talk to Linda as soon as possible, and if he *had* talked to her, surely he would have told Carissa. He knew how worried she was.

Probably he hadn't talked to Linda. Probably she'd died before he'd had the chance, and he'd figured that was the end of it.

Maybe *he* didn't care if those pictures were still out there, but Carissa did. She jumped out of Gavin's car and unlocked Linda's car. Frantically, she searched everywhere. The cell phone wasn't there.

To her horror, the door to the Taylors' home opened when she was only halfway through vacuuming the upholstery. Carissa mopped her eyes on the back of her hand and prepared to tell Gavin she'd been crying over happy memories of Linda.

Chapter 9

"Hey, Fiona. Thanks for meeting with me." Standing on her front porch, Gavin smiled at her. He had Alan's smile—that small grin with the corners raised while the lips stayed together. But Gavin had a gleam in his eyes that made the smile almost mischievous, whereas Alan looked sweet and a little shy. She'd loved Alan's smile. At first.

"Come in," Fiona said. Thank heavens Gavin seemed amiable tonight. She'd prayed fervently that tonight would go smoothly. If Linda's bequest was something valuable, she'd try again—as gently as she could—to persuade Gavin that she had no claim on his mother's assets and she didn't want to create strain in the Taylor family by accepting anything. She doubted she could accomplish this without offending Gavin, but she had to try.

"How goes the painting?" Gavin gestured at her paint-speckled T-shirt. "I see your brain must have started frying."

It took Fiona a moment to recall her joke about grading papers and brain-fry. "Yes. I've been trying like crazy to catch up, but after more hours than I can count of essays and class prep, it was either swap the computer for a paintbrush or do a face-plant on my keyboard. I've been painting the hallway. As you can see, this place needs a ton of work."

"Want some help?"

The offer surprised Fiona. "Thank you, but I'm fine."

"You said you might be painting tonight, so I came ready." Gavin peeled off his jacket and hung it on the coat rack before Fiona could offer to take it for him. He was wearing a faded T-shirt and fraying jeans.

"You really did come ready," she said.

"I changed after my job interview. We'll work and talk. I've done too much sitting around lately. I need to flex my muscles."

Disconcerted but unable to think of a gracious way to reject Gavin's offer when he obviously *wanted* to be put to work, she said, "Thank you. You're very kind."

"Healing my soul through service." Though Gavin's tone was flippant, the topic certainly wasn't.

"How are you holding up?" Fiona asked.

"One day at a time." He scrutinized her. "You look just how Alan described you."

"Do I?" She hoped Gavin wouldn't elaborate. Discussing what Alan had said about her would be an uncomfortable subject. From the way Gavin had reacted at the funeral, he must think she was some kind of demon heartbreaker.

"I'd seen pictures of you, but pictures are limited—a frozen image from a fraction of a second in time. He said you had a regal look. Dignified and queenly and graceful."

Fiona could imagine Alan saying something flowery like that. "This is my most regal paint-stained T-shirt, so thank you for noticing. But I suspect that was Alan's poetic way of saying I look stuck-up."

Gavin laughed. "Maybe your Celtic name evokes poetry. How did you get the name Fiona?"

"I was named after my Scottish grandmother." Fiona turned the conversation. "Tell me about yourself. I know you're two years younger than Alan. You served a mission in Germany. You went to medical school—" She stopped, embarrassed at having rattled out one fact too many. She didn't know why Gavin had dropped out of med school, but maybe it was insensitive to bring it up.

"That's right. Yeah, I started med school, but realized it wasn't for me, so I went into sales. Pharmaceuticals. But the company I was working for was hurting, and I got laid off, so I came home to regroup. Now I'm doing the interview dance, trying to find something that suits me."

"Do you want to stay on the East Coast, or does it matter?"

"I want to stay out east. Near family."

"Do you have a lot of relatives in the area?"

"Yeah. New England, New York, some in Pennsylvania."

Fiona knew Linda had pressured her sons to live as near to her as possible. After Alan and Summer had settled in Virginia, Linda's next Christmas letter had included a paragraph of hand-wringing over how terrible it was to have Alan so far away. Did pressure from Linda have anything to do with why Alan had come back to Massachusetts? The move couldn't have been good for his marriage.

"I hope a good job comes up soon," Fiona remarked, leading Gavin to the hallway she'd been painting. "Here's tonight's construction zone. I was doing the brushwork around the edges."

"I'll start with the roller on the side you've finished while you work on the other wall," Gavin offered. "Don't worry. I'm an old pro at painting. Mom liked to change the color of the walls every couple of years."

"If I ever finish this, I'll leave it the same color until the Millennium."

"Don't blame you." Gavin poured paint into the tray. "I will too, now that Mom isn't here to decide that the color she *really* wanted was 'Seashell' or 'Pine Forest.'" His jaw tightened. "The smell of paint . . . man, that's familiar."

"I'm so sorry," Fiona said. "You don't need to help me with this. Why don't we sit down and take it easy?"

"Since when has *that* ever helped make loss easier to take?" Gavin pushed the roller along the tray, coating the roller in creamy ivory paint. "I think we're cursed. First Dad—did you know I've been scared of fire ever since then? Can't even stand to be near a fireplace or a campfire. Didn't make me much of a winner in Boy Scouts."

"I'm sorry."

He shrugged. "I'd like to be scared of water now, but that involves dying of dehydration."

Fiona couldn't even imagine how traumatic it would be to lose both parents in terrible accidents. "I'm so sorry. How old were you when your father died?"

"Nine. Anyway, I'm guessing you want to know why I asked to meet with you. I told you it was about Mom's will."

Fiona nodded.

Gavin rolled paint onto the wall with rapid, smooth strokes. "She left you some books."

Some of the tension squeezing Fiona's chest went slack. *Books.* Just books. Perhaps a few favorite volumes she thought English professor Fiona would like. A footnote acknowledgment to a woman she'd once thought would be her daughter-in-law. Fiona felt silly and self-centered for how much she'd worried that Linda might have left her a lot of money or an expensive heirloom. Gavin must have been rolling his eyes at her *I don't deserve anything* speech when the item in question was a battered copy of *A Tale of Two Cities.*

"It was thoughtful of her to remember me." Fiona dipped her brush into the paint.

"They were actually Dad's books. His rare book collection. She showed it to you once."

Fiona's relief flipped into horror so swiftly that she dropped her brush into the paint can and had to grab for it before it sank. She'd forgotten about that tour through Linda Taylor's study with Linda proudly pointing out shelves of rare books—including a glass-enclosed, locked and alarmed bookcase—and naming values that had made Fiona's eyes bulge.

"She didn't—leave them all to me, did she?"

"Yeah, they're all yours. She knew you'd appreciate them more than anyone else would."

All Randall's rare books. "Gavin—that's—incredibly kind and generous of your mother. I'm very grateful. But . . . the value of those books—"

"She has all the info. Dad kept it organized in a binder. Not all of the books are valuable. A lot of them are just old books Dad liked but that aren't worth much."

Good. Maybe she was exaggerating the value of the books in her memory—

"The total collection is worth maybe . . . I think it was around three hundred grand. Probably closer to three fifty."

Fiona's heart sank again. She balanced her paint-soaked brush on the rim of the can and wiped her fingers on her jeans. "She must have written her will while Alan and I were . . . she assumed we'd marry . . . then she never got around to changing it."

Gavin snorted. "Did you say she *never got around* to changing it? Mom got around to everything. She was the most organized woman on the planet. The will was current. If she'd wanted something changed, she would have changed it."

Dismayed, Fiona couldn't think what to say. She walked over to where a roll of paper towels sat near the doorway to the kitchen and ripped off a couple of squares.

"You don't look happy," Gavin said.

At least he didn't sound irritated . . . yet. Fiona managed a smile. "I'm overwhelmed by your mother's generosity. But that collection belongs in your family. Something so valuable, and with sentimental value as well—it should go to you and Alan."

"The books were hers, or they were after Dad died. It was her right to do whatever she wanted with them. She was certainly of sound mind when she made the will. The books are yours."

Was Gavin truly not at all troubled that his mother had left books worth three hundred fifty thousand dollars to his brother's ex-girlfriend? Fiona couldn't stop hoping that, for all his insistence on carrying out Linda's wishes, Gavin secretly hoped she'd insist that the family take the books.

Gavin pushed the roller along the tray. "Mom knew you'd appreciate the books more than any of the rest of us would. She wanted them to go to someone who'd love and care for them."

Fiona wanted to point out that if the Taylor brothers didn't care about the books, then they could make a lot of money selling them, but she suspected that was the most offensive response she could give—dismissing the inherent value of Randall's books and suggesting the Taylors treat them as a source of cash.

Unable to think of any subtle way to get her concerns across, Fiona decided to gamble on candor. Considering the way Gavin had reacted to her presence at the funeral, it was a safe bet he didn't like the idea of her exacerbating the problems between Alan and Summer. "I'm afraid Summer won't be happy about this."

"This was Mom's decision. Not Summer's. And she won't be around to complain for long. Alan said he told you he and Summer are getting divorced."

Gavin's matter-of-fact attitude surprised her. "I was very sorry to hear that. But maybe they'll want to . . . wait a little while now, until things settle down. Right after a terrible tragedy isn't a good time to be making life-changing decisions." There was no sensitive way to suggest that maybe Summer and Alan's relationship would improve without Linda around, but surely Gavin was observant enough to know that.

Had Linda mentioned Summer in her will? Fiona didn't dare ask.

"Alan's having a rough time right now," Gavin said.

"I'm sorry. This must be so hard on all of you."

"He sounds really down whenever he calls me. Depressed. Moody."

"I'm sorry." She knew too well what Gavin was talking about. How many phone calls like that had she received from Alan after they broke up? Memories of his bleak, hollow voice echoed in her ears. *Fiona, I need to see you. Just for an hour. I can't take this—it's like I'm freezing to death from inside—*

"His job is suffering," Gavin said. "Some days, he can't get out of bed."

Heavy memories pressed harder on Fiona's shoulders. "Has he—considered grief counseling? A shock like this is more than many people can handle on their own, and especially on top of the problems in his marriage . . ."

"He's not big on counseling."

This was not news to Fiona, but she had to try. "Gavin, when you're sick, you seek help."

"Alan isn't sick," Gavin snapped. "He just needs support right now."

Fiona wiped the handle of her paintbrush with the paper towel and dipped the bristles. "Forgive me for being intrusive, but I know what I'm talking about when it comes to counseling. I wouldn't have survived after Mia Hardy's death if I hadn't had help. Gavin, I've *seen* how Alan can get. Please don't let that happen to him again. Get him into counseling, both for his grief and for his marriage. A marriage is a precious thing. It deserves every chance."

Gavin turned away and drew the paint roller along the wall.

Fiona's cheeks flushed. She was pressing too hard. The last thing Gavin wanted was advice from Fiona Claridge on how to help Alan.

But she didn't want to retract her words. Alan *did* need help, and she didn't want to pretend she hadn't meant what she'd said. "I'm sorry if I've offended you," she said, a middle-ground apology.

Gavin said nothing.

Fiona climbed onto her stepstool and started painting a corner. Should she try to restart the conversation or should she wait for Gavin to speak?

She'd wait. If he wanted to burrow in angry silence, she wasn't going to drag him out.

After a moment, he spoke. "We'd like you to come to Canfield as soon as possible to look at the books and get a better idea of the size of the collection and what it includes so you can plan for transferring it."

"Aren't there legal steps—"

"You'll get an official letter from her lawyer and will probably have to sign some paperwork, but there's no reason for delay. Her wishes were clear, and no one will contest it."

"Summer might."

"She has no claim on those books." He glanced at her and shook his head. "I've never known anyone to complain so much about being given something so valuable."

Simultaneously embarrassed and annoyed that Gavin didn't seem conscious of the strangeness of the situation, Fiona said, "I'm sorry. I didn't mean to sound ungrateful. I'm just stunned. I don't feel entitled to something so valuable."

"Mom thought a lot of you."

This whole thing was crazy. Had Linda assumed that Fiona and Alan would get back together someday and written her will accordingly? Naturally she never would have anticipated dying so young. Had she assumed that by the time she passed away, Fiona and Alan would have been happily married for years? It sounded like she'd done her best to undermine Alan and Summer's marriage, and she *had* taken care to stay in touch with Fiona. Apparently she'd never given up on the thought of Alan and Fiona together.

That thought made Fiona want the books even less, but how could she explain that to Gavin? If he couldn't see how inappropriate Linda's attitude toward the women in Alan's life had been, he wasn't going to understand any better if Fiona tried to explain it. She'd just come across as cold and critical of the beloved mother Gavin had lost under tragic circumstances.

"Thank you for coming to Bennett to tell me about this," Fiona said. "That was kind of you."

"Not a problem." Gavin's voice relaxed. "Like I said, I was in the area. Would you have time to come this weekend and take a look at the books?"

Fiona made one last scrounging effort to find any crack she could crawl through to get out of this situation, but found only the impenetrable knowledge that refusing Linda's generosity would deeply offend a family she had hurt enough already. She could stall, telling Gavin she was too busy this weekend, but what good would come from procrastinating?

"I could come on Saturday afternoon," she said.

"Good. That will work for Alan as well—he'd like to be there."

Wonderful, Fiona thought. Somehow, she didn't think he'd have Summer with him—which would give Summer more fuel for her paranoid certainty that Fiona wanted to steal her husband.

* * *

"What are you doing—auditioning for Slug of the Year?" Kim kicked Nick in the leg. "Get off my couch and help me."

Nick yawned and slumped lower. "Or what? You'll throw salt on me?" He expected Kim to fire back some insult—probably involving the dirt about him that she'd spill to Madison if he didn't get to work—but instead she stalked into her bedroom, clutching her easel and palette.

She was acting weird tonight. Nick had finally called to check on her when she went over twenty-four hours without texting him to demand a ride somewhere. He'd thought she might be sick. She wasn't—but *something* was wrong. He hoped it wasn't anything to do with that creepy campaign against Dr. Claridge. She *was* finished with that, wasn't she? The knife had been a nice grand finale.

When she returned to the room, her eyes looked red. "You okay?" he asked.

"I'm fine," she snapped.

"Is this about your mom coming tomorrow?"

Kim snatched up a box of charcoal pencils and two stray textbooks. "No. I'm cleaning up because it's my life's ambition to become a maid." She marched out of the living room.

Nick rose to his feet and followed her. "I don't mean the cleaning," he said, stopping in the doorway of her bedroom. "I mean the *attitude.*"

Kim was shoving a half-painted canvas behind the clothes in her closet. "It won't be a fun visit, okay?"

"Why are you hiding your art stuff?"

"Because maybe I don't want to get ripped apart again for wasting time drawing lousy pictures when I could be studying to prepare for *business* school. Maybe I don't want to get told that if I'd spend less time doodling, I wouldn't have to copy stuff from the Internet to get by in my other classes and it's a good thing they canceled Paris because sketching the Eiffel Tower would be a stinking *distraction* when I could be studying for the GMAT."

"You know, you need to look her in the eye one of these days and tell her you don't want an MBA anymore. I thought you were looking at switching to biology or—"

"That's none of your business!" Kim slammed her closet door.

Whew. Serious bad mood tonight. He knew she'd been unhappy when she'd learned her mom was coming to Boston on a business trip and planned to stop at Hawkins on the way home, but she seemed even crankier than the situation warranted. Not wanting to set her off, Nick kept his mouth shut and reached for the sketchpad sitting on the foot of her bed.

He flipped it open. The first page was a pencil sketch of a guy in an Oxford shirt and tie writing something on a chalkboard, his mouth partly open like he was talking. He looked familiar—youngish face, glasses, dark hair. Kim really did have talent, Nick thought, flipping to the next picture. It was the same guy, this time sitting behind a desk. Third page—same guy, this time at a lectern. Wasn't he a professor—

"Give me that!" Kim charged him like a solider ready to drive her bayonet through his gut. She snatched the sketchpad so roughly that it hurt Nick's hands.

"Ow! Sheesh, what's wrong with you?"

"Nothing's wrong with me. Maybe you should stop jamming your ugly nose into other people's business." Kim shoved the sketch-pad under her bed. Her cheeks were the same shade as her fire-engine red hoodie.

The familiar face in her sketches finally linked up with a name. "Hey, that's Dr. Hampton. I had him for—" Nick stopped. Kim was crying.

"Hey . . ." Awkwardly, Nick sat on the floor next to where she knelt by her bed. "Sorry. I wasn't trying to be nosy. You, uh—did really good on those pictures of him."

Kim all but slapped the tears from her cheeks. "Why don't you shut up?"

"Why don't you get a grip? You like him, huh?"

"So *what?*"

"So what nothing. I don't care if you've got a thing going with some professor. Maybe your mom will like you hooking up with some smarty-pants older guy."

She looked ready to claw his face. "Nothing's going *on*. He thinks I'm scum."

Oops, Nick thought. *One-sided, huh?* Kim had never struck him as the type to get a girlie crush on a professor, but sometimes she surprised him. And Dr. Hampton looked pretty young—he probably wasn't more than ten or twelve years older than Kim.

"Hey, uh, that's probably better anyway. He'd get in big trouble if he messed around with a student, and you've made enough trouble for teachers here, huh?" He hoped she'd get that mischievous twinkle back in her eye at the reference to Dr. Claridge, but instead she jumped to her feet and stomped out of the room.

Nick swore under his breath. This was girl-to-girl territory; he didn't know how to deal with a female meltdown over unrequited love. Too bad Madison wasn't here. Reluctantly, he followed Kim into the living room.

"Hey . . . sorry," he said, hoping a vague apology would help.

"You think it's stupid, don't you." She folded her arms and glowered at him.

"Think what's stupid? That you have a crush on a teacher? That's totally normal."

"What are you—a psychologist? '*That's normal.*' It's not a crush, Nick. A crush is what you have when you're twelve and get all dopey over some movie star you'll never meet."

She sat down hard on the couch, still glaring at him. Nick would have loved to escape out the front door but didn't think she'd go for it if he suggested he go grab a pizza.

He sat next to her. "Hey, sorry again. I didn't mean to make light of it."

"I really love him. I've never felt this way."

Nick tried to imagine what Madison would do under these circumstances. Probably go all soft and sympathetic and ask Kim about Dr. Hampton, though what Nick wanted to do was shake her and snap *get over it*! "And . . . he's not interested?"

"I thought he was. I really thought he was. But . . ." She shook her head.

"Um . . . I don't think you should take any rejection personally, Kim. He's a professor. You're a student. He could lose his job if he got involved with you." He grinned at her. "Under other circumstances he probably wouldn't be able to keep his hands off you."

"He doesn't even *see* me, not like that," she snapped. "He's in love with Dr. Claridge."

Ohhhh boy. Kim's irrational vendetta against Dr. Claridge suddenly made a lot more sense. "How do you know that? Oh—ah, I get it. That camera in her office. You've been watching them, haven't you? And they're all over each other?"

"No . . . no . . . but he's there a lot, and Nick, I'm not dumb. I can tell he wants her."

"Maybe you're jumping to conclusions. Maybe they're just friends."

"He called me into his office because she accused me of . . . you know. He wouldn't even listen when I tried to tell him what a snake she is. He jumped right to her defense and called me a liar."

"Ouch," Nick said. "Hey . . . you *are* going to quit, right? You had your fun with Claridge."

Kim sniffled. "Think about it. If he calls me in and says he knows what I'm up to and I need to stop and then *poof*, nothing else happens to Dr. Claridge, that's as good as a confession. He'll think he scared me into quitting. But they're just guessing—when they were talking, she even *admitted* she wasn't sure it was me. If I quit now, he'll be *sure* it was me."

"Uh . . ." Nick couldn't imagine a weaker excuse for continuing her harassment campaign. "Keeping it up just increases the chance that you'll get caught. It isn't going to make Dr. Hampton think you're innocent."

"I want you to help me." She grabbed a crumpled napkin off the lamp table and wiped her nose. "If something happens to Dr. Claridge at a time when I couldn't have done it, he'll have to admit I'm innocent."

Nick goggled at her, his thoughts an incoherent mess of profanity. "No way. Come on, I've helped you enough. I broke into her office for you. I drove you to her house. I'm done. I quit."

"You went out with Madison a couple more times, didn't you? And you will again?"

"Listen, our deal was for one date. The fact that she was interested in seeing me again doesn't mean I owe *you* another payment."

"I set you up with the best girlfriend you'll ever have. You still owe me."

She sounded more desperate than persuasive, and Nick couldn't help feeling sorry for her. "You're digging a deeper hole to fall into."

"I need help, okay?"

"You need mental help. I'm not risking getting myself kicked out of school just to help you chase Dr. Hampton."

"You won't get caught, not if you're smart about it." She looked at him with teary eyes. "Do one little thing."

Nick wanted to say he doubted Dr. Hampton was dense enough to suddenly believe in Kim's innocence when—conveniently—the next round got fired at Dr. Claridge when Kim was sitting in Dr. Hampton's class. Anyone who'd ever watched a TV detective show knew *that* strategy.

But Kim was obviously having a tough time right now, and if this would make her happy . . . and his adrenaline *did* give a tickle at the thought of the challenge of it all. Breaking into Dr. Claridge's office *had* been fun. But still, enough was enough.

"How about this," he said. "I'll do one *little* thing for you—if you *swear* this is the end of your war with Dr. C. No more packages. No more nothing. You swear?"

"I swear," Kim said.

Chapter 10

JAMES RAN HIS FINGERS ALONG the stripped wood of the mantel. "You have to wonder why they painted over all this beautiful wood in the first place."

"Painted over it about twenty times, you mean, given the layers of paint I've scraped off."

James pivoted, his gaze moving from the wall where Fiona had painted a test patch of paint to the pile of new baseboards waiting to be hammered in place as soon as she finished painting the walls—sometime in the middle of the next century, at the rate she was going.

"You're amazing," he said. "Where did you learn to do all this?"

"Books, YouTube video clips, trial and error. It helps that I'm not in a hurry. I go very, very slowly. As long as the basics function—water, electricity, kitchen appliances—I don't mind living in a construction zone."

"Want some help? I'd be glad to come over sometime. I'm no pro, but I do know which end of a hammer to hold."

"You have no idea what you're offering. Once I drag you into the black hole of my DIY existence, you're trapped forever."

James laughed. "I think I saw that happen on a Star Trek episode."

"Let me dish up the cake, and we'll go into the study. It's more intact than the rest of the house."

James followed her and watched as she cut pieces from a German chocolate cake.

"Ah, this is the best evening of my life," he said. "German chocolate! My favorite."

"Glad you like it." Fiona didn't feel like mentioning that the cake hadn't been a lucky guess—she remembered Mia's baking a German chocolate cake for James's birthday.

"You didn't need to go to that effort," he said. "I'm almost feeling guilty for inviting myself over."

"You *did* notice the bakery box, right? I didn't exactly go to a lot of effort." She slid a piece of cake onto a plate and handed it to James.

When he was seated on the leather loveseat in the study, James said, "Are you finally going to tell me what Gavin Taylor said to you?"

Fiona stood uncertainly, not sure where to sit. She should have suggested they eat in the living room, despite its construction-zone ambience. The loveseat was the only seat in the study besides her desk chair, and she couldn't sit behind her desk unless she wanted to look like she was conducting an interview. But the small loveseat would put her shoulder to shoulder with James. She was nearly ready to perch on the edge of the desk when James gestured to the seat next to him.

"Sit down and talk," he said. "You sounded stressed on the phone. I want to know what's up."

She sat next to him. "I'm going to need more bookshelves." She told James about the rare book collection Linda had left her.

"Wow. Oh, wow." James swallowed his last bite of cake. "So much for your hoping she'd left you an old stash of Twinkie wrappers."

"I *tried* to come up with a gracious way to refuse it, but it seems impossible—Gavin would tense up every time I tried. I'd love to take the books and hand them straight to Summer, but I'm sure she'd spit in my face."

"Yeah, I wouldn't try that unless you'd like to get beaten senseless with a first edition of *Crime and Punishment*."

"That would be appropriate, anyway."

James scraped up stray pieces of coconut with his fork. "You're stuck."

"Gavin wanted me to come to Canfield this weekend to look over the collection so I can plan how to deal with it."

"And you told him you'd love to but won't have time before you flee the country."

"Sounds like a good plan to me. Let me get you some more of that cake before you take a bite out of the plate. Hold my plate for me while I get you a refill." She swapped plates with James and headed for the kitchen.

With a large piece of cake on James's plate, she returned to her seat.

"Thanks. This is delicious." James picked up his fork. "Know what I think? Just take the books as quickly as you can so that will be the end of your contact with the Taylors."

"I can't figure Linda out," she said. "Why was she so obsessed with getting Alan and me back together—so obsessed that she didn't hesitate to undermine his marriage?"

"Maybe she couldn't admit defeat," James suggested. "Maybe it was less about you than about getting what she wanted."

"Probably. That makes sense."

"Did Linda talk to *you* about getting back together with Alan?"

"She did for the first year, after . . . when I . . . wasn't doing very well at . . . sticking to my guns." Fiona bit the inside of her cheek, thinking of lying on the couch in her parents' living room in Mesa, too heartsick and physically weak to object when Alan kept stopping by to visit her. She'd let herself lean on him emotionally, something she knew was a mistake.

"I know you had trouble dealing with Alan and Linda right after the accident," James said. "I'm talking about later, when you were back on your feet."

"No. She did stay in touch with Christmas and birthday cards, but she didn't nag me about Alan anymore." Fiona sighed. "Let's change the subject."

"Deal. This study is beautiful," James said. "You've done great work in here."

"Priorities. I needed my lair finished first. Though I haven't re-done any of the windows yet, and I still need to get the new outlet covers in here." She gestured at the grimy cover on the wall outlet.

"I hope your electrical system is newer than that outlet cover," James remarked.

"It is. Though I did have a problem the other day. A bunch of the breakers flipped in the middle of the night. It was creepy—especially because I didn't find out about the problem until I woke from a nightmare and couldn't turn on the lights. And naturally I kept thinking I heard someone walking around—too much worrying about Kimberly Bailey, I think."

James frowned. "You thought you heard someone?"

"It was my imagination, James. You'd hear nonexistent intruders too if you had to venture down into my tomb-like basement in the middle of the night."

"Did you call an electrician?"

"Yes. He couldn't find anything wrong. Must have been some kind of power surge. I don't have a clue—electricity is one thing I don't like dealing with, so I leave it to the experts."

"So even the DIY diva has limitations."

"Sadly, yes."

James took a couple of bites of cake, but he still looked troubled. "Was there anything else weird or wrong?" he asked. "Anything out of place?"

"You're as bad as I am, imagining ghouls in the night. No, there was nothing else weird. Just rows of switches in the off position." She expected the tension in James's face to ease, but instead he frowned more deeply.

"The off position? All the way off?"

"I told you something tripped them."

"Do you mind if I have a look at your breaker box?"

"I don't mind at all. Do you moonlight as an electrician?"

"No, though I do know a little about it." James rose to his feet and set his plate on her desk.

"This way." Fiona led him to the basement door. "The pit, minus the pendulum." She led the way down the stairs and pulled the chain to illuminate the basement. "Surprise. It's still creepy."

"Please tell me you haven't walled someone up down here."

"Here's a hint, James. If I ask your opinion on a cask of Amontillado, say you don't drink."

"You scare me." James gave a half smile and walked toward the breaker box. He flipped the panel open and studied it.

"When you had your problem, were the switches here—" He clicked one of the switches to the off position "—or here." He held it partway between on and off.

"All the way to the left," Fiona said. "Off."

"All of them?"

"All the ones that tripped. There were a few that didn't. The switch for the stove, for one. I'm not sure of the others. Oh, I remember the one for the dryer didn't trip either."

"So all the ones for the lights were tripped."

"I'm . . . not sure."

"Fiona . . . you see these instructions here?" James pointed to a line of printing above the switches. "When these switches trip, they end up in the middle. You have to pull them all the way to the left—to the off position—then back to on to reset them."

"What are you saying?"

"I'm saying if the switches were in the off position, they were there because someone put them there. Not because they tripped due to too much current."

A prickle swept from Fiona's head to her feet. "But . . . the electrician didn't say . . ."

"Did you tell him the position of the switches? Or did you just tell him they'd tripped?"

"Just that they'd tripped. James—you're saying someone *was* in my house? That someone did this on purpose?"

"Tell me what you heard. The noises."

"It . . . sounded like someone coming down the stairs and walking around . . . but I told myself . . . I thought I imagined . . . the wind . . ."

"Come on." With his hand on her elbow, James led her out of the basement. "Are you okay? You're pale."

"I'm okay. It's all past now. No, I'm not okay. I'm going to have a heart attack."

"Take it easy." He led her back to the study. "Can I get you anything?"

"How about the SWAT team?"

James drew her onto the loveseat. "Take a minute to recover and we'll go talk to the police."

"What can they do? This was three days ago. And no intruder would be stupid enough to leave fingerprints all over my circuit breaker."

"We can still give them the report."

"What in the world—why would someone—" Fiona drew a deep breath and rubbed her forehead, trying to focus her thoughts. "At least I know the intruder didn't want to hurt me, because she . . . he . . . whoever . . . had the perfect opportunity."

"You don't have to do the she-he legal disclaimer," James said. "It's got to be Kimberly, trying something new."

"I can't believe she'd go this far."

"It fits. Creeping in here, spooking you, but not touching you. She doesn't want a direct confrontation. I'm betting she was careful to make enough noise to wake you up so you'd have to deal with the power outage in the middle of the night—to the tune of creaking footsteps."

Fiona shuddered. "This is far more threatening than leaving a package on my doorstep. If it is Kimberly, she's not just angry—she's crazy."

"I don't think she's crazy. Just angry, immature, and self-centered. I can picture her sitting around with a group of friends and a few beers, fuming about you, and coming up with the idea of sneaking into your house. She probably didn't do it alone."

"I knew I should have replaced those old locks," Fiona murmured.

"Maybe I'm wrong," James said. "Maybe it wasn't Kimberly. But if she's the one leaving the packages, she's got to be the one haunting your house. It's not like you've got a long list of enemies."

"Summer Taylor hates me." Fiona's heart was still hammering. "But it's hard to imagine Summer—"

A thud made her jump. James sprang to his feet. "What was that?"

"Maybe something fell—" Fiona stood and started to move toward the door, but James caught her arm.

"I'll go first," he said.

Fiona felt a twist of queasiness. James thought it was another "gift." She followed him into the hallway. "It came from the front of the house."

"Yes." He walked toward the front door. Carefully, he opened the door a crack then wider.

A large rock sat on the mat. Dismayed, Fiona looked at the gash in the wood of the front door.

"At least she didn't put it through the window," Fiona said. But she'd damaged Fiona's property. Sneaking into her house and switching off the power? And now damaging her property? *Escalation*. What next?

James picked up the rock and closed the door. A folded note was taped to one side of the rock.

"Don't bother to read it," Fiona said. "I have a good idea what it will say."

James's forehead creased as he looked at the rock then glanced at his watch. "Kimberly Bailey is performing in a play tonight," he said. "She told me about it a couple of weeks ago and invited me to come. Her roommate is the lead."

Fiona realized what he meant. If Kimberly was onstage right now, she couldn't have thrown the rock.

"Maybe we've been wrong," Fiona said. "Maybe it isn't Kimberly."

"No," James said. "I think we're right. I think she's clever. When she walked out of class today, right past me, she was talking about the play with a friend. She wanted to make sure I knew she was occupied tonight. Establishing her alibi. She's got a rock-throwing sidekick."

"I'll go ask my neighbors if they saw anything," Fiona said. "Maybe someone saw the car." She knew it was a long shot—even if someone had noticed the car, they wouldn't have noticed the license plate. There would be no proof of anything. Again.

That was Kimberly's game—gloating in the fact that Fiona knew she was guilty but couldn't prove it. Not sure why she couldn't follow her own counsel to James to leave the note alone, Fiona reached over and peeled it off the rock.

James caught her wrist. "Fiona . . . you don't want to—"

"It's okay." She pulled her hand free and unfolded the note. In the familiar, plain black Times New Roman, it read, *Try bludgeoning your next victim, you murderer. And stay away from Alan Taylor or it'll be your skull in pieces.*

It was like tripping over an obstacle in the dark. Jarred and off balance, Fiona stared at the note. *Stay away from Alan.*

"What's wrong? Bad grammar?" Making a feeble attempt at a smile, James took the note out of her hand.

"How could Kimberly Bailey know anything about Alan?" Fiona asked.

James refolded the note and stuck it back on the rock. He looked rattled. "I don't know," he said.

* * *

The familiar rumble of the garage door opening made Carissa start. Steadying herself, she set Jacob's folded shirt in the basket and picked up a pair of jeans. It had taken her a couple years of marriage to realize Brad didn't like it when she rushed to the door to greet him and chatter about her day. It made him feel overwhelmed and pressured—especially if anything stressful had happened at work. She'd learned to bite her tongue and keep doing what she was doing until he approached her. He used to always seek her out for a kiss—even when he'd been working swing or graveyard shift and she was in bed when he got home, he'd always kissed her in greeting. But now, she was lucky if he came near her. He'd disappear into their bedroom or plant himself in front of the TV and stay there until she told him dinner was ready. And good luck on getting more than two words out of him during the meal.

If he was even home for dinner. She'd been delighted when he'd started working day shift, and theoretically, his shift ended at five, but he always seemed to be either late getting home or home and then gone again, working overtime at some community event or attending to some elders quorum president responsibility. Anything except spending time with Carissa. At least he still let her know when he was going to be late so she didn't have to sit wondering if he'd died in a shootout. He used to call her. Now she got one-line texts, things like *late tonight* or *buried in paperwork* or *don't wait dinner for me.*

When was the last time Brad had seemed happy or enthusiastic when he was around her? A few months, at least? She remembered sitting across a restaurant table from him before Christmas, enjoying her stuffed softshell crab while he talked about the sergeant's position that had opened up and how he planned to apply for it. He'd been excited—eager—sure he had an excellent chance at the promotion. He must have been so disappointed when the promotion went to Devin Jensen instead, but he hadn't said much about it, except that Devin was a good candidate. She'd tried to console him, but he hadn't seemed to want her encouraging words—hadn't seemed to want to talk about it at all.

It was difficult to sit calmly folding laundry as she wondered if today was the day rumors about her had finally reached his ears. Had he talked to her friends and asked about Keith? Was Keith still missing?

The tread of Brad's footsteps approached the family room where Carissa sat in the midst of piles of clothes and laundry baskets. She got her smile ready.

"Hi, hon," she said as Brad walked into the room.

He gave her a brief smile, but didn't come forward to kiss her hello. *Would a kiss be too much to ask for?* Carissa wanted to snap. Ashamed that she could feel so demanding toward Brad after the way she'd acted with Keith, she pushed her frustration aside.

"We had chili for dinner," she said. "It's still hot in the Crock-Pot. Would you like me to get you some?"

"I can handle it." He stood watching her match socks. "Sorry I'm so late. Got caught up in an OUI."

She knew how much Brad hated drunk drivers, how angry they made him, so she tried for a sympathetic tone. "Well, when I married a cop, I didn't expect nine-to-five hours. Was it . . . pretty bad?"

"Got the jerk off the road before he killed anyone."

"First offense?"

"Second." From the edge to his voice, Carissa knew Brad didn't want to answer any more questions. He looked so tired, so tense—his face was so tight that his muscles looked like stone. He needed a haircut, Carissa realized. Usually it drove him crazy when his hair got past super-short, and he was very regular with visits to the barber.

Since he was still standing there, not speaking but not leaving the room either, she felt compelled to carry the conversation. "Peter's asleep and David and Jacob are playing in David's room," she said.

He nodded.

"Why don't you go get out of that uniform and I'll get the chili on the table for you?" Carissa rose to her feet and headed into the kitchen, her cheeks warm. Why had he just stood there, looking at her? *Did* he know?

She dished up a bowl of chili, reheated a slab of corn bread in the microwave, and set the meal on the table. Waiting for Brad, she occupied herself wiping a few stray crumbs off the counter. She'd tried to keep everything extra clean lately—as though a spotless house would somehow make him happier and erase what she'd done.

Absently, she wiped at sticky peanut-butter-and-jam fingerprints David had left on the back of a chair. In the center of the table, she'd put a vase of tulips—tulips from the bulbs Brad had planted. He'd planted beds thick with spring flowers, knowing how much Carissa loved the sight of flowers blooming after a New England winter. She hadn't thought about that for a long time—the way he'd shown her the gardening catalog and urged her to choose her favorites, the hours he'd spent planting flowers for her.

He entered, dressed in jeans and a polo shirt. He was a handsome man, with that thick dark hair, muscular build and the kind of face you'd expect to see carved in marble. Carissa wondered if some of the women in town didn't speed on purpose in hopes of getting pulled over by Brad Willis. But Brad would never cheat on her; she was sure of that. He was the definition of integrity. The thought heated her cheeks from warm to scorching, and she kept her face angled away from him as he sat down. He wouldn't cheat on her, but that didn't mean he wasn't completely bored with her—the bubble-brained ex-cheerleader gone to seed. She'd tried to make herself look nicer tonight, exchanging her sweatshirt and jeans for a cute new sweater and khakis. The sage green of the sweater had actually complemented her too-bright-red dye job, and she'd almost felt good about how she looked—until Peter had wiped his sticky ice-cream face all over her sweater and she'd ended up back in the sweatshirt. She'd gone back to the jeans too; the khakis were too tight.

The phone rang, a sharp noise that punched against Carissa's eardrums. She flung her dishcloth into the sink.

"I'll get it," she said hastily, as Brad started to stand. Every time the phone rang, she wondered if it was Keith.

The name on the caller ID surprised her. Alan Taylor. "Hello?"

"Hi—Carissa?" A female voice.

"Yes."

"It's Summer Taylor."

"Oh, hi! How are you doing?"

"Could be worse. I need to meet with you, and I think you'll want to meet with me. Privately and soon." Her voice was hard. "I've got some cute pictures of you that you might want to see."

Fear and shock numbed Carissa's muscles. Had Linda—had she confided in *Summer*? Behind her, Carissa could hear the clink of Brad's spoon against the bowl. She didn't dare turn to see if he was watching her.

"Sure, that would be fine." Carissa did her best to sound breezy. "Hang on a minute." Concentrating on moving at a normal pace and failing—her knees wouldn't bend right— she picked up her cell phone from where it sat on the microwave and exited the room.

In her bedroom, she eased the door shut behind her. "Name the time."

"Uh—Saturday?" Summer sounded off balance, as though she hadn't expected Carissa to be so cooperative.

Carissa fumbled with the cell phone, accessing her calendar. Her thoughts were so jumbled that she couldn't remember if she had anything scheduled for Saturday. What did Summer want? Was she going to lecture her like Linda had? Or threaten to give the pictures to Brad? She knew Summer but not well, and she didn't know what to expect.

"Carissa?"

"Yes, um . . . okay . . . let me check . . . you live in Waltham, right?"

"Yes. How about early afternoon? Say one o'clock?"

"Yes, okay. Brad will—he'll be at work. I just need to find a baby-sitter—"

"I'll come to you."

"Okay." That would give her more flexibility—she wouldn't have to worry about getting home from Waltham before Brad noticed she was gone. Peter would be down for his nap, and she could likely shuttle David and Jacob over to the Elliots—Kristal wouldn't mind having them for an hour or so. No way would she risk her kids' overhearing this awful conversation. "Do you need my address?"

"You're in your parents' house, right?"

"Yes."

"I know where it is. I'll see you Saturday." Summer hung up.

Chapter 11

"TAKE THIS WITH YOU." Gavin handed Fiona the binder where Randall Taylor had kept a meticulous record of each book—where and when he'd purchased it, purchase price, receipts, and details about the book's condition. "It'll help you wrap your mind around everything."

"Thank you." After a tour of Randall's bookshelves, Fiona was reeling. She looked back at the locked portion of the bookcase that Gavin had opened for her. A first edition of *Moby Dick*. A first edition of *To Kill a Mockingbird*. The more books she handled, the less she was able to maintain the feeling that she wished she could reject Linda's gift and walk away. This was a wonderful collection. Linda couldn't have left her anything she'd value more.

Gavin had done nearly all the talking about the books, while Alan remained sitting in an armchair in the corner of the room, watching them, burrowed in a fleece-lined jacket as though he was cold. His face was colorless, and the shadows under his eyes made Fiona want to suggest he go take a nap. Gavin tried several times to engage him, but his answers were always couched in as few words as he could get away with.

It wouldn't have been easy asking him about Summer under any circumstances, but when he was this withdrawn, it seemed heartless to prod him with a painful subject. But she had to try. The message on that rock circled relentlessly in her mind. Could Kimberly Bailey have learned about Alan, Fiona, and Summer's jealousy? That wasn't information she could google—like she could the story of Fiona's accident—unless Summer had been attacking Fiona online, which she hadn't; Fiona had checked. Fiona had casually run Kimberly's name past Alan and Gavin earlier this afternoon, saying she had a student she thought might know the Taylors, but both brothers had looked blank. She was from Portland, Maine, Fiona had added. Even blanker looks, and a comment from Gavin that they'd never been to Maine; Linda had liked to travel south for vacations.

Kimberly *could* have a connection with the Taylors that Alan and Gavin didn't know about, or a connection with Summer's family, or some other source of information about Alan and Fiona, but Fiona *had* to consider the possibility that she'd been wrong about Kimberly. Had the conflict over Kimberly's plagiarism led Fiona—and James— to make unfair assumptions and to interpret things into Kimberly's attitude and behavior that weren't there? It was possible. And if Kimberly wasn't guilty, was Summer?

Fiona thought of Summer's parting words at the funeral: "*You'll get what you deserve.*"

"You'll want to measure to see how much space you'll need," Gavin said. "And as you study the records, you'll see which books are going to need what level of security. You definitely won't want the more valuable volumes in your office at Hawkins. Come on, let's go get a tape measure."

It seemed odd that Gavin would want company on this simple errand, but Fiona obediently followed him out of the room and down the stairs. She wanted to talk to Alan alone, but it would be less awkward asking for that once Gavin finished telling her about the books.

"It's down here," Gavin said, opening the door to the basement. He led the way down the stairs and into a room where shelves held labeled bins of nails and screws. Tools hung from pegboards. Gavin picked up the tape measure and held it out to Fiona.

"Do this on your own," he said. "I'll stay out of the room. It'll give you a chance to see if you can get Alan to open up."

For an unnerving moment, Fiona had the feeling Gavin had read her thoughts—how had he known she wanted to speak to Alan privately?

"You can see what I was talking about the other night," Gavin continued. "He looks awful. You've got to help him."

"I'll try." Fiona didn't know what else to say, even knowing Alan needed more help than she could give.

"If he asks where I am, tell him I'm getting us a snack." Gavin led the way out of the basement, and Fiona headed back upstairs to Linda's study.

Alan was still sitting in the armchair, his expression dull. Fiona forced herself to smile at him.

"Would you mind helping me with this? I need someone to hold the other end of the tape measure, and Gavin bailed out to go fix us something to eat."

Alan rose slowly to his feet. Fiona flipped to a blank page in the back of Randall's notebook and took a pencil from the jar on the desk.

"How are you holding up, Alan?" She drew the tape out as Alan held the casing at one side of the bookshelf.

"I don't know." He glanced at the tape and read off the number. Fiona noted it in the book along with the number of shelves.

"You look tired," she said. "Are you sleeping?"

He shrugged.

Fiona moved to measure the shelf length on the glass-enclosed case. "I'm sorry. I know this is such a hard time for you."

He read off the next number.

Fiona's hands felt a little shaky as she wrote the number down. She never had discovered how Alan felt about Linda's leaving her these books, and she wondered if part of his silence sprang from displeasure at Fiona's inheriting something so valuable. Alan loved reading. He probably would have loved to inherit this collection. "Alan . . . I hope you know that while I'm honored that your mother would leave me such a valuable gift, I feel these books should stay with your family. I'd be happy to sign a document releasing my claim—"

"She wanted you to have them," Alan said flatly. "She always talked about how you would value them more than any of the rest of us, including her. She maintained the collection in Dad's memory but never cared about the books themselves."

"I see." She was glad to hear him speak more than a monosyllable. "Well—I'm very grateful. How does—" Did she dare approach the subject of Summer this way? She couldn't think of a better way to introduce Summer's name into the discussion, so she plunged in. "How does Summer feel about your mother giving them to me?"

Alan's mouth twisted in a bleak smile. "She doesn't know. Not that it would make a difference. She's so angry at me that I don't see how she could get any madder." He set the tape measure down and removed his jacket.

"Alan . . . you know Summer thinks we're . . . having an affair."

"Yes."

"Do you have any idea why she'd think that?"

"No."

"Alan . . ." Fiona looked into his eyes—beautiful forest green eyes. Haunted eyes. An instinctive desire to comfort Alan wrestled with a memory-charged urge to run away. "She must have given you some idea why she suspected us."

"I don't know. Ever since we moved to Massachusetts, she's been . . . angry with me."

"She didn't want to move here?"

"No."

Summer had probably been cringing at the idea of living in the same state as her mother-in-law. "She thought she had some kind of proof against me. Do you know what she was talking about?"

Alan shook his head, turning away. "I don't know. She told me a couple of weeks ago that she knew we were having an affair. She said she had proof. I asked what it was. She told me to ask my mother, which made no sense. She wanted a divorce."

He wandered over to a shelf that held a picture of his parents and stood for a moment looking at it, his back to Fiona. He had a partially healed red cut that ran over his right elbow. She remembered his talking to his aunt Marilyn about the injury—the cut he'd gotten when he was searching for Linda. The thought of Alan's struggling through that storm, frantically searching for a woman who was already dead, made Fiona's eyes sting.

"Did you . . . have a chance to ask your mother about the proof?" Fiona asked.

Slowly, Alan turned to face her. "She didn't have any idea what Summer was talking about."

A couple of weeks ago . . . that was right before Fiona had received the first package. "Do you think . . . is it possible Summer might be angry enough to . . . go after me?"

"What do you mean?"

"I've received some strange 'gifts' lately."

"Strange gifts?"

She told Alan about the packages with their vicious notes, about the circuit breaker and the creaking footsteps, and about the rock thrown at her door.

Frowning, Alan reached out to squeeze her hand. "That's terrible, Fiona. I'm sorry. How could anyone use Mia's memory like that?"

Uncomfortable at his touch, Fiona drew her hand back. "I was convinced the packages were from a student who's furious with me, but when the last note mentioned you, I started to wonder."

"You think Summer might be responsible."

"I don't know. Obviously she hates me, and she knows all about Mia. Do you think she might . . . do something like that?"

"I don't know. It doesn't seem like Summer would . . . but I don't know."

"I got the first package on the ninth, in the afternoon."

His already tight expression went rigid, as though he was gritting his teeth through a surge of pain. For an instant Fiona thought he'd remembered something that indicated Summer *was* guilty, but the date finally clicked. April ninth. That was the day of the storm, the day Linda had died.

"I'm so sorry," she said. "I forgot—"

"Don't worry about it. I was here that day. I'd come to tell Mom that Summer wanted a divorce. She'd just told me the day before. I have no idea what Summer was up to."

The day before that first package arrived was the day Summer had told Alan she wanted a divorce? The day she'd told him she had proof of his cheating on her with Fiona?

She'd been *far* too quick to blame Kimberly Bailey for those packages.

Fiona gave Alan the other dates and times of the incidents, but Alan shook his head to all of them. He'd stayed with Gavin for a few days after the funeral and had no idea what Summer had been doing during that time. And Gavin had gotten him some medication to help him sleep, so even when he was home, he wouldn't have known if Summer had left the house. And it was hard to remember what he'd been doing on any given night.

"Have you given Summer's name to the police?" Alan asked.

"Yes. I'm sorry, but I didn't know what else to do. They wanted the names of anyone who might be angry with me. Have the police talked to her?"

"I have no idea. Do you want to come look around my place?" Alan's gaze was more focused, less remote, a change that relieved Fiona. "Summer's gone this afternoon. She said she was . . ." Alan frowned as though trying to remember what Summer had told him. "Off visiting a friend, I think. You're welcome to search and see if you find any wrapping paper or ribbon that matches the materials used on your packages, or any other evidence."

Fiona hesitated. She didn't like the idea of being alone with Alan in his house, but she couldn't pass up the opportunity to look for evidence—especially not if the culprit might be contemplating further escalation. "Thank you," she said. "I appreciate that."

"Not a problem at all." Alan smiled, and the life the expression brought to his face made Fiona smile. His mood seemed—at least temporarily—to be improving.

"I'm sorry about your problems with Summer," she said. "I hope you aren't giving up on her."

Alan sat on the edge of the desk. "You're not the only one she hates."

"Her relationship with your mother was troubled, wasn't it?" Fiona said cautiously.

Alan said nothing.

"Alan . . . I hope this doesn't sound callous, but you might find it easier to get along with Summer now that there isn't as much . . . potential for conflict."

"Maybe," Alan said, to Fiona's relief. At least he hadn't looked horrified that she would, even obliquely, suggest that Linda's death could have some good results. Did she dare push it a little further?

"I know counseling can be helpful in sorting out problems," she said. "It was a great blessing to me. I think it could help you and Summer."

"Maybe," Alan said.

Fiona risked another nudge. She didn't want to lose this opportunity. "Promise me you'll try it? A marriage is a sacred, precious thing. It's worth any effort to save it."

Alan looked at her. "You just told me you thought Summer might be going after you in some psychotic revenge campaign. Now you're telling me I should preserve a relationship with a woman who would hurt you like that?"

"First of all, I don't know if Summer *did* have anything to do with what's happened to me. My student is still a likely suspect. If Summer was involved, I'm not justifying that. Obviously, she needs help. But I want her to *get* help. You have something with her worth saving, Alan. I want you two to be happy."

He said nothing.

Chapter 12

"HI, SUMMER. THANKS FOR DRIVING all the way out here." Carissa's cheeks burned at how stupid the words sounded. Why was she pretending to be friendly?

Summer smiled, but her smile wasn't any friendlier than Carissa felt. She was very pretty and so *together*. Her shiny brown hair curved perfectly above her shoulders, and her olive skin was so smooth—how could anyone look that good without makeup? No, she *was* wearing a little eyeliner and a touch of mascara, but that was all. Her sweater fit smoothly over the kind of figure Carissa would need surgery to achieve.

Fighting an urge to suck in her stomach, Carissa asked, "Does Alan know you're here?"

"No. I didn't tell him anything, if that's what you're worried about. I haven't blabbed your dirty secret."

Scorched anew with humiliation, Carissa turned away and headed toward the living room. Already, she could feel sweat trickling down her back. Why had she been dumb enough to wear a solid-color knit shirt? Give her two minutes and she'd have huge sweat circles under her arms while Summer remained perfect and cool and scornful.

"Uh—sit down." Carissa said.

"Sit with me." Summer settled on the couch and pointed to the cushion next to her. Carissa sat, certain she'd have been more at ease facing a firing squad.

Summer pulled a cell phone out of her purse. "From the way you acted when I called you, obviously Linda told you about her photo shoot." She held the phone out to Carissa.

Carissa stared at it. "Is that—Linda's phone?"

"Yep."

"How did you get it?"

"I stole it."

"You—stole her phone?"

"Have a look."

Carissa's hands trembled as she took the phone. "Summer . . . it's not what it looks like. I mean . . . I know I was wrong . . ."

"Good for you." Summer's voice was harsh.

Why did Summer seem to be taking this so personally? Why did she care what Carissa did? With Summer leaning toward her, clearly ready to snatch the phone away if Carissa tried to delete the photos, Carissa hastily clicked through them. Keith with his arm around her shoulders as they sat on the rim of the fountain. Keith and her sitting close together in the restaurant booth. Keith holding her hand as they walked. Keith kissing her.

"Who's lover-boy?" Summer asked.

Tears filled Carissa's eyes. "What you see there is all that happened. I swear to you, that was all. I didn't sleep with him."

"Really."

"I'm not excusing my behavior." Carissa wiped her eyes. "I know it was wrong to act like we did. But that's as far as it went. And it's completely over. We only saw each other four times. Please, Summer. If Brad ever found out . . . he'll never forgive me. . ."

"Did Linda threaten to tell him?"

"She said she'd give me two weeks to confess, and if I didn't, she'd step in."

"Sounds like her. Look, sister, quit panicking. Your marital problems are none of my business. I just want a trade. You give me a little info, and I'll delete those pictures and pretend I never saw them."

Carissa shrank back. "You—you're blackmailing me?"

Summer blushed. "Don't be stupid."

The flustered expression on Summer's face brought vengeful satisfaction to Carissa. She could almost hear Summer's thoughts—"*Her husband is a cop! What if she tells him I'm blackmailing her?*"

"Look, I won't tell Brad no matter what, okay?" Summer said. "I won't tell anyone. Like I said, whatever you're doing is none of my business. But I thought maybe you could help me out. As a friend."

Nice backpedaling. "What do you want?"

Summer shifted on the couch and averted her eyes, and Carissa realized the cool, self-possessed look Summer had worn when walking in the door was as phony as Carissa's faux-friendliness. "I . . . think Alan's cheating on me with Fiona Claridge. You and Fiona are friends. I want to know what she's told you."

"Oh, Summer. I'm sorry." The sympathetic words spilled automatically from Carissa's lips, drawn by the pain in Summer's voice. "Did Linda tell you that? I know she said some cruel things to you."

"You don't have to tell me about Linda," Summer snapped. "I'm asking about Alan and Fiona."

"Fiona was *not* having an affair with Alan. She would *never* do something like that."

"How can you be sure?"

"Fiona Claridge? *Fiona?*" Sinking back against the couch, Carissa gave a hoarse laugh. "You don't know her, do you?"

"I know people would have claimed *you'd* never fool around on the side, until Linda caught your Kodak moment."

Carissa's face went hotter than she'd imagined skin could get without blistering. "Fine. Fiona's a better woman than I am."

"I know she used to be in love with Alan. Alan wanted to marry her."

"Is that all you know?"

Summer repeatedly tapped the heel of one boot on the carpet. "I know she broke up with him. And I know after the . . . the accident that killed your sister they got back together for a while, and then she dumped him again."

Carissa sighed.

"Sorry," Summer said. "You probably don't like to talk about that."

"About Mia? Of course I like to talk about her. She's my sister. I'm not going to forget her, whether or not anyone else is brave enough to say her name."

"Good point."

"And Alan and Fiona didn't get back together after the accident. I'm guessing Linda told you that, didn't she?"

Summer nodded.

"Alan visited her a lot after the accident—even got a job that summer in Arizona, where Fiona was living with her parents—but I know Fiona never wanted to resume their relationship. She was just too . . . too sick to stand firm. She had a bad time of it. Not just physically, I mean, though she was seriously injured, and recovery took a long time. But she blamed herself for the accident, and the guilt . . . it was terrible for her. She felt like she should have been the one to die."

From the bright red patches on Summer's neck and cheeks, she seemed acutely embarrassed by Carissa's words. "You—said Fiona didn't want to resume the relationship." Summer traced her thumbnail along the arm of the couch. "But Alan did."

"Well . . . I think he was just trying to be a friend when Fiona needed one."

Summer shot her a disdainful look. "Good grief, you're an awful liar. How did you ever manage to hide your fling from Brad?"

Carissa's face had started cooling down, but at Summer's words, it heated back to a high-temperature blush. "Okay, fine. From what Fiona said, it sounded like he *was* still in love with her."

"Trying to win her back, helping her through that hard time?"

"Probably. They'd barely broken up, and he had a hard time getting over her. But Summer, this was years ago."

"He visited her at Princeton."

"Okay . . . yes . . . a couple of times. But *that* was years ago too. It doesn't matter now. And I swear to you, Fiona would never have gotten involved with Alan after he married you. And she is *not* in love with him. Did Linda tell you they were having an affair? Is that why you tore into Fiona at the funeral?"

"She didn't actually tell me that." Summer picked up the cell phone Carissa had dropped on a couch cushion. "But after we moved here, she kept bringing Fiona up—how wasn't it nice that she'd settled in New Hampshire, and ooh, what a *smart* girl—a master's degree from BYU and a Ph.D. from Princeton!—and now she was an assistant professor of English at some ritzy college and wouldn't it be *fun* to see her for old time's sake?"

"What did Alan say?"

"Not much. He'd try to brush her off—change the subject. But things had been rocky between us, ever since the move."

"You didn't want to come to Massachusetts, I'm guessing," Carissa said.

"Ha! Sure, I was crazy about the idea of living near my darling mother-in-law."

Carissa grimaced. If she'd been in Summer's shoes, she would have wanted at least an ocean between her and Linda.

"She'd been after him the whole time we were in Virginia, nagging him to move closer to home," Summer said. "She'd e-mail him job listings, for crying out loud. It drove me crazy. He had a good job in Richmond. Why would we want to move? At first he was so good at resisting her. But she wore him down. That was Linda—never give up!"

"What made him finally decide to go?"

"I lost my job—I was a manager at a clothing store. The company shut down our location. It turned out Alan was already poking around at the possibility of a job here, and when I got laid off, he jumped at the chance to come back."

"Did he *want* to move? Or was he just trying to get Linda off his back?"

"I don't think he knows the difference anymore. That woman was the devil, Carissa. She *had* to be in control, no matter what it took."

"But she *didn't* tell you Alan and Fiona were together."

"No, but she wanted them to be. And it seemed like Alan and I were always fighting—okay, *I* was fighting and Alan was withdrawing and hiding and going dutifully to visit his mommy almost every week. And then I found this princessy hair comb wrapped in a handkerchief in Alan's drawer. Alan got all shaken up when I showed it to him and he tried to tell me it was Linda's—give me a break! As if Linda ever wore anything that didn't have big fake jewels or glitter on it. And even if it was hers, what was it doing in Alan's drawer? I know Fiona wears decorative combs sometimes—heaven knows I've seen plenty of pictures of her."

"It couldn't have been hers. Or if it was, Alan must have had it from years ago."

"I sorted our whole dresser out before the move, and—no comb. And *then* I heard Linda whispering to Gavin about capturing proof on her cell phone camera and how *someone* needed to face up to what they were doing, and if they wouldn't tell the truth, she would, for the good of everyone involved. She looked so horribly *gleeful* that I was sure she was talking about Alan and me. I thought she had pictures of Fiona and Alan and planned to wave them in mine and Alan's faces to crack our marriage apart. I was fed up with everything—no *way* am I a woman who'll sit quietly by while her husband fools around. I told Alan I wanted a divorce."

"Wait—pictures—"

"Yeah." Summer held up the phone. "I saw her phone sitting on her kitchen counter the day after she died. I swiped it, because I didn't want anyone else seeing the pictures, or showing them to me. I wanted to look at them myself, in private. But I messed up. The pictures were of *you*. Linda was talking about *you.*"

"So you decided to pick up where she left off and come wave them in my face."

Summer shrugged, but she didn't meet Carissa's eyes. "I wanted to know if you knew anything about Fiona and Alan."

"You could have just asked me. You didn't have to threaten me."

"I'm sorry, okay? I thought you might try to protect Fiona."

"So you thought you'd scare me first. Fiona doesn't need protection from me. I'm the snaky little cheater, not her."

"If you're waiting for me to pat you on the shoulder and say don't be too hard on yourself, what you did wasn't all that bad, keep waiting."

Simmering with anger and humiliation, Carissa said, "If you're done interrogating me about Fiona, maybe you should go home."

"We're not done talking." Summer slid her feet out of her boots and settled into the corner of the couch, curling her legs underneath her. Apparently, Carissa had relieved enough of her anxiety that she could settle into a casual pose. "You haven't told me about your guy friend."

"It's none of your business."

"You know you need to vent. I'll bet you haven't told a soul—especially not Fiona, if she's as straight-arrow as you say. I already promised I wouldn't tell anyone, so blab away."

"I don't need you as a listening ear."

"Sure you do, because otherwise you'll explode. And if you don't tell me the facts, I'll assume the worst."

Carissa gave a sharp laugh. It must have been an epic battle when strong-willed Summer and strong-willed Linda went head-to-head. Poor Alan. "He's an old high-school friend. His name is Keith Murray."

"How'd it start?"

Carissa slouched back on the couch. Maybe she *did* want to talk about it. She was sick of keeping secrets, and she didn't want Summer thinking it was worse than it was—not that it wasn't bad enough. "A bunch of us—one of my friends called and said Keith was coming to town and wanted to get together with any of the old gang who were still around. We gathered half a dozen of us—a couple of people came from Boston, and one lives in—" She stopped. Summer didn't care about those details. "Anyway, we went out to dinner. Six of us. I was sitting near Keith, and we talked a lot. He's living in Indiana but is planning to move to Canfield. He's opening a medical practice here."

"Doctor, huh."

"Yes. It was—it was honestly the most fun I've had in a long time. Brad has . . . I'm not excusing myself, but he's been really remote, lately, like he couldn't care less if I fell off the face of the earth. It's been like this for months now. He lost out on a promotion a while back, and ever since then he's just been . . . distant. I spend all day home with the kids, worrying about him, praying nothing bad happens to him. Then he comes home and ignores me."

"Poor you. Great grounds for cheating."

"Too bad I don't have a perfect marriage like you," Carissa snapped. "And you have no idea what it's like being married to a cop."

"I can't imagine Canfield gets much dangerous crime."

At that moment, Carissa would have liked to perpetrate some dangerous crime herself, involving her fist and Summer's face. "A place doesn't have to be LA to make life dangerous for a police officer. Everywhere has problems, and all it takes is one crazy druggie—"

Summer touched her arm, a gesture that surprised Carissa. "Okay. That was a stupid comment, and I'm sorry. Just—go on with your story, okay?"

Carissa was silent for a moment, looking at Linda's cell phone. "Why do you care?"

"Maybe it makes me feel better to know someone else has problems too."

"*There's* a noble motive."

Summer smiled, but the smile held enough melancholy that Carissa suspected Summer's goal wasn't either to gloat in Carissa's problems or to mock her—*she* needed to connect with someone. "Have you told Alan you were wrong?" Carissa asked softly. "That you made a mistake about Fiona and him?"

Summer shook her head. "I wasn't sure I *was* wrong, even when the pictures were of you, not him. I wanted to talk to you first."

"Apologize to him. He's not having an affair with Fiona."

"Thanks for the marriage counseling. So you went to dinner with this guy and he switched on the charm."

Carissa heaved a sigh. "Yes. It was such a high to have some fun, chatting with someone who . . . well, who . . ."

"Who what?" Summer prodded.

"It's going to sound stupid."

"So it's stupid. Like I've never heard anything stupid before."

"He . . . was really complimentary. He'd laugh at all my dumb jokes and tell me how witty I was and listen to my opinions and tell me I was smart—*there's* something I haven't heard in forever. It's not like anyone gives me an A for doing the laundry right. And he kept telling me how beautiful I was, that I'd gotten even prettier since high school, that I looked gorgeous in that shade of green—I was wearing a green blouse. Anyway, it was so nice to be . . . noticed like that. To have someone think I'm still attractive."

Summer gaped at her.

"I know it's shallow," Carissa said, embarrassed at the bug-eyed disbelief on Summer's face. "I used to do such a good job of keeping myself in shape, but since Peter was born, I can't seem to . . . I feel like such a frump. Extra pounds . . . stretch marks . . . and my *hair*—" She ran her fingers through the red strands. "Can you believe this color? I thought it would liven my hair up, but it turned out so fake-looking."

"Uh . . . what the heck do you think is wrong with your hair? It looks fine. And where do you keep those extra pounds? In a safe deposit box?"

"I've gained like—oh, never mind how much—since we got married."

Summer rolled her eyes. "How vain can you get? Maybe you should take a look in the mirror, shut up, and be grateful."

Smarting over Summer's accusation of vanity but grateful for her compliment, Carissa decided to bypass her comments and finish the wretched story. "I saw Keith the morning after the dinner when a few of us went for brunch. After brunch, he asked if he could call me. I knew I should say no, but I told myself it was innocent, we were just old friends, and it didn't mean anything. He asked me to dinner a couple of days later. I pretended to myself that of course it wouldn't be only the two of us—he must have invited someone else along—but it was."

"How'd you explain that dinner to Brad?"

"I didn't. He was working that night, covering a shift for a friend who had the flu, so I got a babysitter, and I was home before he was. He never knew."

"So . . . what happened at the dinner?"

Carissa kicked off her shoes and drew her feet up onto the couch like Summer had. "We . . . got really flirty."

"What do you mean, 'flirty'?"

"You know." She wrapped her arms around her knees. "The looks, the smiles, compliments, that kind of thing. I told myself it was harmless fun; we were just old friends. Honestly it was such a rush. Feeling twenty-one and gorgeous and . . . and admired. I told myself it was no big deal, we hadn't even touched each other. Just because I was married didn't mean I couldn't talk with an old friend. And besides, he was going back to Indiana soon."

"I thought he's moving to Canfield."

"He is, but not until May."

"Uh-huh. And then?"

"He called again."

"And you told yourself it was innocent, you were just old friends." Carissa nodded.

"You must have a master's degree in rationalization."

"I know I was a fool. I already *know*, okay?"

"Sorry for stating the obvious. Go on. So you went out a second time—and . . . ?"

"We ended up sitting close together, holding hands at the table. I kept telling myself it was only flirting—what could be really wrong with holding hands? And then, when we were leaving, we stopped by the fountain in the courtyard in front of the restaurant and he . . . kissed me. I told myself I wouldn't let him, but . . . and then we went on a walk and he had his arm around me and he kissed me a few more times—I kept telling myself just a little more, a little more wouldn't hurt, and then I'd put a stop to it and never see him again. Then he invited me back to his hotel."

"And?"

"I didn't go. But it shook me—made me realize what I was doing. And the awful thing is . . . Summer, I *really* wanted to go." Carissa swallowed hard. "I turned him down and went home, but I kept thinking about him and wondering what it would have been like if I *had* agreed to . . . I was kind of hoping he'd call *and* hoping he wouldn't, you know? And then Linda called me the next day . . . told me about the pictures . . . I couldn't believe what I'd done."

"Nothing like getting a bucket of cold water dumped on your head to wash the stars out of your eyes."

"Seriously. I'd never imagined anyone I knew would see me—we weren't in Canfield; we'd gone to Worcester. There was this new Greek restaurant Keith wanted to try."

"Apparently Linda wanted to try it too."

"Yeah. I was terrified, and I feel horrible. If Brad finds out, I don't think he'll ever get over it. He's so honest. He's the kind of guy who points it out if the checker undercharges him and would rather die than cheat the IRS out of a dollar. And now—his own wife betrayed him. How could he ever get over that?"

"Uh—he's a police officer. How rosy a view of human nature can he possibly have?"

"I didn't say he has rose-colored glasses." Tears trickled down Carissa's face. "And don't you get it? He deals with creeps and dishonest people all the time, but he trusts *me*. And *I* betrayed him. I'm afraid he'll never forgive me."

"Have you told the boyfriend to get lost?"

"I would, but I can't get in touch with him. He's dropped off the face of the earth. I thought he was going to talk to Linda—she'd called him and told him she had those pictures . . ."

"She called him to gloat?"

"No. She called to tell him Canfield is a moral, family-oriented community, and she didn't care if he grew up here, he's no longer welcome—the last thing we need is a sleazy doctor bent on breaking up marriages. She told him to take his medical practice elsewhere, and if he tried to set foot in Canfield she'd make sure his practice failed and he was bankrupt before he could blink."

"She *told* him that?"

"She said she had tons of influence in the community and all she'd need to do is start spreading the word that he was an immoral creep and he'd be scrubbing toilets for a living, because he sure as heck wouldn't attract any patients."

"Wow. Go, Linda."

"She took it personally—said my mother was her best friend and she would *not* let Keith wreck my marriage."

"What did Keith do?"

"He was angry, as you can imagine. He was going to go meet with her, try to smooth things over. I guess he thought he'd have better luck with her in person than over the phone—maybe he thought he could charm and flatter her into keeping her mouth shut. He's good at flattery. But I don't know if he met with her before she—before she died."

"Well, that's one way to solve the problem," Summer said. "Maybe Keith pushed her into the creek."

"That's ridiculous!"

"Sheesh, I'm not making an accusation. I'm joking."

"Do you know if she told Gavin or Alan about me?"

"No idea. But you ought to come clean with Brad, because if Linda told anyone, it's probably too much to hope they'll tumble into a creek and crack their head before they can start rumors."

Carissa flinched. "I'm sorry about what happened to Linda."

"I'll bet," Summer said. "Probably about as sorry as I am."

Chapter 13

"CAN I GET YOU SOMETHING to drink? Hot chocolate?" Alan smiled at Fiona. "That damp wind slices right through you."

"No, thank you. I'm fine." After walking two blocks to Alan's townhouse from the only parking place she could find, Fiona *was* cold, but she didn't want to do anything that would extend this visit. She'd spent the drive from Canfield worrying this was a mistake. Much as she wanted to make progress on figuring out whether Kimberly or Summer—or someone else—had targeted her, the thought of being alone with Alan for an extended period . . . this was not a good idea. She should *not* have talked to him about this, casting herself and Alan as allies with Summer as the outsider. It would have been far better to leave it all to the police.

She could walk out right now, but every time she thought of leaving, she remembered her pitch-black house with footsteps creaking down the stairs. She couldn't walk away without at least trying to figure out if Summer was harassing her. She'd already shared her suspicions with Alan and she'd driven to Waltham to search for evidence. She might as well finish the job rather than miss this opportunity—especially knowing that at this point, the police *couldn't* search Summer's house. They wouldn't have enough evidence for a warrant.

She'd search the townhouse as quickly as she could, and if she found no evidence that Summer had ever wrapped a set of car keys in blue cellophane or put a knife in a candy box tied with a pink and orange ribbon, she'd do what little she could to repair the damage her suspicions had done to Alan's opinion of Summer. Then she'd get out of there and, she hoped, never see Alan or Summer again.

"Let's get started," she said, glancing around the living room. Alan's townhouse was decorated in a simple, clean style—naturally attractive, like Summer, without clutter and frills. It appealed to Fiona.

"I'm not sure where she keeps wrapping paper," Alan said. "But it will either be in the bedroom closet or in the study."

"You check the bedroom," Fiona said. She would *not* accompany him in there, no matter what their errand. "Then we'll do the study."

Alan nodded. He disappeared down the hall.

Fiona sat on the couch and waited. Five minutes later, Alan returned. "Not there. I checked the closet and under the bed—there's nowhere else she'd keep it. Come into the study and we'll look there."

He led the way to a room with a blond oak desk and a computer. Bookshelves lined the walls. Fiona scanned the titles of the books, guilt stinging her at the thought that Randall Taylor's rare book collection belonged here, not on Fiona's shelves. Alan apparently still liked history, Shakespeare, and poetry. There were several titles on container gardening—that must be Summer's hobby. Mystery novels—those must be Summer's as well; Alan didn't like them.

A pillow, folded sheets, and a couple of folded blankets sat on the end of the couch. Fiona hoped this bedding meant a visitor—maybe Gavin—had used the couch in the study. She feared it might mean Alan was sleeping here.

Alan checked the desk drawers and shook his head. "Closet, maybe?"

"Shall I check?" Fiona opened the closet door. On the shelf, labeled bins contained paper, ink cartridges, and other office supplies. Stacked on the floor were plastic storage bins with labels like BEACH TOWELS and CRAFT SUPPLIES. "She's very organized," Fiona remarked. "I envy that. I wouldn't want anyone looking through my closets."

"Maybe it's in one of those bins." Alan pushed the closet door open wider. "What about that box in the back—"

The phone rang. Alan turned and checked the phone on the desk. "I'd better take this. Excuse me." He punched the button on the phone while walking out of the room. "Hello?"

As Alan's voice faded down the hallway, Fiona stood for a moment, feeling awkward at the thought of poking through the closet without Alan at her side. But he'd wanted to check that box in the back, so she might as well finish the closet. She tugged a couple of bins out of the way and slid the tall, thin cardboard box out of the closet.

She folded back the flaps and looked inside. It contained a framed print of Boston Harbor with a ghastly steel frame that looked like strips cut from old hubcaps. Probably a wedding present Summer couldn't bear to hang on the wall and didn't dare throw away.

Fiona returned everything to the closet and closed the door. She turned and surveyed the room, checking for any other likely places to search. The skirt around the base of the couch was pushed slightly outward at one end. Maybe Summer kept a storage bin under there. From the type of things Summer stored in the study closet, it was obvious the townhouse didn't have a lot of storage space, and wrapping paper in a flat box might fit under the couch.

Kneeling, she reached under the couch and felt a hard edge of plastic. She tugged the object out and found a bin containing rolls of wrapping paper. *Jackpot.* She removed the lid. A roll of white, shiny paper embossed with wedding cakes—a roll of brown and blue polka-dot paper—a roll of pink paper decorated with storks and diaper pins. Several other rolls of paper—a bunch of flattened gift bags—five colors of tissue paper. Scissors and tape and ribbon. Nothing in the box matched materials that had been used on the packages Fiona had received.

Searching Alan's townhouse had been a stupid idea. She'd been hoping for easy evidence, but even if Summer had given her those packages, she was probably smart enough not to keep incriminating materials around.

Fiona reached underneath the couch to see if Summer had stored anything else there. Her fingertips touched something hard and smooth. Another bin. The first wrapping paper bin had been crammed full—did she have an overflow bin with more paper? Determined to be thorough, Fiona pulled the bin out.

It had no lid. Inside the bin sat a folded bathrobe, pajamas, a reading light, a poetry anthology, a set of eyeglasses—

Embarrassed to realize she was looking at what was likely a match to the pillow and blanket on the couch—proof that Alan was using the study as a bedroom—Fiona started to push the bin back under the couch when a gleam of gold in the corner of the bin made her pause.

An object lay mostly wrapped in a white handkerchief, with one edge sticking out—a curved gold edge set with pale pink and purple seed pearls in the shape of a flower.

Her heart jolted with a burst of adrenaline so sudden that it hurt. The faint sound of Alan's voice came from somewhere in the house. He was still on the phone.

Delicately, she picked up the object and unwrapped it. It was a large gold hair comb, its rippled edge set with a row of pearl flowers.

Her comb. The heirloom gold-plated comb her grandmother had given her when she'd graduated from high school. The comb she'd scoured her parents' house trying to find when, physically recovered from the accident, she had prepared to move out. She'd given up, assuming she'd lost it, though she'd never been able to figure out how or where.

Alan had loved that comb—loved how it looked against her blonde hair, loved the elegance and craftsmanship of the piece. She could almost feel his arm resting against her shoulders as his finger traced the pearl flowers. "*You look like a queen. All you need is a matching tiara.*"

How had he gotten hold of the comb now? Before Fiona could sort out her thoughts, she heard his footsteps in the hallway.

Holding the comb, she slid the bin back under the couch and rose to her feet.

"Sorry about that." Alan walked into the room. "Gavin was checking in. That guy worries too—" He froze, his gaze on the comb.

In the silence, Fiona could hear her own racing heartbeat. "I was searching for wrapping paper," she said. "I found *this*."

"Fiona . . . I . . ."

"I know I didn't leave it with you accidentally. And even if I did, you should have returned it. You took it. You *stole* it."

"Fiona, I'm sorry." He took a small step toward her. "I know I shouldn't have—I always meant to give it back. I can't tell you how many times I almost—but I . . . needed the reminder. It was . . . all I had of you."

That small, pleading smile resurrected so many painful memories that it was all Fiona could do not to turn and run out the door. "How can you talk to me like this? You're *married*, Alan."

"I should have known it wouldn't work out with Summer. It was a mistake."

"Alan—"

"Please don't be angry," he said softly. "I can't take it right now."

"I need to leave. I shouldn't have come here."

"It's . . . getting harder and harder to open my eyes each morning. I *need* you, Fiona. I need your strength."

The teeth of the comb dug into Fiona's palm. "You have a *wife*. She loves you."

"I don't think so."

"She does. If she didn't care about you, she wouldn't have been so angry when she saw me at the funeral."

"A wife who's threatening you."

"I made a mistake accusing her." Whether or not that was true, Fiona didn't want to deal with it anymore. Let the police handle things. "I panicked. I have absolutely no proof. I was wrong. Please, Alan. Work things out with her."

"I need *you*," he said. "I understand that you don't love me. But I need your friendship. Just your friendship."

All-too-familiar guilt, misery, and frustration flooded Fiona. She pictured Alan here in the study, clutching her comb like a child's comfort object while Summer slept alone in the master bedroom. The picture made her want to shake Alan.

"I'm sorry for everything you've been through," Fiona said. "You've suffered a terrible shock with your mother's death. Get help, Alan. You need to get help. *Please.* Don't let this drag you under."

His jaw tensed. "I need a friend. Not a shrink."

"Talk to your bishop. People care about you. Let them help. I can't come back into your life in any way. It's wrong for both of us."

His voice was dry, like she was being ridiculous. "I'm not asking you to climb into bed with me. I'm asking for your friendship."

Déjà vu rose higher and colder until she felt it would cover her face and drown her. The same arguments, the same manipulation, the same grasping fingers clutching at her emotions, struggling to hold on as she struggled to free herself from a relationship she knew would never work. She'd let the conversation go on too long, let her frustration turn to anger, let the discussion turn to a heated argument while Mia—trying to be polite—had paced in her bedroom waiting for the ride Fiona had promised to give her to the airport. Fiona had finally snatched her keys, grabbed Mia's suitcase, and stalked out the door, leaving Alan in the kitchen while a red-faced Mia followed her, murmuring apologies for inconveniencing her. And she'd driven too fast, too aggressively, worried Mia would miss her flight, her mind on Alan and not on the rain-slick road—

Tears stung her eyes, and no matter how she tried to draw a deep breath, she didn't feel she was getting any oxygen. "I need to go now." She started toward the doorway.

"Wait—we haven't even finished searching . . ."

"We've looked in the likely places. If she had any wrapping paper like I saw on my packages, we would have found it. She's innocent. I made a mistake."

Alan caught her arm as she passed. "Fiona . . ."

"I need to leave. Let go of me." The tears trickled down her face. What a fool she'd been to entangle herself with Alan Taylor again.

"Please," he whispered. "Fiona, please don't leave. I'm sorry about the comb. I was wrong to keep it."

Did he think that was the only issue here? "It doesn't matter. Please let go of me."

The desperation in his eyes clutched at her far more powerfully than his hand on her arm. "Don't run away. Please. Talk to me, for just a little while. I need a friend. Someone who cares about me."

Fiona yanked her arm free, too violently for the light pressure of his fingers; the force of her own motion sent her staggering. *Don't lose control. Don't yell at him. Don't engage. You can't help him; you can't give him what he needs.*

"You're all shaky," Alan said. "Please, come sit down."

Fiona retreated. "I made a mistake in coming here—in coming to your mother's funeral—in upsetting your life. I'm sorry."

Alan followed her but then stood in the living room without speaking, watching as she snatched her coat out of the closet and hurried to the front door, clutching her comb so tightly that the points jabbed into her flesh.

* * *

The twilight sky had darkened to blackness, and her body had stiffened from sitting too long in one position, but every time Fiona tried to put the key in the ignition, panic overwhelmed her and she froze, bloodied images filling her mind.

Her head throbbed and her swollen eyes ached. Her tears had finally dried, but still she couldn't bring herself to pull out of her parking spot two blocks from Alan's townhouse. At least Alan didn't know she was still here or he'd be at her side with his pleas, his demands, his pressure. Desperation, fear, pain, loneliness—all the torment that showed in that handsome face, emotions that dragged at her like a physical force, rousing the instincts that made her want to go to him, put her arms around him, talk to him, comfort him, fix what was wrong.

Even when she knew she couldn't. So she'd walked away. She'd run away.

She felt like a monster.

Put the key in the ignition. You've driven thousands of times since that night. Are you going to call a taxi and abandon your car here? Put the key in.

The ringing of her phone startled her. She pulled the phone out of her purse, but her fingers shook so much that she dropped it. Bending, she picked it up and checked the number. James.

Clumsily, she opened the phone. "James?"

"Hey. Just wanted to see if you were home yet and how things went."

"I'm—not home yet."

"You sound terrible." James spoke sharply. "What's wrong?"

"I . . . things didn't . . . they didn't go well."

"Fiona, what happened? Are you still in Canfield?"

"No, I'm—I'm in Waltham. I'm . . . I'm a couple of blocks from Alan's place. In my car."

"What happened? Why did you go to Alan's house? What's wrong?"

"I . . . it's . . ." She looked at the pearl hair comb on the seat next to her, the gold shimmering in the illumination from the streetlights. It was too much to explain over the phone. "I'm having a little . . . trouble."

"Trouble with what? Fiona, are you hurt? Are you sick?"

"No. I'm . . . it's . . . I can't drive."

"You can't drive?"

"Every time I try to put the key in the ignition I feel . . . so sick that I can't breathe."

James was silent for a moment. "Okay. Listen to me. I need the address and I'm on my way."

"*No.* I have to do this. I can't—I *won't* go back to being . . . I can't let . . ."

"Fiona! You should have called me as soon as you started having trouble. How long have you been sitting there?"

"I'm not sure. Maybe . . . an hour?"

"Give me the address."

New tears filled her eyes. "I can't backslide. I have to do this."

"No, you don't. Not right now. You need to give yourself a break."

"I haven't had this problem in . . . It was just . . . talking to Alan today . . . arguing . . . like before . . . like that night . . ."

"Okay, found the address." Fiona heard the faint click of a laptop closing. "I'm on my way."

"James . . . you shouldn't have to come all the way out here. I need to get through this."

"You *can* get through it—by taking a break and tackling it another day. I'm on my way. Fiona, listen to me. If you've been sitting there for an hour, you must be cold. If you promise yourself you don't have to drive, can you put the key in and turn on the heat?"

"I . . . think so. Maybe."

"Try it. You don't have to go anywhere. You don't have to drive. I'm coming to get you. Just start the engine so you can turn on the heat. Put the key in. I'm right here with you. Can you do it?"

Her keys jangled together as she picked them up in trembling fingers and located the correct one.

"Slow, deep breaths," James said. "Put the key in and start the engine. You're not driving. You're just turning on the heat."

Burning pain filled her lungs, but she shoved the key in the ignition and twisted it. "I did it."

"Nice job. Now get that heat blasting. Then tip your seat back, close your eyes, and rest. I'll be there as quickly as I can."

"Don't drive fast—James, please don't—"

"As *safely* and as quickly as I can. Speed limit all the way. I'll be very careful."

"I'm sorry."

"Don't be. I wish you'd called me earlier. I'm on my way."

Chapter 14

"How's your Monday so far?" James sat in what was becoming his usual spot on the edge of Fiona's desk and peered down at her. "You look great."

"I feel a hundred times better," Fiona said, embarrassed that James's compliment brought warmth to her cheeks. What was wrong with her? James only meant that, unlike on Saturday, she didn't resemble something that had crawled out of the underworld. "I got a lot of rest yesterday. It's amazing what sleep can do."

"You're wearing the comb." James gestured at her hair. "Good for you."

Fiona lifted her hand to the gold comb that helped hold her French twist in place. "I refuse to let what Alan did taint my grandmother's gift. I'm grateful to have it back."

"Good."

"Thank you again for rescuing me." Fiona tried to look at him as she spoke, but eye contact brought deep, razor-sharp guilt, and she hastily averted her gaze. She'd spent all day Sunday trying to forget how peaceful—how safe—she'd felt drifting off to sleep, warm and emotionally exhausted, as James drove her home on Saturday. Knowing she didn't have to keep up any kind of façade for him. Knowing she could trust him completely.

"Are you *sure* you're okay?" James asked.

"I'm a little off kilter, but I'm fine. And you and Troy really didn't need to go all the way back to Waltham to fetch my car. I could have arranged—"

"Troy was glad to help, and you didn't need one more thing to worry about. So you were all right this morning? Driving here, I mean?"

She nodded. "I think Saturday's breakdown was mainly due to too much stress and too little sleep. I'm feeling a lot better now."

"Too little sleep and too much Alan," James said. "I'm sorry you had to go through that."

Thinking of Alan brought the sensation of a weight so heavy it pinned her to her chair. She'd called Gavin late Saturday night to ask him to check on Alan, telling him Alan had been upset when Fiona left his house, and she was worried about him. She'd asked Gavin *not* to tell Alan she'd called—the last thing she wanted was to give Alan false hope. She'd done too much of that eight years ago.

"Thanks again for all your help," Fiona said. "I'll be fine. A little more sleep and a few more ritual slugs of milk, and I'll be good as new."

"Ritual milk?"

"My grandmother's fault. She had osteoporosis, so she was always after her granddaughters to drink more milk. I drink a glass of milk every night before bedtime, in her honor. I'm afraid she'd haunt me if I didn't."

"This haunting brought to you by the Dairy Farmers of America." James grinned. "Warm milk?"

"No. That's disgusting. Ice-cold only."

"I knew you had good taste. Fiona . . . I wish I'd been there with you at the Taylors' on Saturday."

"I wish you had been."

"Will you let me go with you next time? I'm assuming there will be a next time, since you still have those books to deal with."

The prospect of facing Alan again brought an echo of the panic that had paralyzed her on Saturday night. With James by her side, it would be much easier. That thought was so appealing that it took all her willpower to say, "That's so kind of you, but I've caused you far too much trouble already. I'll be fine. You've earned a little time off from my problems."

James adjusted his glasses. He fidgeted like that when he was debating what to say, and she wondered what was going through his mind. "If I wanted time off, I wouldn't keep pestering you."

She forced herself to laugh then wished she hadn't—it sounded phony. "You've already gone above and beyond the call of duty."

He wasn't smiling anymore. "Helping you is not a chore."

"I've been monopolizing your time. I'm sure there are things you'd rather be doing."

Silence filled the office, the lack of sound as painful to the eardrums as shrill noise.

"Maybe I'm spending my time exactly how I want to spend it," he said at last, his voice quiet. "Are there other things *you'd* rather have me doing?"

Blushing, Fiona realized how clumsy her words had sounded. James thought she was trying to get rid of him. "No, not at all. I'm grateful for everything you've done for me—" That sounded equally clumsy, as though she was thanking him for performing a service project instead of acting out of friendship. "I'm sorry. I . . ." Floundering, she finished with, "One of these weekends you need to have some fun."

"Fiona . . . is that what's really bothering you? Guilt over the time I've spent helping you with a couple of things?" She felt the compassion in his voice like gentle fingers, working carefully at the shield concealing her thoughts and emotions. If she didn't push him away, those skillful hands would dismantle her defenses and she'd be telling him everything.

James was looking so intently into her eyes that maybe she didn't need to speak—maybe he'd read everything in her face. "If you want me to stay away, all you need to say is 'Please leave me alone, James.' I'm not Alan Taylor. I'll respect your wishes, no matter how I feel about them."

"Of course I don't want you to stay away." Her voice emerged like she'd developed an instantaneous case of laryngitis. She swallowed. "We're friends."

"May I ask you something very personal?"

Fiona struggled to come up with a light response. "That's the sort of question that usually makes people flee, screaming."

"If you want me to stop, I will." James rose to his feet. "All it takes is, 'Shut up, James.'"

She said nothing.

"I'll take that as permission. Why won't you let anyone get close to you?"

The question threw her even more off balance. "I don't know what you mean."

"I think you do. I've kept up on you, Fiona. Not just through the direct contact we've had, but through your family. A couple of your sisters e-mail me occasionally. I even hear from your mother now and then."

Fiona couldn't figure out why this news made her feel shakier—she knew James had stayed in contact with her family. Rebecca and Shannon had mentioned it several times.

What they *hadn't* mentioned was anything they'd discussed with James regarding Fiona.

Fiona could no longer make any pretense toward eye contact. It was far easier to stare at the silk philodendron on top of her filing cabinet or the watercolor on the wall. "What does my family have to do with anything?"

"They provide another perspective as to what's going on in your life. Such as the fact that you won't attend church singles activities, or any other social event that would encourage interaction with eligible guys. Such as the fact that you don't date. I knew all this before I came to Hawkins, but now I can play eyewitness: your family is right. You're intent on keeping yourself unattached. Why is that?"

"James, when would I have time for a social life? I'm so busy that if I'm not running behind, something's wrong."

"Convenient."

"James!"

"Frankly, I think the perpetual DIY fest is an excuse too. You sent me pictures of your house before you moved in—remember? It didn't look bad at all. But you're always tearing the place up and redoing everything in sight, even though you admit you don't have time for it. And how can you invite friends over when you live in a construction zone?"

The magic words *Shut up, James* twitched on her tongue. She could stop this conversation right now. "Fixing up my house helps keep me sane. And I can't believe you and my sisters talk about me."

"I care about you. They care about you. But we're supposed to never mention your name?"

"There's a difference between mentioning my name and dissecting my social life."

"Why the determination to fly solo? And don't tell me it's a time problem. That's an excuse."

Her tongue was as dry and heavy as concrete. She couldn't go on. This was not for James's ears or her family's ears or anyone's. She'd never even shaped it into formed, rational thoughts for herself, and she didn't want to try now.

"Because of Mia?" James said softly.

Fiona tried to steady herself, but her whole body was shaking. She gripped the arms of her chair. "She was twenty-one. She never had the chance to marry, to raise a family, to live the long, happy life she should have lived."

"So you think the only way you can make up for that is to deprive yourself of those things?"

"I'm . . . just more at peace on my own."

"In other words, you think you don't deserve marriage or children."

"I think we should change the subject."

James came around the side of her desk and stood next to her. "What happened to Mia was an *accident.*"

Pain made Fiona feel like screaming, and the effort to keep her voice low made it come out harsh and hoarse. "Mia died because of *me.* I could have prevented it. I could *easily* have prevented it. I was driving too fast, in the rain. I was driving aggressively. I was angry at Alan, angry at myself, angry at that car in front of me that was driving too slowly—" The memories came sharp and slashing: accelerating and veering left to pass the offending car, a yelp from Mia—"*Slow down, Fiona. Better to miss my flight than get there in pieces.*" Those were the last words Mia had ever spoken, right before the tires lost traction on the rain-drenched freeway and the car skidded—

James reached down and took both her hands in his.

"I took her from *you.*" Fiona forced those last, necessary words out of her mouth.

"Fiona—"

A knock at the door interrupted him.

"I'll tell them to go away," James whispered. "I'll tell them you're not feeling well."

"No—I need to do my job."

James released her hands and went to open the door. Fiona didn't have the strength to stop him. She didn't even have the strength to stand up.

"Hi, uh—" The woman at the door looked past James to where Fiona sat at her desk. Glossy brown hair, a fresh, pretty face.

Startled, Fiona met her gaze. "Summer," she said, not sure what other greeting to offer Summer Taylor. *What do you want? Are you armed?*

Summer's gaze flicked from Fiona to James. "I'm interrupting," she said. "Sorry. I can come back later, whenever it works for you. I just need to talk to you for a few minutes." She aimed an uncomfortable look at James. "Privately, if that's okay."

The meekness in Summer's voice and the embarrassment on her face were not what Fiona had expected. Could she possibly have come to apologize? Apparently Alan hadn't told her about Fiona's accusations.

"Give me two minutes," Fiona said.

"No problem."

James closed the door, stepped toward Fiona, and leaned over her desk. "If you're talking to her, I want to be here."

Still shaken by her conversation with James, she found it difficult to look at him. "You heard how she sounded. I think she's here to apologize."

"You're too quick to think the best of people. Maybe she's here to chuck a rock at your head instead of your door. If you want to talk to her, you need a bodyguard."

"She won't open up to me if you're in here. But if you wouldn't mind staying within earshot . . ."

"I don't like the thought of—"

"I know. But I *want* to talk to her. If I get even the tiniest bit worried that she might try something, I'll holler."

"It's your decision. But I'm standing outside with my hand on the doorknob."

"Deal. Let her in."

James opened the door.

"Thanks." Summer edged into the office. James walked out and closed the door.

Seated across from Fiona, Summer twisted a button on her jacket. Denim jacket, heeled boots, a couple of plain gold bracelets, that beautiful, blunt-cut mahogany-brown hair—she had a stylish and classic look that Fiona had always wished she could master.

"Sorry to interrupt," Summer said. "I thought I'd check your door to see what your office hours were and then come back . . . but when I saw you were here . . ." She tucked her hair behind her ear.

"It's all right." Fiona hoped her voice didn't sound as off balance as she felt. Part of her was grateful for this reprieve from the intensity of her conversation with James.

"I was very rude to you at Linda's funeral, and I'm sorry," Summer said. "I thought you and Alan were having an affair."

"We aren't." Fiona's neck tensed with the need to keep her head facing straight forward. She didn't want Summer to catch a glimpse of the pearl comb tucked in the back of her hair. What if she recognized it? Had she ever seen it? Did she know it belonged to Fiona? "I promise you, I would never—"

"I know. I'm sorry."

"Why did you think we were involved?"

"I misunderstood something Linda said. She was talking about someone else, but I thought she was talking about you and Alan." Summer blushed dark pink. "And when you sent me that note . . . you shouldn't have apologized. I was the one who was out of line."

"I shouldn't have come to the funeral. That was a very difficult day for your family and you didn't need any other concerns."

"Difficult for Alan and Gavin. I'm not a big enough hypocrite to pretend I was sad. I don't miss Linda."

This candor surprised Fiona. "Carissa Willis told me she made things hard for you."

"She always made it clear she didn't want Alan to marry me. She thought our marriage was a mistake, and she was biding her time until it disintegrated. She never liked me."

"Why didn't she like you?" Fiona immediately regretted asking such an intrusive question.

Summer gave a bitter little laugh, but she didn't look offended. "Because I tried to cut the apron strings." She snipped the air with two fingers. "Linda was so . . . so . . . *needy*. She always had to poke her nose in Alan's and Gavin's lives. She was the master of guilt trips and manipulation. You must have been better at putting up with her than I was, because I sure got on her bad side in a hurry."

"It helped that while I was dating Alan, he was at BYU. Linda didn't have the chance to see much of me, which let her imagine I was much nicer than I am."

"I'm amazed she didn't make him find a college within fifty miles of home."

"I think she was willing to endure it as long as it was temporary. To be honest—" Fiona stopped.

"Or . . . you'd rather not be honest?" Summer asked dryly.

"I—was going to say that Linda was one of the reasons I broke up with Alan. It scared me how controlling she was and how difficult it was for Alan to stand up to her. I didn't feel I could handle that in a mother-in-law."

"I can see that. I guess I was way too cocky, because I thought I was a match for her—exactly what Alan needed if he was ever going to break free. And I almost won. When we were dating, he actually listened to me. He *did* start pulling back from her, he'd limit the time he spent on the phone with her, he cut back on his trips home. Boy, did it make Linda mad. When we told her we were engaged—yowza. She went on this weepy rant about what a mistake he was making and how she knew I could never make him happy, and if he'd wait a little longer, Fiona Claridge would come to her senses and he could live happily ever after."

"That's terrible."

"Yeah, it was a nightmare, but I was so proud of Alan. He stood his ground and said he loved me and we were getting married and he hoped she'd be there. She went marching off on one of her martyr walks, and his guilt kicked in and I had to sit on him to keep him from following her—like, literally *sit* on him. I plopped myself on his lap and told him if he wanted to follow her, he'd have to do it while carrying me. And he laughed and stayed with me, and I had eyes full of fairy dust, I guess, because I thought everything would be fine. She freaked out again when he told her he'd gotten a job in Virginia—too far away!—but he held firm. I should have known she wouldn't quit—and Alan wouldn't have the strength to resist her."

"This will probably sound cold," Fiona said, "but the apron strings are severed now. With Linda gone, you and Alan have the chance to start fresh."

Summer looked down into her lap. "I wish. But Alan is so devastated that it's hard to even have a conversation with him. It's like he's in his own world. I mean, I understand that he's grieving, but I have no idea how to reach him, and the bridges are pretty well burned anyway. I . . . I'm the one who asked him for a divorce, right before Linda died. I didn't really want one—I was just so angry at the thought that he was messing around with you. And now, when I try to reach out to him, he seems so *blank,* like he can't figure out why he ought to care about anything I say. So I end up snapping at him, saying nasty things, trying to get him to respond to me."

"He needs time," Fiona said, a response so trite that she wanted to take a red pen and write *cliché* in the margin.

Summer sighed. "Yeah. Maybe. But he moved out yesterday. Moved in with Gavin in Canfield. He's taking some time off work. And time off from me."

Fiona felt chilled at this news. In sharing her suspicions of Summer with Alan, she'd broken the last thread of their relationship.

"He told me about those cruel packages you've been getting lately," Summer said, apparently reading either her face or her mind, "and how you wondered if I was sending them. Not that I didn't know something was up with you already, since the cops stopped by to talk to me."

"Summer, I—"

"Don't you dare apologize. You've done too much of that already. I don't blame you for thinking it might be me after the way I talked to you at the funeral. I wanted to come in person to tell you I didn't have anything to do with those packages or that rock someone threw at your door, or breaking into your house. I'd *never* do anything that psycho."

"I still shouldn't have said anything to Alan. I know that didn't help things between you."

"Oh, brother. *I* would have said something if I were you. You think you're supposed to pretend I'm not the obvious suspect out of, what—good manners? Give me a break. I was a jerk to you. Besides, at this point, nothing can make things worse between Alan and me, and I feel better having him out of the house. Maybe being apart will help clear our heads."

"I hope it does."

Summer rose to her feet. Her tense expression had eased, and it was obvious talking to Fiona had freed her of a burden. "I hope you can get this whole freaky package thing cleared up."

"So do I." Fiona stood.

"Cute picture." Summer gestured at the framed photo sitting next to the philodendron on the filing cabinet. "Your sisters?"

"Yes." Fiona turned and picked up the photo. When she turned back, Summer's almost-friendly expression was gone. She was staring at Fiona, her eyes stony.

"The comb *is* yours," she said. "I thought so."

Oh, no. How could she have forgotten already that she wanted to keep the comb out of sight? "I misplaced it years ago," Fiona said. *Misplaced* was an extreme stretching of the truth, but she feared candor would infuriate Summer. "I didn't realize Alan had it. He returned it to me on Saturday."

"You saw him on Saturday?"

So much for hoping that she could avoid making things worse. Apparently when Alan had told Summer what Fiona had said about the packages, he hadn't admitted he'd met with Fiona personally—or that Fiona had searched their townhouse. "Gavin asked me to come to Canfield. Linda mentioned me in her will, and Gavin wanted to discuss it. Alan was there as well." Much as she hated to bring up Linda's will, she couldn't think of another way to explain what she'd been doing at the Taylors' house.

"What did Linda leave you?" Summer asked.

"Books."

"Alan's dad's ancient collection?"

Fiona steeled herself. "Yes."

"Better you than Alan. If she'd given them to him, he'd have dragged those dusty old things around for the rest of his life, sure he was dishonoring his dad's memory if he sold even one of them." Summer reached for the photograph in Fiona's hand and peered at it. "Five girls, huh?"

Better you than Alan? She'd spent so much anxiety on those books, and Summer didn't even care about them. Feeling ridiculous, Fiona answered Summer's question: "Yes, five girls. No boys."

"All estrogen, all the time," Summer remarked, her voice casual. "I'm the only girl—I have two brothers. What are your sisters' names?"

"This is Kira, the oldest." Fiona pointed. "Then Shannon, me, Lauren, and Rebecca."

"Nice. Listen, thanks for talking to me."

"Thanks for coming." Were they parting on good terms? It seemed so. Thank heavens the comb hadn't resurrected Summer's initial suspicions of Fiona.

Summer started to move toward the door but hesitated. "Uh . . . this is none of my business, but Carissa Willis is having a tough time right now. I promised I wouldn't tell anyone, and technically I'm not—because I'm not telling you the situation—but I know you're friends, and you might want to check in with her."

"What—" Fiona stopped. Hadn't Summer said she couldn't give details? "I'll call her."

"Good. And I don't care if you tell her I'm the one who said to call. I hate it when people do stupid things—like I do all the time—and I don't like sitting there doing nothing to help. I'll see you later." Summer headed out the door.

Fiona expected James to immediately reenter the room, but to her relief, he didn't. He must have eavesdropped long enough to convince himself Summer wasn't dangerous and then moved far enough from the door so he wouldn't embarrass Summer when she exited.

When after a few minutes James still hadn't appeared, Fiona wondered if he'd bailed out altogether. Maybe he'd thought she and Summer would be talking for a while, and since Summer clearly meant no harm, he'd go get some work done. She felt guiltily relieved at the thought that she wouldn't have to face him immediately and finish their conversation.

Fiona took out her cell phone, looked up Carissa's number, and dialed.

"Hi." A young child answered the phone.

"Hi," Fiona said. "May I talk to your mom?"

A pause. Then garbled two-year-old speech about something that sounded like "blue monkey cat."

"Is this Peter?" Fiona asked.

"Yeah."

"Hi, Peter. Can you give the phone to your mother?"

More babbling. Carissa spoke in the background. "Peter! Give it to Mommy." A loud complaint from Peter that Fiona couldn't decipher. "Later, honey. Peter, give me the phone!"

Carissa's voice came on the line. "I'm sorry. I have a determined phone screener."

Fiona laughed. "Hi, Carissa. It's Fiona."

"Fiona, hi!" Carissa's voice was so cheerful it sounded strange, as though in trying to feign good humor, she'd gone overboard. "How are you?"

"I'm good." Fiona ran her finger along the edge of the framed photo of her and her sisters. "I was wondering if I could stop by and see you sometime."

"Oh! That would be—that would be great." Carissa sounded out of breath—almost frantic. "I'd love that. Can you come soon?"

Surprised at Carissa's eagerness, Fiona said, "What day would work for you?"

"Tonight? Brad's working overtime—there's a spring festival at the high school and he's helping with traffic—and the kids will be in bed, so you won't be interrupting family home evening. We could talk." She laughed. "Sorry. What's wrong with me? That's way too short of notice for you. We could do tomorrow—"

"I can come tonight. What time?"

"You can? Thank you—that's great—how about seven thirty?"

"Seven thirty is good. I'll see you then."

"*Thank* you—Peter, I *told* you, no more gummy bears. Fiona, I've got to run. See you tonight."

"Bye." Fiona hung up. Carissa had sounded almost desperate to see her. Thank goodness Summer had tipped her off that Carissa was in need. Whatever was wrong, Fiona hoped she could help.

Fiona picked up the photograph of her sisters and set it back on the filing cabinet. Absently, she rearranged the philodendron vines to trail around the picture. She should try for a living houseplant at some point. It seemed pitiful to have to resort to fabric and wire anytime she wanted a touch of green.

The leaves were getting dusty. Fiona brushed lightly at them. She ought to be more conscientious about—something black amidst the leaves caught her eye. She touched it and felt something hard and smooth. Puzzled, she pushed the leaves aside and found a small, black electronic device of some kind. She turned it over in her hand, examining it. A camera with a microphone.

A *camera?* In her office? Who in the world—why would—

"Hey." James leaned through the open doorway. "Didn't want you to think I ran out on you. I was waiting down the hall—once I figured out there was no screaming going on—and when Summer came out, she stopped to chat with me. How did things go?"

"Fine," Fiona said grimly. She found the switch and turned the camera off. "But look what I found nesting in my fake plant." She held it out.

James took it. "A camera?"

"Why would someone put a camera in my office?"

James's jaw clenched. He shut the door behind him. "Maybe someone was looking for something they could use against you—or wanted to learn more about you so they could figure out more creative ways to hurt you."

"Kimberly?"

"Maybe."

"You and I talked about Alan in here." Fiona took the camera back from James. "If Kimberly *was* spying on me, she could have learned about Alan from that conversation and used that information to make it look like Summer was the one targeting me."

"Could be."

Fiona wanted to smash the camera against her desk. How *dare* Kimberly—or anyone else . . . how long had the camera been there? What else had the culprit witnessed? Fiona thought of today's conversation with James and her cheeks burned.

"You okay?" James squeezed her arm.

"I'm furious."

"Same. Let's search every square inch of this place to see if there's anything else we don't know about. Then you can call the cops again."

"I have them on speed dial," Fiona said through gritted teeth.

Chapter 15

BY THE TIME THEY'D FINISHED searching her office, James had to rush off to teach, leaving Fiona to report to department chair Sarah McKinley that yet another problem had arisen and to hand the camera over to the police. Sarah shared Fiona's anger at this illegal invasion of privacy, but her sympathy for Fiona's ongoing difficulties was clearly waning—would Kimberly Bailey or any student go to the trouble and expense of planting a camera? Likely these problems didn't involve a student at all but were the result of a conflict in Fiona's personal life spilling onto campus—especially given the reference to Fiona's former boyfriend in the rock-throwing incident. Fiona could imagine what kind of conversations would take place as Sarah passed Fiona's report up the chain of command. *"She seemed like such a quiet, stable person at first, but apparently she has a troubled private life, and lately she's been nothing but a magnet for scandal. I'm seriously questioning whether or not Dr. Claridge is an asset to Hawkins College."*

Fiona rested her forehead on the lid of her computer. *You have someone secretly filming you, throwing rocks at your door, breaking into your house and switching off the power, and leaving weapons on your porch—and you're worrying about tenure? That's the least pressing of your problems right now.*

She sat up, opened her computer, and looked blankly at her lecture notes for tomorrow's nineteenth-century American literature class. What was James thinking right now? Distracted by Summer's visit and the finding of the camera, they hadn't resumed the conversation about Fiona's self-imposed isolation, but Fiona knew the reprieve couldn't last much longer. After what James and she had said, they couldn't pretend the conversation never happened. Eventually, they'd have to finish the discussion. But not tonight.

Should she tell James she was going to visit Carissa? She'd better. Tonight, he'd planned to attend the monthly singles family home evening, and as he did every month, he'd urged Fiona to come with him. She'd never given him a firm answer about tonight, and in the camera upheaval, she'd forgotten to mention her talk with Carissa. If she was going to skip out on FHE—again—she'd better tell him so.

She texted a message to James. *Carissa Willis is having a hard time. I'm going to visit her tonight. Won't be able to make FHE.*

For a few moments, she sat with her eyes closed, mentally sanding the edges off her jagged emotions. She'd wasted enough time today. She needed to get to work.

She opened her eyes, put her fingers on the keyboard, and began to edit her notes.

Twenty minutes later, a beep from her phone signaled James's response. *Are you driving to Canfield?*

Yes, she texted back. *I'll be fine.*

Let me come with you.

The thought of two hours alone in the car with James made her hands start sweating—two hours was plenty of time to confront a subject Fiona didn't want to face right now. *Thanks, but I'll be fine. I predict girl talk at Carissa's. No Y chromosomes allowed.*

This time, several minutes passed without a response from James. Fiona swallowed, wondering why her mouth was so dry. Had she offended him?

Finally, her phone beeped. *If you're sure.*

I'm sure. Feeling the need to lighten things, she added, *Congrats on going so long without losing your phone. Have you made it a month yet?*

Funny. I lose it, but I always find it. Eventually.

Absentminded professors should get landlines.

I could lose that, too. Enjoy your elitist evening.

Thanks. She slid her phone back into her purse, grateful James hadn't pushed the issue of her driving. Thinking about Saturday's breakdown embarrassed her. She'd thought she'd grown past that paralyzing anxiety.

She'd have to face James soon and finish the conversation they'd started, but maybe delay would give her time to figure out what to say.

She wanted to be angry with her sisters and her mother for sharing personal information about her—especially when none of them had had the guts to discuss Fiona's solitary life with her directly—but anger seemed pointless. James was perceptive enough and observant enough to have figured it out on his own without any help from Fiona's family.

At seven thirty that evening, following an almost-uneventful drive—uneventful except for the tension in her muscles which led to a painful backache—Fiona rang Carissa's doorbell.

"Come in. Thank you so much for coming. What a pain for you to have to drive all the way here." Carissa's cheeks were red, and she was talking so fast she was almost babbling as she greeted Fiona at the door. "Do you mind if we visit in the kitchen? It's farther from the boys' bedrooms, and I don't want to wake anyone up."

"That's fine," Fiona said. Carissa was holding her hands out, ready to take Fiona's jacket, so Fiona handed it over, but Carissa bypassed the coat closet and carried it with her into the kitchen.

"Have a seat," Carissa invited, frowning at the jacket in her hands as though she couldn't remember what she was supposed to do with it.

Rather than sitting down, Fiona approached Carissa and took the jacket out of her hands. At least with Carissa so transparently rattled, Fiona didn't have to figure out a way to subtly lead into the subject of whatever was upsetting her.

"Oh, let me move all that." Carissa reached toward the stack of clean dishes on the table. "Alan and Gavin came by earlier to return my dishes. I took dinner to them after Linda died and made some cinnamon rolls for Gavin once—he really loves my cinnamon rolls, I put cream cheese in the frosting—"

"Summer Taylor talked to me today," Fiona interrupted. "She came to apologize for how she treated me. She also said you're having a hard time. She didn't tell me what the problem was, but I'm here to help, if I can."

"Summer talked to you?" Carissa set the dishes onto the counter and gave a squeaky little laugh. "That stinker."

"She didn't tell me *what* was wrong," Fiona emphasized. "She suggested I talk to you. Carissa, what is it?"

Tears swelled in Carissa's eyes. "I'm so . . . I'm glad she told you to call, because I've been wanting to—but I'm such a chicken. Fiona, I don't think I've slept more than a couple of hours a night for weeks. I don't know what to do, and I think I'm losing my mind . . ."

"Should we sit down?"

"I've really messed up." Tears streamed down Carissa's face. "You'll think I'm horrible."

"I doubt that." With her arm around Carissa's shoulders, Fiona led her to a kitchen chair. She pulled another chair up close to Carissa's and took both her hands, trying to ignore jolting déjà vu at the memory of the way James had held her hands this afternoon. "What's wrong?"

Carissa clutched Fiona's fingers, her skin cold. "You're not going to believe it. No one would ever think—I've always tried to do what's right—my family would *die* if they knew . . ."

Fiona squeezed Carissa's hands. "Tell me what happened."

"I—I got involved with . . . with another man. An old school friend."

This news *did* startle Fiona, but she was careful not to let shock show in her face, lest Carissa's embarrassment shut down her confession. "How did it happen?"

"Fiona, I never thought I'd do something like that. *Never.* It was all really innocent, I mean it started out that way, a group of old friends getting together. Keith—his name is Keith Murray—was so charming, and it was so much fun talking to him, feeling like he really admired me . . . I'm not excusing myself, really I'm not, but I was lonely . . ."

"Are you still seeing him?" Fiona kept her tone matter-of-fact.

"*No!* No, absolutely not. And I never slept with him. But I did go out with him a few times. He kissed me, and—you won't believe this—the night he kissed me, Linda Taylor was in the same restaurant. We were in Worcester, for crying out loud, but there she was—and she saw us. She took pictures of us on her cell phone."

Fiona tightened her grip on Carissa's twisting hands. "Did she show the pictures to Brad?"

"No. She pulled me aside at church a couple of days later and said she wanted to give me a chance to do the right thing. She'd give me two weeks to talk to Brad and the bishop, and if I didn't, she'd force the issue by giving Brad those pictures. I didn't dare . . . Brad would be devastated; he'd never trust me again. And can you imagine what my parents would think? You know what my family is like—they're wonderful, they're all so good—solid, faithful, stake president and Relief Society president types—I can't believe I . . ." Tears were turning to sobs, chopping up Carissa's words. Fiona moved closer and wrapped her arms around Carissa, waiting until Carissa could speak again.

"I'm sorry." Carissa pulled away and went to grab a paper towel from the holder on the counter. "I'm sorry to lose it like this." She wiped her face, smoothing back wet strands of red hair sticking to her cheeks. "I've been going crazy . . . I was so relieved when you called today. I knew I could tell you, that I *had* to tell you." She ripped another towel off the roll.

"What happened to the pictures?"

"Summer has Linda's phone. She stole it because she heard Linda talking about the pictures and thought they were pictures of you and Alan."

Pictures of Fiona and Alan! *That* must be the "proof" Summer had referred to.

Carissa sank into her chair. "I don't know what to do."

"Yes, you do. This is going to eat you up until you talk to Brad."

"It's gotten complicated." Carissa twisted the paper towel in her hands, tearing it. "Worse, I mean. Linda . . . she talked to Keith too and told him about the pictures. Keith was planning to move back to Canfield. He was opening a medical practice here. But after she saw us together, Linda was determined to keep Keith away. She was sure he'd ruin my marriage and then prey on other married women. She told Keith if he came here, she'd make sure his practice failed. She'd warn everyone in town to stay away from him—and she really could have done it. Linda pretty well knew everyone in town and is probably friends with the whole town council. Keith told me he'd talk to her and calm her down, and everything would be fine, but I doubted it would work . . . he didn't know Linda . . ."

"What happened when he talked to her?"

Carissa looked down at the paper towel she was ripping to shreds. "I don't know. I was waiting to hear from him and then Linda . . . died. I didn't think anything was—I mean, everyone knew Linda went off on those walks in the woods when she was mad. Summer called them 'martyr walks.' And the storm was so bad that day, and Linda wasn't in good shape—we all thought she'd slipped on the bank and gone into the creek. But then Summer—when I was talking to Summer—she joked about how maybe Keith pushed her in, to shut her up. She said she was just kidding, but . . ."

The thought of someone shoving Linda Taylor into a rushing, rock-strewn creek made Fiona shudder. "But you think it's possible?"

Carissa wadded the shredded bits of paper towel into a ball. "I don't know. Maybe it's a crazy thought. Most people don't go around murdering other people, even if they're angry, right? It didn't even occur to me to wonder if Keith would hurt Linda until Summer joked about it. And the more I thought about it, the more scared I got."

"What does Keith say about all this?"

"I can't get in touch with him. That's what's freaking me out. He's missing, apparently. He said he was going back to Indiana, but he didn't show up there. His girlfriend—yeah, while he was dripping compliments all over me, he had a girlfriend—contacted the Canfield police. Brad recognized Keith's name as one of my old friends and called me to see if I knew anything." Carissa's reddened eyes filled with pain. "I admitted I'd talked to him on the phone but said I was just giving him advice on local painters and decorators. I didn't admit I'd seen him after that first dinner, and I didn't tell him what Linda had threatened to do to his medical practice. I hid information! From the police!"

Fiona struggled to arrange the facts logically in her mind. "What you're suggesting doesn't make sense. If Keith killed Linda to keep her from sabotaging his business, then why would he disappear? He'd be moving forward with setting up his practice."

"I don't think he would have *planned* to kill Linda. He probably went to talk to her, maybe to try to bribe her into keeping her mouth shut. Maybe they argued and he pushed her. Maybe he panicked and took off, figuring Linda had already told enough people about him to make the police suspect him."

"I think Brad would have told you if Keith was a murder suspect."

"Fiona, the last time I was able to get in touch with him was the day before Linda died. That can't be a coincidence."

"Yes, it can. Coincidences happen. Carissa, you need to talk to Brad. Do you think telling him will be harder than sitting on this time bomb?"

"I guess not. I just . . . can't stand Brad knowing I betrayed him like that. And it's not just . . . Fiona, if I report this, *he'll* have to report it—about the way Linda was threatening to sabotage Keith's practice . . . Do you understand what I'm saying? There's no way he can report any of this without also letting all his friends know his wife was fooling around with Keith."

No comforting words would do anything to ease Carissa's torment, so Fiona said simply, "I'm sorry."

"So am I, because it's all my fault. I can either hurt and humiliate Brad beyond repair, or I can obstruct what could be a murder investigation."

"You're far too quick to think up worst-case scenarios about Keith. Because he was in conflict with Linda doesn't mean he killed her. Yes, it's odd that he's disappeared, but that's not proof of anything."

Carissa mopped new tears off her cheeks. "The doctor he used to work with thinks he's on vacation somewhere, avoiding his old girlfriend."

"Then that's probably the truth. It makes a lot more sense than assuming he killed Linda."

"True." Carissa sounded a little less panicked. "And it's not like he's the only one Linda caused trouble for. She certainly caused trouble for me—maybe they'll arrest me. Heck, she was on Brad's case, too—he gave her a ticket for running a red light a few months back, and she really gave him a hard time. Obviously he didn't *want* to give a ticket to a family friend, but she nearly hit another car, and he'd seen her run a stop sign just a couple of days earlier. He said either she was getting reckless or she needed her eyes checked."

"Carissa . . . you've got to talk to Brad. Immediately."

"I *hate* myself. I can't believe I did this to my family."

"You made a mistake. Hating yourself for it won't help you get past it. Doing the right thing will. Promise you'll talk to Brad tonight."

"He won't be home until late."

"This can't wait. Promise me you'll talk to him tonight."

"I . . . promise. I guess what I need you to say is, 'If you don't tell Brad, I will.'"

"I'm not sure I want to echo Linda's threat—" Fiona stopped. She hadn't meant for it to come out that way, but on every level, the remark was tasteless—either as a joke about the possibility that Keith might have killed Linda or a hint that Carissa herself had a motive for wanting Linda silenced.

"I didn't kill her," Carissa said. "Is that what you're wondering?"

* * *

Deeply troubled by her conversation with Carissa, Fiona found the drive between Canfield and Bennett far more exhausting than it had been earlier in the evening, and her back hurt so much she finally pulled over at a gas station so she could get out and stretch. Was it possible Linda Taylor *had* been murdered? And was Carissa reluctant to report her suspicions not only because it would include admitting her involvement with Keith but because she knew it could make her a suspect as well?

Carissa couldn't have had anything to do with Linda's death. Sweet Carissa, Mia's bubbly, friendly older sister. Fiona pictured Carissa in their college days, comforting a roommate stressed out over homework or boy trouble, or whipping up a batch of cookies for all of them to enjoy. Always so kind, so concerned about the people around her—including Brad. She thought of the night Carissa and Brad got engaged . . . Carissa displaying her diamond ring and staying up until two in the morning chatting with Fiona and Mia—she'd been so excited, so in love. What had led her to do something as catastrophically hurtful as getting involved with Keith Murray?

Carissa had sworn she'd talk to Brad tonight and had asked Fiona to call her tomorrow to verify that she hadn't lost her nerve. Fiona prayed fervently that Brad would be able to cope with Carissa's confession. Would he believe Carissa's insistence that her involvement with Keith hadn't gone further than a kiss? The thought of Carissa's marriage fracturing like Summer and Alan's—

Please, no.

Stop thinking about this. You can't do anything about it tonight. She wanted to blank her mind, get home, and collapse into sleep. Dreamless sleep, if that was possible, but it probably wasn't. Between her conversation with James today and the time spent with Carissa—Carissa with Mia's brown eyes and so many of Mia's mannerisms—she was going to dream about Mia.

She was so tired. Maybe the stress of this weekend's anxiety attack was still dragging at her. It *hadn't* been very smart to drive all the way to Canfield after emotionally stranding herself in Waltham a few days ago. No wonder she felt so drained.

Emotional exhaustion. She hadn't felt it this heavily in years.

Almost home. Five more minutes and she could crawl into bed.

The road ahead was dark and curving, walled in by trees. She slowed a bit then sped up again; this road was almost always deserted, and she knew every curve—

Headlights flared in her lane only a few yards in front of her. With a scream, Fiona stomped the brake and twisted the steering wheel. Her car skidded, tires screeching, and the crunch of metal and glass tore through her consciousness.

Dazed, unable to catch her breath, Fiona fumbled for the seat belt fastener, but her hand shook wildly and she couldn't find the button. The other car—she'd hit someone . . . she'd hurt someone. *Not again, this isn't happening, this can't be happening.* Her car had swung in a half-circle, and the rear of her car had smashed into the front of the other car. *It's not real, it's not real, it can't be happening.*

Her fingers found the release and the seat belt snapped open. She had to call for help—there were no other cars around; no one had witnessed the accident. Her phone—her purse—she tried to bend over and pick it up and pain rammed her in the chest. *Get the phone. Call for help. The other driver is hurt—dying—*

This isn't happening.

Ignoring the pain, she forced herself to pick up her purse. Her phone—dial 911—her lips numb and her voice a rasping sob as she reported the accident and begged for an ambulance—her head spinning, the voice of the emergency operator in her ear, trying to calm her, promising help.

She shoved her door open and stepped out of the car. Dizziness slammed into her and she fell, landing on her hands and knees on the asphalt, the phone bouncing out of her hand. She had to check—had to see if she could help—

The asphalt scraped her palms as she pushed herself to her feet and staggered toward the mashed-in car. Silent—all silent, no sound from inside the other car—no motion . . . nothing.

"Mia didn't make it. Massive head trauma . . . I'm so sorry, Fiona . . ."

Her hands slammed into the asphalt; she'd fallen again. *Get up, you've got to get up . . . got to help . . .* She dragged herself to her feet and stumbled toward the car.

Headlights. The hum of an engine—the bang of a door. Fiona tried to turn to see who had arrived, but the motion made the ground ripple under her feet.

"Ma'am, are you all right?" A hand caught her arm. Police officer.

"I hit—I hit—I didn't see . . ."

The officer aimed his flashlight through the driver's side window of the car. A motionless figure was slumped over the steering wheel. Long auburn hair—like Mia's—concealed her face.

Blood was everywhere, matting the hair, staining the girl's white shirt, running down the seat behind her.

Horror drowned Fiona. She took a stumbling step backward, the officer's hand the only thing that kept her from falling. She wanted to scream, but she couldn't draw breath. *Let me die—I want to die—*

"How can—what the—" Keeping a firm grip on Fiona's arm, the officer flashed his light around the interior of the car. He grabbed the front door handle. The door stuck then yielded, opening with a painful scraping noise.

Blackness flared and retreated in Fiona's vision, chopping the scene into strobe-like flashes. The officer reached toward the injured woman. To Fiona's astonishment, he grabbed her hair. A wig came away in his hand.

"It's a dummy." He ran the light over the peach-colored balloon that formed the head. "A dummy and red paint." He grabbed the dummy's shoulder and pushed it back against the seat. Taped to its shirt was a note: *Ever consider drivers ed, Fiona? Love, Mia.*

Chapter 16

CARISSA TRIED FOR A WHILE to stanch her tears, not wanting to appear hysterical when she met Brad at the door tonight. After an hour, she gave up and let the tears fall; she was so scared she felt like throwing up. Who cared if she was bawling like a baby when she talked to Brad? The facts were what mattered.

The sound of the garage door opening made Carissa spring to her feet. Fear clawed at her, nearly pulling her backward as she walked toward the kitchen where Brad would see her when he came down the hallway from the garage. *Do it. You got yourself into this mess. Time to face it.*

She forced herself the last few steps into the kitchen as Brad entered from the other direction. His expression made her feel sicker—his face was taut, his eyes clouded. He was already under stress and now—now she would—

He looked at her. Instantly, distraction left his face and the fear in his eyes was so raw it startled her. "Carissa, what is it?"

So shaky that her teeth were almost chattering, Carissa dragged the words out of her throat: "I need to talk to you."

"Okay." His voice was gravelly. "Okay. Let's sit down."

He already suspected. He *must* suspect, or he'd look surprised to find his wife falling apart. He pulled out a kitchen chair for her and she crumbled into it, her confession about Keith Murray spilling out of her mouth.

Brad's face went whiter as she talked, but his gaze was steady and his shoulders straight under his uniform. She had the feeling he was taking refuge in professionalism, attempting to treat this as a confession from a stranger, not trust-shattering revelations from his own wife.

"I'm so sorry." For the hundredth time, Carissa mopped up tears with the soaked wad of tissues in her hand. "I can't believe I did this. But I've told you everything. I didn't do anything else with Keith. I'm so sorry. I can't believe I was so stupid. Brad, I love you."

Brad lips were purplish and his gaze was *too* steady—almost a blank stare. He'd said almost nothing during her confession, and his silence frayed Carissa's nerves.

"Will you *please* say something?" she begged. "Just tell me what you're thinking. I deserve it, no matter how awful it is."

Brad swallowed, but his words emerged croaky like his throat was completely dry. "I'm sorry I wasn't enough for you. I don't know why I ever thought I could be."

"Brad, *no*. I love you."

"Then why Keith?"

"I was—stupid, selfish, trying to recapture some teenage-girl giddiness. I was—I was feeling old and frumpy and dull, and Keith was so charming and said all these flattering things . . . It was—it was nice to hear he found me . . . attractive. But I know that's no excuse, and I'm so sorry. But Brad, I didn't sleep with him. Please tell me you believe me."

"You say the last time you spoke with Keith was when you called him about the pictures and he told you Linda Taylor had threatened to ruin his business."

"Yes."

"That was on April eighth."

"Yes. I tried to call him a couple of times after that to see if he'd talked to Linda, but he didn't answer."

"The last time you saw him was on Friday the sixth, when Linda took the pictures."

"Yes. When Linda talked to me, I realized what a horrible mistake I'd made. I never wanted to see Keith again."

"Amazing how threat of exposure can wake you up."

The words jabbed her, knife-sharp, but she knew she deserved them. "I'm sorry."

Brad reached forward and took her hand. The gesture startled her and brought a gush of hope. It didn't mean he forgave her, but at least it meant he didn't hate her.

His fingers were cold, she realized, so cold she felt the contrast even against her own chilly flesh. "Carissa," he said, "you own a pair of gray gloves with a snowflake pattern on them. Is that right?"

Confused, Carissa nodded. "Yes. They're Fiona's—or they were. Her sister knitted them."

Brad's eyebrows rose. "Fiona's?"

"She left them here last winter when she stopped by during Christmas break. When I called to offer to mail them back to her, she said keep them—her sister Shannon loves to knit, and she'd sent Fiona two new pairs for Christmas. They're great gloves. Why do you ask?"

"Where are they?"

"They're . . . I think they're in the pocket of my coat. Why?"

"Could you get them for me?"

"Right now?"

"Yes."

"Sure." Completely bewildered, Carissa headed toward the coat closet. What did her gloves have to do with anything? Had the stress of this conversation thrown Brad so out of whack that the only way he could cope was to focus on something irrelevant?

She dug into the pockets of her winter coat and found one glove. Where was the other? She checked the pockets of her lighter jacket and the floor of the coat closet. Had she lost it? She hoped not. She loved these gloves, with that intricate hand-knitted snowflake pattern.

She took the glove back to where Brad sat at the kitchen table. "I guess I lost one," she said, putting the single glove on the table.

His expression was so guarded that she didn't have the faintest notion what he was thinking. "Do you have any idea where it is?"

"It could be in the car, I guess. Or I could have dropped it on the way to the bus stop. Brad, why do my gloves matter?"

"Will you please check the car?"

Carissa wanted to say no, this was ridiculous, and why was he so hung up on her gloves, but she headed for the garage.

The glove wasn't in the car. Weary with prolonged tension, Carissa returned to the kitchen. "It's not there. What is this about?"

"Sit down."

She sat. "What's wrong?" she asked then realized how idiotic the question sounded. *What's wrong? Besides the fact that your wife was seeing another man who might be a murderer?* "Why are you so interested in my gloves?"

"When was the last time you wore them?"

"I'm . . . not sure. The weather's been mild, so I haven't . . . I think I wore them when we had that storm a couple of weeks ago, the day Linda . . . or no, maybe I was wearing my waterproof gloves that day . . . why does it matter?"

Brad sat stone-still, his spine straight, his eyes staring through her. "We found Keith Murray."

"You did! Where? What did he say?"

Brad didn't seem to be either blinking or breathing. Carissa wanted to reach over and jostle him back into animation.

"We found Keith Murray's body," he said. "In his car, hidden in the woods. A hiker spotted the car and notified us."

Carissa drew a choky breath. Keith was *dead?* "What happened to him?"

"He was murdered."

The words stunned Carissa. She'd been worrying *Keith* might have . . . and now . . . had she had everything backward?

Her gaze went to the gray glove on the table. Why had Brad asked her about it right before—

Before telling her about finding Keith's body.

Carissa picked up the glove and squeezed it in weak, sweaty fingers. "What do my gloves have to do with this?"

"We found the other glove," Brad said. "Beneath Keith Murray's body."

* * *

Nick tried not to squirm in Kim's armchair while Kim and her mother sat together on the couch with a computer on Aunt Donna's lap. If this discussion of MBA programs went on any longer, his brain would melt into a gray puddle of boredom. How long could they yak about this? If business school was half as boring as talking about business school, Nick knew he wouldn't last fifteen minutes before sinking into terminal snooze mode.

He wasn't sure Kim would last much longer than that. When was she going to get up the guts to tell her mother she'd changed her mind about wanting an MBA? She'd better tell her soon, because it would take Donna a while to adjust to the change in plans and start drilling into the matter of how best to plan Kim's career in cell biology, or whatever Kim wanted to study now that she'd gone crazy over a bio professor.

Yeah, pick on Kim for being a coward. You're the one who doesn't even have the guts to break loose from this conversation. Nick had thought dozens of times about standing up and telling Kim and her mother good night, but he didn't dare. Aunt Donna kept asking his opinion on the schools they were discussing, and clearly she expected him to stay and show interest in Kim's future. A lack of interest on his part might get reported to his parents—who were already on his case about grades that weren't as high as they should have been. Getting Aunt Donna mad at him was about as stupid as napping in the middle of the freeway.

Nick fought back a yawn, his eyes on his aunt with her perfect blonde hair and her burgundy wool suit. Surely she wouldn't want to stay much later. She still had the drive home—but then again, she was one of those hyperthyroid people who could survive on a couple hours of sleep. Up until three in the morning, out of bed by six.

The doorbell rang. Happy for an excuse to move, Nick sprang to his feet at the same instant Kim leaped up.

"I'll get it," Nick said.

"It's *my* apartment," Kim said, and Nick knew she was as eager for a break in the conversation as he was.

"Let him take care of it." Donna tugged Kim back to the couch. "I wanted you to have a look here—"

Tuning out the business school blather, Nick marched to the door and opened it, hoping it was Madison—Kim had said she occasionally forgot her key. Maybe he could grab Madison and go get a late-night burger. Heck, he'd be willing to grab *anyone* who'd give him an excuse for bailing on Aunt Donna.

A man and a woman stood at the door. The guy had red curly hair and freckles, which made him look young, but when Nick looked closer, he realized he wasn't a student—he was probably in his forties, with some gray in his hair. The woman was older too, and both were dressed up like they'd just stepped out of the office.

"Nicholas Cortez?" the man asked.

Uh-oh. That clipped, official tone had *cop* written all over it. He knew the cops had talked to Kim about the stuff going on with Dr. Claridge, but Kim had blinked innocent puppy eyes at them and then laughed with Nick later at how obvious it was that they didn't have anything on her. "*Do they really think I'm dumb enough to admit something?*"

But the fact that they recognized Nick couldn't be good news. That meant they'd been investigating him. They suspected him of helping Kim.

Fake it. Stay cool. "Yeah, I'm Nick. What do you guys need?"

"Is Kimberly Bailey here?"

This timing was bad, *way* bad, with Kim's mother here. Thinking fast, Nick edged out the door and shut it behind him. "Hey, you know, she's really busy right now. She's in an important meeting, discussing business school admissions." It was a stupid excuse, given that it was eleven o'clock at night, but if they didn't have anything against Kim—or Nick—except for Dr. Claridge's accusations, they couldn't force her to talk to them right now, could they? "I can give her a message and have her get back to you." Nick hoped that running interference for Kim wouldn't lead to the officer saying, "*In that case, we'll talk to you instead. Get in the car, punk.*"

The guy reached inside his coat and pulled out what Nick knew would be a badge. "Detective Charles Reid, Bennett Police. This is Detective Andrea Henderson. We need to speak with Kimberly immediately."

"Uh . . ." Nick fumbled to think of a way to stall, but something about a badge in his face jammed the machinery in the clever excuse factory. He couldn't pretend Kim wasn't here; he'd already indicated she was by the way he'd come outside to talk to the cops. "Uh—okay." There was only one way to handle this now: get Kim to come talk to the cops outside or in their car, while Aunt Donna stayed in the apartment in peaceful ignorance. Nick could make up some explanation for why Kim had to run off so urgently.

"Stay right here," Nick said. "I'll send her out to you." He twisted the doorknob and stepped back into the apartment.

"Hey, Kim," he said. "You're needed out here." He aimed his thumb out the doorway.

"We're busy, Nicholas." Donna fired an irritated glance in his direction. "Tell whoever it is to come back tomorrow."

Nick locked eyes with Kim. He wished he could shut the door behind him so the cops wouldn't hear this interchange, but he had the feeling Detective Reid wouldn't be keen on getting the door slammed in his face. "It's kinda urgent," he said, hoping Kim would catch on.

She did—he could tell by the way her cheeks flushed. Heaving a theatrical sigh of annoyance, she rose to her feet. "Sorry, Mom. I'd better take care of this."

"*Kimberly.* I have a two-hour drive ahead of me. Can we please finish looking at Boston College so I know whether or not you want to add it to the list? Your friends can wait."

Kim shot Nick a panicky look.

Nick filled his voice with high-grade politeness. "I think it will just take a minute, Aunt Donna." He didn't know if that was true, but how many more questions could the police possibly have for Kim?

Kim moved toward the open door. "I'll hurry, Mom. I'll be right back."

Donna slapped the laptop onto a couch cushion and stood. Appalled, Nick watched her walk after Kimberly and stop next to her daughter in the open doorway, facing the two detectives.

"Excuse me," Donna said icily, "but this is not a good time. Kimberly is occupied . . ." Her brusque tone faltered slightly, and Nick knew she'd taken a better look and realized the intruders weren't Kimberly's college friends. "Who are you?"

Reid pulled out his badge. "Bennett Police, ma'am. Detective Charles Reid."

* * *

Gentle light glowed from a single lamp, turned low. The rest of the living room was dim, and a slit in the curtains showed black night sky. Fiona lifted her head, battling confusion. Why was she sleeping on her couch?

Across from her, in her recliner, sat James, his eyes closed, his glasses in his lap.

James . . .

Shards of memory began to gather, spurred on by pain that tore through her muscles as she tried to sit up. The accident . . . the police . . . the emergency room . . .

"Fiona." James spoke quietly. He'd obviously heard her stir. He put on his glasses and rose to his feet. "How are you feeling?"

Heavy was the only answer to that question. She drooped back to her pillow and closed her eyes. Everything that didn't hurt was made of lead, and her mind was numb. "Did you . . . take me . . . home from the hospital?"

"Yes. You don't remember?"

"Just . . . a little bit."

"I'm not surprised." James switched on another lamp, removing the gray shadows from the room. "You were out of it. They gave you a sedative at the ER. You were—pretty upset when the ambulance brought you in."

Pretty upset. She remembered that part: the convulsive shaking, the sobs she couldn't control—the sickness that kept seizing her body as her mind jerked between memories of Mia and the new image of a red-haired woman soaked in blood and slumped over the steering wheel. "How did you . . . how did you know what . . . happened?"

James sat on the bare wood floor next to the couch. "You asked a nurse to call me."

"I did?"

"Yes. Don't worry if you don't remember. Drugs—and trauma— can do funny things to your memory."

"Thank you for . . . rescuing me. Again."

He smiled and touched her arm. "I'm honored that you'd call me."

Fiona wished she could remember what she'd said to the nurse when asking her to call James. "I . . . talked to the police, didn't I? Detective Reid?"

"Yes. They talked to me, too."

"To . . . you?"

"Naturally they're thinking this 'accident' was more of the same of what's been happening to you. Since my name is mixed up in that, they wanted to talk to me."

Fiona closed her eyes. *More of the same . . .* James had feared Kimberly would escalate, but this was so far beyond leaving packages or vandalizing a door or even sneaking into Fiona's house that it was hard to believe. Could Kimberly be responsible for this?

"I don't understand how it happened," Fiona murmured. "There was . . . there was no one in the car . . . just a dummy . . ."

"Do you remember what the police told you?"

She thought back, but could remember only fragments of the conversation. "Did Detective Reid say the car was . . . the ignition was off?"

"Yes. The car was parked in the road, blocking your lane. The lights you saw last night weren't the car's headlights. They were spotlights, motion-activated, probably set on the hood of the car."

"But . . . that's such a risky way to . . . target me." Fiona dragged her eyelids open and looked at James. "That road gets almost no . . . traffic at night . . . it's a back way to my neighborhood . . . comes out right next to my house . . . but what if—someone had passed that way before me?"

"The police found two remote-controlled warning lights—the type of flashing light you might see on a barricade, for instance. One was a few hundred yards up the road and one was right before the curve. They're guessing the driver was by the side of the road, watching for your car. If they saw another car coming, they could trigger the warning lights, which would alert the car that there was a problem ahead—causing them to slow down, watch carefully, and avoid a collision. But you had no warning—and with no streetlights and the car being parked just past that curve, there's no way you could have seen it in time to stop."

Fiona pushed herself to a sitting position, wincing at the stiffness in her muscles. "The car . . . was stolen, right?"

"Yes. Two days ago in Boston."

Fiona swung her legs to the floor, dragging the blanket with them, clearing space on the couch for James. "You don't have to sit on the floor."

"You sure you don't want to lie down a while longer?"

"I'm fine," she said, wobbling a little as she fought a gravitational pull toward her pillow. James stood, picked up the blanket, and draped it over her.

"Can I get you anything?"

"No. Thank you. Please, sit down."

He sat next to her. "The doctor gave you a prescription, something to help you get through the next week or so. If you need me to find an all-night pharmacy . . ."

"Thank you." She assumed the prescription was something for anxiety, but at the moment, she was more tired and drained than anxious. "I'm okay right now. James . . . would Kimberly Bailey even *know* how to steal a car? That takes expertise."

"Not if you have a key. The key was still in the ignition."

"This just seems like . . . too much . . . for Kimberly, or anyone . . ."

"She's probably not working alone, Fiona. Here's one possibility—she has a cousin at Hawkins. Nicholas Cortez. I had him in class last semester, and he's a whiz at anything electronic or mechanical—was always happy to fix anything that broke. Kimberly's mentioned him to me—that's how I knew they were cousins—and the police brought up his name last night."

Nicholas Cortez. Had Kimberly roped him into her schemes?

This is ludicrous. How could Kimberly carry her vendetta this far? Stealing a car, setting up the accident—that macabre dummy, soaked in red paint—it was all so out of proportion to anger over a failing grade that Fiona again felt doubts stirring. Maybe she and James were both wrong about Kimberly.

That brought her back to Summer Taylor. If Summer still hated her, why would she have come apologizing? To mislead Fiona? Or had she been ready to believe Fiona wasn't involved with Alan until she saw the pearl comb in Fiona's hair?

Anyone could have known she'd be away from home tonight—or rather, last night; it must be nearly dawn. That information could have come via the camera in her office—she hadn't located it until after she'd made her plans with Carissa. Or, the culprit could simply have driven past her house and seen her car gone.

Was the culprit neither Summer nor Kimberly? The first time she'd talked to Detective Reid, when reporting the knife someone had left on her porch, he'd asked if she could think of anyone who might be seeking revenge for Mia's death, as opposed to using Mia to torment Fiona for other reasons. She'd told him no, she couldn't think of anyone, and Mia's family—especially Carissa Willis—had always been so kind to her.

"I feel completely helpless," Fiona whispered.

"Me too. I can't tell you how much I want to go shake the truth out of Kimberly. But getting in the way of the police doesn't seem like the best way to help you."

"She won't tell you anything," Fiona murmured. "Stay away from her."

James groaned softly. "I will. But it's driving me crazy to be so helpless."

Helpless. The word echoed in Fiona's mind. If the culprit had covered her—or his—tracks too carefully for the police to gather any conclusive evidence, then what? Fiona got to sit and wait for the next strike? Or had the car crash been the grand finale?

Please, yes. Please let this be the end.

"You're trembling," James said. "You need to lie down. Your sister will be here soon."

"My . . . sister?"

"Rebecca."

"You called her?"

"Yes. I hope you don't mind. I thought you might need a sister's help. She's on her way. She jumped in her car so fast I could hardly finish telling her what happened."

"That's a three-hour drive." A spike of panic hit Fiona. "In the middle of the night. James, that's not safe—"

"She'll be fine. She said she doesn't take chances, and if she gets at all sleepy, she'll pull over. She's so worried about you that I doubt she could close her eyes even if she was at home."

"Has she . . . told the rest of my family?"

"I asked her to please not talk to anyone until she talked to you. I wasn't trying to violate your privacy. I just thought you might need her. I did try to ask your permission, but you were not very responsive at the time."

I do need her. The thought of Rebecca's presence brought comfort, but the thought of Rebecca's car speeding along the freeway in the middle of the night . . .

"Fiona, she'll be fine." James drew the blanket up to her shoulders and wrapped his arm around her.

"What time did she leave?"

"Over two hours ago. She'll be fine." James massaged the back of her neck. "Why don't you borrow my shoulder and rest for a while?"

At this invitation and the relaxing pressure of James's fingers on her neck and shoulders, her eyelids went from heavy to leaden, and panic gradually went blunt. Her fear for Rebecca was irrational. Millions of drivers used the freeways every day and never had problems.

"Rest," James said, his fingers lightly stroking her hair. She drooped onto his shoulder, eyes closing.

"Thank you for being here," she murmured.

"I'm here as long as you need me. Rest, Fiona. You're safe. Rebecca will be here soon."

The sleepiness she'd pushed back momentarily rolled forward again in waves of warmth and exhaustion.

Chapter 17

"It's a spaceship! See?" Jacob swished his Lego creation back and forth through the air. "Jump into hyperspace!" he yelled.

Carissa forced a smile as she absently stuck Legos together. "You've been watching too much Star Wars with your brother."

"Whoop-whoop-whoop." Jacob whipped the spaceship in circles and docked it near the plastic bin of Legos. "What are you making?"

Carissa looked at her shapeless conglomeration of multicolored Legos. "Um . . . it's a space station."

"Good guy or bad guy station?"

"Good guy station."

"Yeah, because the bad guy station is all *gray.*"

"Right." Carissa stuck a blue Lego on top of a yellow one. She was tired of faking a cheerful expression—or at least cheerful enough to fool a four-year-old—but she had to keep it up until David came home from kindergarten, and Peter—currently rooting through the stuffed animal box in the corner—took his nap. She would let David and Jacob play the new Wii game together this afternoon, and at last she'd have a few minutes alone to . . . what did she want to do? Cry? She'd done so much of that that her head ached despite the Tylenol she'd taken, and her eyelids were swollen.

She felt nauseated whenever she thought of last night's trip to the police department. She'd insisted that she and Brad go there immediately to talk to the detectives investigating Keith Murray's death. She knew it would kill honest, upright Brad if he concealed the fact that his wife's glove was the one they'd found with Keith Murray, but it would also kill him if he had to be the one to turn her in. The decision had to be hers, and she'd all but pushed Brad out the door, determined to prove she'd had nothing to do with Keith's death.

It hadn't worked out like she'd hoped, or at least she didn't think it had. It had been so hard to read what Detective Tina Merrion was thinking as she'd questioned Carissa. Carissa didn't know Tina very well, though she'd met her several times, and her brisk, matter-of-fact attitude was opaque to Carissa—did she think Carissa was guilty or not? Carissa had told Tina everything about her interaction with Keith—including a fact that had become clear as she'd retraced her time with him: she was sure she'd had both gloves after that last dinner. She remembered holding them on the drive back to Canfield—not wearing them, but holding them and staring down at the white snowflake embroidery, too nervous to talk to Keith after the way they'd kissed. How the glove had ended up with Keith's body, she had no idea.

All of which just made her sound thoroughly guilty. She didn't even know *how* Keith had died, and Tina had deflected Carissa's question when she'd asked. Tina probably hoped Carissa would slip and say something that exposed personal knowledge of the crime.

How *had* that glove come to be with Keith? Maybe she'd dropped it on the porch or the driveway. Maybe Keith had come to talk to her and had seen the glove and had picked it up and put it in his pocket, but she hadn't been home when he'd rung the doorbell.

This was all so insane. What if the police *did* decide she was guilty? What if she was arrested? What would happen to her children? The thought of Brad explaining to David, Jacob, and Peter that Mommy was in jail made her want to start screaming.

You did this. You did this to your family; you did this to yourself. Why didn't you stay away from Keith? You knew what you were doing was wrong.

But I didn't kill him!

"—this one. *Mommy.*"

Carissa blinked back tears. "What, honey?"

"I *said* do you want the purple one?" Jacob waved a purple Lego. "You like the purple ones."

"Yes. Thank you." She took it from Jacob's hand.

Even if the investigation into Keith's death proved she was innocent, what had she done to her marriage? Would she even *have* a marriage when this was over? Brad had been silent last night when he drove her home from the PD. He hadn't even asked how the interview had gone. Unable to endure the silence, she'd rambled out everything that had passed between her and Tina Merrion.

He'd made no comments, and finally his silence had pushed her into silence as well.

I'm so sorry. She couldn't even fathom how hurt and humiliated he must be right now, with his colleagues knowing his wife had been involved with Keith. She'd wondered if he would sleep on the couch last night—or if *she* should offer to sleep on the couch—but she'd been startled when Brad knelt by the side of the bed and looked at her expectantly, obviously waiting for her to join him in their usual prayer. Trust Brad to do the right thing, even when he'd probably rather lock her out of the room than pray with her. It was her turn to pray, but she couldn't even get the first few words of the prayer out without bursting into tears. The body of the prayer ended up three words long between sobs: *"Please help us."*

Brad had kept his back to her all night. She'd hardly slept, and she guessed he hadn't either.

Did he think she'd killed Keith?

Carissa glanced at her watch. She'd expected that Fiona would call earlier than this to verify that she'd talked to Brad as promised. She needed to talk to someone, or her stress would explode and she'd lose any hope of keeping up a calm front for the sake of her sons. She should call Fiona, but Fiona was probably teaching right now.

"Here's a pink one." Jacob handed her another of what he dubbed "girl Legos."

"Thanks." Carissa blinked more tears from her eyes, and took the Lego.

The ringing of the doorbell made her jump. A picture flashed into her head: Detective Merrion, warrant in hand, telling her they'd found her fingerprints on whatever weapon had killed Keith and she was under arrest.

What's wrong with you? How could your *fingerprints be on the gun or knife or whatever the killer used against Keith?*

Carissa rose to her feet, stiff from sitting cross-legged on the floor for so long. "I'll be right back," she told Jacob. "Keep an eye on Peter."

Any hopes that it was the mail carrier ringing the bell disappeared as she saw Tina Merrion standing on the porch along with a tall, red-haired man she didn't know.

"Hello, Carissa," Tina said. "This is Detective Charles Reid. Do you have a moment?"

No, she did *not* have a moment, not now while her children were home and Jacob, who was old enough to understand, might overhear something. But the last thing she wanted was to be uncooperative in any way.

"Sure. Come in." She led them into the living room. "Have a seat. I'll be right back. Let me turn on a movie for my kids." A movie would keep the boys occupied for a little while and lessen the chance that they'd overhear anything.

Thrilled at the prospect of watching a movie when it was not normal TV time, Jacob and Peter bounced into the family room without asking who was at the door. With fruit snacks in hand, the boys settled on the couch and Carissa shoved *Finding Nemo* into the DVD player.

"I'm sorry about that," Carissa said as she sat opposite the two detectives. "I thought it would be better to get them settled first."

"I understand," Tina said. "How old are your boys now?"

This polite personal question surprised Carissa. Was Tina trying to relax her into lowering her guard? *What guard? You don't have anything to hide! You've told her everything.* "David is six. He's in kindergarten. Jacob is four and Peter is two."

"I've got a three-year-old," Detective Reid supplied. "He's a menace. Looks exactly like me."

Carissa managed a little laugh. Reid looked boyish with that curly pumpkin-orange hair and those freckles, and it was easy to picture a three-year-old terror who looked like him. Why didn't she recognize him? Was he new to the department?

"Thank you for taking the time to talk with us," Reid said. "I'm from the Bennett, New Hampshire PD. We're investigating some incidents concerning Fiona Claridge."

"Fiona! What happened to her?"

"She's fine," Reid said. "But there have been problems. Someone has been harassing Dr. Claridge, using references to your sister's death to upset her. It's gone from harassing communications to breaking into her home to property damage and physical harm."

"Physical harm!"

"She's fine but could have been injured if things had gone differently. I believe you've been friends with Dr. Claridge for several years?"

Carissa rubbed her hands on her jeans, drying sweaty palms. She wanted to ask what had happened to Fiona but had the feeling Reid was being vague on purpose. Why hadn't Fiona said anything about this last night? "I've known her for . . . nine years, I guess. My sister Mia and I were roommates with her for a year in college, and Fiona and I have kept in touch since then."

"I'm sorry about your loss," Reid said.

Carissa appreciated that he'd offer sympathetic words even this long after Mia's death. "Thank you."

"How well do you know James Hampton?"

"He dated Mia. I'd see him at our apartment, or we'd double date sometimes, him and Mia and Brad and me. So I guess I know him casually—socially—whatever the right word is."

"He was dating Mia at the time of her death?"

"Yes."

"How serious was their relationship?"

"Um . . . well, I know Mia really liked him, but I don't think I'd call the relationship serious. They were more than friends, but not close to getting engaged or anything, at least as far as I knew. They'd only dated for a couple of months."

"What's your impression of him?"

"Nice guy," Carissa said. "Smart. Very, very kind. I've never heard him say anything cruel to anyone. He's good at reaching out to people and making them feel . . . what word do I want? Important? Valued?"

"How did he respond to your sister's death?"

Carissa bit her lip. It made her squirm to answer these questions about James. Why was Reid asking about him? Maybe because whatever was happening to Fiona had started happening after he moved to Bennett? "He was . . . he grieved, of course. We all did. It was a horrible shock."

"Did you ever have the feeling he was angry with Fiona Claridge for what happened?"

"No. Absolutely not. Exactly the opposite. He did his best to comfort her. He was a good friend to her, and he's kept in touch with her these past years. I can't imagine James would ever want to hurt Fiona, if that's what you're asking."

"I appreciate your candor," Reid said. "After the accident, *was* there anyone who particularly blamed or hated Fiona for her role in your sister's death?"

The question felt strange, as though it twisted part of her body in a direction it wasn't meant to go. There had been comments, of course, from friends and neighbors: "*Why was her roommate stupid enough not to slow down in the rain?*" "*Was she always a reckless driver?*" "*It must be awful knowing if Mia had gotten a different ride to the airport that she'd be alive.*" "*Are you planning to sue her?*" And so on— comments Carissa supposed were meant to be supportive but instead grated and offended. As for the family . . .

"We all grieved, but the person who really blamed Fiona for the accident was Fiona."

"She felt responsible?"

"Yes. Completely. It was rough for her. We all worried about her. She was hurt in the accident, and recovery took a long time—partly, I think, because she felt so guilty that she was alive and Mia wasn't that she wasn't sure she *wanted* to recover. She went to counseling for a while, and that helped, but I doubt she's forgiven herself."

"This is a sensitive question," Reid said, "but I hope you'll answer candidly. Have you ever worried that she might harm herself?"

"No. Oh no, never. When I said she was slow in recovering, I didn't mean to imply . . . no, I can't imagine her ever deliberately hurting herself. What . . . can you please tell me what's been happening to her? She hasn't said anything to me about it."

"She received a couple of cruel notes referring to the accident, and a rock was flung at her house. Last night, she was in an automobile accident—she's not hurt—but it was deliberately set up by the other driver. The driver was gone before we could question him or her."

"A car accident!"

"Meant to stir up memories of your sister. There was a note left in the car, referring to Mia."

Horrified, Carissa ached to ask for more details, but clearly Reid didn't want to give them. "That's the cruelest thing someone could do to Fiona."

"Just to be sure, would you think about it one more time and tell me if there's anyone you know who was particularly angry with Fiona over your sister's death?"

Guilt pressed at Carissa's hammering heart, making the rapid beats painful. "The family didn't blame her," she said, aware that this statement was only *almost* true. The one person who had evidenced as much anger as grief, who had vented privately to Carissa about how at fault Fiona was, and who had never liked her since then, was Brad.

But she *couldn't* say that in front of Tina Merrion. Hadn't she caused Brad enough embarrassment? And it didn't make any difference anyway. Whatever was going on with Fiona couldn't have anything to do with Brad.

"Thank you," Reid said. He looked at Tina as though passing the baton, and Carissa braced herself for whatever Tina was about to launch at her.

"Has Brad seemed at all . . . different . . . lately?" Tina asked.

The question unnerved Carissa. "He's—well, he's been very busy. He's been gone a lot, and he . . . seems . . ." *Curt* and *remote* were the two words she wanted to use, but she changed them to, "He seems to be under some pressure. I think work has been very busy."

"I see." Tina's voice was polite, but Carissa had trouble meeting her gaze. Tina would know if things at the department *had* been unusually busy. What if they hadn't been? What if Brad's absences simply stemmed from a desire to stay away from Carissa and their noisy household?

"Did he talk to you about his conflict with Linda Taylor?" Tina asked.

Carissa's heart bounced inside her chest like she'd hit a patch of turbulence. Linda Taylor, and that stupid traffic ticket. But why would Tina ask her about that now that Linda was dead?

"I know he gave her a ticket for running a red light, and she was furious about it and did a lot of complaining," Carissa said carefully.

"Are you aware that Mrs. Taylor accused him of being under the influence of alcohol when he gave her that ticket?"

Carissa gasped. "She said *what*? That's insane! Brad would never drink! Linda *knew* that."

"She was adamant that she'd smelled alcohol on his breath and witnessed signs of intoxication. And that the light was green."

Carissa's teeth ground together. She'd grown up thinking of Linda as a mixed bag—a strong, talented woman with bossy tendencies. But now she seemed so evilly manipulative that Carissa wanted to go back in time and slap her. How *dare* she say that about Brad? Was she flat-out lying, or was she so wrapped up in her own warped view of reality that she truly thought Brad must have been drunk if he'd questioned her perfect driving? She'd probably told people her suspicions right and left—including Brad's superiors. Those accusations would have devastated Brad.

"Brad has not ever and would not ever drink alcohol—at all," Carissa said coldly. "It's against his religious beliefs, and he's very devout. And his brother was killed by a drunk driver when Brad was a teenager, and he has no patience at all with people who drive under the influence, as I'm sure you know."

Tina nodded. "There was no evidence to back up Mrs. Taylor's accusations. She didn't make the report until the day after she received the ticket."

"Of course not," Carissa snapped. "After it was too late to verify that there was no alcohol in his blood at the time."

"She claimed she'd been so stunned by what her eyes and nose told her that she'd hesitated to report it, especially because Brad was a family friend."

"How convenient." But lack of evidence wouldn't have stopped Linda from spreading rumors, especially since there might not have been any witnesses when Brad pulled her over, and most intersections in town didn't have traffic cameras. Why hadn't Carissa heard about this? Maybe no one had wanted to share the rumors with Brad's wife.

And what of the lost promotion? If Linda had stirred up enough trouble with the people she knew in the town government, could they have influenced the department to bypass Brad? There was no point in asking—no one would admit that unfounded rumors had had any bearing on the decision, but it *was* possible that controversy over Brad had led his superiors to tag someone else for their new sergeant.

No wonder Brad had seemed so stressed lately. It must have been killing him to know that anyone in town might suspect him of drinking on the job. And how had Carissa responded to Brad's distress? By cheating on him.

Carissa inhaled deeply and exhaled, again mopping sweat-drenched hands on her jeans. She needed to calm down. She probably looked ready to go storming over to the cemetery to scream at Linda's grave.

"Linda Taylor either lied or she was insane," Carissa said. "No wonder Brad's been stressed. That accusation would have ripped him up inside."

"I understand," Tina said. "Brad had good reason to be angry with Linda Taylor."

The words jarred Carissa, shifting her vision into a new direction. She'd thought Keith Murray had killed Linda, but now that Keith was dead, that didn't seem likely.

Did the police suspect someone else?

Brad?

* * *

"I could *kill* her!" Kim flung a textbook against the wall with a thud that made Nick flinch. "I really could, I swear it, Nicky. I could strangle her. Or stab her."

"Your mom?" Nick eyed the dent in the wall and took a step backward, ready to flee the room if he became Kim's next target.

"Not my *mom*. Dr. Hypocritical-Underhanded-Sneaking-Lying *Claridge*." Kim slammed another textbook to the floor. "She crashes her car and she blames *me*? She's such a pathetic driver that she *kills* people, and when she gets in *another* accident, she has the gall to tell the police *I* set it up somehow?"

"They think *we* set it up," Nick said roughly. He wasn't in the mood to soothe Kim through a temper tantrum. She wasn't the only one who had spent last night sweating through police questioning. "This whole stupid scheme was *your* baby. Thanks for getting me in trouble."

Kim shoved the books on her wall shelf, knocking them to her bed. "Are you getting hauled *home* over this?"

"Your mom is making you go home this weekend?"

A biology textbook flew toward Nick's face. He dodged, and the book smacked the doorframe. "She's yanking me out of here. For the rest of the year."

"*What?* She's pulling you out of school? For real?"

"Yes, for *real*. She's coming back on Saturday, and I have to be packed up and ready to go."

"You're kidding. But the cops don't have any proof! You didn't fold and admit something, did you?"

"How dumb do you think I am?" she shrieked.

"Dumb enough to yell loud enough for the neighbors to hear."

Kim lowered her voice to a venomous whisper. "Do you think my mom is going to wait for proof?"

"Did you tell her what the cops talked to you about?"

"I had to tell her *something*. I told her someone made a false accusation against me, but it was all cleared up now. I said it was another student, someone who hated me because we both liked the same guy."

"Good story."

"Shut up. Do you know what she did? Do you have any *idea* what she did?"

Given the rabid rage in Kim's eyes, Nick was afraid to ask.

"She called Claridge," Kim said. "At home. First thing this morning. She *called* her."

Nick's jaw fell open. "Seriously? How'd she know what the cops—"

"What do you mean how'd she know? Do you have dog chow for brains? She remembered Claridge's name from that plagiarism dustup. So when the cops came kicking my door down, she got suspicious."

"Ouch." He wasn't surprised Aunt Donna had seen through Kim's story. She was a sharp woman, and anyone who'd raised Kim would know her tendency for lashing out—sometimes irrationally—when she got angry. "So what did Dr. Claridge say to her?"

"She didn't talk to her. Claridge was asleep, apparently, but Mom talked to her sister, claiming she was one of Claridge's colleagues and was concerned about her and wanted to check in and was she all right, and the sister told her Claridge had been in an accident last night, and Mom asked if the police were investigating it, and the sister said yes, someone deliberately set it up, and Mom took a gamble and said she'd heard other bad things had happened to Claridge lately, and the sister said yes, and Mom said do they know who's responsible, but then the sister got nervous and shut up, like she realized she shouldn't be talking about this."

"Does your Mom really think we caused that accident?"

"No. I don't think so. But she does think I did other stuff, which is why the police suspected me."

"Smart woman."

Kim picked up a mug filled with pens and hurled it at Nick. He jumped to the side. The mug hit the doorframe and cracked. Pens shot all over the place.

"I'm out of here," Nick snapped. "If you want to act like a toddler, do it on your own."

"Be all smug and self-righteous if you want. But wait until my mom talks to your mom. You'll be stuck at home working at McDonald's for the rest of the school year, just like me."

"Not a chance. No way will my parents waste a semester they've already paid for. We're not rolling in cash like some people I could name."

"Goodie for you."

"You're an adult, Kim. If you don't want to go home, don't go home. Stay here. Get a job and you won't need the money from home. Tuition's already paid. You just need room and board."

"Oh, and how am I supposed to instantly find a job in a dinky college town where everyone's already competing for every unskilled job in existence? How am I supposed to make enough money to pay my bills and still keep my grades up? And even if I could pull that off, you better believe that next semester they won't pay my tuition after I spit in their faces like this, and no way could I afford it with some burger-flipping gig."

"Student loans—grants—"

"You're full of genius ideas, aren't you? Even if I could get loans or whatever, could I get them before my parents yank all the money out of my account—which my mother will do the instant I refuse to come home?"

"Go home, then. Go home and be good until the money starts flowing again."

"I swear to you, Claridge will pay. I'll make her sorry she ever mentioned me to the cops. She'll *pay*, Nick."

Apparently Kim's urge to commit murder was contagious. Nick would have loved to clamp his hands around Kim's throat and squeeze hard. "*You* started this. I told you it was a bad idea. If you do anything to Dr. Claridge now, you've had it. Quit while you can. At least you're not going to prison. Cut your losses, go home, and *grow up*."

If Kim had been standing any closer, Nick was sure she would have punched him. "She's not getting away with this. She *lied* to the police. *Lied.* She flunks me for cheating and then she *lies* to the cops about a car accident. She is such a—"

"How do you know she lied? Maybe she assumed—"

"Assumed what? She caused the accident and tried to cover up by blaming me."

"I have no idea *what* she did. The cops didn't give me any details of what happened. Did they tell you?"

"No. Just asked me a bunch of questions about where I was, blah, blah, blah, but it's obvious, isn't it? I'll bet she crashed into some lamppost or pedestrian and then gave a sob story about how I jumped out at her and startled her, or maybe we were driving in your car and cut her off, and she had to swerve—you know it must have been some story like that, so the cops think she's not at fault. Since they're already suspicious of me, she knew she'd be safe blaming me. They should yank her license. They should lock her up before she kills someone else."

Nick frowned. "I don't think it was any story like us cutting her off in traffic. The cops were asking me questions about what kind of electronic stuff I've bought lately. Weird questions about lights and stuff."

Kim rolled her eyes. "I'll bet she told them we tampered with her car. To excuse the fact that she's a menace."

"So she's a menace or a liar. Whatever. None of that had better matter to you anymore, or you're going to end up in jail."

Kim kicked her backpack where it sat on the floor near her bed. "So I get hauled home like a kid getting grounded while she struts around all smug and safe, knowing she got the better of me? I don't think so."

Nick had walked into Kim's apartment with a headache, and now the pain pounded so hard he felt it would crack his skull. "You know what? You lost. Face it. Go home before you get us both arrested. Next year you can start over and stay away from her. Your mom's so busy that within a couple of weeks she'll forget she's mad at you and she'll be gone all the time and you can do whatever you want." He grinned at her. "Between shifts at McDonald's."

Kim's face was bright red, and her eyes looked even more manic. Sorry he'd tried to lighten things by teasing her, Nick started to apologize, but Kim interrupted him.

"I'm going home, okay? I know that. You don't change my mom's mind when she decides something like that."

Relieved, Nick flopped to the floor and leaned against the wall. "Good. That's the best way. After you make a ruckus, you have to let things die down. It's only for a few months. You'll survive."

Kim glared down at him. For such a petite girl, she looked ominous towering over him, as though she'd love to stomp on his fingers to see how many bones she could break. "I just have one more present for Dr. Claridge."

"*Kim!*" She *had* to be kidding. No one was that nuts.

"I hate her, Nick. She's not winning this one. Yeah, I'm leaving, but I'll leave *her* a good-bye gift, and I promise you, she'll never dare so much as *look* at James Hampton again. Do you know what I found out? From that last recording? Dr. Hampton was involved with her dead roommate! She killed the roommate and now she's trying to take *him.*"

Nick closed his eyes and banged his head against the wall. "This is still about your stupid crush on Hampton? You can't have him, so you'll make sure she can't either? You are *insane.* You'll go to prison."

"I'm not going to get caught."

Nick had never thought he was the kind of guy who could physically attack a woman, but right now, it took all his self-control not to jump up and slap Kim so hard that he bruised his hand. He was still scared that the police might be able to rustle up a witness who could prove he'd been the one to chuck that rock at Dr. Claridge's door. If they could prove that, maybe they'd leap to the certainty that he'd caused that accident, and he'd be under arrest. All because of Kim's brainless revenge campaign. "The police are watching you, you stupid little flake."

"I doubt it. Not every minute. You can't tell me they have enough manpower to send undercover cops tagging around after every suspect in every crime."

"I'm not playing along this time. Self-destruct if you want. I'm getting out of here." He stood.

"Nick—"

"I'm *not helping you.*" Nick almost started shouting but remembered the neighbors in time to keep his voice down. "You almost landed me in the slammer. I'm not risking everything because you can't come to terms with the fact that *you* got caught cheating. And that you're crazy for a professor who's crazy for someone else. Wreck your life if you want. You're not wrecking mine." He stalked out of Kim's bedroom, heading for the living room where he'd left his jacket.

Kim followed him. "I'm not asking you to do anything except give me a ride."

"No! I said *no!*" He grabbed his coat.

"I'll tell them about Joel Burke."

Nick froze. "You wouldn't do that."

"Why wouldn't I? They'd love to know who did it. Who cost him his college and pro football careers."

"It was an accident! He wasn't supposed to get hurt bad. Besides, he wasn't near as good a player as his dad thought he was. He never would have made the pros."

"Maybe your lawyer can explain that."

Nick spit a mouthful of profanity at her. "If you say one word about me, I'll make sure you go down for Dr. Claridge."

"Really? You want to make things worse for yourself? You're involved with Dr. Claridge too."

"I'll tell them—" His mind went blank. He couldn't think of anything big enough for blackmail, anything as significant as Joel's knee torn apart when he'd slipped on the glossy hardwood floor of his bedroom—a hardwood floor Nick had coated with vegetable oil. Nick had anticipated bruises and embarrassment. Not long-term damage.

Joel's family would sue him for sure. Forget suing him—Joel's dad would murder him.

"You wouldn't do that to me," he said.

"Only if you make me."

She was crazy. Seriously crazy. "Kim—"

"I need you to play chauffeur. That's all. You're the only person I can trust."

"You're poison." She wouldn't rat on him.

Would she?

Chapter 18

"Isn't this gorgeous?" Rebecca held up the half-finished baby blanket. "Shannon would be proud."

"Yes, she would," Fiona said. "She's always proud when she catches another person in her net—her hand-knitted net—and transforms her victim into a knitting devotee."

Rebecca laughed. With her twinkling blue eyes, heart-shaped face, and short blonde hair, she had a mischievous elfin look that made Fiona smile. "I can show you how to do this diamond pattern," Rebecca offered. "It isn't hard."

"How about if you show me *you* knitting the blanket, and I buy your daughter something at the mall? If I try to knit something, I'll never finish."

"Oh, come on. You did finish that scarf. You have to admit it was satisfying."

"Satisfying in the same way it would be satisfying to reach Florida . . . after crawling the whole way."

"You weren't that slow!"

"It took me almost a year. I just don't have time for it."

Rebecca resumed knitting, her fingers and knitting needles skillfully manipulating the soft lavender yarn. "Can I bring you something to drink? Something to eat?"

"After that fantastic pasta Alfredo? I haven't eaten that well in years. You've taken such good care of me that I may never let you go home. How are *you* feeling, after all the work you've done around here today?"

"I'm fine." Rebecca rested her arms on her curving belly. "In fact, I feel so good that I'm afraid Kira will kill me if I admit it out loud."

Fiona laughed, thinking of their oldest sister, suffering through the last trimester of her fifth pregnancy, while Rebecca—twelve years younger and pregnant for the first time—bounced around with plenty of energy and unswollen ankles. "Well, you are three weeks behind her. Three weeks and twelve years."

"I'm still afraid she might punch me." Rebecca gestured at the doorframe Fiona had recently finished stripping. "I love how the woodwork is turning out. This house will be so beautiful when you're done."

"You can bring your grandchildren to admire it, because that's how long it will take me to finish."

"Once I quit work, I'll be able to come up here a little more often. I'd love to help you."

"And I'd love to babysit for you while you paint walls for me." Fiona wished she could freeze time right at this moment—relaxing in her living room, with Rebecca here, everything peaceful and safe. The tranquility of the moment was enough to dull at least some of the horror of last night's accident.

"Fiona . . ." Rebecca's tone went serious, and Fiona knew what was coming. "Why didn't you tell us what was going on with your student and those horrible packages?"

"I'm sorry. I didn't feel like bringing it up. And I don't *know* she's the one responsible—"

"I know, I know. Spare me the fine print. I just wish you'd confided in us. I know we couldn't have done anything about it, but at least we could have supported you. Prayed for you."

"I know."

"I'm glad you had James helping you."

"Yes." Fiona lowered her gaze to the baby blanket Rebecca was knitting. Thoughts of James brought so much confusion that she couldn't look her sister in the face. She wished she could remember more of what had happened last night when James had come to the hospital, but shock and drugs left patches of fog and spaces where time was missing altogether. What had she told the nurse when asking her to call James? What had she said to James?

"He's a neat guy," Rebecca said.

"Yes, he is."

"Good friend?"

"Yes."

"More than a friend?"

"No."

"Really?"

Her sore muscles tightened. She knew she ought to meet Rebecca's gaze and smile away her suspicions, but she didn't dare make eye contact. "We're just friends."

"I didn't mean to make you uncomfortable," Rebecca said. "I'm sorry."

"You're fine. Why would I be uncomfortable?" As soon as she asked the question, she wished she hadn't—she didn't want Rebecca to answer it.

"I . . . can tell he really cares about you, and . . ." Rebecca's voice faded.

"He's just being nice," Fiona said.

"Uh . . . yeah." It was so obvious Rebecca wasn't saying what she was thinking that Fiona wanted to cut off the conversation and flee the room before Rebecca worked up her courage to be candid. But there was no excuse she could offer that would fool Rebecca into thinking she'd exited for any reason other than to avoid discussing James.

"It's been nice having him at Hawkins, hasn't it?" Rebecca said.

"Yes."

"His name's been popping up a lot in your e-mails."

Fiona focused on the fireplace where she'd stacked folded tarps and cans of paint stripper. "He's a good friend."

"I'll bet you have that phrase engraved on a plaque and hanging by your mirror. You read it every morning and night, trying to convince yourself it's true."

"Rebecca!"

"Or maybe you had Shannon knit the phrase into a sweater and you wear it every night, like some kind of hair shirt."

She finally looked Rebecca in the face. "You don't know what you're talking about."

"He's in love with you."

"He's never said that."

"And unlike the rest of us, you can't tell?"

"Does the entire family talk about this behind my back?"

"Of course we do. We're all rooting for you and James to get together."

Despite the lightness of Rebecca's tone, Fiona knew she wasn't joking. Embarrassment made her want to snap that maybe they should mind their own business, but it was her own fault for bringing up James's name so often. How *could* she expect that her family wouldn't wonder about him? She should have been more careful not to give them the wrong idea.

"Let's change the subject," Fiona said.

"Let's not. You love him, don't you?"

The doorbell rang.

Rebecca sighed. "You hired someone to do that, didn't you?"

"I'll get it." Fiona started to stand up. Never in her life had she been so grateful for an interruption.

"No way." Rebecca sprang to her feet. "I've got it."

"This is embarrassing, being waited on by a pregnant woman."

"What is this, the Victorian era? I'm not weak and delicate. And you're hurting, I can tell, so stay still." Rebecca exited the room.

Her fingers unsteady, Fiona fiddled with the border of the afghan Rebecca had insisted on draping over her lap. *You love him, don't you?*

Is that what everyone thought?

What did James think?

She heard the sound of Rebecca opening the front door. A few moments later, Rebecca returned to the living room.

"It's Gavin Taylor," she whispered. "He asked if you're up to visitors, and I said I'd check."

"Yes, that's fine, invite him in." Under any other circumstances, she would have cringed at the thought of facing anyone from the Taylor family, but she'd rather talk to Gavin than field more of Rebecca's questions about James. How did Gavin know about the accident? Had the police talked to him? They might have talked to other members of the Taylor family besides Summer.

Rebecca led Gavin into the room. He was carrying a glass vase filled with a spring arrangement of daffodils, tulips, and hyacinth.

"Hi, Fiona. How are you feeling? No, don't get up." He moved quickly to her side and set the flowers on the table next to her.

"I'm fine," she said. Gavin offered his hand, and she took it. He wrapped her hand in both of his.

"I'm sorry," he said. "What a nightmare. Carissa Willis told me you'd been in an accident."

"Carissa," Fiona murmured. "I was supposed to call her. How did she find out . . . ?"

"Oh!" Rebecca said. "Carissa called while you were napping. I'm sorry. I should have told you, but I fell asleep after I talked to her, and I think the nap wiped my brain. I told her you'd been in a minor accident, but I didn't give her any details."

She should have called Carissa. Thoughts of Carissa, Brad, and Keith Murray had flashed in her mind a few times today, but every time she'd thought of calling, she'd dozed off, woozy from exhaustion and medication.

"I told her you were okay and you'd talk to her later," Rebecca said. "Gavin, can I take your coat?"

"In the presence of an English professor, I think you mean *may* I take your coat." Gavin handed his jacket to Rebecca.

"Not you, too!" Rebecca exclaimed. "I already live in fear of mangling my subject–verb agreement in front of Fiona."

"Please," Fiona said. "When was the last time I corrected your grammar?"

"You don't, but I know you want to."

Fiona laughed.

"Your sister looks a lot like you," Gavin remarked as Rebecca exited the room.

"I'll take that as a compliment, since she's much prettier than I am."

"Liar!" Rebecca called from the hallway.

Gavin chuckled, but his smile didn't last. He studied Fiona. "You sure you're not hurt? You look . . . tired."

Fiona almost smiled at Gavin's awkward tact. She'd seen her haggard face in the mirror and knew what Gavin meant was, "*You look half dead.*"

"I'm sore, but that's all."

"What happened—if you're okay talking about it?"

Gavin's question sent a shudder along her nerves as she pictured the auburn-haired figure slumped over the steering wheel and the seat spattered with crimson. "I'm okay, but I'd rather not give details. The police are investigating."

"Sure, okay."

She knew he must be wondering if she'd been at fault, and that thought made her feel sick. He was wondering if she'd hurt someone. Again. "The accident was deliberately caused by someone else. I'm sorry I can't tell you more than that."

Gavin goggled at her. "Someone *caused* it? You mean they wanted to hit you?"

"They wanted me to hit them and set it up so I couldn't avoid it."

"Crazy! Psycho road-rage nutcases—I hope they catch him."

Or her. "So do I."

"The flowers are from Alan." Gavin touched one of the daffodils.

"That was kind of him. Tell him thank you."

"He would have brought them himself, but he didn't think you'd want to see him. And I was up here anyway—a follow-up on that job interview."

Pretending she *would* have liked to see Alan was more deception than Fiona could muster, so she said, "I appreciate his thinking of me."

To her relief, she saw no condemnation in Gavin's eyes. He walked to the couch and sat down.

"How *is* Alan?" Fiona asked, feeling it would be thoughtless not to ask about him. She wondered if he'd told Gavin about Fiona's finding the stolen comb.

Gavin looked down at the worn wood floor, elbows resting on his knees. "He moved out of his townhouse and is staying in Canfield with me now."

"Summer told me. She stopped by . . ." Was it yesterday? Time was scrambled in her mind. "She stopped by yesterday to apologize for . . . things she said to me."

"About Alan? Yeah, she thought you two were sneaking around behind her back. Summer's a hothead sometimes."

Rebecca hadn't yet returned to the room. Fiona could hear her opening cupboards in the kitchen. She was probably trying to whip up a quick dessert, both in an effort to be hospitable and as an excuse to give Fiona privacy.

"I hope Summer and Alan can work things out," Fiona said.

Gavin pushed his hair off his forehead. He had the same cowlick Alan did but wore his hair longer, so the hair fell to one side of his forehead. "I don't think there's much hope for that. Things are pretty well ruined."

"I'm so sorry."

"Yeah. Alan's really gotten ripped apart."

Fiona wondered if Gavin was including her as one of the sets of claws that had shredded Alan's peace of mind, but Gavin looked weary, not accusatory. "And it doesn't help that the police have all kinds of crazy questions lately." He paused, looking straight into Fiona's eyes. "About Keith Murray."

From the way he was scrutinizing her, Fiona knew he was checking her reaction to see if the name was familiar. She also knew she'd given him an answer: Gavin's words had caught her off guard, and surprise must have shown in her face.

Pain tugged at her strained muscles as she shifted in her chair. "Why are they asking you about Keith Murray?"

"Have you talked to Carissa Willis lately?"

Gavin already knew she'd recognized Keith's name, and there was nowhere else she would have heard about him. "Yes. What did the police tell you?"

"Do you want to turn this into a dance, or can we be candid with each other?"

"I'm not sure what Carissa would want me to say."

"If you're worried about telling me she was fooling around with Keith, you can quit worrying. I already know about that."

"Did your mother tell you?"

"No. She liked to keep her secrets. She told me she had pictures of someone kissing '*another*'—that's how she put it—and how it was going to be a big wake-up and just what their spouse deserved, but she didn't tell me who she was talking about. And I didn't care—it was none of my business. I found out about Murray from the police. He was murdered."

Fiona gasped. "When did this happen?"

"I don't know. They just found his body. I don't think they knew the time of death yet when they talked to me. Apparently after Mom took those pictures of Murray and Carissa, Mom told Murray not to move to Canfield and threatened to ruin his medical practice if he tried. And she told Carissa to come clean with Brad, or she'd give him the pictures." Gavin's gaze went cold and piercing. "Maybe what happened to my mother wasn't an accident."

"But if Keith killed your mother—who killed Keith?"

"Maybe Keith didn't do anything. Maybe it was someone else, someone who panicked, knowing if my mother talked—and if Keith Murray moved to Canfield—she'd never be able to hide what she'd done from her husband."

"*No,* Gavin. You can't be serious."

"Why not? Because she's a sweet Mormon housewife? Some sweet Mormon housewives have secrets. We already know Carissa did."

"Gavin—"

"She's been acting strange. She was weirdly eager to get into my house—offered an excuse about cleaning it for me. I turned her down, but later I noticed that one of Mom's elephants was missing. A big pink porcelain one."

"So now Carissa's a thief?" Fiona said acidly.

"No. I found a little piece of pink porcelain on the floor near the elephant shelves. I think Carissa broke it. I think she sneaked in while I was gone and was searching the place—probably looking for Mom's phone so she could get rid of those pictures. She has a key to the house. Her parents and mine were friends and looked after each other's places during vacations."

"That's a big conclusion to draw from a shard of porcelain."

"She kept showing up. She even offered to clean the cars. She was so insistent that I finally let her do it, but the whole thing seemed weird, and Mom's phone is missing. Carissa must have found it and taken it."

Carissa hadn't said anything to Fiona about searching the Taylors' house. "Summer took the phone. She heard your mother talking and thought the pictures were of Alan and me."

"Summer has it?"

"Yes. Ask her."

"I want to know what Carissa said to you. I want to know *every-thing* she said to you."

Fiona massaged her tense neck muscles. "Carissa would never harm anyone."

"How do you know that? She's nice and you like her—is that your proof? She had a lot to lose. Her husband finds out she's cheat-ing—"

"She never slept with Keith."

"I don't care about the details of what she did or didn't do. Fact is, Mom had pictures of her kissing some guy who wasn't her husband. That would scare her silly. Her husband, her kids, her super-upright-pioneer-stock-parents-on-a-mission, everyone in her ward and neigh-borhood finding out she—"

"I know she was upset." Fiona could no longer hear Rebecca moving around in the kitchen. Had she overheard enough of the conversation to freeze her in place as she strained to hear more? Re-becca wouldn't maliciously eavesdrop, but Fiona couldn't blame her if she'd been startled into wanting to find out what was going on. "But it's a huge leap from being embarrassed and fearing discovery to double homicide. If she were willing to kill to hide what she'd done, she wouldn't have confessed to me. And obviously Summer already knows—she has the pictures."

Gavin's voice went harsher. "Then maybe Carissa talked to you because she knew it was already leaking out and she was attempting damage control."

Fiona stretched her sore body out of her chair and came to sit next to Gavin. "I'm sorry." She touched Gavin's arm. "Even the pos-sibility that someone might have deliberately harmed your mother is horrifying. But Carissa? No. It could be that Keith's death is not linked to your mother's death. Your mother's death probably *was* an accident. Maybe Keith was involved in something else that got him in trouble. Drugs? Gambling? The police will sort it out."

Pain, dark and thick, shrouded Gavin's expression. "I want to know what Carissa told you."

Fiona debated for a moment but could think of no reason to hold back. She told Gavin what Carissa had shared about her interaction with Keith, Keith's disappearance, and her fear that he might have had something to do with Linda's death. "When she talked to me, she didn't know Keith was dead. The police had told her Keith was missing."

"Maybe when she talked to you, she pretended to suspect Keith to deflect suspicion from herself. That's probably the same ditty she sang for the police."

"Is Carissa officially a suspect?"

"You mean is this my crazy imagination or is she a person of interest to the police? Yeah, they suspect her. That was obvious from what they asked me."

Fiona pressed her fingertips to her eyes, wondering how this nightmare had managed to storm the gates of reality. She wanted to defend Carissa again but knew Gavin would shoot down anything she said, since she had no proof beyond the fact that she couldn't imagine Carissa as a murderer.

"I'm—listen, I'm sorry." Gavin spoke quietly, but he still sounded frustrated. "I shouldn't have bothered you, after what you've been through. I was just . . . hoping maybe she'd told you something."

"She didn't confess to murder." Fiona lowered her hands into her lap. "If that's what you were hoping for."

"I know she's a—good—person at heart." Gavin seemed to have trouble pushing the word *good* out of his throat. "If her conscience starts bothering her, she's going to look for relief. She might look for it in a friend. If she tells you anything, do you swear you'll tell me?"

"I'll tell the police. I can't promise I'll come to you."

Gavin sank back against the couch, his small, sweet Taylor smile going crooked. "Point taken. Sorry. I didn't mean to come across as a vigilante. I haven't bothered Carissa at all, in case you're worried about that."

Rebecca's footsteps tapped along the hall, approaching the living room. She stopped in the doorway.

"Are you doing all right, Fiona?" she asked. From the anxious, protective expression on her face, Fiona knew she'd overheard enough to know Gavin's conversation had veered far from his ostensible flowers-and-comfort mission.

"I'm okay." Fiona rose slowly to her feet. "But I think I'll lie down for a while. Gavin . . . I'm sorry. I wish I knew how to help."

He stood. "I'm sorry for upsetting you."

"Reality is reality. I'd rather know what's going on." She walked him to the door. As soon as it closed behind him, she turned to face Rebecca, hovering in the hallway.

"I need to call Carissa," Fiona said.

Chapter 19

JAMES GESTURED TO THE EDGE of the brick planter box in the student center courtyard. "Want to sit down? The weather today makes winter seem like a bad dream."

Fiona sat on the brick edging and sipped from the hot chocolate she'd just purchased. James sat next to her. The weather was beyond gorgeous—high sixties, clear blue skies. Flowering trees sweetened the air, and the breeze scattered stray petals around their feet.

"Nothing like a New England winter to make you appreciate spring," she remarked. "I can't believe how nice it is today."

"It won't last." James pulled a toffee-topped brownie out of a paper bag and passed the bag to Fiona. "It's supposed to rain tomorrow."

"I'll appreciate it while it lasts." Fiona wished she could relax, focusing only on the warmth of sun on her hair and the beauty of the cherry blossoms dusting her feet like a benevolent version of snow. But worry for Carissa, the pain of sore muscles reminding her of the crash, and hyperawareness of James next to her made the knots inside her difficult to work loose.

Carissa hadn't been home when she'd called last night—or if she had been home, she hadn't wanted to talk to Fiona.

"You holding up okay?" James asked. "You really should have taken the rest of the week off."

"To do what? Sit at home and worry?"

"You push yourself too hard."

"Teaching proves to me that I'm still sane."

"Is *that* the sanity test? I'll have to reevaluate my opinion of my grad school professor who wore cleats to class and paused in the middle of lectures to channel Aristotle."

Fiona smiled. "So maybe it doesn't prove my sanity. But I'm hoping it will reduce my ever-increasing chances of getting thrown out of here."

"Fiona, they can't possibly blame you for what's been happening."

"Whether they blame me or simply think I'm an unlucky trouble magnet who's sure to bring embarrassment—or worse—to Hawkins, the ultimate result might be the same."

"You've had a bad time, but it's temporary. They know that. The police will catch the culprit and things will quiet down before most of the college community even knows there was a problem."

Fiona doubted James was naïve enough to think the difficulties would resolve so cleanly, but she appreciated his desire to comfort her—even if there was nothing truly comforting he could say.

"It's been wonderful having Rebecca with me." Fiona changed the subject.

"She's staying longer, I hope?"

"No. She's leaving tonight. She refused to leave until she was sure I was okay back at work—which I am. She needs to get back to work too. Tonight we're going out for dinner and a movie as a last hurrah."

"She drives back tonight?"

"Yes. I'd—rather have her drive during the day, but she told her boss she'd be at work tomorrow morning, and she doesn't want to leave earlier than tonight."

"Do you have someone else who could stay with you? Or somewhere you could go?"

"James, I'm fine."

"Yeah, but . . . you . . . could probably use company right now. You went through a traumatic experience. And whoever set up that accident is still out there."

"I'll be fine." The thought of asking someone to stay with her—or asking if she could bed down in a friend's guest room for a while—made Fiona wince. She was *not* going to let Kimberly or Summer—or anyone, for that matter—scare her into thinking she didn't dare be alone in her own house. What a triumph for the culprit *that* would be, if Fiona fled to cower behind a friend. And when would it end? What if the police couldn't find enough evidence to arrest whoever had arranged the accident? Did Fiona quit her job and run home to live with her parents in Arizona, unable to function on her own?

As helpless, as emotionally paralyzed, as dependent as she'd been after Mia's death?

Fiona breathed deeply, filling her lungs with warm spring air. "I'll be very careful. Rebecca is making anti-theft bars for all the windows today, and tonight while we're out we're going to pick up some motion-sensor alarms for the doors."

"You should hire a security company."

"I will, but I'll be replacing the back door and all the windows within the next few months, so they'd have to redo everything. This will be good enough for now. I'll keep a phone with me at all times. I've got pepper spray. And a crowbar."

"Maybe one of your other sisters could come for a few—"

"James."

He sighed. "You've got a great family."

"Yes, I do."

He broke off a chunk of brownie and offered it to her. "Taste?"

"Thank you." She took the piece of brownie, appreciating that James was willing to yield rather than insisting she needed to find a bodyguard. "Trade?" She broke off a piece of blueberry scone and handed it to him. For a few moments, they ate in silence.

Calm, she thought, her gaze on the pale pink blossoms covering the branches of the tree in front of her. *The last thing the culprit wants is for you to stay calm and in control of your life.*

She'd done relatively well today. She'd stayed focused—mostly—during her classes. When images of the red-paint-splashed dummy had popped into her mind, she'd been able to blank them out fairly quickly. With her car in the shop, it had been natural to ask Rebecca to drive her to work, so driving had not been an issue. She knew she needed to pick up the rental car her insurance would provide, but she hadn't been able to make herself do it yet. She'd do it this afternoon. She'd make herself drive even if it took hours to work up the courage to turn the key. She was *not* going to end up stranded and needing rescue like she had last Saturday.

Finished with his snack, James wadded up the bag and turned toward her. She expected him to speak, but he didn't. Curious, she met his eyes.

"Are you up for a short walk?" His voice was casual, but he was holding her gaze very intently. "It's crowded here."

Tingling spread through her bloodstream. Already, their topics of conversation had been somewhat sensitive—she hadn't worried about being overheard, since the students in the courtyard were all occupied with studying or with their own conversations. If James was seeking privacy now, he was planning to approach a new topic—something so personal he knew Fiona wouldn't risk discussing it in public.

She hadn't been alone with him since the night of the accident. He'd stopped by the house twice yesterday but had urged Rebecca to stay while they chatted.

Not sure if she desperately wanted to talk to him now or desperately wanted to stay safely in the midst of the dozens of students enjoying the sunshine, Fiona followed James out of the courtyard.

* * *

They'd never even *glanced* at her. Grinning, Kim shut the door of the restroom stall and removed the dark wig and glasses. It was such a cheesy, simple disguise, and they hadn't noticed her at all. She'd been able to tail them from Dr. Claridge's office to the student center and then, head bent over a book, to sit only a few feet away while they ate and talked. She hadn't expected much from it—except the satisfaction of knowing that even without the camera, she could monitor them and they wouldn't know it—but it turned out to be the perfect snippet of eavesdropping.

Now she knew Claridge was going to be away from home all evening, out with her sister. This was the perfect chance. Kim would have plenty of time to scout out the territory and get into position.

Pepper spray and a crowbar. What a joke. None of that would help her tonight. This was going to be better than good. It would be absolutely delicious. From watching out of the corner of her eye, Kim could tell Dr. Claridge was already unraveling. She looked pale and tired, and she'd done a lousy job of camouflaging those dark circles under her eyes.

Hatred flooded Kim, searing and stinging. That was the last time Dr. Claridge and James Hampton would go off on a "short walk" to somewhere less crowded. Kim just needed to let Nick know tonight was the night and to talk to Madison to firm up their alibi.

Payback, Dr. C. You lose.

* * *

James led the way to the Murphy Building. Fiona thought they were heading for his office until he veered around the building and stopped next to a bench set near a bike rack. The area was deserted.

"Not the nicest view," James remarked, gesturing at the parking lot to the right. "But private."

They sat. Fiona focused on the lid of her hot chocolate and steeled herself.

"Are you okay?" James asked.

She nodded, a gesture she wished she'd quit making. Her neck muscles were sore.

"Fiona," he said. "If you'd rather not talk now, we can do this later."

She sipped hot chocolate, moistening her mouth. "It's all right."

"We got cut off the other day when Summer Taylor showed up," he said. "And there's something I need to explain to you."

A light brush of dizziness made her scalp prickle. *Stop it. You'll bring on a panic attack. What's wrong with you? What do you think he's going to say?*

"Fiona." James took the hot chocolate out of her hand. "Sorry— you look like you're going to dump that in your lap." He set the cup on the ground. "Do you need me to take you home?"

"I'm okay," she whispered.

"You look scared. Are you afraid of me?"

Afraid of James? It was such a strange question that she thought he was joking, but when she looked into his eyes, she saw no humor there. He looked worried. Grim.

"Don't be ridiculous," she said. "Why would I be afraid of you?"

"I get the feeling the police think it's strange no one ever bothered you until I came to Hawkins."

This comment brought her up short. The police *had* asked her about James after the second package had arrived, but the idea that he'd want to hurt her was so absurd that she hadn't fully realized the police were considering James as a suspect. She tried to remember what Detective Reid had said to her about James after the accident, but her memories were too blurry. She *did* remember James telling her they'd questioned him.

"Please tell me they don't think you had something to do with the accident," Fiona said. "That's ridiculous."

"I don't know what's going on with the investigation." James slid his glasses out from his face, held them for a moment, and pushed them back on again. "But I did know you were out that night. And I know you take that back road home."

"Anyone who can google a map knows about that back road, and it's the most direct way to my house. And anyone could have known I was out that night. I don't have a garage. Either my car's in the driveway or it's not. I'm so sorry that—"

"Don't *you* apologize. This is *not your fault.*"

James sounded so fierce that it surprised Fiona. "James—"

"Sorry. I just don't want you blaming yourself. And I'm not upset that they're investigating me. They're being thorough. That's a good thing. I can live through some embarrassment."

"Still, how stressful for you. And I've never, for even a fraction of an instant, wondered if you might be the person targeting me. The idea is ridiculous."

"Thanks." James slid his glasses off his face and wiped the lenses on the sleeve of his Oxford shirt. "Glad you think so." He switched to wiping the glasses with his tie.

"Have you ever considered contact lenses?" Fiona asked.

"I have them, but don't wear them very often. I hate sticking my finger in my eyes."

"Plus the glasses let you fidget to vent stress."

He settled the glasses back on his face. "Fine, Professor. I'm rattled. It cuts deep to think they're wondering if I'd hurt you—especially when you start looking nervous at being alone with me."

"I'm not nervous at being alone with you." She *was*—but not because she feared for her safety.

"I don't think they seriously suspect me, but they have to ask the questions, since everything happened after I came here—and since the messages all refer to Mia, and I knew her."

I knew her. The apprehension inside Fiona pulled tighter.

"I want to talk to you about Mia," he said. "I know it's hard for you to talk about her, especially after what happened a couple of days ago, but I think it's important."

"It's fine. Go ahead." She focused on the wall of the redbrick science building.

"I've thought a lot about our conversation the other day. About your feeling you don't deserve marriage and family because Mia died before she could have a family of her own. Can you explain to me how it helps Mia—or anyone—for you to punish yourself like that?"

"I'm not punishing . . ." Her words thinned and disappeared. She didn't know what to say. She'd never meant to expose those feelings, that guilt, to anyone, and she didn't know how to rationally explain it. *Because it's not rational. You know that.*

"Fiona, do you think Mia is unhappy now? Do you think God will deprive her of any blessing in eternity because her mortal life ended when she was young?"

"No."

"She'll have the blessings of marriage and family."

"Yes."

"Then why do *you* feel the need to deprive yourself of the chance to move forward?"

"I . . . don't know. I guess I . . . didn't realize I'd made that decision. Like I told you, I'm just more at peace on my own."

James reached down and picked up a twig from the sidewalk. He rolled it between his fingers. "I liked Mia," he said. "But that was all. As far as whether or not our relationship had long-term potential, I wasn't sure, and neither was she. It hadn't gotten to that point yet. Do you think because I dated her when I was twenty-four and she died tragically, that's it—that was my shot at love, and to move on would be to betray her?"

"I never thought that. I know she'd want . . ."

"She'd want what?"

"She'd want you to move on."

"And I have moved on. I mourned Mia, but she died eight years ago. And the truth is, you read far more into that relationship after the fact than was ever there. Did you think it was because of her that I haven't married yet?"

"I did wonder."

"It's not because of Mia. I *have* been looking. I try to meet people. I've dated. I've gone to every blasted singles activity that my schedule will allow. I've gotten into a couple of relationships, but something about them never felt totally right and eventually we both backed off. Fiona, you know that the way you're limiting your life is the last thing Mia would want for you. Let yourself move on. Let *me* move on. Please don't shackle me to her memory."

"I'd never do that to you."

He laughed softly. "That's exactly what you're doing."

Coldness prickled its way across her forehead, over her cheeks and down her neck. He wasn't going to let her dodge this or guide it in a broad, general direction.

"'*I took her from you,*'" James quoted. "In your eyes, Mia and I are still a pair. You won't let yourself think beyond that. You're afraid that unfreezing time means you're betraying her. You're not, Fiona."

She drew rhythmic, deep breaths, gaze focused, trancelike, on the Murphy Building. In her mind, she had one goal: *don't cry.*

James took her hand, intertwining his fingers with hers. "If you want me to back away," he said gently, "all it takes is 'Leave me alone, James.'"

The tears started falling.

Chapter 20

"WHAT ARE YOU SO CRABBY ABOUT?" Kim grinned at Nick, eyes glittering. "You've got the easy part."

"This is so *stupid*." Nick gripped the steering wheel harder. There was no point in holding the wheel, given that they were parked in one of the student lots, but at least it gave him something to do with his hands other than shaking Kim until her crooked brain popped back into alignment. "You're going to get arrested. We're both going to get arrested."

"We're not going to get caught. I don't think she's even going to call the police on this one. A shrink, maybe. Maybe she'll have herself committed."

"You're the one who's crazy. Kim, listen to me. *This isn't worth it.*"

"I say it is. And if I say it is, *you* say it is."

Nick pressed his forehead against the steering wheel. He'd always liked Kim, always thought she was fun to have around, always liked her sense of adventure and her willingness to jump into a prank. But right now, he hated her. She *would* tattle on him if he thwarted her. If there was one thing he'd learned lately, it was that Kim was relentless when someone crossed her. So now he was her slave, unable to back out lest he find himself at the end of a lawsuit or worse, courtesy of the Burke family.

"Come on." She patted his shoulder. "Be a good sport. I'm the one who should be crabby. I'm the one getting yanked out of school."

Nick glared at Kim, her cheerfulness grating on him all the more. "So cut your losses, you stupid monkey. Quit now."

"I would," Kim said, "if she hadn't lied about me. Blaming *me* for her deadly driving and getting my mother riled up. You know Mom will never let me come back to Hawkins." Bitterness poisoned her aura of cheer. "She's probably already picked another school for me."

"You're better off somewhere else."

"Claridge lied about me. And now I never get to . . . I'll never have a chance."

"Never have a chance to—" Nick cut himself off, realizing what Kim meant. *I'll never have a chance with Dr. Hampton.* Dumb kid, making a crush on a professor sound like some tragic love story.

"She's not getting the last word, Nicky," Kim said. "Not after what she did."

"I swear to you, if you get me arrested, I'll strangle you."

"Good luck doing that from a prison cell."

"Fine. I'll strangle you *now.*"

"We won't get caught, okay? Madison will do a great job of giving us an alibi—if we need it. Like I said, I doubt Dr. C will call the police. She might think it's real, or she might think it's a hallucination. Either way, do you think she's going to tell Detective Reid that Mia came to visit? Come on, start driving, and I'll show you where to stop so I can get ready."

Grinding his teeth, Nick started the engine and drove away from campus. *Three more days,* he told himself. *She'll be gone in three days. Get through tonight, and it's over. She'll feel like she won, and she'll be normal again.*

"Turn right on that skinny road." Kim pointed. "Then pull over as soon as you can and stop."

The road was narrow and potholed, pressed by trees on both sides. A quarter of a mile in was a turnaround area. Nick pulled over. "How'd you find this place?"

"Liam and I used to come here before I dumped him. Verrrry private." She smirked. "The road leads to a little farm stand where they sell apples and cider in the fall, but no one's ever here at night." Kim opened a makeup bag and pulled out a jar of white face paint.

"This is so corny." Nick watched her smear paint on her face. "You look like a kid on Halloween, not the tortured soul of Mia Hardy."

"Trust me, it'll work. I copied her clothes exactly—or close enough—from that family blog one of her sisters made. The wig is perfect. And I tried the whole getup on in my bathroom and looked in the mirror by candlelight. It was seriously creepy. And yeah, in daylight and wide awake, Claridge would never fall for it. But at night, by candlelight, with her too doped to think, she'll be weeping and begging Mia for mercy."

"I don't like the idea of drugging her."

"Chill, Nicky. It won't hurt her. It'll just make her dozy and confused."

"How do you know she's not allergic or something? What if she has a reaction?"

Kim checked her face in a hand mirror. "Why would she be allergic?" She dabbed more white cream on a spot she'd missed. "It's just a prescription—"

"*Don't* tell me. Don't tell me anything. I don't want to know."

"Fine. I won't tell you. That way, when they chain you to the rack and torture you for information, you can keep screaming that you're clueless. Which is always true."

"That drug better not be traceable to you."

"It's not. The friend who—"

"*Don't tell me!* What if it doesn't work? What if she doesn't drink the milk tonight?"

"I told you what she said to James Hampton. Every night. Creature of habit."

"This will be the one night she skips it."

"You need to relax. What's wrong with you? You used to like having fun."

"This *isn't fun!*" Realizing it wasn't a good idea to shout, no matter how deserted the road, Nick lowered his voice. "This is *you* self-destructing and dragging me into the explosion."

"Boom," Kim said cheerfully, stowing the white paint. She removed a tube of red. "Hold the mirror for me."

Nick wanted to smack her, but he took the mirror as ordered. Was this the only way she could cope with the disaster she'd created—pretend everything was a joke?

"Hold it steady." Kim squeezed the tube, creating a trickle of red running from her hairline down her cheek. "Good effect, huh?" She created another trickle.

Nick shuddered.

"Let's review." She squeezed harder to create a thicker line of blood. "Your part's so easy I can't believe you're whining about it. We drive to her neighborhood and—"

"I park a few streets away from her house and walk there," Nick snapped. "We can't park closer because the cops are probably patrolling *her* street, waiting for *us*. This is completely idiotic—"

"I wait five minutes so it doesn't look like we're together, then follow," Kim interrupted. "I've got my dark hooded coat to cover everything so I don't look like a freak show. But that neighborhood's so dead no one will see me anyway."

"Unless the cops are out looking for trouble."

"Will you calm down? She's not going to have a cop sitting outside her house. And you'll only be there for a couple of minutes anyway. Just put on your burglar mask, stroll up to the back door, and break in. Easy-peasy for you, and we know she won't be home, so no worries there."

Nick scowled.

"Once I'm in, you leave," she continued, as if Nick didn't already know every detail of this boneheaded plan. "I'll take care of everything else."

"I *know.*"

Kim liked hearing herself talk. "When I'm done, I'll text you with our code phrase—" She paused, obviously waiting for Nick to recite it.

He rolled his eyes. Like he needed to memorize it. He'd know any message from Kim meant *come pick me up*. "'You left your jacket here,'" he said.

"Good. And you come meet me at the same place where you dropped me off."

"Yeah, I'll be waiting there, no problem. Look for the guy in handcuffs with a gun in his ear."

"You didn't used to be such a pessimist."

"You didn't used to be psychotic!"

"Trust me." She squeezed a little more "blood" on her face. "After you get home this summer, we're going to laugh ourselves sick over this one."

* * *

You'd think she'd invest in a dead bolt after the stuff that's happened to her, Kim thought, as she eased the back door shut. Through the window, she caught a last glimpse of Nick, fleeing through the adjoining backyard like a scared squirrel. She'd thought Nick had more guts than this. The older he got, the duller he got.

The back door opened into the kitchen. Kim switched on her flashlight. Keeping the beam aimed low, she made her way to the fridge. First, the milk.

To her delight, about two inches of milk remained in the jug. She'd worried she might have to pour some out if there was too much, since she only had two tablets and couldn't risk diluting them to the point that they didn't work. But this was perfect. With latex-gloved fingers, she took the Ziploc baggie containing the tablets she'd crushed to fine powder and emptied the powder into the milk. She shook the jug vigorously and returned it to the fridge.

She couldn't believe Nick had been so stubborn about this. Couldn't he see that she couldn't just *leave*? If Dr. Claridge wanted to play dirty, Kim could out-dirt her in a heartbeat. And doing this face-to-face and seeing her terror would be a lot more satisfying than dropping off a package.

She thought of the things Dr. Claridge had said to James Hampton today, worrying over her job. She hoped Claridge did get fired. That would be an awesome bonus. Kim had been tempted to go to the English Department chair and make up some more stories about how awful Claridge was, but she didn't dare—it would be stupid to draw too much attention to herself, especially when Claridge might try to call in witnesses to counter Kim's allegations. Better to keep a low profile.

Time to scout out the whole house. Dr. Claridge would probably be too woozy and too terrified to leave her room, but in case Kim had to make a quick exit, she'd better know the layout of the place. She wandered into the living room and shone the flashlight across the bare wood floor and the walls with old wallpaper stripped away. The fireplace was filled with buckets of tools and brushes and cans of paint. This place was a dump. She'd thought Dr. Claridge would have some fancy cottage filled with horsehair chairs—or whatever people sat on in those old novels—where she sat slashing student essays apart and talking to her cat, since, come on, a woman like that would have no social life and zero friends. Except for—

Pain blazed through Kim. She'd skipped all her other classes this week—what was the point of going?—but she'd gone to bio so she could watch James.

And he'd watched her. More than once she'd felt his gaze, but it wasn't the warm, friendly expression she loved. It was guarded. Cold. Because thanks to Claridge's lies, he thought Kim had caused that accident.

Kim blinked, sweeping away tears. She would not cry over this. Let Claridge do the crying tonight.

She strode down the hall. Bathroom. Study, with walls lined with books. A doorway that led down to the basement. No need to check the basement. She wouldn't be going there, and old basements gave her the creeps.

She headed upstairs and found a room with a few pieces of exercise equipment. Yeah, Kim wouldn't want to go to a public gym either if she had scars like Claridge. The closet in the exercise room was probably the best place to hang out. No way would Claridge come in here to run on the treadmill after dinner and a movie with her sister. She'd have her nightcap and go to bed.

Kim opened the closet. Not much in it—good. She'd have plenty of room to hide. She dropped her coat and bag on the closet floor.

This was going to be a blast. Of course, the next few hours would be boring as she waited for Claridge to come home, drink her drugged milk, and go to bed. But Kim had plenty of games on her phone to keep her occupied while she hid.

Now—time to check out the master bedroom, where she'd be doing her haunting. She'd need to figure out where to put the candle so Claridge could see just enough to recognize "Mia." The nightstand would probably be the best spot.

Stifling a giggle, she thought of the cold pack in her bag and imagined what would go through Claridge's head when Mia Hardy's icy hands brushed her face and her anguished voice whispered, "*Don't take my James.*" Okay, Nick was right—it *was* totally cheesy and over the top, but in the dark, it would be enough to terrify anyone—especially a drugged woman already tortured by bad memories.

What a coup it had been when she'd realized the meaning of that last conversation she'd caught before Claridge had discovered the camera. James Hampton had been involved with Mia Hardy, and Claridge felt super guilty over getting involved with him. It wouldn't take much to scare her away from him forever.

Grinning, Kim headed into the bedroom. She flashed her light along the old drapes covering the window, over the bed with its red-and-white quilt, the nightstand, a chair—

The flashlight beam illuminated a figure sitting in the chair.

Kim jumped, her shriek of fear and surprise breaking the silence. Why would—sitting here in the dark . . . Had Dr. Claridge anticipated and asked—

She spun around and ran.

* * *

"Relax," Madison whispered in Nick's ear. "We're supposed to be having fun."

Nick groaned and slouched, resting his head against the back of the couch. "I'm relaxed."

"You're a wreck." Madison's fingertips massaged his scalp.

"If she gets me in trouble, I'll kill her. If she gets *us* in trouble," Nick amended, realizing it sounded selfish to be worrying only about himself when Kim had sucked Madison into her scheme as well, asking Madison to swear—if the police got involved—that Kim had been with her and Nick all night watching movies. Madison didn't know everything that was going on—only that Kim was playing a prank on someone who'd hurt her—but she'd agreed to help. Nick had witnessed a little of the conversation between the two women, and it had annoyed him how skillfully Kim had made it all sound fun and mischievous. He'd had to bite his tongue to keep from telling Madison the truth. He'd known if he scared Madison into backing out, he'd only be hurting himself. Kim would go ahead with or without Madison, and she'd drag Nick along, too. Without an alibi, they'd both be a lot more vulnerable.

Kim had made herself very visible earlier in the evening, laughing loudly as she walked along the sidewalk leading to her apartment, knocking on a neighbor's door to borrow some salt, making sure the maximum number of people saw her around the place. Then she'd snaked her way out the window of her bedroom and, wearing the long platinum wig and a dark coat, had made her way to campus and her rendezvous with Nick. Madison would swear she'd never left the apartment.

"Kim can handle it." Madison massaged Nick's temples, and he closed his eyes, feeling that under Madison's touch, he *might* be able to relax. "She's smart enough not to get caught."

Obsessed edged out smart long ago, Nick wanted to say, but floating in the lake of endorphins generated by Madison's fingertips, he didn't feel as inclined to gripe about Kim as he had a few minutes ago.

"We'd better turn on a movie," Madison said. "So you can tell the cops about the show in case they ask."

He couldn't even think of the titles of the shows they were supposed to be watching tonight, and he was sure the plots wouldn't stick in his head either. Chick flicks. That's what he got for letting Madison choose. "Give me the CliffsNotes summary," he mumbled.

Madison laughed. "Forget it. You're going to have to pay attention—"

Nick's phone buzzed. He fumbled in his pocket and brought it out. *Kim.* The idiot. Why was she contacting him now? She wasn't supposed to contact him until she was done, and that would be hours from now. She was supposedly *here* with him right now, watching movies. Did she *want* to trash her alibi? He opened the message.

Come now.

"*What?* You've *got* to be kidding me."

"What's wrong?" Madison asked.

"I don't know." Nick wanted to hurl his phone through the TV screen. "She's calling it off. She wants me to come get her right now." He showed the text to Madison. What had happened? Had Dr. Claridge arrived home before Kim was ready and caught her by surprise? Had she seen Kim? Could she identify her?

Nick clenched his teeth to keep himself from spewing profanity—Madison thought swearing was immature. "I'd better go get her. I can't leave her standing on the street in that ghost makeup."

"Ghost . . . ?"

"Never mind. She can explain it to you." Nick jumped to his feet.

"Can I come with you?"

"Better not."

"Nick, don't you think I'd better? We're supposed to be together."

"Yeah, but—you might get seen."

"I can wear a hat, or a scarf across my face." She sounded eager. She still believed Kim's sales pitch that this was just a fun prank, and she wanted in on the excitement.

"Good thing it got cold and windy tonight. You'd have trouble pulling off the scarf thing if it were nice out." Nick suddenly liked the idea of Madison seeing Kim in her ghostly corpse regalia. Madison would ask questions, and Kim would have to explain what she'd been up to. Maybe if she was forced to say it out loud to her friend, she'd finally realize it was stupid beyond belief and wouldn't try anything else before she left town this weekend.

Madison ran to her bedroom. She returned a moment later with her long black hair tucked up in a ski cap and a scarf wound around her face, exposing only her eyes.

Nick snorted. "Don't get dressed up *yet.*"

Laughing, Madison yanked off the hat and scarf.

"The scarf's a good idea," Nick remarked. "Better than my ski mask that shouts, "Arrest me! I'm a bad guy!'"

"You can borrow my other one." Before Nick could object, Madison raced back to her room. She emerged carrying a navy blue scarf. "See—not too girlie."

"Thanks." Nick draped it around his neck. He didn't figure he'd be using it to hide his face, but he didn't want to turn down her offer. Besides, he liked the hint of Madison's perfume that scented the wool.

Nick hurried to his car, Madison keeping pace with him, and headed for the rendezvous two blocks from Dr. Claridge's house. At least he hadn't heard any sirens or seen any flashing lights. That had to be a good sign.

He pulled over next to the copse of budding trees Kim had designated as the pickup point and switched off the engine. He expected Kim, swathed in her hooded coat, to rush toward his car, but the area remained empty and silent, except for the rustling of tree branches in the wind. Where was she?

"So we wait right here?" Madison asked.

"Yeah."

"Good spot." Madison peered out the window. "No houses around."

Nick pulled out his phone. "Where *is* she? It's been ten minutes since she texted me. She should be here."

"Should you text her to let her know you're here?"

Nick shook his head. The fewer traceable electronic communications between them tonight, the better. "I'll give her a few minutes."

Ten minutes later, Nick was all but twitching with nervousness, and he struggled to respond to Madison's casual chatter about her plans for the summer. No cars had driven past in that time, but he still felt conspicuous parked here. *Where was Kim?* Had she gotten pinned down at Dr. Claridge's house and couldn't sneak out?

"Better text her," Madison said, an edge to her voice, and Nick realized his distraction was obvious—he'd probably missed responding to something she'd asked him.

"Yeah." He typed a quick message: *You there?*

Blowing the air out of his lungs, he set the phone on his knee and waited for a response.

Nothing.

"Um . . . Nick . . . maybe we'd better go to wherever it is she's pulling her prank," Madison said. "If she was coming, she'd be here by now."

Madison was right. Kim might be obsessed, but she wasn't sloppy if sloppiness might mean a prison sentence. She'd hate the idea of Nick waiting here in the open, fair game for curious eyes. If she hadn't shown up at the rendezvous, it was because she couldn't.

Dr. Claridge must have changed her plans and come home early, with her sister—or with someone else. Nick imagined Kim cowering in the coat closet, unable to leave, while a few feet away, Dr. Claridge was taking a *very* long time kissing Dr. Hampton good night. It would serve Kim right if she had to overhear that.

"I don't want to take the car there," Nick said. "I'll walk. You'd better stay here."

"Forget that. I've been sitting here long enough." Madison grabbed her knit cap out of her pocket.

"Fine. Just—you should know this isn't some spat between Kim and an old boyfriend or someone like that. She has it in for a professor." Quickly, Nick told Madison the story. He trusted her to keep her mouth shut, and she needed to know how high the stakes were.

"Oh *wow*," Madison whispered. "No wonder you're so nervous. The cops must be waiting to pounce."

"No kidding. Believe me, I tried to talk Kim out of it."

"She didn't even tell me her mom was yanking her out of school."

"She didn't want to advertise it."

Madison's lips tightened. "This is really icky. Dressing up like a bloody corpse and trying to scare some poor, freaked-out professor—I can't believe you're in on this."

A surge of anger made it hard not to shout. "I didn't *want* to be, okay? Kim blackmailed me into it."

"Blackmailed you!"

"Yeah, we've known each other too long, and she knows stuff that could get me in big trouble. If I don't help her, she'll blab."

"Wow. She's really . . . I didn't know . . . I thought you two got along really well."

"We *did*. Until she went crackers over that dumb grade and fell in love with Dr. Claridge's boyfriend. Maddie, you shouldn't get mixed up in this. Just stay in the—"

"Sit here alone waiting for the cops to roll by and ask what I'm up to? No thanks. I'm coming."

"Your choice." Nick left the car unlocked in case Kim returned while they were gone and needed a place to hide. Hand in hand, he and Madison strolled—Nick hoped they looked casual, though that was hard with the wind blasting them—toward Dr. Claridge's house. Madison had her hair tucked up in her hat and the scarf loose around her neck, waiting to be used as concealment if needed. Nick kept his ski mask pushed up to the level of his eyebrows. A masked guy wandering the neighborhood would win an instant 911 call.

The lights at Dr. Claridge's house were off. An unfamiliar car was parked in the driveway. A rental car, probably, since her own got mashed up. Her sister was probably doing the driving tonight. Drawing Madison with him, Nick darted along the side of the house and into the backyard. The windows at the back of the house were dark as well.

"It doesn't look like Claridge is home," he whispered. "What's up with Kim?"

"Maybe Dr. Claridge *is* home," Madison whispered back. "She might have gone straight to bed."

"That's what Kim *wanted*; she wouldn't text me and cancel the whole scheme." Too frustrated and worried to be cautious, Nick yanked his phone out and sent another text: *What's up? Answer me.* Nick gripped his phone and waited, willing it to vibrate in his hand with Kim's reply.

Nothing.

He swore under his breath. "Something's weird," he whispered. "I'm going to sneak a look in the kitchen window."

"Be careful. This is giving me the willies."

No kidding. Nick yanked the ski mask over his face and crept toward the house. He leaned his head just enough past the window frame to allow him to see into the darkened kitchen.

The faint light from the microwave and stove readouts were enough to let him see that the kitchen was empty. *What did you expect? Kim sitting at the table, eating ice cream out of the carton and reading* People *magazine?*

Nick hurried to where Madison waited. "This is so stupid," he whispered. "Everything's quiet here. Kim's probably hiding in the closet, waiting for Dr. Claridge. She must have sent that text by mistake."

Even in the dark, he could see the incredulity on Madison's face. "By mistake?"

"Like—she'd typed it in case she needed it in a hurry so all she had to do was hit SEND, and she hit SEND by accident."

"Kim can text faster than she can talk, and that's saying a lot. Why would she need to write the message beforehand?"

"I don't *know.* You explain what's happening, then. She didn't show up at the meeting place, but nothing seems wrong here. And she's not answering my texts—she probably has her phone on silent and doesn't know I'm trying to get in touch with her. This is a waste of time. I'm going home."

"Give it a few more minutes," Madison whispered. "This feels so creepy. We can't abandon her."

"I'd like to shove her off a cliff." Nick stared at the silent house. Kim would pay for this one—assuming they weren't both in jail before sunrise. There was no point to standing here. Nothing was happening.

"I'm going inside to check on her," he said. "She's probably crouching in a closet playing solitaire."

"Good idea. Should I—come with you?" Madison's voice was hesitant, and Nick suspected she was frightened at the thought of actually breaking into a professor's house.

"No. Wait here. Or if you get too cold, go to the car." Nick hurried to the back door. Working fast, he sprang the lock.

He walked through the darkened kitchen, not daring to turn on a light. Kim would probably be hiding somewhere upstairs to make it easier for her to go after Dr. Claridge at the right moment. He headed up the stairs, keeping his gloved hand on the handrail. He couldn't see a thing—should have brought a flashlight. The stairs creaked so loudly that Kim would know for sure someone was here. Or Claridge would know—what if she *was* home and in bed, but she'd skipped drinking the drugged milk? Maybe that was why Kim had called it off—she didn't dare do her spooky act unless Claridge was too doped to yank Kim's wig off and slap her.

This was dumb. With the way the floor creaked, there was no point in trying to keep his presence secret. He fumbled along the wall of the upstairs hallway until he found a light switch and flipped it on.

A filmy white scarf lay on the threadbare carpet that ran down the middle of the hallway. Kim's scarf. The idiot—didn't she realize she'd dropped part of her costume? He picked it up and stuck his head through a doorway. A small bedroom containing a couple of pieces of exercise equipment. Another doorway—the master bedroom. He peeked inside and saw an empty double bed. No, Claridge *wasn't* home—she wouldn't be hanging out with the house all dark unless she was asleep, which plainly she wasn't. Which meant the only person in the house was Kim.

"Kim." He spoke at normal volume. "Kim, wherever you are, get out here. What's up with that text telling me to come get you?"

No response.

"*Answer me!*" He raised his voice. The neighbors wouldn't hear, especially not with the way the wind was blasting. The windows kept rattling, and the whooshy wind noise gave Nick the shivers. Kim must be loving this haunted-house weather.

No answer from Kim. Where was she?

He strode into the master bedroom, flipped on the light, and yanked open the closet door. Clothes and shoes. No Kim.

Swearing, Nick turned off the light, exited the bedroom, and crossed into the room with the exercise equipment. The closet door was open, and Kim's coat and bag lay on the floor. But no Kim.

Nick wanted to kick a hole in the wall. Where *was* she?

He switched off the hall light and stomped toward the creaky stairs. He *was* going to kill her. This was the stupidest—

The sound of a door swinging open made him freeze. The front door.

"Thanks for everything, Becca." A woman's voice came from downstairs.

"Thank *you* for dinner." Another female voice. "Those crab cakes—good thing it wasn't all you can eat, or I'd still be there. They'd have to drag me away from the table at closing time."

"Good luck to the fool who tries to drag a pregnant woman away from her crab cakes."

Laughter. Dr. Claridge and her sister.

"We really *can* do the movie. I swear I wouldn't be too tired afterward. You know I'm a night owl."

"I'll feel better if you get an earlier start."

"No problem. Don't worry about me, okay?"

Sweating, Nick stood paralyzed in the hallway. Had they been able to see the hallway light from the front of the house before he'd switched it off? No. Obviously they didn't think anything was wrong or they wouldn't stand there swapping sister talk.

"Call me when you get home."

"You don't want me calling you that late."

"Yes, I do. Call me. And let me help you with your bags—"

"Don't you dare! Don't *touch*!"

"Rebecca!" More laughter. "I'm supposed to stand here while a seven-months-pregnant woman—"

"*You* are sore. *I* am fine. Honestly, Fiona, get with the twenty-first century."

What now? If he tried to run down the stairs and out the back door, they'd hear him for sure. Hear him, but wouldn't be able to identify him, not with this mask. He'd better make a run for it—but Kim's bag. Kim's coat. He couldn't leave her stuff here. He had to take it with him. The instant Dr. Claridge knew there'd been an intruder, she'd call the police, and they'd come investigate—

Where was Kim? She wouldn't have left without her stuff unless she didn't have a choice. And if she'd escaped the house, she would have come to the rendezvous point.

Nothing made sense, and he didn't dare cause Claridge to get the cops on the scene until he knew what was going on.

"Drive safely. Love you."

"Love you, too." The rattle of the door opening. "You sure you're going to be okay alone? I wish I could stay—"

"No worries. Now shut that door so I can install this silly alarm you made me buy."

Not knowing what else to do, Nick dropped to his belly and army-crawled toward the exercise room, hoping distributing his weight would keep floor-creaking to a minimum. He snaked into the closet with Kim's bag and coat and tugged the door shut.

Chapter 21

FIONA SWALLOWED THE LAST OF her milk and set the glass in the sink. Maybe she should have gone to the movie with Rebecca like they'd planned, but she'd been tired after dinner and had worried about Rebecca's not starting the drive home until late. Intellectually she knew she was projecting her own tiredness onto Rebecca. Rebecca loved late nights and could be chipper and alert until four in the morning, given the chance, but Fiona had buckled to anxiety and canceled their movie date. Now, with Rebecca gone, there was no cheerful voice, no distractions, nothing to keep her mind from the fact that Kimberly Bailey—or whoever had caused the accident—might not be finished with her. And the culprit had already broken into Fiona's home once.

No one is sneaking in here again. Fiona had attached portable alarms to both doors. If Kimberly tried to enter tonight, she'd get her eardrums blown out, and the entire neighborhood would know.

But surely it was over. That car crash *had* to have been the climax of Kimberly's plotting. She wouldn't dare make another move, not with the police breathing down her neck.

If it *was* Kimberly, and not someone so psychologically wounded by Mia's death that he or she didn't care about getting caught.

Try not to think about it. She'd lock her bedroom door as a small extra security precaution, read until she was too sleepy to think, and hope to drift off before she could scare herself too badly.

Good luck. No matter how tired she was or how solidly she managed to convince herself that the culprit wouldn't try anything tonight, her mind would still be stuck in an insomnia-inducing whirlpool of thought and emotion, courtesy of this afternoon's conversation with James.

Conversation? Is that what you call a conversation? Clinging to his hand and crying, unable to speak because you're so shaken by what he's telling you and what you're feeling?

Was she freezing time, afraid that moving on—truly moving on—was to betray Mia? *Was* she chaining James to Mia's memory?

Everything he said was accurate. You know he's right, but you don't know how to cope with it.

Maybe you could start by admitting to yourself that you're in love with him.

"Enough," Fiona whispered. "Now is *not* the time to think about this." Whispering—to whom was she talking? Her imaginary friend? She needed to go to bed before she ended up lecturing the walls and yelling at the woodwork.

Time to double-check each window. This afternoon, Rebecca had wedged thick wooden dowels into all the window tracks. Feeling slightly foolish, but wanting the security of heavy steel in her hand, she picked up the crowbar she'd left propped next to the broom and mop. James had probably thought she was kidding when she'd said she'd keep the crowbar with her.

She checked the living room and kitchen windows, then turned down the hallway and went into the study. Everything was secure—or as secure as it ever got in this rickety old house. She stepped into the downstairs bathroom and flicked on the light.

Fiona screamed. Sprawled in the bathtub was a woman with long auburn hair. Her face was pasty white and streaked with red. A blood-ied hammer lay on the floor of the bathtub.

It's another dummy, it's just a dummy. The logical side of Fiona's mind shouted at her as she jerked backward, slamming into the towel rack. *Look at it. It's a dummy.*

Blinking, she stared at the woman, expecting her cleared vision to show another peach-colored balloon, another auburn wig. It *was* a wig—askew, partially covering the face—but it was not a dummy. The face . . . the flesh of the neck . . . the hands . . . the blonde hair exposed where the wig had slipped. Fiona's gaze returned to the face, looking past the pallor, the bloodied wound on the forehead, the streaks of red.

Kimberly Bailey.

Horror vaporized in fury. One step up from a dummy. This time Kimberly had posed herself, waiting for Fiona to find her. She expected Fiona to rush away to call the police; meanwhile, Kimberly thought she could go out the window, leaving Fiona with nightmares and no proof.

"It's *over*, Kimberly." Fiona knew it was foolish to yell at her, but rage and adrenaline ignited the words. She gripped the crowbar, swinging it up to a strike-ready stance in case Kimberly jumped at her. "It's not working this time."

Kimberly didn't move. She was so still—*too* still—was her chest moving at all? *Stop it. She's posing—faking—*

The room smelled of blood. Dizziness buzzed in Fiona's head, and her limbs turned to stone. "Kimberly?" She was faking. She had to be faking. Fiona brought the crowbar forward and jabbed Kimberly in the shoulder. Kimberly didn't react.

"*Kimberly?*" Panicking, Fiona leaned forward and pressed her fingers to Kimberly's throat, feeling for her pulse.

Nothing.

The breath trapped in Fiona's throat splintered into sobs. *The police—call the police—*

She stumbled out of the bathroom, her hand fumbling in the pocket of her pajama pants for the phone she carried with her. The phone slipped out of her fingers and skittered across the hall floor. She bent to retrieve it, swaying as she reached for it. Her shoulder banged into the wall. She was so woozy, it was hard to move. *Get the phone. Get out of the house. Whoever killed her might still be here.*

She grabbed the phone and staggered toward the kitchen. Creaks . . . heavy thuds—someone was coming down the stairs. What was wrong with her legs? She couldn't run—she kept stumbling—

Hands seized her from behind.

Fiona tried to scream, but a surge of dizziness dampened the cry into a moan as the hands dragged her backward. She glimpsed a black mask and dark jacket.

"Don't panic, please don't panic, I'm not going to hurt you." A male voice, rapid words that made no sense; a rough hand wrenching the phone out of her grip. He'd killed Kimberly Bailey . . . Kimberly was dead . . .

The intruder dragged her into the living room and shoved her onto the couch, facedown; the cushions muffled her cry of terror. She couldn't fight him off. Why was she so dizzy? Her arms wouldn't cooperate. Her legs were made of lead. He pulled her arms behind her back and something dug into her wrists. She tried to twist away from him, but her body was too slow, too weak, and his weight pinned her down, crushing her legs.

The weight lifted and she felt his hands on her ankles, yanking them together, binding them. Through the haze dulling her thoughts, Fiona waited for a blow to the head or the burning pain of a knife. Kimberly's blood—Kimberly was dead—

"Who are you?" she whispered.

* * *

What have I done what have I done what have I done? The words blurred in Nick's mind as he stepped back, watching Dr. Claridge wriggle against the makeshift bonds—Kim's white scarf around her wrists, Madison's navy wool scarf around her ankles.

What have I done? When he'd heard her scream then shout Kim's name, he'd panicked. Everything was completely out of whack. What was Kim *doing*? Why had she ignored Nick's attempts to contact her? And she wasn't supposed to go after Claridge before she went to bed. The house was supposed to be dark and Claridge drugged out of her mind. Why hadn't Kim waited? It hadn't been that long since Dr. Claridge had drunk the milk—Nick had heard the fridge open and close. She'd been too alert when Kim had made her move. She'd recognized her. And when he'd come down here and seen Dr. Claridge rushing along the hall, a phone in her hand, Kim nowhere in sight— she was going to call the cops—*Where was Kim?*

Dr. Claridge twisted her head, struggling to look up at him, but he figured all she was seeing was a ski mask, and not clearly. She looked plenty doped now. The drug must work fast. No way would she be able to give the police any identifying details about him.

"Stay quiet and I won't hurt you," he said, trying to sound rough and anonymous. He should gag her, but the two scarves had exhausted his resources, and she didn't look like she was going to scream again anyway—her breathing was shallow, and she looked bleary, her expression a mix of terror and confusion. She kept squeezing her eyes shut and opening them again like she couldn't focus.

Maybe the best way to find out what was going on with Kim was to ask Claridge directly. "What scared you?" he asked. "Why did you scream?"

"I found . . . her. Why did you kill her?"

Nick's nerves froze to threads of ice. "Kill who?"

"Kimberly . . . Kimberly Bailey."

Don't panic. Don't panic. Remember the makeup? She's supposed to look dead.

But she wasn't supposed to look like herself. *She's going to prison,* Nick thought in despair. *We're both going to prison.*

"Where did you see her?" he asked.

Foggy blue eyes stared up at him. "Who are you?"

"Tell me where you saw her."

Dr. Claridge's gaze shifted toward the hallway. "Bathroom. She's . . . the blood . . ."

"Stay still," Nick said. "Stay quiet." He turned on rubbery legs and walked down the hall. The light was on in the bathroom, and he leaned his head through the doorway.

Nausea smashed into his gut.

"Kim. *Kim,* don't do this, this is a joke, right?" He grabbed her by the shoulders and shook her. Her head flopped back; the wig fell off. The blood—that wound on her forehead—and blood covering the side of her head, soaking her hair . . . She hadn't created any fake wounds on her scalp—

"*Kim.*" Nick ripped off a glove and prodded her throat, searching for a pulse, hoping that at any moment, she'd grab his wrist and start laughing.

No pulse. No breath coming from her lips. A bloodstained hammer lay on the bottom of the tub, a few inches away from her.

"Kim." Tears blurred his eyes. Without thinking about what he was doing, Nick slipped his arms behind her back and beneath her knees and started to lift her out of the tub. He couldn't leave her sprawled like that, in that sickening, blood-spattered basin—blood— he was getting her blood on him. *What are you doing? You can't help her now.*

Nick released her and stepped back, blinking tears out of his eyes. His knees shook, and he had to grab the edge of the sink to steady himself. Who had done this to her?

Dr. Claridge.

But you heard her come home. Nick's gaze moved dully around the bathroom. One of the towel racks had been knocked off the wall. The ceramic soap pump lay on the floor, in pieces. The mirror was smashed, countless lines spidering outward from a missing chunk of glass in the right-hand corner. Above where Kim lay, several tiles were broken.

But Nick had heard no sounds of a struggle—no thuds, no shattering glass, no shouts from Kim. Nothing until Claridge had screamed.

Limbs moving mechanically, chest aflame with pain, Nick walked back into the living room. Dr. Claridge lay motionless on the couch, her eyes closed. Could she have come home earlier, killed Kim, gone to dinner with her sister, and then returned home to "find" the body?

No. It hadn't been that long since Kim's last text. The timing didn't work at all.

Just get out. You can't get caught here. Go home and let the police figure it out. Get out.

But his feet didn't move.

Kim. Kim's dead.

Dr. Claridge couldn't have known Kim would be here. If she'd found her unexpectedly and attacked her, there's no way she could have concealed that from her sister. Wasn't her sister staying with her?

But who else would be likely to kill Kim in Dr. Claridge's house?

Nick stared at Dr. Claridge's pale, still face. Trying to think was like trying to throw hoops over those pegs in that carnival game where the hoops never landed right.

"Did you kill her?" he asked.

She didn't stir.

Savagely, Nick shook her shoulder. She opened her eyes.

Nick pulled her to a sitting position and kept her there with his hands gripping her upper arms. "Did you kill her?"

"Mia?" she murmured.

Nick's fingers tightened. Was that a confession? Kim had been dressed as Mia. "Tonight," Nick said. "The girl in the bathroom."

Her head tipped sideways. Nick curved his hand around the back of her head, steadying it. "Kimberly Bailey," he said.

Fear darkened the mist in her eyes. She tried to pull away from him, but the movement was weak and uncoordinated. "Why did you kill her?" she whispered, looking up at Nick.

Nick released her. She slumped onto the couch. He untied Madison's scarf from her ankles and reached for his pocketknife to saw through the scarf around her wrists, but changed his mind. Who cared if he left Kim's scarf? The cops would find all her stuff. Find her stuff and find Kim. He turned and trudged out the back door. The wail of a door alarm followed him as he fled across the yard.

* * *

Madison Brower smeared more makeup around her eyes, trying to conceal the redness, but every time she thought of Kim, more tears welled, undoing her work. *Stop it. You can't look upset before the police tell you what happened.*

How could she ever have thought being questioned by the police would be fun? It had seemed like a game when Kim, grinning, eyes sparkling, had asked Madison to provide an alibi for her and Nick. Madison had imagined herself using all her acting skills to convince frowning officers that Kim and Nick had been with her the whole night, and then laughing later as Kim regaled them with stories of the prank she'd pulled. It was all fun, with just enough risk to make it exciting. Kim had been emphatic that she wasn't going to do anything *really* bad—she was just wreaking a little well-deserved revenge on a stuck-up jerk who richly deserved it. Madison had imagined some bratty ex-boyfriend getting his car filled with sand and maple syrup.

When Nick had come sprinting toward the car where Madison—too cold to stay in Dr. Claridge's yard any longer—was waiting, and had jumped in the car and sped out of the neighborhood without a word to Madison, the look on his face had told her something had gone horribly wrong. They were back at Madison's apartment before Nick could even answer her questions, but finally he'd choked out the words: Kim was dead.

She'd hoped he was joking—hoped *she* was the victim of Kim's prank, that this was all a setup, and in a moment, Kim would pop out of the apartment with a gleeful "Gotcha!" But tears were streaming down Nick's face, and his body shook like crazy as he clutched Madison's hands and told her he'd found Kim in the bathroom, bludgeoned to death with a hammer.

This wasn't a prank.

She'd begged him to stay with her, but he'd taken off, desperate to change out of his clothes—he'd gotten Kim's blood on his jacket—and desperate to vacuum out his car in case any strands of Kim's wig lingered there, and to shove everything in some random Dumpster. They didn't have much time—that alarm on Dr. Claridge's back door would alert the whole neighborhood, and someone was sure to call the cops. "*If the police come talk to you, stick to the story, but leave Kim out of it. You and I were here all evening watching movies. We have no idea what Kim was up to.*"

Kim's blood on Nick's jacket. He'd said he'd panicked and tried to pick her up. That image was so horrible that Madison feared she'd throw up just imagining it.

How long until the police knocked on her door? They'd want to know when she last saw Kim, if Kim had said anything about her plans for tonight, and so on.

I didn't know! she wanted to yell. *I had no idea. I thought it was a silly prank.*

Dr. Claridge must have killed Kim. She'd seen Kim in her freaky ghost costume and she'd lost control. *But that doesn't make sense. You heard that car pull up; you heard Dr. Claridge talking to her sister while they walked up to the house. Kim must have already been dead, or she would have answered Nick's texts—*

"You don't have to figure it out," Madison whispered, staring at her puffy-eyed face in the mirror. "You just have to stick to the story." She ought to go to bed. It was nearly midnight, and if the cops did come tonight, it would seem less suspicious if their knock awakened her. Plus, sleep would help excuse her bloodshot eyes.

Someone rapped on the front door and Madison jumped, dropping the tube of concealer into the sink.

I can't do this. I can't. They'll know I'm lying. I'll get arrested.

Another knock, harder this time. Soon they'd be shouting, "*Police! Open the door!*" and the whole complex would hear. *What does that matter? Do you think you can keep it a secret that Kim was murdered?*

Desperate, Madison splashed cold water on her face, patted her eyes dry with a towel, and went to answer the door.

Chapter 22

SITTING ON THE COLD STONE bench in the hotel courtyard, Fiona closed her eyes and breathed in the damp air, fighting to keep a grip on the last fragments of her self-control. It had taken an hour of arguing and persuading to get Rebecca to consent to let her go outside alone. After spending most of the day in a hotel room, she'd desperately needed the fresh air—and needed a few moments alone to sort out her thoughts. Rebecca had been worried but had conceded there was no way Kimberly Bailey's murderer could know where Fiona was staying right now.

Oncoming rain had rendered the courtyard deserted, to Fiona's relief. The wind tore at her hair, blowing wisps across her face. Inside her head, everything seemed broken and random, as though the circuits in her brain no longer connected. All she had were separate, terrifying images: Kimberly, blood dripping down her face, her clothes like Mia's; the dark-masked intruder; Kimberly smiling at her at the jogging track; Detective Reid's freckled face; the set of car keys in that first package; Kimberly yelling about how unfair Fiona was; the auburn-haired dummy in the driver's seat of a car.

Raindrops spattered her head. At any moment, Rebecca would be out there hauling her inside. Bless Rebecca, turning around and driving back to Bennett to rescue Fiona again.

James. Did he know about any of this? She wanted to call him, but Detective Reid had asked that she not contact anyone outside the family for the time being.

"Fiona."

At the sound of her name, she turned to see a familiar face—worried hazel eyes, long light brown hair drawn back in a ponytail.

"*Shannon.*" Jerkily, Fiona rose to her feet. "When did you—how did you get here?"

"I flapped my arms really fast. How do you think I got here?" Her older sister threw her arms around Fiona and squeezed hard. "Let's get inside before we're drenched." With her hand on Fiona's arm, Shannon hurried her toward the hotel. Fiona mopped away the tears on her cheeks, hoping any passersby would take them for raindrops.

Rebecca was waiting near the door to the hotel suite. Without asking permission, she pulled Fiona's jacket off and wrapped her in a blanket. Fiona wanted to say she was fine, it wasn't that cold, but Rebecca's pampering was comforting.

Shannon guided her to the couch. "Oh, Fiona, I'm so sorry." Shannon sat next to her and wrapped her arm around Fiona, her cheek against Fiona's hair. Rebecca sat on the other side and held Fiona's hand.

Any thought she'd had of reining in her emotions dissolved in the warmth of the women on either side of her. She sagged against her sisters and cried in a way she hadn't cried since Mia's death, her shoulders heaving, her sobs so wild that she was gasping for air. Her sisters held her, their arms intertwining. Shannon wiped her face, tossing aside each tissue as she soaked it; Rebecca stroked her hair and rubbed the back of her neck, her voice a soothing murmur. "Good girl, let it out, let it go."

Fiona couldn't have stopped it even if she'd wanted to; she could only let the pain flood out until her muscles were slack, her eyes swollen and her throat raw. When the tears finally stopped, she was so weary she couldn't move. Shannon had to steady her head so she could drink from the glass of water Rebecca pressed to her lips.

"Do you want to lie down?" Shannon asked.

"I'm okay," Fiona rasped.

Shannon smoothed damp hair back from Fiona's face. "Let me help you into bed."

"No. I'll . . . sit here. I'm . . . sorry about your shirt."

Shannon touched the soaked fabric covering her shoulder and smiled. "It'll dry."

"Hello, she has three kids," Rebecca said. "Do you think she wears dry-clean only? Come on, lie down. Here—" Rebecca grabbed a throw pillow and put it on her lap. "Put her here, Shan."

Fiona would have found it easier to protest if her head hadn't been throbbing and her muscles made of jelly. At Shannon's hands, she soon found herself full-length on the couch with her head resting on the pillow on Rebecca's lap and the blanket covering her.

"Good thing you're not having twins," Fiona murmured. "Or there wouldn't be any room for me."

Rebecca laughed. Her fingers rubbed Fiona's forehead, easing the headache. "You up to a report?" she asked. "Detective Reid called while you were outside."

"What did he say?"

"They've got a warrant for the arrest of Kimberly Bailey's cousin, Nicholas Cortez."

Startled, Fiona started to sit up. "Her cousin!"

"Lie down." Rebecca pressed Fiona back onto her lap.

Fiona sank into the pillow and the comfort of Rebecca's fingers kneading her scalp. "Do they think he killed Kimberly? I thought they suspected him of helping her."

"He did help her," Rebecca reported. "They questioned Kimberly's roommate—who was also Nicholas's girlfriend—last night. At first she claimed they'd been at her place watching movies all evening, but under pressure, she cracked. Apparently what happened at your house started as Kimberly's final prank on you. Nicholas didn't want to help her, but she blackmailed him into it—according to the girlfriend, Kimberly had some secrets on him. Kimberly drugged your milk to make you too woozy to sort fantasy from reality and planned to haunt you while she was dressed as Mia Hardy. She wanted to scare you half to death and warn you to stay away from James."

Fiona blinked swollen eyelids. "To stay away from James?"

"Apparently Kimberly was obsessed with him and jealous of you."

"Nicholas was the one in the mask," Fiona murmured.

"Yes, the girlfriend said that was him. Apparently he was hiding in the house when we got home."

Fiona shuddered. While she'd been walking around checking windows, he'd already been in the house. "So Detective Reid said he . . . killed Kimberly?"

"Detective Reid wasn't saying, but I got the impression . . . well, he said the girlfriend admitted Nicholas was furious with Kimberly.

I got the feeling Reid thinks Kimberly tried to manipulate Nicholas one too many times, and he lost his temper, and . . . anyway, Reid said they do have some evidence—he didn't say what."

"That was my hammer," Fiona said, her throat burning as she pictured the bloodied hammer lying in the bathtub. "I'd been using it to nail the new baseboards in place. I'd left it in the hallway."

"That's awful." Rebecca stroked her hair. "He must have seen the hammer, and he was so angry with her . . . they probably argued . . . he never meant to hurt her . . ."

"Poor girl," Shannon said. "I feel sorry for both of them. But at least . . . it's over."

It is *over*, Fiona realized. No more tension, no more fear, wondering what Kimberly's next nightmarish move would be. It was over, but at a hideously high price.

"Can Fiona go home?" Shannon asked. "Or are they worried Nicholas Cortez might . . . bother her?"

"I'm not worried about that," Fiona said. "If he wanted to hurt me, he would have done it last night."

"You can go home," Rebecca said. "Detective Reid said they're done with the house and it's been—cleaned."

Fiona tried not to picture someone scrubbing Kimberly Bailey's blood off the tub.

"Do you *want* to go home?" Shannon asked. "You ought to take some time off. Come to Nevada with me."

"Or to Connecticut with me," Rebecca offered. "It's much closer. And I'm a nicer person."

"I have two nieces and a nephew for you to play with," Shannon countered with a smile.

"I have peace and quiet," Rebecca fired back.

"I'm a better cook."

"I have two pounds of Swiss chocolate."

"Truce." Fiona sat up. "Thank you both, but I want to go home."

Shannon studied her, anxiety in her eyes. "Fiona . . . are you *sure*?"

"I need to get back to normal, and I have a job I need to get back to."

"She has a *James* she needs to get back to," Rebecca said, and she and Shannon got matching smirks on their faces.

Fiona felt herself blushing. "That isn't—"

"This is the part where she claims they're just friends," Rebecca stage-whispered. "Which is a complete lie."

"You are such a—"

"Now that you have clearance from Detective Reid—he said it's okay for you to talk to James—I'm sure you'd like to call him. Shan, grab my phone off the dresser, will you? Fiona's phone is at her house."

Shannon snatched the phone and offered it to Fiona.

To avoid giving her sisters any satisfaction, Fiona thought about pretending she wasn't desperate to talk to James, but she rejected that idea in a millisecond and touched the buttons.

"Maybe we should take a walk, Becca," Shannon suggested.

"It's not going to be that kind of conversation!" Fiona protested, but Rebecca and Shannon were already heading for the door.

* * *

Giggles, squeals, and roars led Carissa to the bedroom David and Jacob shared. She stood in the doorway, watching the chaos. On the floor, the two boys were climbing all over Brad, bouncing on his back, messing up his hair, tickling his sock-covered feet. He'd lie still for a moment, then rear up, roaring, and grab one of the boys to tickle him. The shrieking and laughing were enough to be heard in the next time zone; it was a miracle Peter hadn't awakened.

Watching Brad wrestle with the boys made everything seem so wonderfully *normal*. Brad used to play with the boys all the time—nothing delighted David, Jacob, and Peter more than a wrestling session with Dad.

She'd planned to talk to Brad as soon as all the boys were in bed, to ask him what was going on. Had Tina Merrion talked to him? Did Tina consider Brad a suspect in Linda's death? The police couldn't be *too* suspicious of him, or he wouldn't be walking around in uniform, carrying a gun—or maybe they suspected him, but didn't have enough evidence to suspend him. Did he know if they still suspected Carissa? Did he know anything about what was happening to Fiona? And why hadn't he told her Linda Taylor had accused him of being under the influence of alcohol when he gave her that ticket?

Brad noticed her in the doorway and sat up. The boys collapsed on the carpet, panting and giggling.

"We're busted, guys," he said. "It's bedtime."

Looking into his face, Carissa could see the strain beneath the joking—he was *trying* to relax a little, trying to make things feel normal for the boys. Suddenly she couldn't bear the thought of bringing up painful subjects tonight. Let him have one evening that wasn't riddled with stress.

"It's okay," she said. "They can stay up for a few more minutes. I'll go finish the dishes."

"Tickle attack!" Jacob yelled and both boys tackled Brad. Carissa retreated, smiling while tears stung her eyes. How many more father-sons happy family moments would she get to witness? In the future, would those moments take place out of her sight while the boys were at their father's house and Carissa was living elsewhere? Would their family crack in half, splitting along the fissure she'd created? How could she have been so selfish? Brad was an incredibly good man, and a wonderful father. And she'd forgotten that—for a few evenings of flirting, she'd forgotten it.

She finished sweeping the kitchen floor and tied the top of the full garbage sack. Was it still raining? Drops still clung to the window glass, but she couldn't hear the patter of falling rain. Without trading her rubber-soled slippers for sturdier shoes, she headed for the trash cans by the side of the house. The motion-sensitive lights flared, illuminating puddles on the brick path. She *should* have put on better shoes.

As she reached the cans, something hard crunched beneath her foot, poking at the sole of her slipper. She bent and picked it up. A piece of amber glass. A few more pieces were scattered near the trash can. Puzzled, Carissa lifted a chunk of glass containing most of the label.

A beer bottle? What was a beer bottle doing in her side yard? Maybe Brad had picked it up—he was the type of guy who'd clean up someone else's litter. But it wasn't like him to drop a bottle to the sidewalk and only pick up some of the broken pieces.

She opened the lid of the trash can. More pieces of broken glass were scattered on top of the other bags of trash. A sack caught her attention—a sack from a grocery store Carissa rarely patronized; it was farther from home than the store she preferred. She poked the grocery sack and heard the clink of bottles hitting together.

She set her bag of kitchen trash on the sidewalk and reached for the grocery sack. Inside it were three empty beer bottles and a crumpled sourdough pretzel bag. Sourdough pretzels. Brad's favorite snack.

Maybe he'd gone out with some of his work friends after that elders quorum presidency meeting last night. She didn't know what time he'd arrived home—she'd been sound asleep, for once—but she hadn't gone to bed until ten, and usually his meetings didn't run that late. He must have gone out afterward. *The pretzels are Brad's; the beer belongs to the friends. Brad was driving, so the trash ended up in his car.*

But what kind of outing would involve Brad's bringing the trash home—as opposed to his friends throwing away their bottles at the bowling alley or sports bar or wherever they'd been hanging out? And it was strange that Brad would break a bottle and not pick up all the pieces. He was usually so meticulous.

Tina Merrion's report on Linda's allegation that Brad was drinking dug deeper into her thoughts.

That's ridiculous. Absolutely ridiculous. Brad would never touch alcohol. Linda just couldn't handle the fact that he'd cited her for speeding. Besides, I certainly would have noticed if he had alcohol on his breath.

Assuming he got close enough to me for me to notice.

Shivering in the chill wind, Carissa stared at the grocery sack. She ought to ask Brad about the bottles. He wouldn't mind. He'd tell her which friend they belonged to, and she could uproot these illogical worries.

After another moment of hesitation, she reached into the trash can and pulled out the grocery sack along with the tied trash bag she'd put there yesterday morning. Compulsively, Carissa grabbed the next trash sack in the can. Beneath it lay a damp paper bag with a rolled top that Carissa knew she hadn't put there. She grabbed the sack and opened it. It contained half a dozen crushed Heineken cans.

Pulse thudding, she threw all the trash back into the can and shoved the lid down tight. *What's wrong with you? They're not his! Brad would never drink.*

So why don't you just go ask him where those cans and bottles came from?

Chapter 23

"*THAT* WAS FUN," JAMES MUTTERED under his breath as he and Fiona exited the administration building housing President Kregg's office.

"I'm just hoping they're as successful at keeping this low key as they'd like to be." After a two-hour-long meeting in the president's office, Fiona was already so tired that she wanted to go home and sleep—and it was only ten o'clock in the morning. At least the damp, cool wind against her face was refreshing, though the dark clouds in the sky reminded her that she'd forgotten her umbrella.

"Rumors will spread," James said. "They can't stop that."

"Both the Hawkins administration and her parents will want as little of this to be made public as possible. Did you see how sketchy the article in the paper was this morning? Kimberly was found dead under suspicious circumstances, and the police are seeking her cousin, Nicholas Cortez, for questioning. Period. No mention of me, no mention of Kimberly's vendetta, no mention of you."

"The truth will get out—or some version of it." He shook his head. "Walk you to your office?"

"Thank you."

They were walking up the stairs to the Gilmore Building before James spoke again. "I still can't believe . . . I wish I could have broken through to Kimberly before it was too late."

"You tried, James."

"Tried and failed." He pushed up his glasses and rubbed his eyes. "I'm sick about this."

"At least you tried. If I'd done a better job of connecting with her in class, maybe this downward spiral would never have begun."

"Kimberly's choices are not your fault."

"I know. But I wish I'd tried harder to reach out to her."

"I'm sure her parents feel the same way." From the grim tone of his voice, Fiona knew he was thinking of the conversation he'd reported on in their meeting: Kimberly's mother had called him yesterday and had torn into him, demanding to know if he'd been messing around with Kimberly or if he'd led her on in any way.

Fiona unlocked her office and stepped inside. James followed her and closed the door.

"Are you okay?" Fiona asked. "That must have been awful to have Kimberly's mother interrogating you like that."

James shrugged. "Given the circumstances, I understand why she'd wonder about me. Same kind of questions the police and the Hawkins crew are asking."

"Please tell me the police don't think—"

"I don't think they do. I don't think Kregg does either, but . . . if rumors . . . it's a good thing I know how to flip burgers and bus tables, if it comes to that."

Fiona rested her hand on his arm. "James, you're not going to get fired over Kimberly's obsession."

"I hope you're right." James interlaced his fingers with hers. "But weren't you the one reminding me the other day that you don't have to be responsible for a scandal to get thrown out over it?" He groaned. "And here I am worrying about my job when Kimberly is dead and her cousin is wanted for murder. I don't think my problems will win any contests."

"I'm grateful they haven't accused me of murder," Fiona said. "If Nicholas hadn't left me tied up, I'm sure I would have been their first suspect."

"But Rebecca was with you the whole night."

"Not the whole night. And if Kimberly died right before I got home, the window for the time of death might have included—" She shivered. "Never mind. I don't want to talk about this."

"How are you holding up?"

"I'm on my feet and I'm coherent. I can't ask for more than that yet."

"May I take you and your sisters to dinner tonight?"

"You're sweet, but I suspect Shannon already has something planned—if I can get her and Rebecca to put the catalogs down. They've decided my yard needs some new bushes and flowers and they're on a landscape-planning frenzy. I don't have the heart to tell them that anything they plant will die of neglect after they leave."

James grinned. "Shannon doesn't have anything planned for tonight. I already talked to your sisters."

"You did?" Fiona felt her cheeks reddening as she wondered if James and her sisters had discussed anything besides dinner. She slipped her hand out of James's grasp. "In that case, it's a deal."

"Cheesecake for dessert afterwards. *My* cheesecake. Homemade."

"You made cheesecake?"

"Couldn't sleep last night. Baking seemed like a better idea than pacing."

"I know the feeling. Maybe I'll bake cookies next time insomnia hits."

"I'd better go," he said. "Got an appointment with a student."

"Thank you, James. For everything."

He squeezed her shoulder. "Take care, Fiona." He exited and closed the door behind him.

Fiona took out her laptop and sat at her desk, but instead of starting on her backlogged work, she sat thinking about the sadness in James's eyes. He'd known a different side of Kimberly than Fiona had—a smart, funny young woman, a top student. She could have had a wonderful future.

Kimberly dead . . . her cousin accused of murder . . . it would tear that family apart. Fiona rested her forehead against her fingertips and closed her eyes.

A knock on the door brought her head up. Grateful for an alternative to being alone with her thoughts, she called, "Come in."

The door swung open. A young man with his chin covered in dark stubble stepped into her office and, without asking permission, closed the door behind him. He looked familiar, but it wasn't until his hand came forward, brandishing a knife, that Fiona recognized him from pictures Detective Reid had shown her.

Nicholas Cortez.

"Don't scream," he said. "If you stay quiet, I swear I won't hurt you."

Fiona silently exhaled the huge breath she'd drawn. Screaming would be futile. There was no way help could get to her before Nicholas did.

"I won't hurt you," he repeated. He was breathing so fast he was almost gasping. "I promise, I won't hurt you. I just need to talk to you."

Fiona wanted to push back from her desk to put more distance between herself and the long blade of the kitchen knife in his hand, but she feared if she moved, it might set Nicholas off. "If all you want to do is talk, put the knife down."

"If I put it down, do you swear you'll talk to me?"

"Yes."

"You'll hear me out? You won't scream or call the police until we're done?"

"I promise."

"I guess you wouldn't lie about that." Nicholas laughed crazily. "Someone as honest as you, right? No mercy on plagiarists? Though Kim swore you lied about the accident."

"Put the knife down, Nicholas."

"It's Nick. The only person who calls me Nicholas is—is—is Aunt Donna—" Another ragged laugh escaped. He was shaking, Fiona realized, the knife jiggling in his grip.

Too scared to decide if Nick's agitation made it more or less likely that he'd sink the knife into her chest, Fiona tried to sound calm and firm. "Drop the knife and we'll talk."

His teeth clenched as panic contorted his face. "Don't scream. Please don't scream. I've got to tell you . . . it's not how it looks—the police are wrong—"

"I'll start listening as soon as that knife is on my desk."

He slapped the knife onto the desk and shoved it toward Fiona. That complete of a capitulation startled her. Before he could change his mind, she snatched the knife and dropped it into her center desk drawer.

"I'm sorry. I'm sorry about the knife. I didn't know how else to get you to give me a chance, to keep you from screaming for help the second you saw me. I know the police think I'm a killer—"

Fiona wondered if he'd slept since Kimberly's death. His eyes were bloodshot with bluish shadows beneath them. "Sit down," she said. He took a step backward and slumped into one of the chairs facing her desk.

"You don't have one of those panic buttons back there, do you?" he asked. "Like in a bank?"

"Does that sound like standard Hawkins office equipment to you?"

"Guess not." He rubbed his eyes with the heels of his hands. "I didn't kill Kim."

Why did he feel the need to protest his innocence to her? "Tell me what happened."

He described getting Kim's message, going to the rendezvous, going to Fiona's house, and ending up in the closet. "When you screamed, I knew something was really wrong. Kim hadn't answered any of my texts, and no way would she have ignored me when I was in your house hollering her name—she would have come out to shut me up. Plus, she never would have made her move so early. I came running downstairs and saw you were about to call the cops—I panicked—you remember this part, right?"

"Most of it." Fiona's frantic heartbeat was starting to slow. It seemed Nicholas *did* want a listening ear, not a victim. "It gets blurry."

"After you told me where she was, I went and . . . at first I thought she was faking. When I realized she wasn't, I . . . freaked out. I picked her up—got her blood on me, my fingerprints everywhere—I'd taken my glove off to check for a pulse." The nervous flush in his face had faded; he was chalk white. "Ah, Kim, you dumb little . . ." He choked on the words and jammed his fingers against his eyelids.

Fiona waited for him to regain control of himself, but when it looked like that wouldn't happen soon, she asked quietly, "When was the last time you ate or slept?"

Nick mopped his face with the sleeve of his sweatshirt. "Uh . . . I ate a . . . handful of crackers at the apartment where I swiped the knife. Only had like . . . five bucks on me when I ran. I've been scared to show my face in too many places . . . saw my picture in the paper . . ."

Fiona opened a desk drawer. "I have some . . . let's see . . . grape juice, an apple, and a muffin. Here." She put the items on the desk where Nick could reach them.

He swiped more tears away. "Thanks." He grabbed the juice, tore off the lid, and gulped.

"Nick," she said, "you need to turn yourself in."

"I know." His voice was still shaking, but he looked calmer. "I had to talk to you first. You've got to understand what happened. I did *not kill Kim.*" He ripped the muffin wrapper.

Fiona waited until he'd finished devouring the muffin before she said, "You and Kimberly were close?"

"Yeah. Since we were born, just about. Grew up together. I never would have hurt her. I *threatened* to, plenty of times." His mouth twisted in an expression that was half humor, half anguish. "She could be a total punk. But I never meant it. What do the cops think happened?"

Was there any reason she shouldn't tell him this? She decided to be candid. "That you fought with Kimberly. Your girlfriend said you were furious with her for forcing you to participate in this . . . stunt at my house. I don't think anyone believes it was premeditated. They think you lost your temper."

"Maddie . . . poor Maddie . . . should've known she couldn't lie to the cops over something this big . . . she was a wreck when I told her what happened to Kim. Does she think I killed her?"

"I don't know."

Nick bit a chunk out of the apple. "I didn't kill her," he mumbled through a mouthful of apple. "And I know you didn't kill her. I would've heard a fight if it'd been you."

"You need to tell the police your side of the story. Running away doesn't exactly make you look innocent."

"I panicked, okay? When I realized I'd left my fingerprints there and I'd gotten her blood on—and I saw the cops coming to my door—I took off. Out the back window. Later I . . . came back . . . asked my roommate—he told me what the cops had said and I could tell they thought I killed her . . ." Anger exploded in his eyes. "I *told* Kim it was a rotten idea. I *warned* her, over and over, but she was nuts. She couldn't see anything but how much she hated you. But it was more about Dr. Hampton than about that grade. She thought she was in love with him, and it made her crazy that you two were together."

Fiona almost corrected him but decided trying to explain her relationship with James was beside the point.

"And when you crashed your car and told the police she was responsible, she snapped," Nick said.

"I did not tell the police she was responsible. I told them what happened. They drew their own conclusions."

"Look, all I know is she didn't have anything to do with it, and neither did I. Yeah, she did the packages with those cheesy notes, but we didn't have anything to do with any car wreck."

"The rock thrown at my door? The camera in my office?"

Nick hesitated then gave a jerky shrug. "Yeah, whatever, that stuff was us. But not the car crash."

Fiona studied Nick's haggard face. She could understand why he wouldn't want to admit to causing the accident—it was a far more serious charge than chucking a rock at Fiona's door. But it seemed so futile to admit to some of Kimberly's stunts and deny the rest.

Nick devoured the rest of the apple. Finished, he set the core on the empty muffin wrapper.

"You admit you and Kimberly used Mia Hardy's memory against me before and after the accident," Fiona said. "But somehow, in the middle of it, someone *else* stole Kimberly's theme and set up an accident with a blood-soaked dummy made to look like Mia Hardy. Is that correct?"

Nick frowned. "A dummy?"

"In the car, with a note from 'Mia.' That sounds like Kimberly's touch to me."

"Maybe, yeah, but it *wasn't her.*"

"What about the circuit breaker?"

"Huh?"

"Breaking into my house. Tampering with the circuit breaker."

"We never did anything like that."

"Maybe Kimberly—"

"Are you kidding? She had no clue how to spring a lock." Nick's eyes brightened, and the look of growing excitement on his face confused Fiona. "This is *it.* I knew it. That's what I thought; that's why I came to you." He laughed, sounding so relieved that Fiona wondered if his sanity had fractured. "Someone else *is* after you. Who is it?"

"I—have no idea what—"

"Kim must have run into someone at your house. That's why she tried to call things off, sending me that text telling me to come get her."

"Why wouldn't she have run out of the house?"

"Not sure. I thought about it. I'll bet the killer blocked her escape, so she locked herself in that bathroom."

"But that's hardly a secure—"

"She wouldn't have thought she was in danger of getting killed—just detained and arrested. You don't assume everyone you meet is Jason from *Friday the 13th,* right?"

True. Fiona swallowed, wishing she had some of that grape juice she'd given Nick. Her throat was parched.

"I'm guessing she texted me quick so I'd be there to get her. That window in the bathroom is big enough for her, right? She was pretty small. I'll bet she thought she could climb out while the killer was off calling the cops on her, but he broke in before she could do it."

Fiona thought of a couple of facts Reid had told her: the safety bar in the window track had been removed, and loose paint chips from the old window frame lay in the track, indicating Kimberly might have jerked at the stubborn old window trying to open it. And damage near the flimsy door lock made it clear the assailant had kicked his or her way in.

Nick pushed his hands through his hair, leaving it even more disheveled. "That killer was there for *you.* Kim must have surprised him—or her."

"That's insane. There's no reason to think—"

"*Who is it?*" He leaned toward her and Fiona tensed, ready to grab the knife from her desk drawer if she needed to defend herself.

"Sorry." He sank back, raising both hands. "I didn't mean to scare you again. But I swear to you, I did *not* kill Kim. And we had nothing to do with your accident and whatever happened to your circuit breaker. If *you're* telling the truth, someone else is after you. That's got to be who killed Kim. Which means you're in big trouble. So who's mad at you? Who else besides Kim wanted to cut your throat?"

A sick feeling of *not again* made it hard for Fiona to respond. She'd been so sure it was over. *But why should you believe him about the accident, about Kimberly's death, about anything?*

"Who's mad at you?" Nick repeated. "Kim told me about that woman who thought you were sleeping with her husband. Alan."

"She came and apologized and admitted she was wrong, which you should know if you checked the final transmission from that camera you planted."

"Maybe she was faking you out," Nick suggested.

"I thought of that," Fiona conceded. "But it's a stretch to imagine—"

"Hey, that makes sense. If it was a woman Kim met there, maybe that's why she didn't think she was in real danger. She wouldn't see another woman as a big threat."

Fiona pictured Summer. She wasn't a big woman—probably not much taller than petite Kimberly—but she looked like she was in good shape. "Maybe," she said. "But I already gave her name to the police."

"But since they think I killed Kim, they wouldn't have even thought of her this time around. And what about this Alan guy? Does he have a grudge against you?"

Fiona tried to picture Alan creating a dummy of Mia Hardy and dousing it in red paint, or bludgeoning Kimberly with a hammer. "I . . . it's difficult to imagine . . ." He'd begged her for help, and she'd pushed him away. She'd snatched the pearl hair comb back, the object he'd treasured all these years, and stalked out of his house, completely rejecting him. His mental health was troubled. And with the shock of his mother's recent death . . .

Fiona's mouth was so dry she couldn't speak. She swallowed. *No.* Not Alan.

Nick grinned. It was a wild expression, but filled with relief. "Could have been him, huh? Yeah, I can tell you're thinking it. You've *got* to tell all this to the cops."

She swallowed again, unsticking her dry tongue from the roof of her mouth. "I have. I will. But it wasn't him." Alan would never want to hurt her or anyone else. He was *not* a violent man. "Let me call the police. Now."

Nick's grin crumpled. Slouching in his chair, he rubbed his eyes. "Yeah. I . . . okay. This is going to be great. Getting marched across campus in handcuffs."

"If it would be easier for you, I can tell Detective Reid we'll meet him on the east side of campus at the back of the faculty lot. You'll have less of an audience there."

"*We'll* meet—you'll come with me?"

"Yes. Obviously there are some things I need to discuss with Detective Reid."

"Prison," Nick mumbled. "If Kim were alive, I'd kill her. I told her we'd end up in the slammer."

"Nick . . . Dr. Hampton has taken some heat over this. Questions about possible involvement with Kimberly."

"What? Sheesh! No. He didn't do anything. That was the whole problem—Kim was loony over him and he wouldn't even look at her."

"Will you confirm to the police—"

"Yeah, yeah. I'll clear his good name. Whatever."

Fiona reached cautiously for the phone on her desk, her eyes monitoring Nick. "I'm calling now."

Nick nodded. Fiona picked up the phone.

"You're a lot nicer than I thought you'd be," he muttered. "I don't know what Kim's problem was."

Chapter 24

"Unreal, James." Rebecca took another forkful of chocolate cheesecake, a dreamy expression in her eyes. "Mmm, this is divine."

"Got the recipe from my grandmother." James lifted a bite of cheesecake on his fork and displayed it as though it were the Mona Lisa. "She swore if I could do chocolate well, I'd have my pick of women. So far, her theory has been total bunk, but the cheesecake is good."

Rebecca and Shannon both laughed. Fiona smiled, but laughter didn't come. She couldn't break her thoughts away from Nicholas Cortez and his frantic protests that he hadn't killed Kimberly—that someone else had, someone who was after Fiona. And even if she did manage to shift her thoughts for a moment, they turned directly to thoughts of Kimberly dying a few yards from where Fiona was sitting.

Shannon glanced at her, and Fiona widened her smile. "This *is* delicious, James," she said, knowing if she let her anxiety show, the conversation would instantly turn back to Nick's visit this afternoon. She didn't want to talk about it right now. She'd already scared everyone enough with her report of Nick and his knife, and they'd spent all of dinner discussing it—a dinner switched at the last minute from a restaurant to takeout in Fiona's dining room, since no one felt like going out in public after Nick's visit.

Neither Rebecca nor Shannon had seemed to put any credence in Nick's words—naturally he would protest his innocence, no matter how obvious it was that he'd killed his cousin. Nick had admitted that he and Kimberly had been tormenting Fiona, and it was beyond comprehension to think that more than one person might have targeted her simultaneously. Kimberly and Nicholas were guilty, period. Nick was in jail. There was no reason to be afraid any longer.

What did James think? She was having trouble reading him. Outwardly, he'd seemed to agree with Rebecca and Shannon, but his eyes wore a veiled expression very atypical for him, and Fiona had the feeling there were things he didn't want to say.

"Would anyone like a glass of water?" Fiona asked.

"Me," Rebecca said. "Rich desserts always make me thirsty. But I'll get it."

"I've got it." Fiona rose to her feet, trying not to move stiffly lest both sisters leap up to serve her. "Shannon?"

"Thanks."

Fiona headed into the kitchen. The scrape of a chair and footsteps behind her told her James was following her.

She opened the freezer and took out an ice cube tray. "Have to do this the old-fashioned way," she remarked, twisting the tray. "Needless to say, the kitchen isn't plumbed for water to the fridge."

James took four glasses out of the cupboard and set them on the counter. "You doing okay?" he asked, his voice low.

"Yes." She dropped ice cubes into the glasses. "No. I'm faking it. I have one frayed thread left holding my nerves together."

"I thought so." James's hand closed on her shoulder. "Every time I think about that kid pulling a knife on you—"

"He wouldn't have hurt me. Besides, he's in custody. We don't have to worry about him."

"Do you believe him? That he didn't kill Kimberly?"

So that's why James had followed her—he wanted to see if she'd be more candid without her sisters listening. "Half of me wants to believe him."

"So half of you *doesn't* want to believe him?"

Fiona thought of Nicholas crying in her office. "I don't want him to have his cousin's death on his conscience. I'm not sure what to think."

James's grip tightened on her shoulder. "If *he* didn't kill her—"

"I know. I've been through it all with Detective Reid. But if it wasn't Nicholas, who was it? I can't believe Summer or . . . well, I suppose anything's possible."

"I don't think it's wise for you to be staying here right now." James lowered his hand. "You should go back to the hotel."

"Shannon got a handyman out to replace that rickety back door and install a dead bolt, and a security company came today—the whole place is so wired that I can hardly twitch without setting off alarms. No one's getting inside without the police here to meet them. The police *and* Rebecca and Shannon with baseball bats. Or, once my parents get here on Monday, it'll be my father with the bat."

"Your parents are coming?"

"Yes. They wanted to come sooner, but my mother just had minor surgery and needed a few days to recover. I tried to tell them I'm fine, but they want to see me."

"I still think you should go to the hotel. I'm not just talking about the possibility that you're in danger here. I'm talking about what you experienced."

"That's why I can't leave."

"I don't understand."

Fiona took two glasses to the sink and filled them. "If I run away now because I can't cope with the fact that Kimberly was murdered here, I'm afraid I'll never be able to cope."

"What do you mean?"

"It won't be my house anymore—it will be her tomb. I can't let that happen. I've got to push through this."

"I think you're pushing yourself to run too fast."

She set the glasses on the counter. "I know how I can get, James. After Mia, I . . . there was so much I couldn't do, so many places I couldn't go—still can't go—because they remind me of her. I shut myself off—it took me a year and a half before I could even get behind the wheel of a car, and even then, I had so many panic attacks that I didn't think I'd ever be able to . . . and then when I started backsliding last weekend . . . and now after what's happened . . . *no*. I'm not going that route. This is *my* house. I don't care if I don't get a wink of sleep for the next month. I'm staying here."

James touched her cheek. "Okay. I understand. And I feel better knowing you won't be alone. I just wish the police could confirm whether or not Nicholas Cortez is guilty or if Kimberly really did run into someone else here."

"I can't picture Summer—or anyone else—lurking in my house, waiting to attack me." She looked away from James's probing gaze, unable to openly state that she'd wondered about Alan.

"Maybe whoever was here wasn't planning to attack you," James suggested. "Maybe they were here for a different reason, but when Kimberly surprised them, they panicked."

"What kind of reason?"

"Maybe—searching for something?"

"Searching for what?" Fiona picked up the other two glasses. "I don't have much worth stealing, unless there's a black market for caulk and paint stripper that I haven't heard about."

"I hope this doesn't offend you," James said. "But Alan Taylor has made it clear that his feelings for you are less than healthy. That comb he stole and hoarded all those years—the way he acted when you found it—you can't tell me you haven't wondered about him."

Words came painfully. "I did . . . think about him. Detective Reid already knows the whole story. He's probably already checked Alan and Summer out. I wish it didn't have to be this way. I doubt Summer or Alan was involved with any of this, and getting questioned about it is going to drive them further apart."

"Are you still waiting for happily-ever-after for Alan and Summer?"

Fiona sighed. "Summer still loves him."

"Which isn't going to do her a lot of good if he's obsessed with you."

"But with Linda gone . . ."

"Linda's death didn't immediately heal all the damage she did to their relationship." James looked strained and tired, as though away from Shannon and Rebecca, he didn't feel the need to keep up a cheerful façade. "Maybe they'll get through this. Maybe they won't. It's not your problem. And I think you need to stay as far away from Alan as you can. Maybe you—"

The doorbell rang. Fiona and James looked at each other.

"Want me to take care of that?" James asked.

Fiona shook her head. "I'll answer it. But come with me." It probably sounded pathetic that she wanted moral support to answer her own door, but James nodded and followed her along the hallway.

The sight of Alan standing on her porch gave Fiona the startled, guilty feeling that she'd been gossiping only to turn and see the victim of her gossip standing behind her. "Alan," she said.

"I apologize for intruding." His tone was courteous, but his gaze kept jerking from Fiona to James, and he looked ill—face flushed and eyes fever-bright.

"You're not intruding," Fiona said, automatically polite, but as she spoke the words, she realized they were a mistake. Even politeness might give him the impression that she was glad to see him, and the last thing she wanted to do was create false hope. The wind blasted a gust of rain under the porch overhang, and Fiona shivered. Alan was getting soaked.

"What do you want?" James spoke flatly, moving to stand beside her.

Alan gave him a hard look. "I need to talk to Fiona."

"I think Fiona has already said everything she wants to say to you." James edged a little in front of her. This behavior was surprisingly protective—almost aggressive—for James, and Fiona realized he'd meant what he said when he'd suggested Alan as a suspect in Kimberly's murder. Standing here looking at Alan's familiar face made that thought seem ludicrous. She'd never known Alan to be violent in any way.

"Maybe you ought to let her speak for herself." Alan's voice got louder, surprising Fiona—she'd never heard Alan raise his voice. "Are you afraid of what she might say?"

Fiona touched James's arm, not wanting him to respond and escalate this confrontation. "I'm sorry, Alan, but I don't have anything to discuss with you. Please go home."

"Go home and wait for the police to come knocking on my door again asking questions about you? Fiona, I would *never* do anything to—" He reached forward as though to touch her, but James moved fully in front of her, shielding her.

"Taylor, you need to—"

"James." With her hand on his arm, Fiona pulled him aside so she could see Alan. Alan's eyes were filled with pain and confusion, not anger. "Alan, I promise you, I didn't accuse you of anything. The police asked for the names of anyone who might have any reason to be upset with me. It's a routine question. They already have a suspect in custody, a student at Hawkins."

"They have a suspect?"

"Yes." She was standing close enough to James that their arms were pressed together, and she could feel the tightness in his muscles. She knew he wanted to slam the door in Alan's face, lock it, and call the police.

Alan rubbed his forehead, his hand trembling. "You wouldn't have mentioned me if you didn't think it was possible I was guilty."

"Alan, they already knew your name from that message I got earlier. The rock thrown at my door, remember? I told you about that message. I'm so sorry the police bothered you, but they had to be thorough. They talked to Summer, too, right?"

"Yes. She told me." Again, he reached toward her. James started to move, but Fiona touched his hand. He stopped.

Alan lowered his arm. Another gust of wind blew rain onto the porch, pelting Fiona with icy drops.

"I would never hurt you." Alan seemed oblivious to the rain soaking his hair and coat. "You know that. What's *happening* to you? Are you all right? Are you hurt? The police were asking about that girl, the student, the one you mentioned, Kimberly Bailey. She's dead? What's going on?"

"She was trying to play a prank on me, and someone . . . she was murdered."

James nudged Fiona. She glanced at him and read the message in his eyes: *Cut this off now; he needs to leave.* She pictured Alan— agitated and angered by her refusal to answer his questions, afraid for her, furious at getting sent away—driving home in the rain, his mind anywhere but on the road. The image made her feel sick to her stomach. She couldn't send him away like this.

She could believe Alan would sneak into her house to search for a keepsake to replace the comb, but she couldn't for anything picture him bludgeoning Kimberly Bailey. Alan wasn't a killer. And no matter what, Fiona was not in danger now, not with James and her sisters here.

"It's all right, James," she said. "Alan, come sit down. You're soaked, and you look exhausted. I'm going to call Gavin and have him come pick you up."

Alan gave a dry laugh. "Don't do that. He'll jump down my throat for being here. I'm not sick. I just need to know what's happening."

"Come in." Fiona tugged James back a step, allowing Alan to enter the house. She led the way to the living room.

"Wednesday," Alan said. "The police were asking about Wednesday night."

"Yes," Fiona said. "That's when Kimberly died."

"I was with friends. For dinner." A shadowy version of his smile curved his lips. "I get a lot of dinner invitations. I'm a popular service project."

"Alan—"

"I was there all evening. At dinner. I couldn't have killed your student." He glared at James. "How about you, Hampton? Where were you Wednesday night?"

"Sit down," Fiona said hastily, before James could reply. "I'll bring you some hot chocolate."

Alan sat on the couch. James trailed Fiona into the kitchen.

"You have *got* to be kidding me," he whispered, face tense with more anger than Fiona had ever seen there. "What are you thinking, inviting him inside like that?"

"Did you take a good look at him?" Fiona whispered, pouring milk into a mug. "He's so agitated he can't walk straight, let alone drive. It's a miracle he made it here. I can't let him drive home like that."

"Then call the cops. Call an ambulance. Just *get him out of here*."

"Alan! Hey, long time no see!" Rebecca's bright, cheerful voice came from the living room, followed by Shannon's warm, "Hello, Alan."

"What a pleasure." Alan's greeting was a little tremulous, but he was plainly attempting his usual courtesy. "How are you ladies doing?"

"Go in there," Fiona said. "I'll call Gavin."

"Tell him to get over here immediately or he'll be picking up his brother in jail."

"James, he has an alibi for Wednesday. He couldn't have killed Kimberly."

"Maybe it's solid. Maybe it's not."

"Check with Detective Reid."

"I will."

Fiona set the mug inside the microwave. "And please don't crash heads with him tonight. He's upset enough as it is. Keep things calm and I'll get Gavin here as quickly as possible."

"Fine." James stalked out of the room.

Chapter 25

"THANKS FOR LETTING ME COME OVER." Carissa stepped over the threshold into Summer Taylor's townhouse.

"I figure your life stinks as bad as mine if this is the best thing you can think of to do on a Friday night." Summer closed the door. "And talking to you is better than staring at the walls."

"Not much better, I'll bet."

"Look, you did something rotten, but at least you realize you made a horrible mistake. Unlike Alan, who can't see anything except some glorious delusion where angel Fiona waits at the gates of happiness."

"Oh, Summer—"

"Skip it. I don't want sympathy. Come into the living room."

Summer's living room was decorated in a tasteful, understated style—everything clean, straightforward, and elegantly simple. Like Summer. "Beautiful place," Carissa said.

"Thanks. Sit down. So what do you want to talk about that you couldn't say over the phone?"

Carissa sat on the cobalt blue couch. "I guess we could have done it over the phone, but it seemed . . . better in person."

"Let me guess. Brad's gone tonight, and you're tired of wall-staring too."

"I'm twitchy to the point of insanity. Sick of sitting at home worrying."

Summer plopped into a striped wingback chair and curled her stocking feet underneath her. "You look way tired," she said. "Maybe you should have gone to bed early tonight instead of driving to Waltham."

"Because ceiling-staring is *much* better than wall-staring?"

Summer sighed. "Yeah. I know what you mean. What do you want to ask me?"

"First of all—I swear to you, I did *not* kill Linda."

Summer's eyes widened. "Congrats on your self-control. Do the police think you did?"

"I don't know."

"Good grief, you didn't come hoping to find out if *I* killed her, did you? Did Brad and his police buddies send you to record my confession?"

"Oh, please. Like Brad would talk to me long enough to work something like that out."

"Did you tell him about Keith?"

"Yes. I told him everything."

"And?"

"I don't know. He hardly talks to me. I don't know what he's thinking." She tried to smile. "At least he hasn't kicked me out. But we're both . . . I think the police are suspicious of both of us. In Linda's death, and Keith's. You did hear about Keith, didn't you? That he's dead?"

"Yeah, I heard. Why would they suspect Brad? In Linda's death, I mean. I can see why he'd want to kill Keith."

Avoiding Summer's gaze, Carissa ran her finger along the cold pewter of the vase on the table next her, before stopping to think that Summer probably didn't want fingerprints on her polished vase. "Sorry." She moved her hand back to the arm of the couch.

"Um, I really don't care if you touch my vase. Does this look like a museum? What's wrong, Carissa? Quit stalling and say what's on your mind."

Just tell her. You drove all the way here to ask her about this—are you going to lose your nerve now? "Apparently Linda made a lot of trouble for Brad after he gave her a traffic ticket. She accused him of being intoxicated when he stopped her. Even though there was never any proof, if she complained to enough people, she might have cost Brad a promotion. She knew everyone in town and was always bragging about chatting with the mayor or someone on the town council or the chief of police."

"Typical Linda."

"And regardless, it would have just about killed Brad to know that *anyone* thought he might have been working—and driving—under the influence."

"So Brad's boss thinks he might have cracked and pushed Linda into the creek?"

Carissa braced herself. "Summer . . . did *you* ever hear Linda say anything about Brad's drinking?"

"Yeah. She was complaining about him when we were over there for Sunday dinner a while back. Said he ticketed her for running a green light and she smelled booze on his breath. I sat there trying not to laugh—it was so ridiculous. Alan pretended to be concerned, but on the way home, he admitted she was out to lunch—Brad Willis drinking? She just couldn't stand that a family friend would dare give her a ticket. She had to find a way to blame Brad. I've driven with Linda, and I can tell you, that ticket was *way* overdue. Have you talked to Alan or Gavin?"

"I tried. I stopped by their house this morning and talked to Alan for a little while, but then Gavin got home, and he was so cold to me that I left as quickly as I could. I'm sure he thinks I killed Linda."

"You're not worried Linda was telling the truth about Brad, are you?"

Carissa lowered her gaze. A spot of salsa from lunch had stained the leg of her jeans. She hadn't noticed it before she left. Summer must think she was a slob.

"You *are* worried?" Summer asked. "Really?"

Carissa scraped at the stain. "No . . . I don't think so . . . but . . . last night I was taking out the trash and I found . . . beer cans and beer bottles in the outside trash can."

"Whoa. Did you ask Brad about them?"

Carissa shook her head. "I wouldn't have even noticed them if there hadn't been a broken bottle on the ground. *That's* super weird. Brad is meticulous—not obsessive-meticulous, but he puts his dirty socks in the hamper, puts the dishes in the dishwasher after he has a snack—you know, he likes things neat. If he dropped a bottle he would have made sure every piece was picked up, unless . . . well . . . unless he wasn't thinking straight."

"You mean unless he was drunk? Get a grip. Don't you think you'd notice if your husband was coming home reeking of Coors?"

"We . . . haven't spent a lot of time together lately. Do you have any idea what happened on the day Linda died? Were you in Canfield? Or did Alan say anything?"

"You really are afraid that Brad killed Linda and Keith."

"I didn't say that! Brad would never—I just . . . need to know if there's anything out there . . . evidence that might be misinterpreted . . ."

"I don't mind telling you everything I know, but it's not much. I wasn't in Canfield that day. Alan had gone to tell Linda we were getting divorced, and no way did I want to be there for her hip-hip-hoorays. Then Gavin called me late that night and told me Linda was dead. While she was out on one of her martyr walks, she'd fallen into the creek. That's all I know."

"If she would have been happy about the divorce, why the martyr walk? I thought she did those when she was upset."

"Who knows? Maybe Alan was licking her shoes and missed a spot."

"Do you have any idea whether or not Keith ever met with Linda? You overheard her whispering about the pictures of me and Keith—did she say anything at all to indicate that she'd met with him?"

"Nope. I don't know squat about your doctor boyfriend—" Summer stopped.

"What is it?"

"A doctor. Huh. It probably doesn't mean anything, but—"

Carissa sat up straight. "What is it? Something about Keith?"

"Don't get so hyper. A couple of days after Linda died—when Alan came home—he'd stayed with Gavin for a few nights . . . anyway, he had this gash on his elbow that had been stitched up. He'd fallen when he'd been out searching for Linda in that storm."

Carissa winced.

"I keep track of all our bills, and I asked him for the paperwork from the emergency room, or wherever they stitched him up, but he said he didn't have any paperwork and mumbled something about the new doctor guy doing it for free. It didn't make sense, but I didn't press him. He looked so trashed—I wasn't going to hound him about a receipt when he was devastated about Linda. I figured a bill would come in the mail eventually, but I haven't seen it yet."

"New doctor. He could have been talking about Keith. Keith was opening a practice in town."

"Could be. But if your boyfriend had a beef with Linda, why would he stitch up Linda's son for free?"

"I don't know. Maybe he came over to the Taylors' house and found Alan hurt and offered to help him in order to . . . soften Linda up?"

Summer shrugged. "I have no idea. Ask Alan."

"I've talked to Alan." Carissa's interest deflated as she remembered what Alan had told her. "Never mind. I'm not thinking straight. Alan already told me he's never met Keith."

"Linda's death probably *was* an accident," Summer said. "But how did Keith die?"

"I don't know. But the police said it was murder."

"Seems pretty unlikely he'd kill Linda and then get killed by someone else. Two killers in little Canfield?"

Carissa swallowed. "I've thought of that. And so have the Taylors, and so have the police."

"I'm sorry." The sympathy in Summer's voice surprised Carissa. "I wish I knew something that could help you."

"Thanks," Carissa said tiredly.

"Are you hungry? I've got a quiche in the fridge that I could heat up. And some cinnamon bread I picked up at the bakery. I'll bet you haven't had dinner yet, and neither have I."

"That's . . . very nice, but . . ."

"Look, we're both sick of worrying alone with no one to talk to. Stay for a while." Summer stood up. "You can make the salad."

* * *

Carissa hurried through the rain toward her car, a block away. It surprised her that she'd almost been able to enjoy her dinner with Summer. By the time they were finishing off the quiche, they'd been confiding in each other like old friends, with Summer telling tales of Linda Taylor that had left Carissa's head spinning. Poor Summer. Poor Alan.

She unlocked her car and started to slide inside when the sight of a figure in the passenger seat startled her so much that she cried out.

"Shut the door," Brad said.

"What did you—how did you—what are you doing here?"

"Shut the door." Brad gripped her wrist and pulled her the rest of the way into the car.

* * *

From her seat on the couch next to James, Fiona watched as Rebecca and Shannon engaged Alan in friendly conversation, keeping the discussion focused on harmless topics like Alan's job and Shannon's children. She could tell Alan was struggling to keep up his end of the conversation and he kept looking at Fiona and James, but he made polite, appropriate responses.

When the doorbell rang, James started to rise, but Fiona caught his arm and shook her head slightly.

Alan's courteous smile flattened. "You didn't—Fiona, you didn't call Gavin, did you?"

"Take it easy," she said. "I don't want you driving when you're this tired."

"Fiona—" Alan moved to stand up, but Shannon leaped to her feet and pointed at Alan's chair with a firm, motherly gesture.

"Don't you dare get up. You're supposed to be relaxing, and you haven't tried James's cheesecake yet."

"I'll get you a piece," Rebecca said. "Stay right where you are."

Fiona hurried out of the room, leaving her sisters to deal with Alan. She hoped they would manage to keep him there. She wanted a few minutes to talk to Gavin alone.

Moist wind blew into the house as she opened the door. "Hey," Gavin said. "Is everything okay?"

Fiona nodded and gestured Gavin inside. "He's calmer," she whispered, shutting the door. "My sisters are here, and James Hampton. They've been talking to him, keeping things light." Well, Rebecca and Shannon had. James had been watching Alan in alert silence. "Thanks for coming."

"Not a problem." Gavin spoke in a low voice, obviously picking up on the fact that she didn't want Alan to overhear. "Are *you* okay? Alan told me something about the police questioning him about you. What's going on?"

"Some . . . bad things have happened to me . . . or near me . . . lately. It's a long story."

Gavin's eyes narrowed and he pushed his wind-tousled hair back from his forehead. "You don't think Alan . . ."

"No." She didn't add how relieved she'd been to learn Alan had an alibi for the night Kimberly had died.

Still frowning, Gavin whispered, "Hang on a minute. I'm going to get a box out of my car."

Puzzled, Fiona stood in the doorway while Gavin hurried through the rain and retrieved a cardboard box from his trunk.

When he reached the porch again, he whispered, "Where's Alan?"

"Living room."

"Do you have an office? A study where you keep books?"

"Yes."

"Okay. Take me to Alan."

Fiona led the way.

"Hey, Al." Gavin's voice was casual. "How are you doing?"

"Fiona overreacted." Alan kept his gaze on the plate of chocolate cheesecake in his hand. "I'm perfectly capable of driving home."

"Better safe than sorry. And it gave me an excuse to start delivering these books." Gavin tilted his chin toward the box in his hands. "Eat your dessert. Fiona's going to show me where she wants these."

"This way," Fiona said, taking her cue. She led Gavin into the study. Gavin set the box on the desk and silently eased the door shut.

"These aren't really your books," he whispered. "They're a few of my old books and some clothes I threw in the trunk a few weeks back, planning to drop them at the Salvation Army."

"Quick thinking," Fiona said.

Gavin shrugged. "It'll give us a few minutes worth of time to talk privately. Not that Alan will really fall for it, but at least he'll be less embarrassed in front of your sisters. Now *what's going on?* Alan told me last weekend that someone had been sending you cruel messages about Mia Hardy and had even broken into your house. Then the police showed up to talk to him. He wouldn't tell me much—either he didn't want to give me details, or didn't know them. Then tonight, he slipped out—didn't tell me he was leaving—and here he is on your doorstep and you're freaking out. What's going on?"

"I'm not freaking out. I'm just worried about Alan." As concisely as she could, she summarized what had taken place over the past few weeks. Gavin stared at her, silent, his gaze so intense that he seemed to be absorbing and analyzing every word she spoke.

"I never accused Alan of anything," Fiona said. "But given that his name was included in one of the messages, naturally the police talked to him."

"You never accused him," Gavin said. "But did you suspect him?"

Fiona tried to edge around the question without touching it. "I've never known Alan to be violent in any way. And he's not under suspicion—he has an alibi for the night Kimberly died."

"What night was that?"

"Wednesday."

"Wednesday . . . Wednesday . . . oh yeah. He was back in Waltham that night—he's been staying with me, but some friends from his ward called and invited him to dinner. And you said the police have arrested the cousin anyway. So it's over. They caught the guy."

"I'm . . . not sure. Nicholas admitted to helping Kimberly with several of the stunts but denied having anything to do with the accident. And he swears he never would have harmed her."

"It would take a pretty stupid criminal to admit to murder." Gavin sank onto the loveseat and sat slouched, hands in his jacket pockets. "I'm sorry, Fiona. Nightmare for you."

Fiona absently toyed with the cardboard flap of the box Gavin had set on the desk. "Gavin . . . this is a tactless thing to ask, and I'd appreciate it if you'd keep it confidential. But . . . how well do you know Alan's wife?"

Gavin raised one eyebrow. "Ah," he said. "You're wondering if her jealousy might have made her crazy enough to . . . do something stupid."

To Fiona's relief, he didn't look offended. "It's a long shot. And she *did* come to me and apologize for accusing me of having an affair with Alan."

"But you're not sure you trust her. Summer is . . . I don't know, Fiona. I don't see it. If she got mad enough, I can see her driving a knife into someone's chest, but it would be a face-to-face battle. Sneaking around . . . setting up that accident . . . creeping into your house . . . Summer? I'm no criminal profiler, but . . . I can't see it."

"Thanks for being honest, and I'm sorry to even suggest—"

"You're scared. I get it. But I think you're getting paranoid. The truth seems obvious. I don't think you have anything to worry about."

"I hope not." Maybe he was right. She'd let herself get too affected by Nicholas's snow job—affected by the fact that she didn't *want* him weighted with the guilt of killing someone he loved. "And I'm sorry my . . . conflict with my student has caused so much upheaval for your family."

Gavin shrugged.

"How are you doing?" Fiona asked.

"I'm all right." The bleakness in his eyes made him resemble Alan more strongly than he usually did. "Alan's not so good, though."

"Have you . . . talked to him about seeing a doctor?"

"Not yet."

"He might be more willing, now that your mother isn't here to argue against it. I know she felt mental and emotional issues were setbacks people should be able to climb out of on their own, but it's not true."

"Yeah. I keep thinking of the things she used to say—how head doctors were quacks, and therapy was a bunch of fluffy words and handholding by shysters making a buck off people too weak to manage their own lives."

"You know that's wrong."

"Yeah." He stretched his legs out and stared at his rain-wet shoes. "I'm not too good in this role. Trying to . . . I don't know . . . Alan's my older brother. I thought he'd take care of *me.*"

He looked miserable—miserable and lost, the same way Fiona had seen Alan look so many times. Gavin must be under unbelievable strain, struggling to deal with his grief over his mother's death while trying to help Alan stay mentally afloat—all while hunting for a job. Fiona wondered if she'd be pushing her luck to suggest Gavin seek counseling as well.

"Is there anything I can do to help you?" Fiona promptly wished she could retract her offer. What could she possibly do to help the Taylors? She only had the power to make things worse.

"No." Gavin rose to his feet. "I should take Alan home."

"Would you like some cheesecake?"

"Thanks, but I'll skip it. Listen . . . maybe there is something . . . it's awkward asking you this, but it might make the difference. Like I said, I'm not very good in the dad role. I know I need to get Alan some help, but if he refuses—and he will—I can't force him. But if you back me up, I think we'd have a shot at succeeding."

"I've told him many times he needs to get help. He won't listen to me."

"He won't listen to me either. But the two of us together—maybe that will tip the balance."

"Do you want to bring him in here and we can talk to him together?"

"No, not now. That's asking for trouble. He's already annoyed at both of us. Let me soften him up. Set the stage. If I call you in a day or two, would you be willing to come and back me up?"

Torn, Fiona looked away. She didn't want to refuse—especially since she'd just asked if she could help him—but how could involving herself more deeply in Alan's life be anything but damaging?

"Gavin . . . I think having me there would only make things . . ."

Gavin held up a hand. "Hang on. I wasn't clear on what I was asking. I know you're worried about giving him the wrong impression. I'm not asking you for long-term involvement—that would be a mess. I'm asking you to sit down with Alan and me *once,* and for you to back me up when I try to convince him he needs professional help."

"I shouldn't—" Looking at the exhaustion and anxiety in Gavin's face, she couldn't finish the refusal. She'd urged him to get help for Alan—would she now refuse to take any steps to help him follow through? And she wouldn't be spending time alone with Alan. She'd be with Gavin every moment—Gavin, who was finally willing to get Alan the help he needed.

She could easily understand his edginess about confronting Alan. How *could* it ever be easy to tell your brother he needed professional help, especially considering the way Linda had regarded counseling? It *would* help if Gavin had someone to back him up—someone Alan trusted.

"One time," Fiona said.

"Once. That's all I want." Gavin pushed his damp hair away from his forehead. "I'll get some recommendations and get together a list of good doctors." He took out his cell phone. "Give me your numbers."

Fiona recited them and Gavin punched them in.

"Okay," Gavin said. "I'll work on him for a while then give you a call. We'll ambush him before he knows what's happening." Gavin gave a feeble grin. "Now I'll go see if I can get him in my car without a smackdown."

Chapter 26

"SHUT THE *DOOR*, CARISSA," Brad said. "You're getting soaked."

Carissa shut the door, her heart hammering. "I was visiting Summer Taylor—"

"Why?" Brad released her arm. In the streetlights, his face was an eerie collage of shadows.

"I wanted to see if she knew anything about the Taylors, about the day Linda died, about Keith . . . Brad, what are you doing here?"

"Waiting for you."

He'd followed her. He'd thought she was going to meet another boyfriend. While she'd talked to Summer, he'd gotten in her car to wait for her. To confront her. *At least he's not sitting there silent,* she mocked herself. *Isn't this what you wanted?*

"I went to Summer's." She tried to sound calm. "That's all. I would never . . . I would never again—I swear there's not . . . we can go ask Summer if you want . . ."

"Why didn't you tell me where you were going?"

"You weren't home!"

"You used to let me know if you had plans for the evening."

"I . . . I didn't think it mattered. You said you wouldn't be home until late, that you were helping John Bridger lay that tile in his kitchen—"

"He had more than enough help there. I left. Called you on my way home to tell you I was coming home early. I got Annie on the phone. She said I'd barely missed you."

But Carissa had told her babysitter she was "visiting a friend." How could Brad have known where—

"I saw your car as you were turning onto Davis Street." Brad answered the question before she spoke it. "What did you want to ask Summer about the day Linda died?"

"Just—what happened that day. What she knew."

His voice was almost too quiet to be heard over the drumming of the rain. "You think I killed Linda Taylor and Keith Murray, don't you? And hurt Fiona?"

"*What?* No!" She looked out the windshield, watching the rain stream down the glass. "You know about Fiona?"

"The Bennett detective talked to me, too."

"I know you'd never hurt anyone."

He was silent. This time the silence would stretch on forever if *he* didn't break it, Carissa thought, because her throat was so tight that she'd be lucky if she could make a sound.

"I deal with a lot of good liars," Brad said at last. "You're not one of them."

She swallowed. "Brad—I could never think—"

He touched her hand. The sudden contact made her start. He drew his hand back.

For another long moment, they sat without talking, the rain pounding on the roof of the car.

"You sneak out of the house," he said. "I touch you and you jump."

"You startled me."

"Your hand is freezing."

It was more than freezing. Carissa could feel the clammy dampness of her skin and knew Brad had noticed it too. "It's cold outside." She fumbled with the keys, wanting to start the car so she could turn on the heat. "I'm not afraid of you. I'm a suspect too."

"But you know *you* didn't do it." She could feel how he was studying her, but she didn't dare meet his gaze. How long had she wished he would look at her, focus on her, pay attention to her? And now she couldn't even make eye contact. She tried to put the key in the ignition but dropped the keys instead and had to grope on the floor near her feet, hunting for them.

"Do you think I'm going to kill you?" he asked.

She laughed. It sounded hysterical—almost crazy. When she'd seen Brad sitting in her darkened car, she'd been more than startled—she'd been frightened, but frightened of what? Frightened Brad might think she'd been sneaking off to meet another man? Or frightened he might—he might—

No. Not Brad.

Tears filled her eyes. What was happening to her—to them—that she could have even the tiniest flicker of doubt about—

"I believe you about what happened between you and Keith," he said. "You were telling the truth then. You're not now."

Another crazed laugh, and tears spilled from her eyes. "Do they teach mind reading in the police academy?"

"Tell me the truth."

Her fingers fumbled along the floor mat. Where *were* those keys? "I could never suspect you. You're the most upright person I know."

"You're still lying."

Carissa abandoned the keys and sat up, words flooding from her mouth. "My head is so messed up I can't think. I feel like I don't know you anymore. And you don't know me. We hardly talk. All those problems with Linda and that traffic ticket and her accusing you of drinking—why didn't you *tell* me, Brad? All I could see was you pulling away from me. Now your cop friends are breathing down my neck, asking me questions about you, about whatever awful things have happened to Fiona, if I know anyone who hates her, about Linda, about what she did to you. Gavin Taylor thinks I'm a murderer, and everyone knows I'm a lying, cheating, unfaithful—wrecking my family . . . I don't blame you if you think I killed Keith . . . or Linda . . . and then I'm taking the trash out last night and there's a broken beer bottle on the ground and a bunch more cans and bottles in the trash—where did those come from?"

"Hold on—beer bottles in our trash?"

"Yes. And cans. And a broken bottle on the ground."

"You found them last night?"

"Yes."

Slowly, he leaned over and picked up the car keys.

"Thanks," Carissa said. *Thanks,* all courteous, as though this were a normal interaction—as though Brad hadn't followed her to find out if she was cheating on him again, as though she hadn't implied that he was drinking, as though the police didn't suspect both of them of murder. She held out her hand for the keys, but Brad kept them.

"You're not driving," he said.

"I'm a careful driver." More laughter. "Never had a ticket. You know what's crazy? Mia was always a wilder driver than Fiona. Don't you think that's ironic?"

Brad reached over and took her hand. His grip was hard, as though he were trying to keep a current of hysteria from sweeping her out to sea.

"You never understood Fiona, never understood her at all," Carissa babbled. "Do you have any idea how much she blamed herself for Mia, how much she hurt, how much she *still* hurts? You won't ever be able to forgive her, will you? How about me? Will you ever be able to forgive me? You're here holding my hand. Is that a good sign? Or are you about to arrest me?"

"Carissa."

Carissa breathed deeply, trying to calm herself.

"Carissa, I did not put those bottles there."

That surprised her. She'd expected him to say he'd thrown them away for a friend. "How did they get in our trash?"

"I don't know. But they're not mine. I've never drunk alcohol. Linda Taylor was lying. Or maybe she was stubborn enough that she convinced herself she'd seen things she hadn't—but deep down, she must have known she was wrong, or why didn't she talk to you?"

"Talk to me?"

"Think about it. When she took those pictures of you and Keith, what did she plan to do with them?"

"Show them to you," Carissa said. "She made a big deal about how it was for my own good."

"And she didn't think alerting *you* that I had a drinking problem was for my own good? If she really believed I was drinking, she would have rushed to tell you."

He had a point. Linda would have delighted in warning her. Instead, she'd only vented to people who hadn't passed the word along to Carissa.

Who had put those bottles in the trash? Someone who *wanted* her to think Brad had a problem?

The person who had killed Keith Murray?

"I'm taking you home," Brad said.

"What about your car?"

"Forget about my car. We can come back and pick it up tomorrow. Do you want me in the house with you? Or do you want me to find a hotel?"

Why couldn't she stop shaking? She tried to tighten her muscles to steady herself. It didn't work—it made the trembling come in jerky waves. "I love you," she said.

The tension in his face and in his grip remained. Carissa knew she hadn't answered the real question: she loved him, but did she trust him?

She pictured herself telling Brad not to come home. She pictured him checking into a hotel, knowing Carissa was too afraid of him to let him in the house.

That she thought he was capable of murder.

Did she think that?

She closed her eyes and leaned against the seat. She could hardly feel Brad's hand anymore despite the firmness of his grip. His flesh must be as cold as hers.

Brad said nothing. He was waiting for her to make her choice.

"Let's go home," she said. "Both of us."

* * *

"*Don't,* Fiona." James's tone was so adamant that Fiona saw her sisters exchange a wide-eyed glance. "Alan Taylor's mental health is *not your responsibility.*"

"I know that." Fiona kept her voice quiet. "I'm not making it my responsibility."

"If you agreed to help Gavin talk Alan into seeing a doctor, then you *are* making it your responsibility."

"Maybe Gavin will be able to take care of things without calling Fiona," Rebecca suggested. "Alan seemed really cooperative when he left with Gavin."

Fiona hoped Rebecca was right. Gavin *had* done a skillful job of teasing and bullying Alan out of the house, and by the time they were leaving, Alan had seemed glad for his brother's taking control.

"I can't imagine it will be that easy," James said. "Not with Alan Taylor. He's going to use this as a way to get close to Fiona."

"I won't let that happen," Fiona said. "Gavin and I were clear on the terms. He's asking me to come *once,* with him, to talk to Alan. I won't ever be alone with Alan."

"Alan is not your responsibility!"

Fiona stared at James.

"I'm sorry," James said, and Fiona had the feeling he was struggling to rein in his emotions. "I'm sorry. I'm worried about you."

"I promise I won't let either Alan or Gavin turn this into more than a one-time visit."

"You *think* you're promising one visit. What happens when Alan's dragging his heels and Gavin's still begging you for help, trying to convince you you're the only one who can fix things—maybe one *more* visit . . ."

"James," Rebecca said. "Give Fiona some credit."

"I am. But I know it was extremely difficult for her to disentangle herself from Alan the first time. Alan is good at playing on her guilt. It sounds like Gavin is too."

"That's not fair," Fiona said. "I asked if I could help him."

"You offered because you're a compassionate, charitable person. If he had any sense, he would have turned you down."

"He's scared, James. He just lost his mother. His father died when he was a child. His brother is struggling, and he's trying to hold everything together."

"I'm very sorry for what the Taylors are experiencing. But you know the scripture that says 'I give not because I have not, but if I had I would give'? This is a textbook case of that situation. You'd help them if you could, but what they need, *you can't give them.* Didn't you already tell Alan that?"

She *had* told Alan that, but the circumstances were different.

Weren't they?

She glanced at her sisters, sitting together on the couch. Rebecca looked anxious, the skin creasing between her eyebrows. Shannon was frowning and running a finger over the half-finished baby blanket Rebecca had left on the lamp table.

"If Gavin is feeling overwhelmed, he should call on family members or call his bishop or Alan's bishop," James said. "This should *not* be on your shoulders. By getting involved, you'll throw fuel on whatever feelings Alan has for you and maybe put yourself in danger."

"You talked to Detective Reid. Alan couldn't—"

"So he has an alibi for the time Kimberly died. I'm not suggesting he's a murderer. But you need to stay away from him."

"I'm not an idiot, James. I said one visit and I meant one visit. Alan has needed help for years. Gavin—who knows his brother much better than I do—thinks my help might make the difference. Can't I give at least *that* much to the Taylors?"

James's jaw tightened. "If you'd stop thinking with your guilt and start thinking with your mind, you'd see what a bad idea this is."

Before Fiona could respond, Rebecca interceded. "She'll be smart about it."

Shannon shook her head. "I'd think about it carefully. James is right—it's too easy to get tangled up in something you didn't plan on. Better to stay away."

"I can't avoid the Taylors forever," Fiona snapped. "There are still those books Linda left me."

"Send someone else to get them," Shannon said.

"I can't do that. What does that say to the family? That I have such disdain for them that I won't set foot over their threshold?"

"Hey, enough!" Rebecca waved her hands. "Enough, okay? I think we're all too worn out to discuss this rationally. Why don't we call it a night? After a few hours of sleep, maybe we can talk without snarling at each other."

James rose to his feet. "Fiona, may I speak to you privately?"

Fiona wanted to say no. Her conflicting emotions about Alan and the whole situation enclosed her like jagged shards of steel; no matter which direction she moved, they'd cut her. But if she refused to talk to James and sent him out the door angry, worried, frustrated—it was still pouring rain, water dashing against the house—

Stop it. He's not you, and he's not Alan, and he's not Mia. Talk to him because you want to talk to him, not because you're afraid something catastrophic will happen if you don't.

"Fiona!" Shannon's voice went sharp, and Fiona realized her expression must have exposed her fear. "What's wrong?"

To say *nothing* would sound unbearably phony, so she shook her head and stood to follow James out of the room.

James led the way into the study and closed the door. She expected him to launch into another round of why acceding to Gavin's request was a bad idea, but instead he said, "I'm sorry. I've overstepped my bounds tonight, trying to tell you what to do. I'm just worried sick for you. What can I do to help?"

Speechless, she stood for a moment, hesitating, then stepped toward him. He wrapped his arms around her, and she rested her head against his shoulder.

James stroked her hair and gently massaged the back of her neck. Tears trickled down her face as she leaned against him, letting her tight muscles relax.

"If you're determined to help Gavin, at least let me go with you," he said. "You told me you wouldn't face the Taylors alone."

"You know that wouldn't work." She closed her eyes, letting more tears fall, draining away stress. "If you're there, Alan will be so defensive that Gavin and I won't make any progress with him at all."

"Even if I'm not inside talking to him, I want to be there. I'll wait outside the house. I'll park down the street, if you want, so Alan doesn't know I'm there. But if you're going to do this, I don't want to be more than a few seconds away. Remember what happened when you confronted Alan about that comb?"

Fiona thought of shivering in her car outside Alan's townhouse, unable to drive home. "That won't happen again . . . I hope," she murmured.

"It would be a miracle if it didn't, Fiona, after everything you've been through this week. I want to be close by. Will you agree to that?"

Having James close enough to arrive instantly if things got too stressful . . . "Yes," she said. "I'd appreciate that."

"I'll be there. Call me when you hear from Gavin. And Fiona . . . don't let yourself get sucked in. You set your terms. Stick to them."

"I will," she said.

* * *

The swish of the windshield wipers, the hum of the engine, and the friction of tires on wet pavement were the only sounds, but for once, Carissa didn't mind the silence between Brad and her. It was a warm, calm silence, not a tense one.

Brad reached over and touched her hand. This time, she didn't jump.

"I love you," he said.

The words felt new, as though it were the first time Brad had spoken them. "Even after what I did?"

"You weren't the only one who messed up. I hurt you, and I'm sorry. I took you for granted. Got my priorities backward."

"I . . . wondered if you were gone so much because you didn't want to be around me. Because you were bored with me."

"Bored! Are you crazy? I don't know what I was thinking, but I wasn't trying to stay away from you. Maybe I was just . . . I don't know. Trying to prove to everyone that I was a decent guy, despite what Linda Taylor said . . ."

"Out there helping everyone who needed it?"

"Yeah . . . and working all the overtime I could get . . ."

"You've always been a guy who gives more of yourself than you can spare," Carissa said lightly.

"I should have been there for you, first off. You and the boys. I'm sorry. If I'm gone too much . . . if I'm ignoring you . . . tell me. Just say it right out. I need to know when you're hurting."

"And please tell me when *you're* hurting. I had no idea what you were going through. I feel awful that I didn't know."

He intertwined his fingers with hers. "You're beautiful," he said. "I can't figure out why you've been feeling . . . whatever it was you said. Dull? That's nuts, but I'm sorry I didn't do a better job of telling you how I feel."

"You . . . really think I'm beautiful?"

Brad grinned. It had been a long time since she'd seen him smile like that—amused, flirtatious. "You're gorgeous, and you always will be. You'll be a stunner when you're a great-great grandmother."

Carissa laughed. "Stunning people because I'm still around at a hundred and ten. Brad . . . I'm so sorry I got us mixed up in this trouble over Keith. Do you know if we're still considered suspects? Or are they looking at someone else now?"

"I don't know what evidence they've gathered. They're keeping me out of the loop, for obvious reasons. Did Summer tell you anything interesting?"

"Not really. She wasn't in Canfield the day Linda died. She did tell me something that made me wonder if Keith *had* come over to the Taylors' to talk to Linda and had seen Alan—until I remembered Alan had already told me he's never met Keith. Total strike out."

"What did she say about Alan?"

"Alan had stitches on his elbow. He'd slipped when he was out searching for Linda and had gashed his arm on a rock. Summer asked him about a bill or receipt, and he didn't have one—he said something about how the 'new doctor' had stitched him up, but was so upset that Summer didn't press . . . What is it?" Brad's hand was constricting around hers.

"Alan Taylor had stitches in his elbow?"

"That's what Summer said."

"And she didn't know where he got them?"

"That's right. What is it? What are you thinking?"

"In Keith Murray's office that he was setting up here, one of the few things in the trash was the remains of a suture kit and some bloodied gauze," Brad said. "None of the staff that he was in the process of hiring knew anything about it—the office wasn't even open yet, and there were no records of any procedure being done. But it seems clear Dr. Murray treated someone there."

"But Alan said he never met Keith."

"Maybe he lied."

"Why hide it? Alan has no motive for wanting to hurt Keith."

"Because the motive isn't obvious doesn't mean it isn't there." Excitement animated Brad's voice. "I need to let Tina know about this. They need to look harder at Alan Taylor."

Carissa's heart thudded. If Alan had lied about not seeing Keith, what else had he lied about?

Chapter 27

AT SIX THIRTY IN THE morning, the phone rang. Fiona immediately swiped the phone off her nightstand, not wanting the noise to disturb Shannon or Rebecca. "Hello?" she said quietly, already knowing from the caller ID that this wasn't a call she felt prepared to take.

"Fiona? It's Gavin."

From those three words, Fiona could read the stress in his voice. "What's going on?"

"Things are bad. I need your help. We both woke up early, so I tried to talk to Alan about counseling—dropped a few hints—and he lost it. Shouted at me. Took off into the woods like Mom used to do. He's out there now."

"Do you think you should go after him?"

Gavin gave a hoarse chuckle. "He'll come back on his own. He's not as good at this as Mom was. He doesn't stay out long. Could you come over now? If you're here when he returns, he might listen to you, and the way he's acting—we can't wait any longer to confront him."

"If you're worried he might be a danger to himself, then you need to call the police."

"It's not to that point, not yet. That's what I'm trying to head off. Will you come?"

She'd already agreed to help Gavin talk to him, and considering how panicky he sounded, she couldn't turn him down. "Yes. I'll be there in an hour."

"*Please* hurry. And don't come to the front door. Come to the studio at the back of the yard. I've got a better view of the woods from here. I'm watching for him."

"Okay."

Fiona hung up. Now she needed to jolt James out of sleep on a Saturday morning to tell him they were going to the Taylors. She dialed his cell phone number.

Voice mail. She hung up. She'd expected that he'd keep his phone close at hand, considering how worried about her he'd seemed. But maybe he was so exhausted that he'd missed the ringing.

She dialed again. Still voice mail.

She texted a message: *Gavin called. He tried to talk to Alan. Alan ran off. Gavin's worried sick and wants me to come now. Can you come?*

She wanted to rush out the door but figured she'd better give James a few minutes before she tried to call again. She left the phone on the bathroom counter and stepped into the shower. Seven minutes later, showered, dressed, and with her wet hair in a ponytail, she checked the phone to find that James had returned her text.

Sorry. Barely woke up. You go ahead. I'll meet you there.

The message brought a wave of relief. James seemed to understand and sympathize with the urgency Gavin was feeling. And they needed to take separate cars anyway, if James was going to set up his stakeout down the street from the Taylors'. She couldn't exactly ask him to drop her off, thus leaving Alan and Gavin wondering where her car had gone.

She texted James: *We're meeting in the studio at the back of the Taylors' yard. Stay out of sight unless I call you.*

OK.

Fiona penned a quick note for her sisters. *Gavin called—he's worried about Alan and needs me to come now. James will meet me there.* She left the note on the kitchen table and headed outside.

The sky was still overcast and the branches shook in the wind, but last night's rain had stopped, to Fiona's relief.

She hated driving in the rain.

Her stomach churned as she slid the key into the ignition, but she forced herself to start the engine. She would *not* leave Gavin pacing, desperate for help because she didn't have the courage to drive.

Traffic was sparse and the trip to Canfield went quickly. Fiona parked in the Taylors' driveway. She checked her phone for any additional messages from James—none—and turned the ringer off. It certainly wouldn't help Gavin if the shrill noise of Fiona's phone interrupted what was going to be a sensitive and difficult conversation.

Praying silently that she'd know how best to help Alan, she walked around the side of the house, keeping to the flagstone path so she wouldn't soak her shoes in the grass. Light showed around the edges of the curtains in the small, rectangular studio. Fiona knocked on the door.

The door opened. Alan stood there, pale and unshaven, his hair disheveled.

"Hello, Alan." Fiona wished she'd made it here more quickly so she could have consulted with Gavin before Alan returned. But at least he was safely home instead of wandering among the trees and alongside the creek where Linda had died.

"Come in." Clearly, he wasn't surprised to see her. Gavin must have forewarned him.

She stepped inside. The room was warm, pleasant in the chilly morning, but dust coated everything and spiderwebs decorated the corners of the room. A couch covered with a sheet sat near one wall. An upright piano was positioned at the edge of a braided rug. Stacks of boxes indicated the studio was being used for storage.

Fiona unzipped her sweatshirt. "Are we going into the house?"

"We're talking here," Alan said.

The studio wasn't the most appealing venue for a conversation, but perhaps Alan was more comfortable here—the house might evoke too many memories of Linda.

Alan had tossed his jacket onto an empty desk, but Fiona didn't want to do the same—her sweatshirt would come away covered with dust. She set her sweatshirt and purse on the sheet-covered couch.

"Where's Gavin?" she asked.

Alan closed the door and twisted a key in the lock. He put the key in his pocket and smiled at Fiona. The strange, bright look in his eyes made her nerves prickle. "Alan, where's Gavin?"

"In bed. He doesn't like getting up early."

"In bed! But he called me."

"We sound a lot alike on the phone."

A splash of adrenaline burned Fiona's chest. "That was *you* on the phone?"

"I knew you'd come for him. You wouldn't come for me. Not after the way you treated me last night, like I belonged in the nuthouse."

"I didn't—"

"He told me he fed you some story about how he was going to get me to a shrink and you were going to help him. He was right— you *do* think I'm crazy."

"No, I don't." Fiona kept her voice calm, but all she could think of was Alan's turning that key in the lock. A double-keyed lock. He'd locked them in.

The memory of Kimberly Bailey's lifeless body filled her mind. Had she been wrong—fatally wrong—about Alan? Was his alibi faked? Had he manipulated his friends into covering for him?

"Alan, we need to go wake Gavin. I'll come with you. Unlock the door."

"You'd make a good psychiatrist," Alan said. "You've got the soothing voice down pat."

Was James here yet, parked down the street? But he wouldn't have any idea she needed help.

She should have recognized Alan's voice on the phone, but it hadn't occurred to her that he'd sunk to the point of impersonating his brother to manipulate her. Why had Gavin forewarned him about enlisting Fiona's help?

"Alan, I'm not comfortable with this situation," she said firmly. "You and I shouldn't be alone together."

He laughed. It was an odd laugh, far too hyper—almost giddy?— for Alan. "Worried about scandal?"

"Unlock the door."

"You're good at that voice too," he said. "The stern teacher. Summer's better at it, but you're passable. I'm not unlocking the door. If I do, you'll leave. I need to talk to you."

"If you unlock the door, I'll go with you. We'll talk to Gavin together."

"No," he said quietly. "No, Gavin would stop me."

"Stop you from doing what?"

One side of his mouth jerked upward, a hybrid of his usual smile and a scowl Fiona had never seen on his face. "'Stay away from her, Alan; she's poison, Alan; don't trust her, Alan; she doesn't care about you; she's ruining your life.'"

"Gavin said those things?"

"He doesn't understand. You're the only one who understands."

Fiona swallowed to moisten her dry tongue. Why would Gavin have sought her help if he thought she was hurting Alan? Or were his harsh words his way of trying to persuade Alan to forget her?

"James is coming," Fiona said. "Open that door, or I'm calling him and telling him you've locked me in."

"Okay," Alan said. "Call him."

What game was he playing? Warily, Fiona removed her phone from the pocket of her purse.

"I know you must have him on speed dial," Alan said. "One button. Call him."

It was a warning. If she tried to call the police, Alan would yank the phone away from her before she could finish punching 911.

Why would he let her call James? He must know James would immediately call the police. Was he planning to hold her hostage— maybe demand something from James? Did he *want* James to know he'd trapped her? If Alan decided to—if he—there was no way James or anyone could get to her in time—

"Go on," Alan said.

Heart thudding, she stepped back to put more distance between Alan and herself and pressed her finger against the button to dial James's number.

The loud ring of a phone shattered the quiet in the studio, making Fiona jump. Alan reached into his pocket and pulled out his cell phone. Instead of answering it, he stepped forward and held the phone out to Fiona so she could see the number on the caller ID.

Her number. That was James's phone.

Alan hit the button to silence the phone. "*Go now*," he quoted, moving his thumbs to mime texting. "*I'll meet you there.*"

James hadn't answered her text this morning. Alan had. James didn't even know she was here.

Fighting a terrified urge to scream for Gavin, Fiona kept her voice even. "How did you get his phone?"

"How do you think? It was on the couch in your living room last night. It must have fallen out of his pocket. I figured you'd try to call him before you came here. He was certainly playing watchdog last night."

"He's still coming," Fiona said. "I left him a message on his land-line as well."

"He doesn't have a landline."

"You don't know—"

"Give me a little credit, Fiona. There's no listing for him, and from his call record, I see he makes calls on his cell phone morning, day, and night—including times when he'd be at home. He doesn't have a landline. Are you *this* scared of me now? You don't dare talk to me without a bodyguard in the room?"

She couldn't let Alan rattle her. That had always been her mis-take—letting him upset her and play on her guilt, leaving her fum-bling ineffectually to coax him out of her life, afraid to stand firm lest she hurt him more than she already had. But when she finally *did* stand firm, he'd always backed down—at least temporarily.

She needed that reprieve now. "Alan, I will talk to you, but *not* under these circumstances. You can open that door and we can go get Gavin, or I'm calling the police."

She held his gaze and held her breath, praying for him to turn away, shoulders sagging, and reach for the key in his pocket.

Instead, he smiled. "I knew you'd be this way."

"Open the door."

"You're strong. I know that."

Fiona opened her phone.

Alan lifted the jacket lying on the desk and picked up a knife that lay underneath. With a swift motion, he raised it and brought it to his throat, pressing the tip of the blade into his flesh.

"Drop the phone," he said.

Frozen, Fiona stared at the knife. "Alan, please don't do this. *Please*. Drop the knife."

Emotions emptied from his face: the hysteria-tinged humor, the mockery when he'd told her to call James, the annoyance when he'd talked about her bodyguard. Only a hollow remained.

"I'm a murderer," he said.

* * *

James searched the pockets of his Dockers and dropped them back into the hamper. Not there, not in his jacket, not in his car. As soon as someone invented a phone that could be surgically implanted into the customer's ear, James would be the first to sign up. Maybe *then* he could go a month without losing his phone.

He should have gotten a landline. Using a cell phone only had seemed sensible—at least until the first two times he'd misplaced the phone. Even with insurance, this was getting expensive.

He'd sprung to adrenaline-laced awareness at seven this morning, realizing he'd forgotten to plug in his phone to charge it. Though he still had adequate battery left, with his current worries about Fiona, he wanted a full charge at all times. But when he'd jumped out of bed to plug in his phone, he couldn't find the phone. Anywhere.

He must have left it at Fiona's last night. What if she'd tried to call him only to hear his phone ringing uselessly under her couch cushion?

Cursing himself, James yanked on a sweatshirt and jeans, grabbed his car keys, and rushed out of his apartment. It was too early on a Saturday morning for an unannounced visit, but Fiona didn't usually sleep in. She'd told him once that any time after seven was fine for a phone call, even on weekends. But after the stress of the past few weeks, she might have finally collapsed with exhaustion, ready to sleep until noon—at least until absentminded idiot James started hammering on her door.

As he pulled up to her house, he saw two cars—one in the driveway and one parked on the street. Rebecca's car and Shannon's rental—but where was Fiona's rental?

So much for worrying about waking her up. She'd probably awakened early and slipped out to grab a jug of milk. It would be like Fiona to force herself to drive on an errand, despite the excruciating stress she likely experienced right now when she got behind the wheel of a car.

He tapped his fingers on the steering wheel and studied the house, trying to figure out what to do. Maybe he should knock softly on the front door. If no one answered, he'd assume Rebecca and Shannon were still asleep and wait for half an hour or so to see if Fiona returned. He hoped she wouldn't see his behavior as over-protective, but he was edgy at the thought of her having no way to contact him. What if Gavin Taylor summoned her? She'd sworn to call James if that happened, but how could she do that if his blasted phone was AWOL?

He walked up to the house and rapped lightly on the door. Almost instantly, he heard the shuffle of footsteps approaching. Thank heavens.

"Hey there, early bird!" Rebecca was wearing a neon-yellow bathrobe and her hair was tousled.

"Sorry," James said. "I hope I didn't wake anyone up."

"Weren't you meeting Fiona there?"

"Meeting her where?"

Rebecca frowned, confusion clouding her eyes. "The Taylors. Her note said you were meeting her there."

"The Taylors!" Without waiting to be invited, James stepped inside the house. "What note? What did it say?"

"That you were—here, I'll show you." Rebecca hurried toward the kitchen, one hand on her bulging stomach. "Didn't she talk to you?"

"I don't have my phone. I lost it. I think I left it here last night."

"Here." Rebecca picked up a page torn from a notepad and held it out to James.

James felt sick. He knew it wasn't rational to be this worried, but he'd promised Fiona he'd be there for her if she needed him, and now he'd missed the boat. "She must have tried to call me and couldn't reach me."

"Were you planning to talk to Alan together?" Rebecca asked.

"No. I was going to wait for her, out of sight of the Taylors, so in case she needed support, I'd be nearby."

"Oh, that's a good idea. I'm surprised she went without you."

"Gavin probably made it sound like the sky was falling, and she didn't dare wait. But why would she assume I was meeting her there if she couldn't get in touch with me?"

Rebecca gripped his arm. "Take a deep breath. She probably left you a message and assumed you'd get it as soon as you woke up and you'd come after her."

"How long has she been gone?"

"Not long. I heard her go out the door around six forty-five."

James glanced at his watch. Seven forty. She'd probably barely arrived in Canfield.

"I'm sure she's fine, James. Let's find your phone so you can listen to her message." Rebecca headed into the dining room. James followed her. Within a couple of minutes, they'd searched every possible place the phone could have fallen last night. No phone.

Rebecca picked up Fiona's landline. "What's your number? I'll call it."

He told her. She dialed. They both stood silent, listening for a ring tone. Nothing.

James gritted his teeth. "I know I had it last night."

"Let me call Fiona, but I'll probably have to leave a message—she'd never answer her phone while driving." Rebecca dialed and waited. "Hey, Fiona, it's Becca. James is here—he lost his phone and didn't get the message that you were going to Canfield. He's on his way now. I'll send my cell phone with him in case you need to get in touch with him." She hung up. "Let me get my phone for you."

She exited and returned a moment later with her phone. "Here it is." She winked. "Try not to lose it."

James grabbed it. "*Thank* you."

"No problem. Go find Fiona."

"Thanks." James shoved Rebecca's phone in his pocket and raced out the door.

* * *

Alan's confession struck like a kick to the ribs, knocking the air from Fiona's lungs. She forced a shaky breath down her throat. "No one suspects anything. You can put the knife down."

"The police were back last night, asking more questions. Asking about the stitches. They'll figure it out. Maybe they already have."

"What stitches?"

"I deserve to die. Would you like to watch? You'll remember me forever."

She was going to pass out. Her head spun and her arms hung useless, as though fear had paralyzed the nerves. "You didn't mean to kill her."

Relief lifted some of the darkness from his face. "You understand. I knew you would, if I could keep you here long enough to listen to me. You're the only one who *can* understand."

"Please put the knife down."

He rolled the handle of the knife between his thumb and forefinger so the blade puckered his skin. With a little more pressure, the tip of the blade would sink through his skin, heading straight for his jugular vein.

"I'll start listening when you put the knife down," she said, remembering the words that had worked on Nicholas Cortez.

"Put your phone down," he said. "We'll talk."

Fiona struggled to think. He'd confessed to murdering Kimberly Bailey. Did he plan to kill her, too? Why else would he have tricked her into coming and trapped her here?

"Are you going to kill me?" she asked.

He squinted as though her words had jarred the world out of focus. "Why would I—I could *never* hurt you. Don't you know that by now?"

He expected her to believe she was safe with him when he'd left Kimberly dead in her bathtub? "You admitted you killed Kimberly."

"Kimberly." He frowned. His arm dropped slightly and the knife lost contact with his throat. "No, not Kimberly, not your student. Why would I hurt her? I never even met her. I killed my mother."

"Your mother!" The words rode on a disorienting sense of being tossed from nightmare to nightmare. "But that was—I thought that was an accident. She slipped—"

"She slipped because I pushed her." Alan brought the knife back to his throat and gave the handle another twist.

Panicking, Fiona dropped her phone on the rug. "Put the knife down. You can talk to me. What happened?"

Alan grinned. "I knew you'd understand. Mia died, but you didn't mean it. I didn't mean it either. But we both killed someone." He blinked, and tears trickled down his face.

Grinning, laughing, crying—how long until his jumbled emotions exploded? "Tell me how it happened."

"I came to tell her Summer wanted a divorce. It was her fault. And she laughed." Alan's face hardened. "She *laughed*."

"I'm sorry."

"She told me she knew Summer was worthless, that Summer had never loved me, that I'd made a huge mistake marrying her, and I should have waited for *you*. Over and over again, that you were the one for me, when I knew you hated me, when you'd told me you never wanted to see me again. She was so *happy.* To her, Summer didn't matter—she was gone already. Mentioning the word *divorce* had wiped her off the map. Mom was so triumphant. She'd won."

He *did* love Summer, Fiona realized.

"From the beginning, she'd been trying to drive Summer away, but Summer held on. Summer is strong. But after we moved back . . . we shouldn't have left Richmond, but Mom wouldn't stop hounding me. I thought if I gave her *that* much, maybe she'd give me peace, and it *was* a good career move . . . But Summer was furious . . . didn't want to be here. We kept fighting. And Mom wanted to see me all the time, almost every weekend, and she kept talking about you. Summer hated that. She hated it, but she kept coming with me." Alan's arm lowered slightly, paused, then lowered all the way so he was holding the knife at his side. Fiona tried not to look too relieved. She didn't want his guard going up again.

"Then she found that pearl comb, your comb." Alan's voice was leveling out, his usual polished cadence returning. "I'd forgotten about it. It had been in a box of old college papers and mementos for years. I'd meant to send it back to you, but it was easier not to think about it. When I was sorting things before the move, I found it. I left it in the box, but after we got settled here, Summer and I were fighting so much, and I thought it would be comforting, to . . . remember. I took the comb out of the box and put it in a dresser drawer. It was foolish."

"When she found the comb, did she know it was mine?"

"No. She suspected, but she didn't know. It was something Mom did that made her snap. I don't know what, but when we came home from Canfield the day before I . . . before Mom died, Summer claimed Mom had proof that you and I were having an affair, and she wanted a divorce. When I accused Mom of manufacturing phony evidence, she told me not to be ridiculous and that Summer was making things up. But Summer wasn't a liar."

The pictures. Linda's pictures of Carissa Willis and Keith Murray, the ones Summer had thought were of Fiona and Alan. That's what Alan was talking about. "Summer made a mistake—" Fiona began, but from tension that reappeared in Alan's expression, she knew she shouldn't have spoken.

"I know she made a mistake," he said. "I didn't know that at the time. And Mom started rattling on about how she was still in touch with you and we should go to Bennett and visit you. She wouldn't listen to anything I said about Summer. She'd driven Summer away from me and she didn't care."

"What did you tell her?"

"I tried to tell her what she'd done to Summer, what she'd done to me. She kept saying I'd be so much happier now. When I got angry with her, she stomped out on one of her walks. Martyr walks, Summer called them. It was storming, snow and rain, but that's how she liked it. Bad weather made her exit more dramatic."

"Did you go after her?"

"I swore I'd let her stay out there until she froze, but I couldn't . . . I couldn't . . . we always . . . if I didn't, I'd never hear the end of it . . . she'd moan for months about how unloved she was . . ."

"I'm sorry."

"I went after her. She was standing on the edge of the slope that leads down to the creek. When I walked up to her, she gave me this . . . look. She was trying to appear sad, but inside she was laughing. She knew I couldn't fight her. She knew she'd always win. I . . . everything erupted inside me. I . . . pushed her. She rolled down the bank, and before I could do anything, she was in the creek. I went after her—fell and cut my elbow—but it was too late. Her head—the current had grabbed her, thrown her into a rock."

Alan stood motionless, his expression remote, and Fiona knew he must be remembering the sight of Linda tossed by the foaming current.

"I know you didn't mean to hurt her," Fiona said.

Slowly, Alan's mouth curved. "I did, actually. I wanted to hurt her. I wanted her sorry for what she'd done."

Fiona forced herself not to look at the knife in his hand, but she was so hyperaware of it that she might as well have been running her finger along the blade. "But you didn't mean to kill her."

"No. But for that moment—that one moment—I was stronger than she was." He studied Fiona, that eerie smile distorting his mouth. "It felt good."

"Alan—"

"She hurt me. But for one moment . . . I was stronger."

"Let's go sit down," Fiona suggested carefully. "You can tell me about—"

He lunged at her. The movement startled her so completely that before she could turn to run, he shoved her backward. She landed hard on the couch, her head snapping back. Dazed, she twisted wildly, falling to the floor, trying to roll away before he could stab her, but he caught her and dragged her onto the couch. *Where was the knife?* Both his hands were holding her, yanking her against him so her back was pressed to his chest.

"I'm stronger than you, too," he said.

That shove had jounced the air from her lungs, and it was hard to talk. "Let me—go—Alan—"

With his arms encircling her, he gripped her wrists, pinning her bent arms against her body. "You said you'd listen to me."

"Not like—not like—this—" She thrashed, attempting to break his grip, but his arms were stone. Finally, Fiona sagged, muscles throbbing. She could see the knife now, on the rug where he'd dropped it.

"Don't worry," he said. "I won't hurt you." He gave a small, quiet chuckle. "But I *could,* Fiona."

Chapter 28

STAY CALM, STAY CALM, Fiona repeated in her mind. If Alan planned to kill her—at least right away—he wouldn't have dropped the knife. "I know you *could* hurt me, but I know you don't want to. You've always been kind to me, Alan."

"I've always loved you." His arms weren't quite as rigid and his fingers shifted slightly, loosening enough so they weren't digging painfully into her wrists. Fiona breathed slowly, resisting the urge to try to break free again. If she fought, he'd tense up, and in physical combat, she didn't have a chance.

"I didn't mean to kill her." She couldn't see his face, but from the shakiness of his voice, he was crying. "She was right. That's what rips me apart, Fiona—she was *right*. When I saw you at her funeral—when I realized you *had* come back, that you did care, just like she said—she was right, and I killed her. I should have trusted her."

Horrified at the realization of what she'd set in motion in Alan's head when she'd gone to Linda's funeral, Fiona tried to think how to respond. Should she feed his delusions and hope that would calm him enough for her to break free, or should she work to disengage him from Linda's cruel distortions of reality? She risked a try at the truth.

"She *wasn't* right. You love Summer. Summer loves you. You belong with Summer. Your mother—she was using the memory of me to try to manipulate you. That's all it was, Alan. We didn't have some kind of destiny together. There's nothing special about me. Your mother just didn't like Summer taking your attention away from her and she used my name as a tool to try to separate you. If *I* had taken you away from her, she would have hated *me*."

She could feel Alan trembling. "No, she was right," he said softly. "She knew you were the one for me." He shifted his grip, passing both of her wrists into his right hand. His long fingers twined around her wrists, still gripping them tightly, but she could yank her hands free now, if—

No. Not yet. Stay calm. Breaking free for a moment would do her no good at all, especially locked in this studio with the key in Alan's pocket. She couldn't risk provoking him, not until a better opportunity for escape arose.

With his free hand, Alan traced a finger along the side of her face, following the scar that curved from her hairline to her cheekbone. "You know how it feels," he said. "You didn't mean to hurt Mia, but she died. Tell me what to do, Fiona. I can't live this way. Every night she talks to me. My mother. I can't even sleep unless Gavin gives me something. Please help me."

Fiona resisted the urge to jerk her head away from the feel of his finger caressing her scar, over and over. "I *can* help you, if you'll let me. But I can't do it alone. Alan, please listen to me. Let's go get Gavin. Together we'll help you."

"Gavin doesn't understand." Alan's hand settled on her forehead and tipped her head back so it was resting against his shoulder. Fiona breathed slowly, keeping her muscles relaxed.

"He *should* understand," Alan said. "He of all people should understand. But he was just a kid. Nine."

"Just a kid when . . . what?"

"When Dad died. The fire."

"That must have been so traumatic for both of you, losing your father like that."

"It was bad. Gavin felt horrible. He had no idea it would spread like that."

"That—what would spread?"

"The fire. Mom had told him to leave the matches alone. Gavin didn't always listen."

A new shiver passed through Fiona.

"He didn't even know Dad was in the cabin," Alan said. "He thought he'd gone on the hike with Mom and me. He thought he was alone."

"Gavin—Gavin accidentally started the fire that killed your father?"

"He didn't mean it. You didn't mean to kill Mia."

Drenched in icy sweat, Fiona tried to gather her thoughts. Poor Gavin! What a crushing, heartbreaking burden for a child to bear. "I'm sure Gavin—I'm sure he understands you didn't mean to hurt your mother either. Let's go talk to him."

"Hiding hurts too much," Alan said. "But Gavin says that's best. Mom said that's best. 'Mother knows best.' Isn't that the old cliché?"

"It's not always true."

"Hiding hurts. Too many people die. That doctor was kind." Alan chuckled. "He didn't even charge me for the stitches."

"What stitches, Alan?" Fiona made an extra effort to speak calmly. Alan was sounding less and less coherent.

"My elbow. I told you I hurt my elbow. When Mom died."

"That's right. I'm sorry."

"I got back to the house—didn't know what to do. I was bleeding like crazy. That doctor—Murray. Keith Murray. He was at the door. He'd come to talk to Mom. I had blood all over my arm. It kept dripping on the floor. He said he could help me. Took me to his office and fixed me up. He was talking about Mom—something about her being mad at him but that she didn't understand the situation, and he wasn't a bad guy . . . I didn't know what to say . . . he was talking about Mom . . . but she was dead . . ."

Keith Murray. Keith who had been found murdered. "Alan . . . did . . . Dr. Murray figure out what happened to your mother?"

"No. I don't know. I didn't tell him. But I was upset . . . crazy . . . wasn't thinking straight. Gavin said Murray would figure it out— from the crazy way I'd acted, he'd know . . . Once they found Mom, he'd figure it out. He'd seen me right after . . . he'd know . . . he'd figure it out . . ."

"You told Gavin what . . . happened with your mother?"

"Yes. He was worried—thought Murray would figure it out and tell the police . . . you've got to hide things like this, he said. You hide it, or they lock you up."

"Alan . . . did you kill Keith Murray?"

"No. I didn't want him to die, but Gavin said there was no choice . . . he said it was quick, he hit him on the head, he never felt any pain . . . you're shaking, Fiona." His hand rested against her cheek. "Are you scared?"

Deep breath. It had never occurred to her to be afraid of Gavin. He'd seemed to be the stable one, the one taking care of Alan. *He was taking care of Alan. He killed Keith Murray so Keith couldn't tell the police he'd met a dazed, soaked, bloodied Alan right after Linda tumbled into that creek.*

"Alan, you told me Gavin doesn't understand. You need to get help from someone else, someone who does. Come with me, back to Bennett. I know a doctor—"

"They'll lock me up."

"They'll *help* you. You're ill."

"They'll lock me up. And you'd turn the key yourself, wouldn't you?"

"I only want—"

He clamped both hands around her wrists. "You have to love me, Fiona. She said you would."

"Of course I care about you. I want to help you."

"I knew you'd help me." He sounded relieved, but he was still holding her so tightly that her hands were going numb.

"Can you trust me enough to come with me?" Fiona spoke gently. "If you don't want to see a doctor, why don't we go to my house?"

"Your house?"

"My sisters are there. You know how kind they are. You'd be safe while you figure out what to do."

"That's . . . not a good idea." But the words were hesitant. He was uncertain.

"Let me help you. Come with me."

He shifted, his grip loosening a little. "Maybe we can talk for a while. Talk here."

"All right. We can do that."

"Fiona." His grip relaxed a little more. His fingertips moved, stroking her wrists. "I love you."

"Remember when Mia first introduced us at that football game?" Fiona made her voice light. "And she told you I was working on a master's in English, and you told me about that English teacher you had in high school who worshipped Dickens and sounded like Jeeves?"

"'Very good, sir,'" Alan quoted in a perfect British accent.

"I never did understand football very well," Fiona said. "I'd just cheer when everyone else cheered."

The tension in Alan's arms eased a little more. "If you hadn't tried to read Steinbeck during the games, maybe you would have caught more of the fine points of first downs and field goals."

"Steinbeck, football—both involve pain. Why not combine them?"

Alan chuckled. "Remember that day when we went up Provo Canyon for a picnic and read Shakespeare all afternoon?"

"*Much Ado About Nothing*," Fiona said.

"I would have chosen *Romeo and Juliet* but thought I'd be pushing my luck."

To Fiona's surprise, her laugh came naturally. "That was a wonderful afternoon. It's one of my favorite memories."

"It is?"

"We had a lot of fun. Remember that a cappella festival on the night when it was snowing so—"

The click of a key in the lock made Alan jump and tighten his grip on Fiona. The door to the studio swung open and Gavin stepped inside.

New terror tore through Fiona. *Stay calm. Don't show that you're afraid of him. He doesn't know what Alan told you.*

Moving slowly, as though he didn't want to spook Alan, Gavin closed the studio door. "I wondered where you'd gone, Al," he said. "You weren't in your room. And I saw a car parked out front."

"I needed to talk to Fiona." Alan sounded defiant.

Gavin scratched his head. His messy hair and stubbly chin indicated he'd just climbed out of bed.

"How did you get her here?" Gavin asked.

"I called and told her I was you. You told me she'd agreed to come if you called."

"Nice."

"It's all right," Fiona said. "We're chatting about old times." Considering the way Alan had her pinned against him, she knew the statement would strike Gavin as absurd, but he'd understand she was trying to keep Alan from panicking.

Gavin spotted the knife. He picked it up and set it on the desk. "Why did you want to talk to her?"

Alan didn't answer.

Gavin picked up Fiona's phone.

"That's mine." Fiona tried to sound matter-of-fact, as though she assumed Gavin would give it to her.

Gavin slid her phone into his pocket. He walked across the room and sat on the couch on the other side of Alan. "You thought she'd help you, didn't you?"

"She *will* help me."

"She wants to take you to a doctor, doesn't she?"

No answer from Alan.

"She said that, didn't she, Al?"

"She . . . said she knows a doctor in Bennett . . ."

"I warned you, didn't I?"

No answer.

"I do want to help him," Fiona said. "He knows that."

"Let me translate," Gavin said. "'I want to help you' means 'Do you want your straitjacket in a small, medium, or large?'"

"That's *not true*. Gavin, you *know* Alan needs a doctor. We talked about this last night. You asked me to—"

"Did you tell her everything?" Gavin asked.

Alan shifted, readjusting his grip on Fiona. "I . . . she . . . cares about me."

"You thought you could trust her?"

Alan said nothing.

"But she wants to lock you up, doesn't she?"

"Alan, tell your brother to go away and leave us alone," Fiona said. "We were having a good conversation before he barged in here."

"She wants to lock you up," Gavin continued. "Lock you up in some creepy psych ward. That's all she wants for you, brother. She'd do anything, say anything, to get rid of you."

"That's not true." Fiona tried to twist around in Alan's grasp so she could look at Gavin. "I only want—"

"—what's best for you," Gavin finished. "That's the line they give right before they slam the door and you spend the rest of your life in a nuthouse. Will you let her do that to you?"

Alan's hands trembled, his grasp on Fiona tightening and loosening. "I need her. I love her."

"Remember when she was poking around your house and she found her hair comb and you asked her for friendship—only friendship? You told her how lonely you were, how much you needed her? What did she do, Alan?"

No answer from Alan.

"She spit in your face and walked out," Gavin said. "Remember? The only reason she's acting like she wants to help you now is because she's scared of you. She thinks you're a lunatic who'll stab her if she doesn't pretend to love you. She's faking. The instant she gets out of here, she'll call the police and tell them everything."

"Alan, that's not—"

Gavin cut across Fiona's protest. "And as soon as they lock you up, she'll wash her hands, forget about you, and go back to James Hampton."

"*No*—Alan—"

"She destroys everyone around her. She tore you up and threw you aside. She killed Mia Hardy. She killed Mom—Mom would never have gone out on that walk if it weren't for her. She kills and she destroys and she never pays. She destroyed that student too, the one the police asked you about. Did you know that? She ruined that girl's life, and then the girl died in Fiona's house. Who do you think killed her?"

"Alan, you *know* I would never—"

"You can't let her keep hurting people. She's killing you little by little." His voice was soft. "We need to free you."

Alan's fingers had gone lax, and Gavin hadn't locked the door behind him. Focusing all her strength, Fiona twisted violently, throwing herself off the couch. She landed on her hands and knees on the carpet, scrambled frantically to her feet, and leaped toward the door.

A weight crashed into her, throwing her forward. She hit the ground full-length, the impact so jarring that for an instant, she was too stunned to move. Someone yanked her arms behind her so savagely that pain ripped through her shoulders.

"Al, help me. Hold her hands."

Choking down a breath to reinflate her lungs, Fiona struggled with all the strength she had. It was useless. She felt Gavin—Alan?—winding something rough around her wrists. The room had started spinning. She was going to vomit—hands on her ankles, rope digging into her flesh.

Standing above her, Alan spoke, his voice dull. "The police will come for me anyway."

"No, they won't."

Fiona twisted her neck, looking up at Alan. "Alan—*please*—"

"They know Keith Murray was here," Alan said. "They know about the stitches."

"So? That doesn't prove anything. They suspect Carissa Willis killed him. Mom told me Carissa and Murray were having an affair, so I put Carissa's glove with Murray's body. She's a better suspect than either of us."

"Carissa's . . . glove?"

"Mom had it. Carissa had dropped it at church on the day Mom told her about those pictures. And I planted some stuff at the Willises' house to give Carissa a few doubts about Brad's character. You know how Mom insisted he was drinking? I figured it would be good if Carissa thought so, too. The more we can pit them against each other, the less they'll help each other—or lead the cops to the truth."

"It's not going to work," Alan said bleakly.

One hand in the pocket of his jacket, Gavin moved to stand next to Alan. "No worries, brother. We'll be fine. Let's get you back to the house." He put his arm around Alan's shoulders.

"I don't know . . . I can't . . ." Abruptly, Alan stepped backward and grabbed his own shoulder.

"Easy, Al." Gavin dropped an empty hypodermic syringe to the floor. "You need to take it easy. We'll get you back to the house where you can rest."

Rubbing his shoulder, Alan took another step away from his brother. "I don't want to sleep."

"You don't have to. It won't knock you out. It'll just help you relax. Same stuff I gave you the other day. Don't worry. Everything will work out." He took Alan by the arm and led him toward the door. Alan looked over his shoulder at Fiona, his gaze bleary and filled with pain.

"Come on." Gavin prodded him through the doorway and shut the door behind them. Fiona heard the key click in the lock.

Chapter 29

TEARS OF FEAR, FURY, AND self-hatred spilled from Fiona's eyes. *Gavin?* Could she possibly have been any blinder? As soon as he got Alan settled, he'd be back. He'd killed Keith Murray to protect Alan. He'd kill Fiona, too.

Kimberly? He must have killed Kimberly. But why?

How long did she have until Gavin returned? She could scream for help on the miniscule chance that, early on a Saturday morning, someone had wandered close enough to the Taylors' isolated property to hear her. But it was far more likely that the only one to hear her would be Gavin, who'd rush back to gag her—or slit her throat. There had to be a better—

The knife. Gavin had left the knife on the desk. If she could get to it, maybe she could cut the ropes and climb out the window. Desperately, Fiona rolled toward the desk.

Contorting her body, she managed to pull herself to a sitting position and then to her knees. Fortunately, the knife lay near the edge of the desk. Unsteadily, she pushed herself partway to her feet and, using her chin, dragged the knife over the edge of the desk. She twisted around and fumbled behind her until her fingers grasped the knife handle.

Fingers clumsy, she tried to angle the blade to bring it into contact with the rope. This wasn't going to work. *It will work. It has to work.* Fiona repositioned the blade again and drew it downward. Lava-hot pain in her forearm told her she'd cut flesh, not rope. *You can do this. Try again. Do you want James attending your funeral next week?*

Another slice, and this time, she felt the roughness of the rope beneath the blade. *Again.* Another flash of pain; she clenched her teeth, feeling warm blood trickle over her hand. She adjusted the knife and tried again. *You can do this.*

Faster. Hurry. Fiona sawed frantically at the rope, ignoring the pain when the blade missed the mark, ignoring the way her hands were cramping. Every few seconds she'd pause and twist her wrists, yanking against the rope, hoping to weaken it further, and then resume sawing. Soaked in sweat, she finally gave one last wrench and felt the rope snap. She pulled and shook her wrists free of the loops of rope.

Half-numb fingers slipping on the sweat and blood coating the knife, she sawed at the rope binding her ankles. Her legs free, she staggered to her feet. She tucked the knife, handle down, into the back pocket of her jeans—she didn't want to leave the knife for Gavin.

She'd better go out the back window, cut through the woods until she was far from the Taylors' house, and head for the road. She lurched to the window, slid the curtains aside, and fumbled with the latch. It wouldn't release. It was a keyed lock.

Biting back a scream, Fiona whirled around to look for something she could use to smash the window. The piano bench. She grabbed it, swung it back, and slammed the end of the bench into the window. Glass shattered. She swung again and again, knocking glass shards everywhere.

The bang of a door hitting the wall made her spin around. Gavin stood in the open doorway.

He leaped toward her. Fiona dropped the piano bench and lunged toward the window. She had both legs over the sill when Gavin caught the back of her shirt. She screamed, thrashing, struggling to break his grip, but he yanked her backward. She landed hard on her back on the studio floor. Before she could fight through the breath-stealing jolt of pain, Gavin shoved his hand beneath her and yanked the knife out of her pocket.

Fiona threw her body to the side, rolling, crawling, finally staggering to her feet near the storage boxes stacked against one wall.

Gavin didn't come after her. He moved to the open door and closed and locked it. Now the broken window was the only way out, and she'd never be able to beat him to it. No wonder he wasn't moving faster—he had her cornered. No need to hurry now.

He walked toward her, but stopped with a couple of yards between them. He held the knife at his side, his arm loose, the tip of the blade pointing toward the floor.

The back of her legs stung and she felt the heat of blood where glass had cut her when Gavin had dragged her over the shards rimming the window. "If you kill me, Alan will never forgive you."

"He helped tie you up," Gavin said. "That ought to tell you something."

"He'd never want—"

"You don't understand how ambivalent his feelings are toward you. Part of him still worships you. But in his head he knows you're destroying him, just like he knew it with Mom." Gavin stood silent for a moment, studying her. He looked grim and rigid, as though he was bracing himself.

Blood trickled over her palms. She glanced down and was startled at the amount of blood on her hands and forearms. She'd been so frantic to cut herself loose that she hadn't felt half of what she was doing to herself. She clamped her hands around opposite wrists, hoping to slow any significant bleeding.

"Why did you give me that speech last night about needing my help to get him into counseling?" she asked. "What was the point of that?"

He shrugged. "Just gathering evidence for Alan's benefit. You wouldn't stoop to help him when he begged you for friendship, but when you thought I was offering you the chance to get him locked up, suddenly you're ready to jump in and help."

"That is *not* a fair interpretation of anything I said to either of you."

"The best thing I can do for Alan is to get you out of his life." Gavin spoke in a near-whisper, and Fiona wondered if he was talking to her or to himself. "He knows that."

"I don't want to be in his life."

"Then maybe you shouldn't have come back, stirring everything up again." He took a step toward her. "Do you know what it *did* to him when you showed up at the funeral? I'd calmed him down—managed to get him to understand that it wasn't his fault, that Mom asked for what she got, he didn't mean to hurt her, he didn't have to feel guilty about it; she'd been wrong about everything, wrong to try to manipulate him. Then *you*—there you were at the funeral, the fulfillment of her prophecy."

"Gavin—I had no idea—"

"That night he was raving, out of his mind—I thought he was going to hurt himself. He kept talking about how she'd been right, and he hadn't believed her. I wanted to kill you. Hadn't you done enough to him in college? You almost destroyed him then, and here you were to finish the job."

"I'm so sorry. I never would have come if I'd thought—"

"You're sorry. *That* makes a difference." Gavin took another step toward her.

With nothing at hand that she could use as a weapon, Fiona grabbed the top storage box, hoping she could use it as a shield. It turned out to be so heavy she could hardly hold it, let alone maneuver with it; it must be full of books. She dropped it. The thud shook the floor.

Gavin still didn't attack. He stood several feet away, drumming the flat of the knife against his thigh. "I should have killed you the first time. Headed things off before they got worse."

"The . . . first time?"

"That's why I was in your house—turned off the power—I thought maybe I'd . . . but I changed my mind. Alan was positive that you had come to the funeral because you wanted to give your relationship another chance. I figured I'd better give *you* a chance, for Alan's sake. I gave you chance after chance, and what a winner you turned out to be. You were so disdainful—didn't want to contaminate yourself with Dad's books, never mind how much they were worth—wouldn't stoop to help Alan in any way, even when he begged for your friendship. You'd even parade your new boyfriend in front of him. You were destroying him—torturing him to death. At least Mia's death was quick."

"The—accident. With the dummy of Mia. Was that—you?"

"Yes." He used the point of the knife to push his hair off his forehead. "It was easy to get the car. Classmate of mine from med school has a grandma who lives in Boston. I remembered him talking about how his grandmother was going to get her car stolen someday because she always kept a spare key in one of those magnetic key cases attached to the bottom of her car. I just had to find her address. Wasn't hard—unusual last name. I remembered it from that conversation."

"But why go to so much trouble to hurt me?" Fiona asked.

"You deserved it. And it's the kind of thing your angry student would have done."

Part punishment, part misdirection. He'd wanted the police to think Kimberly was escalating, so when Fiona was murdered, they'd blame her. "Did you—Kimberly Bailey? Were you waiting for me and she found you—or you found her?"

"She found me. Bad luck."

"You were going to kill me that night."

He nodded.

"Why *didn't* you wait for me, after—? You could have . . ."

"I panicked. Took off. Figured I'd try again later. She's your fault too, Fiona. Your cruelty brought her to your house. You hurt, you kill, and you destroy. It's over now. You're not hurting Alan again."

Dizziness made her skin tingle. Gavin didn't *want* to kill her. He'd had far better opportunities than this, chances when she'd been completely off guard. But he'd always backed off. Had he feared Alan's reaction?

"My sisters know I'm here," Fiona said. "I left them a note. The police will come straight to you."

"It doesn't matter what your sisters say." His eyes stared straight into hers, a gaze so cold it made her shiver. "We're leaving anyway. You saw what Alan's like. He's in no shape to deal with the police again, and they're already breathing down his neck about Keith Murray. He'd crack for sure."

"Gavin—this won't help Alan—"

Raising the knife, he sprang toward her.

* * *

James had originally intended to park out of sight of the Taylors' house so his presence wouldn't derail whatever progress Gavin and Fiona were making with Alan, but by the time he reached Canfield, worry for Fiona had overridden any thoughts of staying out of the way. He tried repeatedly to tell himself that his mounting fear was irrational—and probably rooted in jealousy of Alan—but nothing worked. All he could feel was a frantic need to get to Fiona *now.* Let her be angry with him for interfering, but he *had* to see her in person and confirm that she was all right.

Fiona's rental car was parked in the driveway of the Taylors' big white colonial. James parked on the street and hurried toward the front door. When he reached the porch, he hesitated. Now that he was at the point of actually interrupting the conversation, the message his rational mind had been shouting for the whole trip—that he was overreacting, and badly enough to irreparably damage Fiona's opinion of him—began to temper his anxiety. What was he so afraid of? Alan Taylor couldn't have murdered Kimberly. Fiona should *not* be there with the Taylors, especially not if Alan was acting in a way that had upset Gavin into calling her at six in the morning—but how would it help if James hammered on the door and embarrassed everyone?

If it was possible to check on things without causing a disruption, that would be ideal. *What are you going to do? Peek in the windows? Your mother would be so proud.* If Fiona caught him spying like that, she *would* throw him out of her life—and get a restraining order.

The curtains were drawn over the front windows anyway. Frustrated, James stared at the silent house. He couldn't just—

A faint thudding noise caused adrenaline to fire through James's veins. What was that? Something heavy hitting the ground? But the noise hadn't seemed to come from inside the house. Outside? In back?

Uncertainly, James stepped off the porch and started around the side of the house. The noise probably had nothing to do with Fiona's conversation with the Taylors, but checking it out was better than standing on the porch like an indecisive fool.

James followed a flagstone path toward the backyard. A small, white-shingled building stood at the edge of the trees. Must be a guest house or studio—

A scream came from inside the building.

"*Fiona!*" James hurtled toward the door and grabbed the doorknob. Locked.

"*Fiona!*" he yelled. He backed up and slammed his foot against the door. The force of the collision sent pain tearing up his leg, but the solid door didn't yield. He kicked again. Nothing.

Another cry came from inside the studio. James spun around and snatched one of the rocks edging the flowerbed. He slammed the rock into the window.

"*Fiona!*" James wielded the rock over and over, smashing out the rest of the glass. He reached through the opening and jerked the curtain out of the way.

Fiona was stumbling, arms raised as she tried to fight off Gavin—Gavin holding a knife, Fiona's shirt stained with red—

"*Get away from her!*" Grabbing the sill, James started to hoist himself into the room.

Someone struck him from the side, knocking him away from the window.

* * *

At the sound of James shouting her name, Fiona felt a frantic surge of hope and energy. Gavin froze, his gaze on the door. Taking advantage of his distraction, Fiona grabbed another box and hurled it toward Gavin. He jumped aside, and the box hit the floor.

"Get out now and maybe you'll have a chance," Fiona said. "Run!"

Thuds shook the door—James, trying to break in. Fiona opened her mouth to yell at James to come around the back, the window was broken there, but the words emerged as a cry as Gavin struck again. She threw up her arm to try to ward off the blade and felt it slash her forearm. The sound of glass shattering filled the studio.

Gavin struck again; Fiona jerked to the side and the blow missed her. He swung around to follow her and struck. The knife sank into her shoulder.

Fiona screamed and kicked Gavin, trying to force him back enough so she wouldn't be pinned between him and the wall. He stumbled. Fiona lunged to the left, but Gavin threw himself toward her, grabbing for her arm. He caught it and yanked, swinging her around. One of the storage boxes she'd tossed to the ground tripped her, and she fell.

She thrashed wildly, trying to roll away from Gavin, trying to knock the knife aside, feeling it slash along the back of her arm—sharp pressure in her side, pain flaming in her ribs. If she could ward off a lethal strike for a few more seconds, James would have time to—

Gavin sprang on top of her, his weight pinning her to the ground. His face was crimson, his eyes fiery as he drew the knife back. With no way to elude him, Fiona flung her arms up in what she knew would be a final, futile effort to ward off death.

The explosive noise of gunshots smashed against her eardrums. On top of her, Gavin jerked and went still, his mouth open, his eyes wide, his hand still holding the knife high. His hand shook, bringing the knife down in a zigzag motion, finally dropping it onto the carpet. He fell forward, his body a suffocating weight on top of Fiona.

A thud made the floor tremble and a moment later, Gavin's weight rolled off of her. Fiona looked up and saw Brad Willis leaning over Gavin, a gun in his hand. Another thud, and a uniformed police officer approached from the direction of the front window. The officer was speaking into a radio, calling for medical assistance, calling for backup.

Brad turned and dropped to his knees next to Fiona. "Lie still," he said. She closed her eyes, feeling Brad prodding her, turning her, assessing her injuries. Another thud marked a third person entering through the window. Fiona opened her eyes and saw James approaching.

He knelt next to her. "*Fiona . . .*"

"I'm sorry," she said hoarsely. "James, I'm sorry . . . you warned me . . . bad idea . . ."

"Shh, stay calm." James's face was so gray that Fiona wondered if he was going to pass out.

"Use your sweatshirt," Brad snapped, pushing his own folded jacket against Fiona's side. "Her shoulder."

James yanked his sweatshirt over his head and pressed it against Fiona's shoulder where pain burned. Her blood, staining his sweatshirt. How much blood was spilling out of her? Her thoughts skidded backward: the accident, the broken, bloodied mess of her arm and leg, blood streaming into her eyes, Mia's motionless body, trapped by mangled metal and glass—*Mia*—

"Fiona, stay with us." Brad's voice. "An ambulance is coming."

"Gavin." She focused on Brad. "Gavin killed Kimberly Bailey . . . and Keith Murray . . . I never thought . . . how did you . . . know I was in trouble?"

"Alan called me," Brad said.

Chapter 30

AT THE SOUND OF THE door opening, Fiona turned from where she'd been standing at the window, looking at the sunlit flowering cherry trees in the hospital courtyard.

"Arrest her, Brad." Carissa, holding a vase of yellow roses, elbowed her husband in the arm. "I'm sure her being out of bed is a felony."

Fiona reached for the front of her robe, tugging the edges a little closer together to make sure she was at least somewhat ready for visitors. "I only stood up for a moment."

"Then I'll give you ten seconds to get in bed before I call for backup." Brad spoke with a half smile on his face, and Fiona tried not to show her surprise. Brad Willis, joking with her?

Gripping her IV pole, Fiona shuffled toward the bed. The brief trip to the window had been more than enough exertion, and already she was beginning to feel lightheaded.

Carissa set the roses on the nightstand and came around to meet her.

"Is there anywhere I can hug you that doesn't hurt?" Carissa smiled, but her eyes were starting to overflow. "Or would you prefer a virtual hug?"

Fiona leaned into Carissa's embrace. Almost every movement aggravated one or more of her injuries, but she still wanted the comfort of her friend's touch.

"I can't believe you're on your feet." Carissa pulled back, wiping her eyes.

"It wasn't a good idea." Fiona didn't want to admit *why* she'd dragged herself out of bed—how much she'd needed to remind herself that she *could* walk, that she could move both arms and both legs, that it was not eight years ago.

"Are you dizzy?" Carissa asked.

"A little."

"I can tell. You're as pale as the bedsheets. Lie down." Carissa helped settle her in bed.

"I'm not as fragile as I look," Fiona said. "Only two of the wounds were deep. The others . . ." She stopped, figuring Carissa didn't want a detailed account of exactly where the knife had slashed, where it had nearly missed her and caused only a scratch, or where a potentially lethal wound had been averted when the knife hit a rib.

"Want me to tip the bed back a little more?" Carissa asked. "You need to rest."

"I'm all right." Fiona looked at Brad, who was fingering the stem of a rose and studying the wall. "Brad, I never had a chance to say this, but—thank you. And I'm sorry you had to . . . it must be difficult . . ." Unsure of how to finish, she fell silent. Brad had known Gavin Taylor personally, and he'd had to pull the trigger.

"Given another half second, Gavin would have put that knife in your heart," Brad said. "I did what I had to."

"What did Alan say when he called you?" She was still reeling from the knowledge that in the end, Alan had been willing to sacrifice both himself and his brother to save her life. "Did he call you or did he call the department?"

"He called me. I was home, off duty. He was incoherent, rambling about how he loved you, but you were dangerous and wanted him locked up and Gavin was going to kill you and you needed help. He sounded both drugged and off his rocker—I couldn't even make out if you were in Canfield or at home—but I figured I'd better get to the Taylors' immediately. I had dispatch send another car in case the trouble wasn't all in Alan's mind and had the Bennett police check your house as well."

"Thank you."

"It's my job. You don't owe me thanks."

"I owe you my life. Thank you. How is Alan doing?"

"He's undergoing psychiatric evaluation. He's been very cooperative."

"I talked to Summer this morning," Carissa said. "She's in a daze, pretty much, but she's hanging in there. She was going to check to see if she could visit Alan."

This news surprised and warmed Fiona. Despite everything, Summer wasn't giving up on him. "I hope he—they—are finally able to find peace."

"Brad, we'd better leave." Carissa leaned over and touched Fiona's hair. "Fiona looks exhausted."

Fiona wanted to protest, but fatigue was crushing her. "Thank you for everything."

"Call me if you need anything," Carissa said. "Day or night. Do you have help when you go home?"

"My parents are here now. I'm in good hands."

"Good. Sleep, okay? I'll talk to you soon."

"Thanks, Carissa."

She watched Brad and Carissa head for the door, with Brad's hand resting lightly on Carissa's back. She didn't need to hear it in words to know Brad and Carissa were working things out.

Brad paused near the door and looked back. For a moment, he studied her in silence, and Fiona felt a stirring of the uneasiness she usually felt around Brad Willis. He spoke at last, his voice brusque. "If you for one instant think anything Alan or Gavin Taylor did is your fault, then you're crazier than the two of them put together. Are you clear on that?"

Startled, Fiona said, "I never should have gone to Linda's funeral."

Brad strode toward the bed with the authoritative gait Fiona imagined he used when approaching a criminal. He stopped at her bedside. "How is it your fault that both Alan and Gavin had severe psychological problems that their mother did everything possible to make worse?"

"I . . . didn't . . ."

"Do you realize she wouldn't even allow Gavin to see a counselor after his father's death? We learned that from Alan. She never told anyone how that fire started. It was Gavin messing around with matches, by the way. Gavin had some issues from the start. But she made him keep everything secret—thought it was better if he locked it inside and pretended it never happened."

"Oh, Gavin . . . that poor boy . . ."

"Yeah, it's a tragedy on every level. But it's not your fault."

Fiona glanced at Carissa. She was goggling at Brad, plainly as surprised as Fiona was.

"Both Alan and Gavin were unraveling long before you walked through the door of that church," Brad said. "Do you think if you hadn't gone to the funeral, that would somehow have cured both of them? And brought Linda Taylor and Keith Murray back to life?"

Fiona didn't try to answer Brad this time.

"If you're crazy enough to accept the blame Gavin tried to pin on you, then good luck to your shrink," Brad said.

"You have a great bedside manner, Brad," Carissa said dryly.

"You're going to talk to someone, right?" Brad gaze locked with Fiona's. "Someone who can help you deal with this? You might find yourself dealing with a lot of posttraumatic stress. You can't carry that solo."

"I know I can't," Fiona said. "I won't try."

"Take care, Fiona."

"You, too."

He put his arm around Carissa. "We will," he said.

* * *

When Fiona opened her eyes, her hospital room was dim with waning twilight. Blinking, she reached for the button to switch on the light, but before she touched it, the light clicked on. James was sitting in the chair next to her bed.

"Hey," he said.

She smiled. "How long have you been there?"

"Just a few minutes. Hope I didn't wake you."

"No, you're fine."

"How are you feeling?"

"Okay." James had already come to visit her twice, but the first time he'd brought Rebecca and Shannon, and the second time, Fiona's parents had already been here. This was the first time she'd seen him alone.

Moving carefully, she found the button to raise the head of the bed and pressed it.

"You okay?" James asked. "Maybe you shouldn't sit up."

"It doesn't count as sitting. The bed is supporting me."

"How's the pain?"

"Not bad." Fiona looked down at the bandages on her arms. "Good thing I'll have plenty of new scars. I was . . . getting bored with the old ones."

James pulled his chair closer to the bed. "How are you really doing?"

Tears blurred her vision. "James . . . I should have listened to you. You were right. You warned me—"

"*Stop*. I had no idea what Gavin Taylor was capable of, any more than you did."

"You warned me about Alan."

"Fiona, if I hadn't been such an absentminded idiot who can't hold on to his phone for more than twenty minutes at a time, you never would have ended up in that situation. Alan got bold enough to lure you there because he knew he could trick you into thinking I was on board. *I'm sorry*."

"James, no. It's not your fault."

"You were trying to do what was right. You made some mistakes. So did I. And you weren't wrong about Alan. He *didn't* want to hurt you. He's the one who got Brad there in time."

Fiona closed her eyes, letting the tears trickle down her cheeks. "I didn't want to die. I kept thinking . . . James . . . I didn't realize how much I wanted to live until Gavin . . ."

James touched her face, wiping away the tears. Opening her eyes, she turned toward him. "I love you," she whispered. The words came so naturally, so easily, that for a moment, she couldn't believe she'd said them.

James smiled. "I love you, too. In fact, I've felt that way for a while now."

"You have?"

"Yes. Truth is, I fell for you long distance."

"Long distance!"

"Our e-mails. Texts. The occasional phone calls. All the friends-staying-in-touch stuff."

Friends staying in touch—the contact that had begun when James kept checking in with her during her recovery from the accident. "I had no idea."

"I swear I didn't have any ulterior motives, not for a long time. I just considered you a good friend. I gave the whole dating scene due diligence and then some, but nothing ever seemed to gel. I found myself thinking about you more and more. And when I got to the point where I'd sit there on a date hoping she'd go to the ladies' room so I could check my e-mail to see if there was anything from you, I knew I was in trouble."

"You never let on."

"Come on. I knew you." James took her hand, his fingers gentle. "The only shot I had at getting close to you was to wave a backstage friend pass. If I didn't tread cautiously, you'd panic. But you have no idea how long and hard I prayed that I'd be able to find a job in New England so maybe I'd have a chance with you, face-to-face."

"You did?"

"I'm certain the Lord got me into that position at Hawkins just so I'd stop pestering Him."

"James . . . thank you for being patient with me."

He rose to his feet and leaned over her. With his hands on her face, he tilted her head back and kissed her. Desperation, hunger, fear, love—so many emotions flooded out of Fiona at the touch of James's lips on hers that by the time he straightened up, she felt too weak to even keep herself steady.

"You look exhausted," he said, lowering the head of the bed. "Get some rest."

"Don't leave yet. Please."

"I won't." James pulled the blankets up to her shoulders. "I'll sit here with you and recite love poems."

"Do you know any?"

"If you'll turn your back for a minute, I can google a few."

"Not necessary. Just be with me."

"I love you. How's that for poetry?"

"It's perfect," she said.

About the Author

Stephanie Black has loved books since she was old enough to grab the pages and has enjoyed creating make-believe adventures since she and her sisters were inventing long Barbie games filled with intrigue and danger or running around pretending to be detectives. She is a three-time Whitney Award winner for Best Mystery/Suspense, most recently for *Cold as Ice* (2010).

Stephanie was born in Utah and has lived in various places, including Arizona, Massachusetts, New York, and Limerick, Ireland. She currently lives in northern California and enjoys spending time with her husband, Brian, and their five children. She is a fan of chocolate, cheesecake, and her husband's homemade bread.

Stephanie enjoys hearing from readers. You can contact her via e-mail at info@covenant-lds.com, or by mail care of Covenant Communications, P.O. Box 416, American Fork, UT, 84003-0416. Visit her website at www.stephanieblack.net and her blog, Black Ink, at www.stephanieblackink.blogspot.com.